Totally Bound Publishing books by Jennifer Luna

Emerald Mafia
Dove
Clipped Wings

I0662146

Emerald Mafia

CLIPPED WINGS

JENNIFER LUNA

Clipped Wings
ISBN # 978-1-80250-761-4
©Copyright Jennifer Luna 2024
Cover Art by Kelly Martin ©Copyright February 2024
Interior text design by Claire Siemaszkiewicz
Totally Bound Publishing

CLIPPED WINGS

Dedication

To my daughter,
You are currently five days old,
Sitting in my lap as I write.
I hope the glare from Mama's laptop isn't too
terrible.

Acknowledgements

First and foremost, to you, the reader. Thank you for supporting debut and indie authors, small press and independent publishers. There are so many amazing stories out there that deserve to be seen and heard. I am beyond grateful to every single one of you.

I'd like to thank my husband for being so supportive, for listening to my crazy ideas about sexy underground fighters and criminal overlords, for trying not to speed-read through the steamy scenes. But mostly, for giving me the greatest gifts of all — your love and our children.

Breanne and Autumn, for proving that thousands of miles can't come between fifteen years of friendship. To my alpha readers — Heather, Tissa and Sebrina — I couldn't have completed this story without you. Your encouragement and unfiltered opinions feed my creative soul. To my most precious writer friend, Luisa Raegan, thank you for checking in on me, whether it be book or baby related.

As a relatively new author with a glamorous case of imposter syndrome, I like to enlist all the editorial help I can get. Lexie Eldridge at Morally Gray Edits, your manuscript critique is a godsend. The publishing process can be complicated and overwhelming, but Totally Bound Publishing helped every step of the way. Specifically, Anna Olson and Rebecca Scott for your guidance and attentiveness.

Lastly, to the Smuthood, thank you for being such a supportive group of individuals. Your recommendations are on point. I really enjoyed going down the rabbit hole with everyone and can't wait to continue exploring romantic literature. Your open-mindedness, inclusivity and humor are a breath of fresh air.

Prologue

The Grecian sun glinted off the incoming waves, refracting rainbows of light that welcomed me into the sea. The sand was warm, the breeze balmy. Rays of sun kissed my skin, now tan from two full weeks under it. The soothing water seeped over my toes, my feet sinking farther into the wet powder with each rush of the tide.

As I submerged myself in the Aegean Sea, serenity embedded itself in my bone marrow. My fingers flitted across the rippling water, dancing in the early afternoon light. I lifted my hands to my hair, brushing back the long strands, heavy with briny drops from the ocean.

I'd been with Jack O'Connell for nine months, although it felt like he'd always been there – a staple in the life of Emma Marshall. Where I went, Jack followed.

But where Jack went, I wasn't allowed.

There was a shift in the current and a cool burst of water stroked my naked calves, a riptide that had changed direction. The wind strengthened, taking tendrils of my hair along with it. A change was coming. I could feel it in my heart, the way it fluttered faster beneath my ribs. Not in anticipation but in preparation.

My life was inextricably tied to Jack's and, unbeknownst to him, we were on borrowed time. A dragon was slumbering, dreaming of revenge. This dragon thought I belonged to him.

But if I belonged to anyone, it was Jack O'Connell. I was learning him on a trial-and-error basis. I'd rile him, then analyze his reactions. That was the way to study a devil. It wasn't a safe method, but it was effective nonetheless.

I'd gleaned one important fact throughout my relationship with the leader of the Irish mob. He was protective—to a bloody fault—of the few people he held dearest.

And I was his most prized possession.

Chapter One

Jack

I entered the bungalow, balancing grocery bags under each arm. They were filled with ingredients from the Mediterranean. I was excited to work with fresh produce, though not as excited as I was to see Emma. I'd been gone less than an hour, but a tightness in my chest had formed from the need to have her close again.

After I set the bags on the kitchen counter, my gaze found her. If anything, the magnetic force between us had grown over the past few months. I was attuned to her presence at all times, even when she wasn't aware. I stopped to stare, my breathing uneven.

The fact that a creature like her lived in the same dimension as a demon like me was baffling.

Emma was an angel, sitting on the terrace in her white, see-through cover-up. She wore nothing underneath, the little temptress. Her hair, lighter than usual, was damp and beginning to wave. She had it pulled over one shoulder in an attempt to control the wayward locks. As Emma sat on a cushioned armchair, legs crossed, her eyes were glued to a thick text. She held a glass of white wine in one hand, idly swirling its contents.

I set a jug of milk onto the stone countertop, the noise stirring her. She looked at me, that slow smile spreading over her full lips, rising higher on one side like she was thinking something naughty. Her wide brown eyes grew smaller as her cheeks lifted, her smile turning into a full-on grin at the sight of me.

Her awe-inspiring effect was in no way diminished from the first time I'd laid eyes on her.

Circling the counter and walking the length of the living area to the terrace, I knelt in front of her. As I pulled her legs away from her body, she set her book and glass of wine on the side table. With her legs stretched out, I was able to see all of her. She was a tiny thing — average height for a woman, but thin and small-boned. She'd taken up a more rigorous form of exercise than she was used to. Her new muscle tone was slight, but long and lean. As delicate as a dove.

I kissed the side of her knee, tasting sea salt, and admired the goosebumps that formed in response to my touch.

"I thought we said no work," I murmured against her skin, sliding my hand up her thigh to reach her hip.

"It's not for school," she insisted, wiggling.

So impatient.

I trailed kisses and little bites along her inner thigh. Her hands flew to my hair, where she sank her fingers into my haphazard curls. I groaned as her warmth soothed the ache in my chest, melting it into nonexistence.

She tugged on the crown of my head, pulling me up until our faces were level. Her half-lidded eyes were filled with the same heat as her touch.

"I'm never going to see Santorini if you keep doing this to me." She pouted, cupping my rugged jawline.

I leaned forward to kiss the dip where her collarbones met, teasing the handcuff charm on her necklace. "It's nowhere near as interesting as you."

Her wild hair smelled like the ocean, fresh and salty. She'd been swimming, but I recognized the underlying notes of apples and lavender in it. Her skin, normally ivory, was now the color of warm honey and twice as sweet. The new freckles adorning her nose were adorable. I'd kissed them a thousand times since they had appeared.

Summer Emma might have been my favorite version, but I said that every season.

"I'm a history major, Jack," Emma argued, as she was prone to do. She was one of few people on Earth I enjoyed sparring with. "My professors would kill me if they knew I went to Greece and barely even made it out of bed. Do you know how much there is to see here?"

I shook my head against her chest, watching with satisfaction as her nipples pebbled. "You'll have to enlighten me."

I had my reasons for not taking Emma into town. They were entirely selfish, and I knew it. Emma and I were both so busy back in Manhattan. We didn't see each other as often as I wanted. I could count on two hands how many times we had been able to sleep in the same bed. This was a vacation to Greece for Emma. It was a month of unfiltered access to my girl for me. I didn't give a shit about ancient history. Having Emma by my side every second of the day was the best thing I could ever hope for.

Before she could dispute further, I ripped the light fabric over her chest and pulled her breast into my mouth. Her spine arched off the chair, her body pushing into me of its own accord.

"Jack." She moaned my name. "That was expensive."

"I'll buy you ten more."

I licked my way down her flat belly, pressing the heel of my hand against my groin to quell the ache there. Emma groaned, her head falling back as I approached my goal. She was ready, as I knew she would be, her pink little pussy glistening for me.

"Move in with me," I breathed against her sex.

She shuddered with pleasure, then stiffened. "No."

I flattened my tongue, dragging it through her folds in one long, languid stroke. I swirled her clitoris twice, then pulled back. "Move in with me."

It had to have been the hundredth time I'd asked her to move into my apartment in the city. If she lived with me, we would have every night together. It would also ease my worries about her safety. If she wasn't on campus or working at Roisin's, I got antsy. Ideas of her being kidnapped invaded my mind, making me useless during work.

Alas, we'd had this conversation before. Emma's little sister, Ella, was moving to the city at the end of summer to attend Tisch, NYU's prestigious drama school. Emma wanted to be there for Ella during her first year at college, which included sharing an apartment with her.

Emma's ability to care for others was admirable, but exhausting. She was a genuine person. She aced her classes, was never late to work or school and emptied her wallet to the homeless. She didn't even eat meat. She was everything that I was not. When people thought of me, words like "selfish," "controlling" and "hard-ass," came to mind. Emma was soft and innocent. Everyone fell in love with her…and I was no exception.

Emma churned her hips toward my mouth, desperate to get off. A moan slithered from her throat, her chest rising and falling with heightening arousal. I licked and sucked, tugging her abused clit into my mouth. The moment her muscles seized, I stopped, denying her orgasm.

"Move in with me," I pleaded.

She roared—an adorable little tiger cub—and slammed her legs shut on either side of my head, pinning me to her. She knew I was taunting her with the edge, trying to persuade her to move in while she was hot and suggestible, and it was pissing her off.

"I'll smash your beautiful face if you keep doing that," she warned, her eyes flashing with frustration.

"Is that a threat, sweetheart? Because I can't think of a better way to die than suffocating in your pussy."

When a magnificent blush stained her cheeks, I smirked. Emma couldn't hurt me if she gave it her all. I could easily slip my head out from between her thighs, but I enjoyed driving her crazy. She did the same to me without trying. Even if it wasn't in a physical sense, Emma had a power over me that she was entirely unaware of. She was the one person on the planet who could put me in my place, and she just so happened to be less than half my size. My name had most men trembling in their boots, but Emma could bring me to my knees with a single glance.

"We'll go into town tomorrow," I said, my eyes roaming her delicate features. Her gaze was fixed on my mouth, greedy. "We can do whatever you want, dovey."

I bent my head, seeking to fulfill her wishes. My goal had and would always be to keep my little dove smiling.

* * * *

The setting sun had turned the sky a pinkish purple, the twinkling cliffside of Santorini a distant landscape. Emma, exhausted from hours of lovemaking, went to take a hot shower. I thought of joining her, but decided to start on dinner instead. When it came to her, I fought tooth and nail for some form of self-control. I had to remind myself that the poor girl needed a break from my ever-present sex drive, not that she ever complained.

Listening to the waves rolling onto the beach, I pulled the mussels and herbs from the fridge, setting the ingredients on a large cutting board. Cooking, along with exercise and fucking, was a way for me to get out of my own head, to step back from the unbearable coil of anxiety and anger that hissed beneath my skin.

I hadn't experienced much inner turmoil during the past two weeks and it had everything to do with Emma. She was my own personal medicine. *If only I could take her in pill form when we return to Manhattan.* We were halfway through our vacation, and I found myself wishing it could be permanent.

My phone buzzed from its charging station on the counter. I glanced at it wearily. We'd promised each other no work for a month, but Emma had already broken that. I knew the book she was reading had been assigned for summer break. Besides, she was in the shower. She wouldn't even know.

Leaving the cooking, I gathered my cell phone and pored over ten missed calls. Seven were from Shannon, three from Kieran, and they'd started around one in the morning New York time.

Shit.

I clicked on Shannon's picture, dialing my sister-in-law. She was two months from her due date, but anything could happen. If I missed that baby being born, Connor would kill me and Shannon would help dig the grave.

"Connor's gone dark," Shannon said by way of answering. Her voice was laced with fear and cracked as she spoke, putting me on high alert.

"How long?" I asked. It wasn't like my brother to go dark, especially without Shannon by his side. He was just as protective of her as I was of Emma, more so now that she was carrying their child. He stayed in contact with her at all times and didn't even let her out of the penthouse if things were getting dicey.

"He never showed in Boston last night." Shannon panted. I could hear her shoes clapping on marble floor. She was pacing at home. "Tom called and asked if I was with him."

Fuck. That had been over twelve hours ago. Something was wrong. Something was very fucking wrong. I spun around, turning the stove burners off.

"Who's with you?" I asked, making sure she wasn't alone while she waited for word.

"Just Guillermo," she replied, her anxiety worsening at the sound of mine.

Guillermo was their personal chef. Where was my younger brother? "Kieran?"

"Scouring the streets."

"Stay calm," I told her, although I felt anything but as I jogged into the bedroom.

Emma was just getting out of the shower, her hair still soaking wet and a plush towel wrapped around her torso. I reached into the closet, snatched the first dress I felt then tossed it to her.

"We'll be there tomorrow," I informed Shannon, ending the call. I hoped she would take my advice. It wasn't good for the baby to feel such stress, but it was inevitable given the circumstances.

When Emma saw my grim expression, her eyes widened. She slipped the dress over her head, yanking it down to her thighs as she stepped into a pair of sandals.

"We're leaving," I stated, throwing her phone, laptop and a few other necessary items into a backpack. I'd have the rest of our belongings shipped to us.

Thinking, as I had, that it was about the baby, Emma's nerves bled into her tone. "Charlie's not due yet."

I swung the backpack over my shoulder, grabbed Emma's hand and all but dragged her out of the bungalow. She struggled to keep up, her untied halter dress sliding off her shoulders. I bent down, scooped her into my arms, and carried her the rest of the way to the car. My brother had already been missing twelve hours and we wouldn't land in New York for another twelve. I was pressed for time.

"Get a flight plan set to La Guardia," I ordered the pilot, cell phone pressed to my ear as I buckled Emma into the G-Class. "We need to be in the air in an hour."

The pilot acquiesced without hesitation. I slammed Emma's door and rounded the front of the vehicle, throwing the bag into the backseat. The tires kicked up gravel as we sped onto the small street, well hidden from Santorini's higher-traffic tourist areas. I dialed another number and my younger brother answered over Bluetooth on the second ring.

"How far out?" Kieran asked, his monotone voice echoing throughout the interior of the vehicle. It sent a renewed jolt of panic through my bones. I hadn't heard his tone like that in years. Out of the three of us, Kieran was the least uptight.

"Twelve hours." I swerved past an old pickup truck, the bed of which was filled to the brim with potted plants destined for a local vineyard. Emma grabbed the side of the door to steady herself. "Call a meeting."

"With who?"

"Everyone. Meet at the northern safe house."

"Done," Kieran said, ending the call before I had the chance.

"What is it?" Emma's voice was faint. She knew something bigger was going on. This wasn't how I would react to the news of a baby coming.

"It's Connor," I gritted out, my jaw twitching as I admitted it aloud. "Someone got to him."

Chapter Two

Emma

We were aboard the O'Connells' private jet, putting space between us and the aqua sea, in just over an hour.

I didn't know how he'd gotten a flight plan and clearance in that small amount of time, but I'd stopped being shocked by Jack's capabilities long ago. The people who worked with him, and for him, knew better than to fail an order.

My stomach was in knots. The O'Connell brothers — Connor, Jack and Kieran — were the three-headed demon that governed the Irish mob in New York. They were close and, as such, trusted no one more than each other. They'd suffered together under the wrath of their father Frank. Sharing such a violent and abusive childhood had bonded them. With Jack not knowing where his sibling was, my heart ached for him, even if he hid his emotions behind a meticulously controlled mask.

On the other hand, Shannon would be wrought with worry. I wished I could offer her comfort, but it was impossible to make a phone call aboard the small aircraft. We would be dark for the next half-day, just as Connor was, but everyone was abreast of our whereabouts. No one knew where the face of the O'Connell family was.

Jack's gaze burned my profile as I looked out of the window, the sea now a solid expanse of blue beneath us. We passed above a few clouds, their white puffs like spun candy. Despite the stress of the situation, I was painfully aware that I wasn't wearing panties. I'd barely had enough time to put the sundress on.

By the heat of his stare, Jack was alerted to my missing undergarments as well.

Where most people would be still and pensive with worry, Jack was not. The more agitated he became, the more he craved physical release. He needed a punching bag to get his emotions out, and there wasn't one on his plane. Just me.

He was changing the way I reacted to stress, too. If I had a hard day, Jack was the sole person who could take my mind off it. We were addicted to each other. Some turned to drinking or drugs for comfort. We turned to one another.

I recrossed my legs, trying to quell the errant pulse in my core. Jack's gaze flitted to the hem of my dress, absentmindedly smoothing his finger over his bottom lip. He leaned back in the leather seat, his arousal growing in his jeans. The ever-present tether between our bodies hummed through the air, tantric and desperate.

I stood, walking across the cabin toward him. I took his hand, giving him a tentative smile. His hooded eyes met mine, pupils dilated.

"How is it you always know what I need?" he rasped, tightening his grip on my wrist. His features were indifferent, but shadows danced behind his green eyes like monsters lurking in an enchanted swamp. I was desperate to rid him of them, if just for a moment.

"Because I pay attention," I answered. "I watch, I listen, I learn. When necessary, I react."

He tilted his head, the intensity of his scrutiny enough to make my thighs tremble. "When necessary?"

"We have ten more hours in the air and the pilots are locked in their cabin." I ignored his question, straddling his lap. His gaze dipped to my cleavage, his throat bobbing as he swallowed. "Tell me exactly what you need, devil of mine."

"You, dove." Jack explored the bare skin at the base of my spine with his fingertips. He cradled me against his chest, his nose tracing warm circles behind my ear. "I'll always need you."

* * * *

When the elevator deposited us into the Upper East Side penthouse, Shannon was seated on the huge sectional in the living area. At the sound of our arrival, she stood at once. Or, she stood as quickly as a woman in her third trimester could.

"Have you heard anything?" she begged, holding her arms out.

Jack crossed the room with purposeful strides, enveloping her in his embrace. I stood behind them, the knot in my stomach growing from nausea to a cold, immutable pain.

Shannon melted while Jack held her, her fingernails embedding into his biceps as if she'd fall if he let go.

Her eyes were closed, but her wayward red locks and blotchy features told me she had been fretting nonstop.

Her stomach seemed to have doubled in size since I had last seen her. Three weeks ago, she'd been glowing, the type of woman who made carrying a child look simple. Now, she was too pale. Her belly jutted from her body like a foreign object had been shoved inside her.

Jack helped Shannon to the couch, glancing back to make sure I was following. I hesitated, deciding to make myself useful in the kitchen. Jack had this handled. As I turned on the burner and located some chamomile tea, I listened to their conversation, occasionally glancing at them from under the suspended cabinets.

"Any word from Kieran?" Jack asked.

"No." Shannon's voice broke. "It's like Connor disappeared off the face of the earth! He would never do this to me. Not now."

"I know, Shan," he soothed, brushing her hair away from her face. "We're going to find him."

She put her head in her hands, distraught. "I can't do this without him."

"Don't fucking think like that, okay?" Jack tilted her chin, meeting her watery gaze. "We *will* find him."

It sounded like Jack was reassuring himself more than Shannon, but I kept my nose to the ground, grabbing mugs from the cabinet below the espresso machine. I'd been to the penthouse many times. Shannon and I had spent hours choosing paint colors and decorations for Charlie's nursery. We fawned over organizing the changing table and hanging his miniature clothes in the closet. Sometimes I would just pop in after a shift at Roisin's.

Connor was rarely home, but on the off-chance he was, he greeted me with a warm, if not tentative, smile. He was glad that Shannon and I had grown so close. At least, I thought he was happy about our friendship. Like Jack, Connor guarded his emotions from everyone apart from his wife. But whereas Jack's aversion to exposing his feelings came from trauma, Connor's was a business tactic. He was the family's first line of defense, Kieran was the sweet-talker and Jack was the last resort. If a problem landed itself in front of the Emerald Devil, as Jack was often called, it didn't resurface.

Or so I'd been told, both by Shannon and Luca Nic—

A hand brushed my elbow and I startled, nearly dropping the kettle to the floor.

Jack took the steaming pot of tea from my hand, setting it on the marble countertop. "Can you do me a favor?"

"Of course," I replied without hesitation.

"I know we had a long flight," he started, peering at me from under his thick lashes. It had been a long flight. A long, sleepless, toe-curling flight. "But can you stay here with Shannon for a while?"

Every muscle in my body twitched with fatigue, but I didn't let it show. Shannon needed me. Jack needed me. The exhaustion I felt was nothing compared to what they were going through.

"Of course."

Jack cupped the nape of my neck, dusting his thumb over my cheekbone. He was uncomfortable but forced a smile nonetheless. He tugged me in for a kiss, his lips tight against my mouth like he couldn't bear the taste of me knowing he had to leave.

"I'm going to find my brother," he promised, his forehead pressed against mine.

"Please be careful," I begged. I didn't know everything going on in his world, but my emotions were in reaction to his. Something was horribly wrong. Jack wouldn't cut our vacation short for anything that didn't constitute an emergency. Connor hadn't lost cell service or decided to go for a joy ride. Someone was keeping him from getting in contact with his family. Or worse.

He kissed me one last time, his lips parting for a moment, before he turned and stalked off. He disappeared as the elevator doors slid shut.

Chapter Three

Jack

"I've been tryin' to call a meeting fer six months," Peter McKenzie fumed, cigarette dangling from his lips. A fleck of ash fell, flaring bright red before it landed on the cement ground and sizzled out. "Me men going missin' aren't important, but when an *O'Connell* disappears, everyone fuckin' listens!"

We were gathered in a large, dimly lit room. It was often used as an underground casino, but it'd been cleared for this meeting. Dust and smoke stained the air, thick and pungent. The other heads of house sat around a card table, but Peter and I stood, facing off.

"We don't give a fuck about what happened to your men," Kieran spat. He looked as weary as I felt. His mop of dirty blond hair was a mess, his clothes were wrinkled, and his face shone with sweat and filth. He'd barely made it back in time for the meeting.

I held a hand up, silencing my younger brother "Yes, we do. If our men have been going missing for this long, it could be the same people that got to Connor."

"Oh, so it's *our* men now, eh?" Peter scoffed. "Where were ye bastards when I had two Willies wash up with their throats slit?"

"I was at your home that day," I volleyed, "helping track their last movements."

It wasn't a lie. I had been with the McKenzies on that day back in November. I remembered because I'd been trying to cut the meeting short to call Emma before she went to sleep. I should've paid more attention to the deaths.

Two McKenzie recruits had surfaced along the Hudson, throats slit and almost all the blood drained from their bodies. As far as I knew, no one could say when or where they had been abducted. They'd disappeared into thin air. Like Connor had. Only these men had floated back up forty-eight hours later. It'd already been a day since Connor's last communication. If the same person or persons were involved, we were running out of time.

Peter McKenzie grunted and sat on a metal folding chair, lighting another cigarette to show he was done complaining. I continued to stand, my legs jittery like I needed to sprint. To where, I had no idea.

"Anyone else have disappearances we don't know about?" I asked, pacing to give myself something to do in the interim.

We had the heads of the McKenzie, Sweeney and Murray families gathered under one roof. That hadn't happened since Jeremiah Murray had been killed in prison. The three clans were entities unto themselves, but Connor governed them at a distance. With him missing, they answered to me. Whether they — or I, for that matter — liked it or not.

"We have a similar story," Michael Sweeney stated, twirling an ace of diamonds between two fingers. He was a quiet man in his mid-forties with mousy brown hair and small, inquisitive eyes.

I lifted my brows, a signal for him to continue.

Michael adjusted himself in his seat, dropping the playing card on the table. "About two weeks ago, my nephew disappeared on his way home from a yacht party. Found him a couple days later, dumped in the alley behind one of our restaurants in the Meatpacking District. Throat cut so deep he was nearly decapitated, the poor lad. All the blood gone."

A chill skated down my spine. Someone was picking off the Irish, that was obvious. I hoped to God whoever was doing this didn't have Connor, but the odds of it being anyone else were slim. We had many enemies, but Eoghan kept track of their movements. This threat had to be unknown to slip under his radar.

"Any leads?" I demanded.

Kieran shifted restlessly, coming to the same conclusion as me. We had a day, if that, to find Connor alive.

Bryan Murray rose, looking worse for wear. Their war with the Mafia wasn't going well. His father was in the hospital recovering from a shot to the head. With his eldest brother dead, nineteen-year-old Bryan was left in command of his family.

"I've heard rumors," he said, addressing me. He was pale and slim, his chin still housing the acne of youth. "Nicoletti brought someone over from Italy. Another family member."

"Luca Nicoletti ships people back an' forth from that godforsaken country every five minutes." McKenzie swore with vitriol, running a meaty palm through the orange scruff on his cheek. "We can't keep track of every Rickie or Vinnie coming an' going."

"Let the boy speak," I snapped, all too aware of the hand on my watch ticking. Was it moving faster or was that my imagination?

Bryan cleared his throat, proceeding. "I have a mole. She's in a position close to the Nicolettis. Said the men have been talking about some sort of 'enforcer' that Don Luca recruited to inspire fear, even among his own. The disappearances, the bodies, they all started around the time he brought this man to the States."

"Who's the mole?"

Bryan shuffled his feet, scuffing the toe of his boot along the cement floor. "I'd rather not say."

Kieran shot out of his seat, nearing Bryan. "Our brother is gone, and you'd rather not fucking *say*?"

I stepped in front of Kieran, keeping my focus on the Murray kid. "Where can I find her?"

"I'm not sure she'll be comfortable meeting with you." Bryan eyed me with evident worry. "She's in deep."

"I don't give a fuck what she's comfortable with!" I was starting to lose my sanity. Minute by minute, I was slipping, letting the rage take over. This was why Connor handled leadership. I was too volatile, too unpredictable. "Tell her to meet me at Roisin's at six this evening. If she objects, drag her ass in there yourself, Murray."

Bryan nodded obediently, turning to leave. I shot a text to update Arthur, Connor's first lieutenant who had refused to blink until my brother was found, then began instructing the remaining men. We were going to tear this city apart brick by brick. My father and his men were searching Boston, but I had a feeling Connor was closer to home.

Chapter Four

Emma

Shannon fell asleep on the couch a little before six. I grabbed a blanket from a nearby ladder shelf and laid it over her misshapen form, then cleaned the kitchen. Guillermo had left earlier, but I'd reheated tikka masala and urged Shannon to eat some of it. Her color had been making me nervous.

That wasn't the sole root of my anxiety. In Santorini, Jack had told Kieran to organize a meeting. But he'd left hours ago. Why wasn't he back yet? Why hadn't I heard from him? They obviously hadn't found Connor. He would've called Shannon to let her know.

The elevator dinged and I jogged toward it. My heart thrummed in anticipation, the need to see Jack overtaking my exhaustion. But when the doors slid open, a tall, leggy woman stood behind them. She wore a form-fitting blue dress and heels so high they would kill me if I tried to move in them. She was striking, with bright green eyes, auburn hair and glossy lips.

"Where's Shannon?" she asked, her voice low and throaty. She made her way into the foyer, walking past without so much as a glance in my direction. Her heels clicked on the marble, vibrating my eardrums.

"Sleeping," I whispered. I let my manners slip as I added, "Who the fuck are you?"

The woman turned, facing me. Her smile was sultry, her unapproving gaze skimming over my body. "Who the fuck are *you*?"

"Emma M-Marshall," I stammered, her challenge catching me off guard.

She wasn't an enemy of the O'Connell family if security had let her up here—the Shannon building was well guarded—but this woman also didn't appear friendly. By her pixie features and fire-hued hair, she wasn't related to the brothers. Then that must mean—

"I'm Faye Walsh," she announced with authority. "Shannon's aunt."

"You look more like a sister," I mumbled.

How old was Faye? Thirty? That was impossible. Shannon's parents died in a car accident when she was nine. She had been raised by her Aunt Faye, although she had told me Faye was a little wild and rarely home. I'd been picturing someone older with a bad dye job and cigarette breath. Not this...goddess.

Faye winked at me. "Good genes. Are you the housekeeper?"

My mouth popped open at her blatant disrespect. I was about to tell her off when I realized I was holding a dirty dishtowel. I set it on the entrance table, choosing to give her the benefit of the doubt.

I forced a sweet smile onto my lips. "I'm with Jack."

Faye's immaculate eyebrows disappeared into her hairline, the disbelief evident on her face. "Jack O'Connell?"

"That's the one." Sarcasm dripped from my words. I didn't like this woman. If I had fur, it'd be standing on end.

Faye laughed, but it wasn't joyful. "Jackie Boy got himself a girlfriend?"

I narrowed my eyes, refusing to respond. I was fully aware that Jack had been a womanizer before me. He'd never kept a girl around for longer than a day, which resulted in many one-night stands. He had broken the mold with me, but what the hell did Faye know about him? She'd stayed in Boston when Shannon and the brothers had moved to Manhattan five years ago.

"Well, I wouldn't get too attached, sweetheart," she cooed, her eyes wide like she cared about my feelings. I was under the impression that this woman didn't care about anything other than herself.

My spine stiffened. "Why's that?"

"I just ran into Jack downstairs in the restaurant. He had his arm around some pretty brunette. A little skanky in my opinion, but who am I to judge?"

My jaw dropped, but I recovered. "Keep an eye on your niece."

She chuckled darkly as I scooped my cell phone off the glass entry table. I stepped into the private elevator and jammed the button for the lobby over and over, forcing the doors to close.

I didn't believe a word that nasty woman said, but it didn't stop the jealousy from choking me like a sandstorm in the desert. I hadn't known I was a jealous person. I had no reason to be until I met the likes of Jack O'Connell. Wherever we went, he turned heads.

Waitresses, hotel staff, even random women on the street tried to flirt with him. They got dazed looks on their faces, their mouths turned up in sexy smiles despite my presence. Jack never gave them the time of day, taking his eyes from me only when necessary.

He's looking for his brother, Em. Calm down.

Still, my heart was in my throat as I descended sixty floors. My fingers curled into fists, then I flexed them again. I was dead on my feet, an emotional wreck. My feet were bare, and I'd been wearing the same tiny sundress for more than twenty-four hours.

I exited the elevator and padded toward the entrance of Roisin's, thankful I'd had the foresight to steal a pair of Shannon's panties. I was vulnerable enough as it was.

A few of my fellow servers eyed me with suspicion as I carved a path through the restaurant, the dim lights reflecting off crystal dining ware and bronze crown molding. As usual, the place was packed with patrons. I was a fish out of water in my less-than-formal attire. Air blasted from the vents, making me shiver from both the chill and an impending mental breakdown.

I banked left down a darkened hall, approaching the solid oak door to the private room. Upon twisting the knob, I discovered it was locked. Hushed voices conversed on the other side. I recognized Jack's deep tone immediately. The other was a woman.

Lungs burning, I pounded on the door.

A girl my age opened it. She was taller than me in high-heeled boots and her dark brown hair was curled to perfection, ending just above her hip bones. Her clothes were skimpy but expensive, and she was attempting to stuff a wad of crisp hundreds into her impressive cleavage.

Jennifer Luna

She was a sex worker. By the looks of it, a high-end call girl.

"You're in my way," she chided, her displeasure evident.

Jack reached for the girl, tugging her toward him. He couldn't see me standing there, his peripheral blocked by the half-closed door.

"I'm not done with you," he growled, his hand still wrapped around her twiggy upper arm.

Stepping into view, I let my gaze rake over him, my skin sizzling with fury. Jack's clothes were wrinkled, his chocolate curls a sexy mess. He had dark circles under his emerald eyes, which froze once he saw me. His already sharp face hardened to stone, his jaw clenched. There was a pained look in his eye, but the rest of his expression was one of annoyance.

"Go back upstairs, Emma." His words were soft, but it was clearly an order.

The rage almost blinded me, but I refused to blink. If I did, the tears would fall. His betrayal hit me like a sword to the gut, spilling my entrails. I wanted to double over — vomit, scream, hit him — but I didn't. I had to keep some shred of dignity.

"Fuck you, Jack," I cursed with vehemence, the words struggling around the lump in my throat.

He ground his molars, preparing a retort. I didn't give him the chance. I spun around and left the damn restaurant. *Screw him and his orders.* I wasn't going upstairs to be with Shannon and her awful aunt. If he was fucking other women while his brother was missing, he didn't deserve my devotion.

I repeated this over and over to myself, trudging across Park Avenue, still barefoot. A few heads turned in my direction as I sped toward the subway, but I was numb to my surroundings. The tears were falling, burning an acidic path down my cheeks. My nose started to run. I wiped at it angrily, MetroCard in hand as I descended into the underground.

Fuck him.

Chapter Five

Emma

When I got to my empty apartment, I forced myself to shower. I felt like crashing in my bed and crying myself to sleep, but I was filthy. After walking the streets and riding the subway barefoot, I should've checked myself into quarantine for a bleach bath and skin-melting steam.

But the shower would have to do.

I washed myself methodically, focusing on scrubbing my feet and legs as hard as I could. Images of Jack and the woman flitted through my mind, making me choke. I took my anger out on myself, cleaning until my skin turned red and raw, digging into the crevices between my toes to make sure I rid myself of the city.

When I had nothing left to distract myself, I threw the loofah over the shower curtain, hoping it landed near the trash bin next to the sink. My fury was fading, and so was I.

My legs lost their battle with gravity. My spine slid along the cool shower wall, and I fell with a thud. I pulled my knees to my chest and tucked my head into them, letting the water drown out my sobs.

Exhaustion would take over soon and that would be the only relief, assuming my dreams weren't as dark as my reality. I knew I should get out of the shower and go to bed, but I was scared to move. Turning off the water and stepping into the central air would force me to face the circumstances of what I'd just seen.

Connor was missing, and Jack hadn't sought me for comfort. He'd returned to his old method of stress relief — fucking and fighting. He met with his men, then hired a prostitute to curb his appetite. Not that he needed to pay for sex. He could grab a girl at random off the street and she'd climb into bed with him, no questions asked.

I'd always known something like this would happen. It was one of the reasons I had refused to move in with him, to jump into this relationship with both feet. There was always a deep-rooted fear that I wouldn't be enough for Jack. Apparently, I'd been correct.

Don't think like that.

It wasn't my sole responsibility to keep him happy. And if I wasn't enough for Jack, then I wouldn't bend over backward trying to meet his needs. He might be going through something horrible, but he was still a piece of shit for cheating on me. I'd made my stance clear in the restaurant.

The shower curtain was suddenly yanked to the side. I jumped, a small scream escaping my throat. Ava, my roommate, had moved out over a month ago. She was staying the summer with her parents in Connecticut before moving to Milan. Until my little sister arrived for the fall semester at NYU, I had the apartment to myself.

"What the fuck do you think you're doing?"

Jack was angrier than I'd ever seen. He was seething, his chest rising and falling as if he'd sprinted across the park to my building. His eyes were bright green, in stark contrast to the bluish-purple shadows beneath them. Even furious, his beauty was severe. The perfection annoyed me, lighting a fire under my ass and giving me a renewed burst of energy.

"The door was locked," I snapped, getting to my feet and turning the water off. My legs trembled, but I did my best to hide it. I would not show weakness. Not in front of him.

"I made myself a key." He grabbed a pink towel from the rack, thrusting it at me. "Now tell me why I got a call from Eoghan saying you rode the subway wearing practically *nothing*?"

I wrapped the towel around myself and exited the bathroom. "I told you to stop having me tailed."

He was hot on my heels as I made my way through the apartment to my bedroom. "If you stopped using the subway, my men wouldn't have to tail you."

Once in my room, I rounded on him. "You have some balls walking in here being upset with me for breaking our promise when you were fucking someone at Roisin's!"

Jack reeled back like I'd slapped him, which I was very close to doing. He froze, his temper ebbing at my words. His features softened, as if he couldn't believe

I'd come to that conclusion. "I didn't cheat on you, dove."

His words settled in the air, but I didn't give myself a chance to process them. Adrenaline was making it difficult to string two thoughts together. I pulled clothes on at random — ripped jeans, floral blouse, mismatched socks. Whatever was left on the floor after packing for Greece.

Jack neared, reaching for my hand like he was attempting to tame a wild animal.

"Don't fucking touch me," I bit out.

He grabbed my wrist anyway, pulling me against him with a huff. His chest was warm and familiar, his scent welcoming. I fought to break free of his iron grip, hating the way my body responded to him.

"She's a mole," he murmured into my wet hair. "I was paying her for information about where Connor might be."

My breath caught in my throat. I stopped struggling, shame flooding through me. I screwed my eyes shut, the stinging tears threatening to return. Damn it, I'd messed up. I was so quick to believe that Jack had betrayed me. I'd let my own insecurities get the better of me.

"Faye told me she saw you..." I trailed off, my voice strangled as I tried to explain my reasoning. God, I'd acted immature, foolish.

Jack held me at arm's length, his emerald eyes melting into me. He caught a stray tear with the pad of his thumb, licking it clean. "Faye loves drama."

My upper lip curled in disgust. "Her niece is eight months pregnant with a missing husband. How much more drama does she need?"

Jack grimaced, but his half-smile was apologetic. *I should have been the one apologizing.*

I nuzzled into his hand, attempting to do just that. "I'm so sorr —"

But I was cut off by Jack's cell phone ringing. He retrieved it from his pocket and answered, keeping one arm around me. He gave my shoulder a reassuring squeeze, letting me know we were okay.

"Go," he ordered.

I waited, still soaking in embarrassment. The rush of emotions — jealousy, anger, despair — had all been for nothing. If I'd followed his orders and stayed at the Shannon, he would've told me as much. I was even more drained than before, but my mind shifted gears. We were back to the one thing that mattered — finding Connor.

"Send me a pin."

Jack led us back into the living room. He tossed a pair of white sneakers at me, and I hustled to put them on. While I tied my hair into a low ponytail, Jack pulled his revolver from his waistband. He looked it over, checking the cylinder before snapping it back in place. The metallic click pierced my eardrums, sending an ominous chill down my spine.

"Where are we going?" I asked, trying to keep the fear from my voice. This had been the longest twenty-seven hours of my life and, although they were frequent in Jack's line of work, guns made me nervous.

"They found the vehicle Connor was using. It's parked on a street in Brownsville. Our men are casing the block." He tucked the revolver into his jeans and looked me over, terror flitting across his face so fast I wondered if I'd imagined it. "Stay by my side."

"Always," I answered, taking his hand as we exited my apartment.

* * * *

Over the past couple of months, I'd grown accustomed to Jack's favorite mode of transportation. The Icon Sheene and I had become fast friends, pun intended. Once the temperature got above sixty degrees, Jack had me on the back of his motorcycle, squealing as we tore through the streets of New York. He was crazy about the damn bike. No one apart from me was allowed to touch it, let alone ride it. Jack said he'd never been possessive in his previous relationships, but I didn't think he'd factored in his Sheene.

I joined him so often on the powerful piece of metal that he'd given me a custom helmet for my twenty-second birthday this past spring. Like his, mine was matte black and connected to his phone's Bluetooth, but the smoky halo adorning the back was a personal touch. Jack was a fearless conductor, but he exercised restraint with me as a passenger.

That was not the case today.

My body fused with his as we barreled south through Manhattan, weaving in and out of traffic. Like every other aspect of my life with him, it was easier to let him guide. I leaned into him as we tilted, pulled my knees tight when he took a sharp turn. Even my lungs synced themselves with his.

When we reached the Brooklyn Bridge, our helmets rang with an incoming call, startling me. Jack's phone had been silent for the past twenty minutes, which was uncommon for one of the wealthiest arms dealers in the world.

Jack answered in a monotone, his mind clearly elsewhere. "I've got Wings."

"I've got Wings." That was his way of letting his men know I was listening in on the call. The phrase had become a running joke. Whenever Eoghan was tasked with driving me around town, he called it Wing Duty. At the gym, members of the mob I hadn't even met referred to me as Wings. Jack had no idea what he'd started by referring to me as his angel.

"We've narrowed the location down to one building," Kieran stated, his voice laced with anticipation. "Where the hell are you?"

"Five minutes out," Jack clipped.

"Fuck it. I'm going in."

"No, you are not!" he roared, rattling the bones in my skull. "Wait for me, Kieran. I'm five min—"

"I'm going in, Jack." Kieran ended the call.

"God fucking dammit!"

Jack revved the engine. It vibrated beneath me, the humid wind whistling through my helmet louder than it ever had. I cinched my grip around his waist, no doubt crushing a few of his ribs, but Jack didn't seem to notice. I was afraid to open my eyes and look around. We had to be going dozens of miles over the speed limit. Every muscle in Jack's body was hardened, the tension thick as ropes under my arms.

When we began to slow, I allowed myself to peek at my surroundings.

The sun had just set as Jack pulled us to the curb outside an old three-story Brooklyn warehouse. A few people stood outside, their shadows long against the brick wall. They were O'Connell men I recognized from the St. Patrick's Day celebration at the Emerald. At that time, they'd been plastered, goofing off and laughing. Now, their faces were somber as they guarded the vaulted entrance.

Jack killed the engine. I jumped off the bike, setting my haloed helmet on one of the side mirrors. He grabbed my hand as we jogged along the sidewalk, but our path was stopped by one of Jack's men.

"Get the fuck out of my way, Cathal," Jack snarled. The lines of his face were etched in misery, like he knew what was on the other side of the door. The ache in my belly worsened, adrenaline blurring my vision.

Cathal bristled, but his tone was gentle, soothing. "We've cleared the area, Jack, but you don't want to go in there."

Jack's nostrils flared, his throat working on a swallow. "That's an order."

Cathal glanced in my direction, seeking my help. When he got none, he stepped aside to let us through. He kept his gaze locked on mine as we passed by, a beacon of warning in his eyes. The hair on the nape of my neck stiffened. I thought I might vomit, but I hadn't eaten anything for more than a day.

Jack's head hung lower and lower the farther we traveled down the ill-lit hallway, like an anvil was crushing him under its weight. My legs trembled, but I followed his retreating form. I couldn't stop. I had promised I would stay with him.

A dark-haired man was seated on the floor to the right of an open doorway at the end of the hall, his back pressed against the brick, his head dangling between his bent legs. If defeat had a posture, this man embodied it. I'd never met him, but I'd seen him guarding Shannon on a few occasions. And if he had been tasked with ensuring Shannon's safety, that meant he was close with Connor — probably high in the chain of command.

The man's fingers twitched upon our arrival, but he didn't look up as Jack brushed past him and into the large room. I continued after him, despite the cold draft escaping from the doorway.

When we entered, Jack halted with a quick intake of breath, his gaze shooting up toward the vaulted ceiling. I almost ran into him but caught myself. Jack stood just ahead of me, his arm outstretched behind in a protective gesture. I followed his line of sight, my knees wobbling when I saw what he was staring at.

It was Connor, but I wouldn't have recognized him apart from his signature Brioni suit. He was dangling upside down from the rafters high over our head, a thick rope tied around both feet. His eyes were closed, his face covered in his own slick blood. His throat had been slit, the sea of dark red on the concrete floor beginning to dry. He'd been hanging there, dead, for hours.

Kieran was kneeling underneath his eldest brother, his jeans soaked in blood. He held his head in his hands, shoulders shaking violently. He was sobbing, but I couldn't hear anything apart from the loud ringing in my ears. My brain had gone fuzzy, like I'd been transported into one of my nightmares. Except I hadn't had a nightmare since last fall, and this was too horrific to be fake. A few seconds passed in utter silence, but they felt like an eternity.

I looked at Jack, my mind refusing to process anything.

He turned away from his dead brother, leaning his forehead against the brick behind us. His eyes were screwed shut, his teeth gritted in pain. Reality came spinning back to me when Jack punched the wall repeatedly, the bones in his hand cracking.

I ran to him and grabbed his wrist, holding him back. I wasn't strong enough, but he stopped anyway. I wrapped my arms around him as best I could, holding him upright until his legs gave out. We fell to the ground together.

"*Fuck!*" he howled, his voice cracking.

It was a long, terrible, heartbreaking wail that left my teeth chattering. It was a cry I recognized. A roar of deep agony, of soul-splitting loss. I cradled him, my fingers numb with shock. My breathing was hitched, the air leaving my lungs in short puffs.

Jack pressed the side of his head against my chest. I held it there, my palm on his cheek. His body went limp, and he shook against me. I rocked back and forth, clinging to him with every ounce of strength I had.

Silent tears dripped down my face as sirens approached.

Chapter Six

Emma

I slid the black blazer down my arms, setting it on the arm of Jack's leather couch. I took my heels off and tucked them under the furniture, out of Fiagaí's sight. The house panther had a thing for my shoes, in particular. He would tear them to shreds once he found them, but I'd let the cat do his worst.

The apartment was dark, the sole source of light coming from those of the city. The view through the glass wall was staggering, despite the immense sadness that hung in the air. Jack's grief was palpable, even if he hid it well. And here, alone in his safe space for the first time in a week, it emanated from him like a tangible force. As if a demon inhabited the room with us, feeding on the stagnant energy.

Turning, I helped him out of his suit jacket, careful not to nudge his bandaged hand. He studied me as I removed the material from his arms, his face unreadable, but there was an emotion in his eyes I didn't like. Immense sorrow, yes, but something else as well. Whatever it was, it made my heartbeat quicken.

It'd been a long seven days filled with funeral arrangements, hushed conversations, stifled sobs and the occasional questions from law enforcement. I had stood by Jack's side through it all. Even if I had wanted to step away—which I never did—he wouldn't let me out of his sight. If so much as a foot of space came between us, his arm reached out of its own accord and pulled me back. Like his subconscious couldn't stand the distance.

The only time we had separated was when he had to speak with his men. We'd been confined in the penthouse of the Shannon, but it was large enough to house us all and then some. Their meetings had been held in the dining hall, and no one was permitted into that wing until they were over. I imagined it had been turned into some sort of war room, with members of the Irish mob dropping in unannounced. They carried flowers or home-cooked meals into the kitchen, then disappeared down the hall to join the others.

During the time I had been alone, I'd seen to my own biological needs—using the bathroom, showering, changing my clothes—but mostly I had sat on the bed in the guest room that Jack and I shared, my head in my hands. I'd focused on the simple act of breathing, trying to decompress as best I could.

"I need to show you something," Jack muttered now, taking my hand in his uninjured one.

His footsteps echoed down the hallway as we neared his bedroom. The apartment seemed even bigger than usual, and empty. Fia was nowhere to be seen. He was probably prowling the many rooms, hunting for spiders. Jack's housekeeper—a skinny, balding, middle-aged man with red hair—had been watching him while we'd been gone.

Jack led me into his closet and flipped on the lights. I'd been in here many times before, but it never ceased to impress. The room was huge, accented with dark wood and brass furnishings. Custom black dress suits lined half of one wall. The other half housed a series of drawers where Jack kept everything else—jeans, T-shirts, underwear, over a dozen designer watches in a glass case. There was a black granite island in the middle with more storage area, a vase of fresh red roses sitting atop.

The other side of the closet—the side Jack had designated mine—was remarkably bare. A few dresses and jackets hung on the racks, other basic essentials stuffed into a drawer or two. I hadn't wanted to give him the impression that I was moving in, but that was before.

Given the circumstances, I would relocate to Jack's luxury apartment overlooking Central Park without a second thought. Jack's needs far outweighed my own insecure reasons for hesitating.

Jack crossed the closet and opened a large antique armoire. Instead of clothing or more storage space, there was a giant metal door with a digital pad on it. I'd seen the safe before but hadn't paid it any mind. Jack wouldn't make any *Forbes* lists because of how he obtained his money, but he was a billionaire. And apart from the pistol in the kitchen, he didn't leave weapons lying around the house. It all had to go somewhere.

"Memorize this, Emma," he ordered.

I stood behind him as he entered the code. It was long, but I committed it to memory.

"Got it?"

"Yes." My voice came out as a whisper, startling me. We'd conversed so little with one another over the past week. Hardly anyone had spoken at the wake, apart from Frank O'Connell, but no one had paid him any attention. I hadn't seen Jack's father since Christmas, and I hadn't missed him in the slightest. He had a few new scars, and his nose was bent from where his son had beaten him to within an inch of his life. Even so, I had hung around Jack. I wouldn't have put it past Frank to try to start something, but he had altogether ignored us.

Jack swung the heavy door open and gestured for me to enter. Bewildered, I did as I was told. Lights sprang to life, buzzing along the ceiling. I blinked a few times, adjusting my eyes to my surroundings.

Well, I'll be…

The safe was not, in fact, a safe. It was a hidden room. The shelves on either side were filled with dozens of weapons, each seated in its own charcoal foam case. I didn't know anything about arms, but it was obvious few of them were legal. Sniper rifles, automatic machine guns, dozens of different pistols, shotguns. Not to mention grenades, flash bombs, throwing knives, brass knuckles, Kevlar vests. It was overwhelming, but it didn't end there.

At the other end of the room, gold bars were stacked against the wall. Next to those sat a series of metal briefcases, one on top of the other, and a large filing cabinet with a heavy lock on it.

"It's a panic room," Jack said, shutting the door behind us.

As he did so, claustrophobia descended on me. I ran my thumbs over my palms, conscious of the clamminess on them. "Why are you showing me this?"

He ignored my question, his gaze locked on me, intent and severe. "You have the code memorized?"

"Yes, but—"

"We're the only two people who know it." He raked his hand through my hair, pushing one side over my shoulder, then gave me a feather-light kiss. My lips tickled where his brushed mine. "Take this."

He removed a black Amex from the pocket of his slacks and put it in my hand. The prestigious credit card felt heavier than it should.

"I don't—"

"Each of these has a million in cash." Jack gestured toward the five silver briefcases sitting next to the pile of gold. "If you need more, I've left a business card for my finance officer next to your sink in the bathroom."

My breathing grew erratic. "Jack, you're scaring me."

He wrapped his arms around my smaller frame, tugging me to him, pinning my hands against his iron chest. He smelled heavenly. Woodsy, smoky, rainy. Like a thunderstorm.

"I have to take my brother home," he murmured into my hair, his words choked.

He was talking about Connor's body. "To Boston?"

He shook his head, burying his face in the crook of my neck. "Ireland."

"I'll pack a bag."

He dropped his hands to my hips. "I can't bring you with me, dove. I need you to take care of Shannon."

Tears welled in the corners of my eyes. "She has Faye."

"Faye is unreliable at best. Shannon needs someone like you by her side right now."

He was right, of course. Shannon hadn't spoken since that fateful night. She just stared into space. She would eat or drink, but only if someone set it in front of her. She would sleep if someone tucked her into bed, but she was vacant. It was torture to look at her. For the first two days, the one person she had allowed in her room had been her aunt, which concerned me. I didn't trust Faye to see to the needs of a grieving, pregnant woman.

Reluctantly, I nodded. Jack cupped my face in his hands, the gauze on his knuckles scratching my cheek.

"I know I'm asking too much of you, as usual," he started. When I began to protest, he continued with renewed vigor. "But I need you to do one more thing for me."

"Anything."

"Please, for the love of God, keep yourself safe. Don't go anywhere alone. Always use a driver. Don't take the subway. I'm leaving Eoghan under your command."

I'd already assumed Jack knew more about what had happened to his brother than he let on. There was still a threat out there. Whoever had mutilated Connor hadn't been caught. No one knew just how the culprit—or culprits—had caught Connor unaware, and the vehicle that had been found in Brownsville had been wiped clean. The FBI was looking into it now. Connor's was the fourth body to turn up in such a way. It was a miracle the media hadn't caught on yet.

Jack held my hand as we exited the panic room. The code had to be entered to get out once the door had shut. He locked it behind us but made me reopen it. He wanted to be positive I knew how to get myself in and out. If I got stuck inside, there was a button I could push, but it would ping the entire mob. They would show up in tactical gear, seeking to neutralize a threat. The image of them descending just to find me trapped in the room was mortifying. There was no way I'd forget the code.

When we got back into his bedroom, the lights inside the apartment were still off. The reflection of the city shone in Jack's dilated pupils, desperation blanketing his features.

"I have an hour."

I was already slipping out of my pencil skirt. Jack was quick to undress himself, then helped me with the buttons on my blouse. The care he took in getting me to bed was slow and methodical. His lips danced over mine as he positioned himself above me. He lowered his body, his erection pressing into my belly. His hands moved like honey, slow and sweet, caressing my skin. He kissed me everywhere, setting my senses ablaze, not an inch of skin going untouched.

Each time Jack entered me, it was a new experience. Sometimes I got his darkness, his demons. Other times, he was playful, lighter. He challenged me, his approach to sex changing like a mood ring. I was obsessed with every emotion he gave, because he rarely graced anyone else with so much as a second glance.

But I wasn't sure I liked this form of fucking. It wasn't rough, or caring or anything in between. Perhaps I was wrong. Perhaps it was everything in between. When he finally slid into me, our breathing was fast, but he kept the pace slow. Like he never wanted it to end.

This was a goodbye.

The intensity built as Jack moved his cock in and out, in and out. He kept his hooded gaze on mine, rotating his hips to massage my most sensitive areas. His gaze flitted across my features, committing them to memory.

I bit my lip, telling myself not to let the tears fall. Even if he could see them pooling in the corners of my eyes, I would wait until he left. I didn't want his parting memory of me to be one of sadness. The entire week had been one long grievance.

Let him have this moment.

Hell, let me *have this moment.*

Jack broke our stare first, sinking his teeth into my neck, marking me.

"*Mo anam cara*," he growled, his breath hot.

He nipped at the throbbing pulse in my throat. My skin misted with sweat. I tilted my hips, wrapping my legs around his middle to allow him deeper. Our chests pressed together, hearts beating in sync.

"W-What does that mean?" I stuttered.

As an answer, Jack quickened his pace, bottoming out over and over. He locked his mouth over mine, swallowing my moan. He licked and sucked, biting my bottom lip with a subtle sharpness. When I reached down, digging my nails into his backside, he hissed, punishing me with his desire.

"*Mo. Anam. Cara.*"

He repeated the words with every flex of his hips, pounding them into my womb. The familiar tingling sensation was like an illegal stimulant in my veins. My muscles tensed with the inevitable. I didn't want this to end, but my body betrayed me, greedy for release.

"Are you with me, baby?"

"Always," I answered, as he knew I would

"If I don't finish now, I'll never let you go."

His eyes blazed with heat, catching mine as he gripped the base of my thighs. I reached up, caressing his jaw in one hand, fisting the sheets in the other. The power behind each ensuing thrust was enough to knock the breath from my lungs. I didn't want him to let me go, but my orgasm came regardless.

"Jack!" I moaned his name, letting it pour over my lips.

My channel twitched around his thickening cock. The ball of sorrow, of grief, exploded from me in an ongoing disaster. My body went limp in his arms as Jack neared his own finish line.

"Fuck, fuck, fuck," he whispered, his voice cracking in the darkness.

When he came, he kept his face bowed, his brow drawn. A strangled sob escaped him, and I found the willpower to pull him against my chest. I held him there while we both calmed, running my fingers over the smooth contours of his back. He turned his face to me, peppering my skin with slow, loving kisses.

Time passed, neither of us willing to move. He let himself soften inside me while we lay there, intertwined. I ingrained this moment in my mind—his stormy scent, the sound of his steady breath, the way his large body molded perfectly around mine. I didn't know how long he would be gone. He hadn't said, and I didn't want to ask. He was going home to bury his brother. It would take as long as it took.

When he rose, he took care in untangling our limbs. My skin chilled. I got to my knees as he slid from the bed, already aching from his absence.

Silent, he dressed in jeans and a T-shirt, a ball cap and Converse. He had a bag sitting by the door, but it'd been too dark for me to notice when we had walked in. My eyes were adjusted now, but I still wasn't ready to watch him go.

He knelt by the bed, his face level with mine, and leaned in to kiss me once more. I parted my lips for him, letting him taste me. His lips were electric, the energy between us at an all-time high. As if it knew we would be parting and was fighting to hang on.

When he pulled away, we both had to catch our breaths. He held my face in his hands, his forehead pressed to mine. While he kept his eyes closed, I studied him. His long lashes, the steady slope of his nose, the strength of his jaw, the dark stubble along it.

"Mo anam cara."

His words from earlier floated back to me. Were they Irish? Jack and his brothers had taught themselves the language when they were younger as a means to converse without Frank being in the know.

"What does it mean?" I asked again.

Jack opened his eyes and looked straight into mine. The green of his irises pierced right through me, striking me at my very core. Like an arrow parting the flesh of an animal.

"I love you, dove."

A persistent tear broke loose, burning a path down my cheek and falling onto the white comforter between us. We'd never told each other that before, although we both knew it was true. It'd been on the tip of my tongue since Thanksgiving, but I had been too much of a coward to admit it aloud, to recognize how much a part of me he'd become.

"What took you so long?"

"I was struggling to find the right words…to tell you how strongly I feel for you." Jack's lips twitched into a grim smile. "I've concluded that they don't exist in the English language, but 'I love you' will suffice."

The joy at finally hearing those words spill from his mouth was diminished by the fact that he was leaving. "I love you, Jack."

As if he'd been waiting for that confirmation, he dropped his hands from my face and rose, grabbing his bag on his way out. He never once turned back. I listened to his feet speed down the hallway. Then the elevator dinged shut.

He's gone.

I sat, naked and kneeling, on the bed for a while after, wishing he'd reappear in the doorway. But I knew better. He wouldn't be returning. Not for a while, anyway.

I wasn't sure how much time had passed before I fell onto the pillows. I pulled the blankets under my chin, curled into a little ball and rid myself of whatever tears remained.

Chapter Seven

Emma

The very next morning, I broke my promise.

I was standing in the foyer in nothing but one of Jack's dress shirts, staring at a framed photo on the side table. I tapped my spoon against a plastic carton of blueberry yogurt, contemplating.

Shannon had taken the photograph on New Year's Eve. It was a shot of Jack and I right when the ball dropped. We were locked in a kiss, unaware of the camera. Jack's giant hand encompassed my jaw, tilting my head to the side in the way I loved. The tiniest bit of tongue glistened, the lights of the nightclub dyeing our skin a neon purple. Our mouths were turned upward in silly, buzzed smiles.

Fiagaí circled my legs as I studied the couple in the frame. Was I still the same woman? Because the woman in that picture had been content to take whatever Jack could give her. She'd sworn not to push him too far, not to delve into the details of his work or past.

I loved Jack, but he was only letting me love half of him.

"Don't use the subway, never go anywhere alone, Eoghan is yours to command."

Jack had left me in the dark, without so much as a single explanation. I knew there was a threat, but I wasn't sure what to look for. How long would I have to glance over my shoulder, searching the streets for unidentifiable enemies? How long would Jack be gone? When would I hear from him? Would anyone bother to let me know when it was safe again?

Two hours later, those questions still plagued me as I sat on the stiff mattress in room 1523 of the Booker Hotel. I took a cab, having confirmed that Eoghan was tracking my MetroCard usage. It was the simplest explanation for why Jack was able to find me so fast whenever I used the subway.

I scrolled through my phone while I waited, although I didn't have any notifications. Jack would still be in the air, and my family thought I was in Greece. I hadn't had the time or the energy to fill them in on all that had occurred. Instead, I poured through my camera roll. Images of Jack. Of both of us together. The aqua sea in Santorini. A snapshot of him fighting in the octagon. A selfie from his birthday. A candid I had taken while he slept in bed, the winter sun kissing his bare chest.

Anything to distract me from the wait — but it took a mere thirty minutes for Don Luca's men to show. Without a word, I stood and allowed them to place a cloth bag over my head, holding my wrists together for them to tie. I'd been through the process just once, but

I knew the drill. I left my purse and cell phone behind as the men pulled me from the room, taking me to him.

Jack thought he was protecting me by keeping me out of the loop, so I was forced to seek answers from the very last person I wanted to see. The man I thought I'd never return to, although he'd said he would leave his door open for me — figuratively, of course. If anyone knew what was going on in the underbelly of this city, it would be him.

"Hello, little one."

Another hour had gone by. I'd been shoved into an idling vehicle and driven in silence to the don of the New York Mafia. Luca Nicoletti was as immaculate as ever. Dressed in a luxurious buttoned shirt and slacks, he appeared youthful despite his age, his handsome features reeking of foreign aristocracy. The don was a dragon slumbering beneath human skin. I, in turn, donned my mask as well.

"Do you know who's been murdering the Irish?" I asked, seeking to skip his pleasantries. It was worth a shot, but I should have known better. I was on his time. It didn't matter how badly I wanted answers. He might have been a monster, but he was also a stickler for manners.

Don Luca gestured for me to sit, his smile oozing with wickedness. We were in his study adjacent to the billiard room. His large mahogany desk was clear apart from a small laptop, but that was closed. The walls were lined with books and awards, commendations from his many donations to local charities and law enforcement. It was racketeering at its finest.

I sighed, planting my butt on a plush leather armchair. Don Luca did the same, claiming a seat across from me. His expression was almost one of pride, as if he were delighted I'd come to see him. It made me ill.

"Amara," he called into the other room. I was surprised to discover we weren't alone. "Make Emma and me something to drink."

"It's nine in the morning," I protested. Don Luca didn't seem like the type to indulge so early in the day. He was a busy man.

His grin widened. "Amara makes a delicious cappuccino."

I glanced at the entryway to the billiard room. I could hear glasses being set down and feet shuffling on the hardwood floor.

"Can she hear us?"

The rest of the Mafia didn't know why Nicoletti and I were meeting. He liked to keep it private. If they knew what I did, they would turn on him.

"She is my niece," he explained, always taking care to enunciate his words, English being his second language. "She knows all about our little... arrangement."

Meaning she knew her uncle had paid to have his own daughter murdered. She knew he'd had Jeremiah Murray framed to get access to him in prison, then he'd had Murray killed to kickstart a war. She thought, as the don did, that I had a letter in my possession that could take him down. That I was holding it over his head in exchange for safety.

Don Luca watched me with practiced scrutiny, twiddling his thumbs in his lap. He had one ankle crossed over his knee, his lean form a picture of ease.

"I do happen to know who has been taking the Irishmen out," he spoke, inclining his head in admission.

I cleared my throat, impatient. "And?"

"I have an associate that likes to be referenced not by their given name, but the name that has grown infamous in our ranks. The Babau."

"Babau," I repeated. My lips pulled at a smile before I realized he wasn't joking. "As in 'the bogeyman'?"

"I'm not surprised you know the Italian version of the legend." The don applauded. "It's no longer popular to use fear to inspire children's obedience, but the Babau was once an effective parenting tool. A child was less likely to forget their place or speak out of turn if they knew a monster would steal them from their beds and feast on their blood."

I fought to keep my emotions under control, but recalling the way Connor had been found shook me to my marrow. Even at the viewing, Connor's face had been so pale. They had put him in a black turtleneck under his suit to hide the gaping wound at his throat. It truly had looked like some evil mythical creature had consumed him, but this was the real world. Where every monster was human.

"Why would your man target Connor?" I asked, my voice barely above a whisper. "We had a deal."

"Ah, we still have a deal," Don Luca corrected, leaning back in his chair. The movement was smug. "I swore amnesty for yourself and the Emerald Devil. Jack O'Connell, yes?"

My eyes burned with fury. We both knew he hadn't forgotten Jack's name, but his point was clear. He had made a promise not to kill Jack. Everyone else was fair game.

Don Luca sighed in pity. "I do admit, I never gave a direct order to have the eldest O'Connell brother killed."

"Sounds like the Babau has issues following your command," I snapped, interlacing my fingers on my knee to keep from fidgeting.

"He has been instructed to eliminate any threat to my enterprise. His one caveat is not to kill you or your Irishman until I give the go ahead."

His insinuation was in no way subtle, but he spoke like we were discussing an average business deal, not life and death.

"Your war is with the Murrays. How was Connor a threat?"

Before the don could answer, a tall woman entered the room carrying a tray of coffee and *sfogliatella*. She wore a black pantsuit and matching heels. Her greasy hair was situated in a long braid, tied at the end with a diamond butterfly barrette. It looked like an heirloom, childish in nature. Her expression was blank, and her skin was brutal in its pallor.

I'd met her once before. Last December when I had confronted Nicoletti's men at the Booker Hotel and demanded to see him, she'd been the one to zip-tie my hands. Her movements were precise and practiced — cold, even.

She'd looked older back then, but I could see now that she was around my age. And, apparently, Luca Nicoletti's niece. The one person I knew of who the don trusted with information regarding our deal.

"I think it funny that you came here last Christmas even though I easily could have killed you," Don Luca continued, forcing my gaze away from the new addition to the room. "You came here because you are in love with Jack O'Connell. You wanted to ensure his safety, but he doesn't even bother telling you about his business, does he? Doesn't keep you informed? How odd you lay your life on the line for him, but he refuses to trust you with basic information. Information that could keep you safe."

Don Luca took a porcelain cup from the tray that Amara held, thanking her. Amara turned, her black eyes meeting mine as she offered me a cappuccino. I took it out of sheer politeness, chilled by her abysmal stare. Did the woman ever blink?

"He doesn't want me implicated in anything," I said, my voice stony.

The excuse was weak. Jack's reasoning for keeping me hidden from his world was for my protection. But look where I was now. Being kept in the dark had pushed me into one of his enemy's homes.

"He is very protective of you," Don Luca concluded, as if reading my mind. A spark of realization lit his dark eyes. "He does not know you are here. Did you tell him about our last meeting?"

I shuddered at the thought of Jack discovering where I was. He didn't even like me riding the subway. If he knew the risk I was taking, he'd tuck me away for good. Screw tying me to his bed—he'd lock me in the panic room.

Don Luca laughed wholeheartedly this time, his hand on his stomach. Hearing the sound was like having rusty nails driven into my eardrums. Amara smirked, standing dutifully by his side. Her gaze was locked on me, noting my every micro-expression.

"You two will destroy each other before I get the chance," Don Luca joked, coming back to himself. Acid churned in my stomach. "Keeping such secrets from the ones you love."

My heart threatened to burst from my chest. I wasn't getting enough oxygen, but I had to keep my breathing even. I held my hands in my lap, the whites of my knuckles glowing.

Luca took notice of my panic. "Relax, little one. I will not tell your lover about our little chats. If I did, I would never have the pleasure of seeing you again, and I do so enjoy our time together."

It was odd, but the don seemed sincere in his sentiment. Although I knew his greatest source of joy was watching me struggle to parry his attacks, analyzing me as he tossed threats against my armor. He was chipping away at it, bit by bit.

I had my answers, but they had cost me. Luca now knew I was keeping things from Jack, and he could hold that over me. Nate's suicide note – the one I said would bring him down – was looking flimsier as each day passed.

"Thank you for brightening my morning, Miss Marshall." Don Luca stood to shake my hand. I slid mine into his, wishing I was burying it in shards of glass instead. "Amara, take Emma into the hall and prepare her for the trip back to the Booker."

Amara did as she was told without hesitation. I followed her out of the study and across the billiard room, her heels clicking while my sneakers stayed silent. Her braid swayed as she walked, the diamonds in her barrette twinkling in the artificial light. Her movements were stiff, as if the mundane task of attending to me was beneath her.

When we entered the windowless, carpeted hall, she turned on me, her face inches from mine. She was over a foot taller – though her heels weren't that high – and she had to bend forward at an awkward angle. Her breath smelled sickly sweet, like coffee creamer and mud.

"My uncle may have a soft spot for you," she whispered, her accented words hitting me square in the face. The air leaving her body was glacial. "You were his grandson's lover and the sole connection he has left to his memory. But it's a matter of time before he demands to see Nathaniel's suicide note. Then, we will discover just how long he'll keep you around. Once he realizes you've been lying to him."

I widened my eyes at her revelation. She knew I'd deceived Don Luca. My knees weakened as she gnashed her teeth at me. Her nails were long and sharp at either side of my head, caging me against the wood-paneled wall. Her sinewy arms were deceptively strong.

"My uncle hates betrayal over anything else," she warned as a pair of men rounded the corner, approaching us. "You know that as well as I do."

And I did. Luca Nicoletti had ordered the murder of his own daughter because she had betrayed him. Gotten pregnant, married without his blessing, fled the city then carried on an affair with Jeremiah Murray. An Irishman. It was a classic Shakespearian tragedy, too violent and twisted to be real, except in the world of organized crime.

In Don Luca's mind, Maria's biggest disloyalty had been keeping Nate, his grandson, from him — from the Mafia. Once his daughter was out of the way, the don had aimed to take his grandson under his wing, but things hadn't gone as planned. Nate saw more than he should've and, as a result, killed himself.

In my bed while I had slept in ignorance beside him.

Amara released me from the wall, teeth bared in what must be her version of a smile. She tugged the cloth bag over my head, leaving me without sight.

* * * *

Jack

Emma hadn't responded to my text, but it was still early in Manhattan. I'd hardly let her out of my sight all week, drawing on her strength whether I wanted to or not. She was in need of rest and, I hoped, sleeping in.

The thought of her tiny body in my bed — maybe cuddling a pillow — made my chest burn, like it was missing a vital organ. I wanted to call her, but the sound of her voice would worsen my symptoms. That soft, sweet tone would just remind me of the inescapable distance between us.

Eoghan was tracking her cell phone and MetroCard. Emma would go ballistic if she found out, but I had to be sure she was safe. It would make being away from her a bit easier. I hadn't told her of the danger because I didn't want her to live in fear, but I hoped I'd been grave enough to make her follow my command.

The Italian informant, Sofia, had told me about Luca Nicoletti's pet with a penchant for slitting throats. The Babau. Sofia, working as a call girl for the Mafia, hadn't overheard the man's legal name. She had it on good authority that the Babau came from Italy with his own small crew. Only they knew his true identity, along with the don.

If Emma didn't follow my order to keep herself safe, Eoghan would know about it. That gave me some comfort as I stared out of the window, watching Ireland's soft green hills speed by, the hearse plowing through the fog. The sun was setting, but we would make it to the farm before it disappeared along the western horizon.

The farm where I'd spent the first seven years of my life had been on its last limb. The land was an infertile sludge. The animals that hadn't died yet were starving, as were we. There were holes in the roof. We were constantly battling rats — and losing that battle.

Today, my family home was a sprawling manor. Hundreds of acres, two stables, three guest houses, an inn for visitors and fields of oat and barley. It was funded by the mob, an international criminal organization that my eldest brother had started and which had now been forced onto me.

The weight of responsibility lay on my shoulders, straining the muscles as if it were a physical presence. I'd been integral before — I made decisions, I held my own — but being the face of the mob was on a whole new level. It required finesse and balance, and in no way did I want the position.

Aside from preferring to stick to the shadows, I wanted my brother alive. To be there for Shannon. To raise their son together. I wanted to be back in Greece, losing myself in Emma, not a care in the world. I didn't want to be driving my brother's body through a marsh to bury it in our family cemetery.

What I wouldn't give to turn back the clock.

My mum greeted me with open arms, tears like a fountain down her soft, plump face. Her embrace was something I hadn't known I needed. It melted me a little, relaxing the knots in my neck. She held on for a long time, but I was grateful for it. When she turned to address Kieran, the stone resettled in my stomach, lodging itself there as it had when I had found Connor hanging from that rafter.

While our family laid my brother to rest, the entire town came to pay their respects. There were hundreds of villagers, but I recognized just a few dozen. I'd returned to Ireland a handful of times since moving to America, but not in the past two years. The small hamlet of Banshire had grown, largely due to the contributions from our family.

Kieran, Mick, Mum, Nan and I stood as they lowered the black coffin into the ground, bagpipes blaring. Distant relatives backed us, their hands out to comfort, but I kept myself from reach. There was one person who could soothe me right now, and she was across the Atlantic Ocean.

It wasn't long until the priest finished the Rite of Committal. The villagers dissipated, the O'Connells set off to prepare the wake and Mum and Kieran drifted away, arm in arm.

I knelt in the mud, thick drops of rain coating the sparse grass. The skies had given up, opening for the inevitable downfall. In the distance, thunder boomed across the forest canopy, carrying with it a long, shrieking wail. It was far too late for omens, so I ignored the inhuman sound. I ground my molars to keep emotion from overwhelming me, fisting my hand in the wet earth. The earth that would be my brother's home for eternity.

"*Go n-éirí an bóthar leat, dearthháir,*" I whispered into the night.

May the road rise up to meet you, brother.

Turning my back on the open grave, I followed the others out of the cemetery, weaving through the ancient tombstones of my ancestors. The oldest grave postdated the Rebellion, which was when our bloodline had fled south to avoid British colonization. Emma would love it here — the history, the folklore, the ghosts.

The lights of the manor were a beacon, guiding me down the sodden hill. People poured into the modern castle, singing at the tops of their lungs. I rubbed my temples, massaging the migraine that was furrowing its way into my brain. If I couldn't have my girl, I needed a bellyful of whiskey.

On my way to the ballroom, I ran into Kieran, who was exiting the library. His eyes were sunken and bloodshot, much like mine. I hadn't shed a tear since boyhood, but my body displayed all the physical evidence of grief. It was nothing in comparison to the knives raking against my chest, to the agony weighing down my heart.

Kieran gripped my dress shirt, his face screwed up in pain. His teeth were gritted, panic and rage seeping from his pores. "What do we do now?"

I placed my hand over his fist, squeezing once. "We kill them all."

Chapter Eight

Emma

I rounded the corner of Canal Street, breathing a sigh of relief. I was officially out of Little Italy. There was something to be said for being off Nicoletti territory.

It had been a horrible mistake to visit Don Luca, just as much as the last time. I might've gotten the information I wanted, but I was starting to dig my own grave. I thought Nicoletti would know something about the murders, but I should've considered the very high possibility that he was involved. I was foolish for not thinking that one through. I had made my decision to see him out of desperation, and he knew it.

What had Amara said about Luca Nicoletti having a soft spot for me? Sure, Don Luca had wanted to meet with me last winter because of my relationship with Nate, but the don didn't have a soft spot for anyone. He had a reptilian brain. I still hadn't discovered a weakness, even though he was tallying mine against me.

Lost in my own head, I hadn't walked five feet toward the subway before someone grabbed my arm and threw me into the backseat of an idling car. A scream clawed its way up my throat, but settled once I recognized Eoghan's baseball cap.

"Want to tell me what the fuck you're doing?" he roared, pinning me against the inside of the door, gripping my arms.

The look on his face was pure fire, the lines around his mouth set in stone as the SUV lurched into traffic. I struggled against him, glancing toward the front seat for help, but the driver was hired security. He would only answer to the O'Connells, which I was not.

"You've been following me?" I gasped, looking down at Eoghan's hands digging into my biceps. The pain was sharpening. Any more pressure, and he would leave bruises.

"I've been tracking your phone," he snapped, his hazel eyes boring into mine.

With his usual boyish smile and charming demeanor gone, I could see why Jack had assigned him as my guardian. He could flip the switch to 'fatal' as easy as his boss. Everyone in the O'Connell mob was capable of snapping a neck at the drop of a hat.

Eoghan knew where I'd been. Not all of it, of course. The Mafia had me leave my belongings in the hotel before sneaking me out through the back entrance. Still, Eoghan knew I'd visited a hotel owned by Luca Nicoletti and, from his point of view, I'd stayed there for hours.

My heart raced, throat constricting. If Jack knew who I was with... "Did you tell Jack?"

"Not yet," Eoghan threatened. "He's burying his brother tonight. How could you do this to him?"

I shook my head, arguing. "You don't know the whole story."

"You've been feeding information to the Mafia!"

Eoghan leaned forward, the door handle carving into my spine. The driver glanced at us in the rearview mirror, then went back to minding his own business. Out of the corner of my eye, the city spiraled past. People sped down the sidewalk in business attire, out for a quick lunch.

"No!" I flinched, tears welling in my eyes at the suggestion. "I can explain."

"Go," Eoghan ordered, his jaw twitching.

I shook my head again, looking toward the driver.

Eoghan understood my hesitation. "Take us to Roisin's," he ordered.

The driver nodded once, putting his blinker on.

Eoghan let me sit properly in the seat, but kept his hand wrapped around my biceps. He wouldn't be letting go anytime soon.

* * * *

When Shay set the custom vegetarian stew in front of me, I practically inhaled it. It was two o'clock, and I hadn't eaten since the wake. Even then, it had just been a nibble when Jack had been watching. I'd thrown the rest of my plate out, my appetite diminished. It had felt disrespectful to eat in a room full of mourners.

"You're telling me that you threatened the don of the New York fucking Mafia," Eoghan repeated, eyeing me like he'd never seen me in the right lighting before. He tilted his seat back, arms crossed over his chest.

We were dining in the private room at Roisin's. Both doors, the one to the dining area and the one to the kitchen, were shut. Shay had just dropped off our meals and exited via the kitchen. She'd given me a strange look. I hadn't been in to work since we had left for Santorini, but no one asked questions. They knew there had been a death in the O'Connell family, and that the feds were poking around.

"Not only that," Eoghan continued, straightening. "You threatened him with an incriminating letter. A letter that doesn't even *exist*, am I right?"

I swallowed a carrot medallion whole. "The letter exists. It just doesn't say what he thinks it does."

Eoghan stared, open-mouthed. It made him look younger than me, although we were around the same age. The deadly man from a couple hours ago had vanished and he was, once again, the Eoghan I'd grown accustomed to—frazzled hair, distressed jeans, inquisitive eyes.

"Why haven't you told Jack any of this?"

I set my spoon down, readying myself. "What exactly did Jack tell you before he left? Regarding how to handle me."

Eoghan looked uncomfortable, but answered, nonetheless. "He said to keep you safe and to follow your command."

"Well, I'm safe. So where does that leave you?"

His expression turned scrutinizing. He didn't want to say it. "Under your command."

I folded my hands on the table. "Good. First command—I decide what to tell Jack. If he doesn't want me to know about the Babau, then I don't know about the Babau. And we *don't* tell him about my visit with Nicoletti or the deal I have with him. He'll turn around and fly home immediately. He needs to bury his brother in peace."

Eoghan looked sicker and sicker as I spoke. He ran a hand through his messy hair, brows raised. "He's my boss, Emma."

"*I'm* your boss, too," I reminded him. "As long as you keep me safe, you're still upholding Jack's command. Every other order you're to follow comes from me. Got it?"

Eoghan cursed, leaning back in his chair. His loyalty to his boss was admirable, but Jack had given him to me. If Jack wanted to pass his second lieutenant around like an old iPad, so be it. I'd decided on the drive to the Shannon that I could use someone on my side, someone who knew how knee deep in shit I stood with the don.

"Fuck it," he said, a rush of air leaving his body. "Anything else?"

"Just a simple question. How long have you been tracking my phone?"

He shrugged, like stalking wasn't a big deal. I supposed in their world, it wasn't. "Since January when I accompanied you and your sister on the subway. I've also been hacking into the transit system database for alerts on your MetroCard usage. Phones don't always send a location ping underground."

I couldn't stop my mouth from forming an 'O' in disbelief. I had known he was capable of tracking my whereabouts, but breaking into citywide transportation data was on another level. "Hacking? You're a hacker?"

"Yup." He popped his lips sanctimoniously. "I'm pretty good, too."

"Huh," I mused. Eoghan didn't look like someone who spent too much time with computers. He was tall, tan and dressed like a grunge kid who smoked too many cigarettes outside a convenience store. "I never would've guessed you were a techie. You don't look the part."

"No?" he asked, the corner of his mouth lifting in a mischievous grin.

"You look like the kind of guy who yells at his friends to shut up while the Yankees are playing."

He snickered. "I don't like baseball."

I furrowed my brow. I had never *not* seen him in a Yankees cap. The royal blue of his hat was worn, lightened by the sun and frayed along the brim. He put his elbows on the table, noticing the direction of my gaze.

"I don't like baseball, Em," he repeated, locking his eyes with mine. "But I enjoy the players."

"Oh." I pondered his words, following the insinuation. "Oh!"

Eoghan chuckled, but it sounded shaky. "Jack doesn't know I'm gay. I'd like to keep it that way."

"Why the secrecy?" I asked, tilting my head. "Jack isn't homophobic. Kieran is bi."

He grimaced, the apples of his cheeks pinkening. "Still, it's a touchy subject."

I held my hands up in retreat. "All right. Say no more. Your secret is safe with me."

He regained his usual knowing grin. "Anything else, ma'am?"

He didn't say thanks for my discretion, but it wasn't like I was expecting it. A person's sexuality was their own business. It wasn't my place to tell Jack anything about his employee's sexual preferences, especially when he was keeping my own secret from his boss.

I smiled at him, feeling privileged that he felt he could confide in me. "You got family, Eoghan?"

That caught him by surprise. We hadn't spoken much about his life before the mob. Most of our conversations were playful in manner, and centered around Jack. That was, until now.

"In Louisiana," he answered. "But we don't speak."

"Any hobbies besides tracking my whereabouts?"

He smirked. "I tinker."

"Tinker?"

"I'll leave it at that."

"Whatever." I shrugged. "Go tinker. I'll call if I need you."

He narrowed his eyes in suspicion.

"Don't worry. I'm going to check on Shannon, then I'll have a driver take me home. I'm sure you can verify it with your stupid tracker."

Eoghan stood, winking at me. "I'll be keeping my eye on you, Emma." He turned to leave, muttering as he went. "…insane…threatening Nicoletti…"

* * * *

Upon entering the penthouse, I waved to Guillermo. The quiet Salvadoran man was cooking dinner with a pained expression. I thought about asking him if everything was all right but froze when I heard the television.

"'…violence in the city is reaching a new high as Manhattan real-estate mogul and businessman Connor O'Connell was found dead in a warehouse in Brooklyn. O'Connell's is the fourth body discovered since November. The FBI has been called in to investigate the mysterious deaths, but has yet to comment on whether O'Connell is connected to other slayings throughout the Burroughs… Questions about whether we have another serial killer stalking the streets… Would be the first confirmed serial murders since the nineties…'"

Rushing into the living room, I found Shannon sitting by herself on the sofa. She was a ghost, her wet eyes glued to the news. I found the controller, turned the television off then sat beside her.

She continued to stare at the black screen, unblinking. I watched her chest rise and fall just to be sure she was breathing. Her stomach was looking bigger by the day, or maybe it was just the rest of her body that seemed to be shrinking under the weight of her grief.

"Shan," I murmured, taking one of her hands in mine. They were unnervingly cold. "Where's Faye?"

Guillermo walked in from the kitchen carrying a plate of salmon, rice and veggies. He set it on the coffee table in front of Shannon, eyeing her with trepidation.

"Miss Faye left a few hours ago," he informed me. "She didn't say where she was going or when she'd be back."

Sighing, I thanked Guillermo. "If that happens again, please call me and I'll come right over."

By the look on his face, he'd been uncomfortable watching over Shannon for that long. I could understand why, with her being so pregnant and in a near-comatose state.

"If you're finished, feel free to go home for the evening. I'll stay with Shannon."

Guillermo inclined his head toward me. "Thank you, Miss Emma. I'll be back tomorrow morning."

Guillermo cleaned the kitchen and gathered his things while I prodded Shannon to eat her dinner. Once I set the dish in her lap and the fork in her hand, she cleared her plate without a word. The penthouse was silent apart from the hum of the air conditioner and Shannon's utensil scraping the plate.

When she was finished, I wrapped a blanket over Shannon's thin shoulders and took the dish to the sink. Shortly after, I led her to the master bathroom to run a bubble bath. She stripped and I helped her into it, washing her vibrant red hair as she did her pale body. Her movements were robotic. It hurt my soul to watch.

When we finished, I guided her out of the tub and into a set of soft maternity pajamas.

"Will you stay with me tonight?"

I jumped out of my skin at her crackling voice. I hadn't heard it in days, not since her guttural scream upon hearing of her husband's death. That scream — along with Jack's strangled howl and the image of Kieran kneeling in a pool of blood — continued to haunt my dreams.

Shannon sat upright in bed, hands in her lap, eyes red. She was so fragile in the giant California King. It looked as though it were eating her alive. Her belly seemed to be pulling her down through the floor.

"Of course," I answered, slipping out of my sneakers and into the bed.

Shannon laid her head on my chest, the weight of her womb close to crushing me. She slid her leg over both of mine and wrapped an arm around my middle, holding me to her in a tight embrace. Wet hair soaked my shirt, and her ivory skin was warm from the bath.

"He's going to push you away."

Again, Shannon startled me. I jolted, causing the baby to kick my side. I shuddered at the odd feeling. How strange it must feel for her to have someone constantly wiggling beneath her skin.

What did she just say?

"Jack," Shannon continued, as if I'd asked for clarification aloud. "I know how he deals with stress. And loss. He'll push you away."

Her voice was strained, like it took a great amount of energy to speak. It made what she said all the more important.

I combed her long, thick hair away from her face. "He can push all he wants."

"He'll make you hate him." Her words sent a violent warning down my spine, but I didn't move in case I disturbed the baby again.

"That's not possible," I whispered. There was nothing Jack could do that would make me hate him. There was nothing that could change the way I felt about him.

"You will. You'll hate him, but you'll love him more. You need to remember that you love him more, okay?"

I was unnerved with her premonition, to say the least. She spoke like Jack's leaving me was inevitable. Or worse, that I would want to leave *him*. The idea was asinine.

Realizing Shannon was waiting for an audible response, I muttered an "okay" and let her settle into me.

She fell asleep soon after, whimpering in her slumber. I couldn't seem to work the ice from my bones, but I didn't move a muscle. I would lay there for as long as Shannon needed, letting her cuddle my body for comfort. Jack had asked me to be there for her, and that was exactly what I was going to do. I'd already broken one promise.

I wouldn't be breaking this one.

Chapter Nine

Emma

The next morning, I untangled myself from Shannon's hold and crept out of the master bedroom, careful not to wake her. It was seven o'clock and she was in serious need of rest, even if it was riddled with sobs.

Guillermo was in the kitchen prepping breakfast. I waved as I entered the sprawling living area. He gave me a lazy salute and continued mixing batter.

I plopped myself on the couch and grabbed my phone, anxious to hear Jack's voice. I hadn't heard from him since his text about landing safely the day before, which meant Eoghan hadn't told him about my visit with Luca Nicoletti. It also meant he was probably too busy to talk.

Fuck, I thought as I perused my notifications. I had five missed calls from my mom, three from my dad and a series of texts from my little sister.

Ella: OMG have u seen the news?
Ella: Mom and Dad r freaking out
Ella: R u still in Greece?
Ella: Dad says he'll be @ ur apartment in the am

Double fuck. The goddamn news. My parents knew about Connor's murder, and they'd guessed that I was no longer on vacation. I dialed my dad, hoping to catch him before he left Connecticut.

"Do you know how worried your mother and I have been?" he barked, the engine of his sleek Mercedes purring in the background. He was already on his way to the city.

"I'm sorry, Dad. Things have been nonstop since we got back." My excuse was even flimsier out loud. I should've assumed the media would chomp down on the story of Connor's death. He was wealthy, mysterious and attractive—the kind of person made for headlines.

"I'm just so happy to hear you're safe." The vulnerability in his tone made me feel horrible. I should've taken the time to inform my parents that I'd come home early, and the morbid reason for it. "What the hell happened to Jack's brother?"

I puffed my cheeks, resigning myself to a lie. "We don't know yet. The FBI are still searching for answers."

"Are you in danger? You know... Because of Jack's...work?"

My father was the one member of my family who knew what Jack did for a living. Being a lawyer, he'd pulled strings and gotten a few gritty details on Frank O'Connell from his colleagues. Fortunately, Jack and his brothers had evaded the law thus far, unlike their father.

"No," I lied. "This was unrelated."

Whether he believed me or not, I could sense his relief. And I hadn't *technically* lied. I was safe from the Babau as long as Luca Nicoletti continued to grant me amnesty. I wouldn't let myself think about what would happen if he changed his mind or didn't keep his word.

Although I assured him everything was copacetic, my dad insisted on coming to the city and taking me out to breakfast. I protested, using Shannon as an excuse not to leave the penthouse, but he demanded the address and said he would see me in thirty minutes.

When I ended the call, I looked toward Guillermo, who was still busying himself in the kitchen.

"We're gonna have one more dining with us, chef," I grumbled.

Nearly thirty minutes to the second later, my father's gaze raked over me from across the dining table as I shoved bite after bite of cheesy eggs into my mouth.

"You've lost weight."

I reached for a third piece of buttered toast, nodding. "My appetite is just coming back."

My dad smiled, but it was forced. He hadn't touched the gourmet spread Guillermo had set in front of us. Gregory Marshall was a black coffee for breakfast kind of person. Sometimes he'd spice things up with a bran muffin.

"How's Shannon?" he asked, sipping at his cup.

I spoke through a mouthful of bread. "Terrible."

Guillermo had retreated to the master bedroom to serve Shannon her breakfast. He was a caring person. He would ensure she had enough to eat. I didn't know how much time I had to consume my own food before checking on her, hence the sloppiness.

"The street is flooded with reporters." My dad inclined his head toward the picture window behind me. "The police have shut down a section of Fifth Avenue. I had to flash my work badge to get through. They're under the impression I've been hired to assist in Connor's estate."

I was aware of the media frenzy downstairs. After I'd hung up with my father, news outlets had descended on the Shannon like a storm of locusts. Connor's death had gone viral. The story was now global news. The city was buzzing with rumors about a serial killer targeting white men. The idea that even someone as handsome and affluent as Connor O'Connell couldn't escape death was being sensationalized. It infuriated me.

"Are you sure about all this?" Dad asked, his expression inscrutable.

"All what?"

"Jack. His...*life*. I worry about you, Emmy. I know he cares for you, but I don't want you caught up in his world. Jack might be all right, but the people he deals with are dangerous."

I set my glass of orange juice down, contemplating my response. My father was a smart man, top of his class at Yale Law. He didn't buy the line of bullshit the media was spewing. He knew Connor's death had everything to do with the criminal underworld.

Still, my appetite vanished at his suggestion. Leaving Jack was out of the question. I'd known this conversation was bound to arise eventually, and I aimed to nip it in the bud.

"I love him, Dad," I said, willing him to see the depth of emotion reflected in my eyes. "I'm not going anywhere. Please don't suggest it again."

He tilted his head, analyzing my resolve. His chest rose as if he planned to say something more, but Guillermo suddenly appeared in the dining room, pale and flustered.

"Is Shannon all right?" I asked, rising from my chair.

Guillermo shook his head, panicked. "It's the baby, Miss Emma. He's coming."

* * * *

I paced the bright hall of New York Presbyterian, phone pressed to my ear. The line rang off and I cursed, jabbing my finger on the "end" button before the voicemail picked up.

Jack wasn't answering. Neither were Faye or Kieran.

A pregnant woman walked by, wobbling as her husband guided her down the hall. I gave them a short smile, then returned to my frantic dialing. Why wasn't anyone answering? It was four o'clock in the afternoon in Ireland.

Shannon was in the room behind me, hooked up to a steady flow of pain medication. The baby would be coming soon. She was already eight centimeters dilated. The doctors had tried to slow her labor, but to no avail. That baby wanted out — *now*.

It was understandable. The warm, loving body he'd been growing in had turned cold and grief-stricken. It wasn't Shannon's fault, of course, but the baby could probably sense it was time to leave his mother's womb and try his luck on the outside.

My father and Guillermo were waiting in the lobby. We'd escaped the media with ease, thanks to the vast wealth of security Connor had left behind. The elevator in the penthouse descended straight into a private underground garage, which was reserved in its entirety for the O'Connells' fleet of vehicles. We had been met with row after row of sleek cars in every shape and size, from basic to luxury. The armed drivers — which were kept on rotation — had immediately stepped forward to assist us with Shannon, their calm authority welcome during the panic. Connor's first lieutenant — Arthur, I now knew his name to be — had insisted on accompanying us, although he looked haggard, as though he hadn't rested in weeks.

Guilt and grief hadn't affected just the family members.

After they had made sure she'd arrived at the hospital, Shannon had thanked our three male companions and asked that only I enter the Labor and Delivery ward with her. By now, she'd already requested Faye's presence twice, and my anxiety was through the roof.

I didn't want to be alone with Shannon while she gave birth. I'd never seen anyone go through that. I didn't know how to encourage her, especially with Connor gone. She was going through hell and, if no one else showed up in time, I would have to face the fire with her.

"Hello?"

Finally! Mickey Kelley's gruff voice was like a lighthouse for a ship lost at sea. He was with Jack and Kieran in Ireland. He could tell them to get their asses back here.

"Mick!" I screamed, then lowered my tone when a nurse glared from her station. "Shannon's having the baby. Like, *now*. Are you with Jack?"

"Shit…" I could hear laughter in the background, along with Irish rock music and yelling. "She's not due for another month!"

"Tell that to the baby," I huffed. "I tried calling Jack, but he didn't answer."

Mick was silent again. On his end of the line, glasses clinked and people spoke over one another. Were they at a pub? I knew the O'Connells liked to party, but it seemed a little gratuitous to be celebrating so soon after Connor's death. Then again, they were Irish.

My suspicions were confirmed when I heard a woman's voice, soft and feminine, say, "Here's your drink, *a ghrá*." Jack responded, but he was too far from the phone for me to discern his words, or his tone.

"I'll let Kieran know." Mick grunted. "He should be on the first plane tomorrow morning."

"And Jack?" I asked, biting the side of my thumb. Why wasn't Mick answering my questions about him? Did Jack know I was on the phone? Was he purposefully not taking my calls? I was being paranoid. The hospital setting wasn't helping. "Is he coming back?"

Mick cleared his throat. There was something in his voice that I disliked — pity. "Jack's handling some business here, lass."

"Is he okay?"

My heart galloped inside my chest. Mick wasn't telling me something. What was it Jack was doing in Ireland that made Mick uncomfortable to talk about? My mind immediately jumped to conclusions, but I refused to breathe life into them.

"Jack is…" Mick stammered. "He just misses you is all."

I released the air from my lungs. "So, is he coming home with Kieran tomorrow?"

Mick swore. "Sorry, Emma, bad reception. Text me updates!"

Click.

Damn it.

"Emma?" A nurse materialized in the hall, shutting the door to Shannon's room. "It's about that time. You'll need these."

She held out a navy-blue set of scrubs, shoe covers, a hairnet and a surgical mask. The blood rushed from my head, but I took the items between two hands like I was receiving a flag at a military funeral.

"I know this is a rough situation, sweetheart," the nurse said, her face open and honest. I slid the loose pants over my jeans. "I assume Shannon's husband is the one that's been on the news?"

I nodded, slipping the hair net over my messy bun.

The nurse shook her head, somber. "I need you to look at me, sweetie."

I did, eyes huge and panicked. The nurse squeezed my shoulders, earnestness adorning her strong features. She had a slight Southern accent, which I found comforting.

"Now, I don't know how you're related to Shannon, but you're all that girl's got right now. When you go in there, you need to be strong for her. You hold her hand and you don't leave her side for a second. The only way she's gonna get through this is with you helping her."

The nurse's reassuring words washed over me. My panic went from full-fledged to a small trickle in the recess of my mind. Shannon needed me. It didn't matter that I'd never been through this before because she hadn't either. She was about to give birth and the father of her child, the love of her life, was dead. No one else was here but me. I had to be enough.

I closed my eyes and took a deep, settling breath. When I opened them moments later, the nurse had disappeared into Shannon's room. I followed her, leaving my self-doubt behind. This wasn't the time or place for it.

* * * *

"I can't do this!" Shannon screamed, her red hair plastered to her forehead. She was curled to the side and holding her stomach, her thighs clenched shut. "I can't do this without him!"

"Shh," I soothed, brushing the perspiration from her face. I pulled gently on her shoulder in an effort to get her to lay flat, but she wouldn't budge. Her muscles were as stiff as corded ropes. She was fighting with all her might to keep that baby in.

The nurse exchanged a look with me, a warning in her eyes. This baby was coming, and Shannon needed to get ready.

"Give us a minute," I said to the nurse.

She retreated, leaving the door open a crack. The doctor would be here any second. Shannon was fully dilated, her water had broken and it was now or never.

"Look at me, Shan," I commanded, willing the power into my voice.

She kept her face hidden against the pillows, a grimace marring her shriveled features.

"Shannon O'Connell, you look at me right now!"

The volume of my words shocked her into submission. Her eyes met mine, horror shimmering in those grassy depths. A gut-wrenching, free-falling face of terror, like she'd been pushed from an airplane without a parachute.

I took her hand, and she crushed mine with her own. I bit the inside of my cheek to hide a wince, then chose my words with care.

"I can't even begin to imagine the level of agony you're in right now," I started, praying I was going in the right direction. This was a pep talk of epic proportions. "Not just because of labor. I know you feel dead inside with Connor gone, but you *aren't*, Shan."

The lines of Shannon's face smoothed as I spoke, tears traveling the expanse of her pale cheeks. Her lower lip trembled, but her gaze stayed locked on mine.

"You aren't dead, Shannon, because there's a little life inside of you that wants to come out. There's a living, breathing piece of Connor right in your belly that can't wait to meet you. Charlie needs you to be strong. If you can't do it for yourself, do it for him. Do you hear me?"

"Are we ready?" the doctor sang as she waltzed through the door, stethoscope swinging from her neck. She was short and thin, and I couldn't help but wonder how the hell she was going to pull this baby out. But the fact that she was a woman was consoling. We needed fierce feminine energy right now.

I glanced toward Shannon, surprised to see that she was sitting upright in bed—knees bent, legs spread, hands fisting the starchy sheets. Her eyes were narrowed with determination and her face was pink. She glanced at the doctor, gritting her teeth.

"Yes," she snarled.

Chapter Ten

Jack

Mick's words floated to me from another universe. They were diluted, echoing aimlessly around my skull like I was being held underwater.

"I'm catching the next flight." Kieran slammed his pint down, rising from the table. The pub was riotous, but he spoke with definition. "Jack?"

Raising my head, I met my brother's gaze. It wasn't even eight o'clock at night and I was shit-faced. I had been all day. My movements felt slow and fuzzy, but my brain was whirring from Mick's information.

Shannon had given birth. The baby was healthy. A month early but a solid eight pounds, six ounces. Mick had just gotten off the phone with Emma. I wanted with all my being to throttle Mick, to demand details about the call, to ask if Emma was okay.

But I held back. I was so inebriated, even Mick could take me down if he tried. More importantly, I had to keep distance between myself and Emma. Work needed to be done. I couldn't go home yet, and just the thought of having my girl in my arms made me want to get on the fucking jet.

I shook my head at Kieran. "You go."

"You're not coming?"

I locked eyes with my brother, my expression hard and resolute. "No."

That ended his line of questioning. Kieran raised his brows, shrugging as he walked away—which I took as his goodbye. He would be on the next flight out of Dublin. He was going home. Envy burned its way through my veins. Or maybe that was the whiskey.

I took another swig, seething. Kieran could do as he pleased. I, on the other hand, had to think of safety first and foremost. And vengeance—vengeance was a close second.

With that in mind, I rose, climbing on top of the bar stool, then onto the table. Mick's eyes widened as he watched, stepping back from the circular table and into the crowd behind him. Fellow patrons turned to observe, their faces expectant. The pub was packed wall to wall, shoulder to shoulder. The young woman who'd brought our drinks smiled at me coquettishly, raising her glass with a wink. I paid her no mind, focusing on the villagers of Banshire.

"Oy!" I yelled, commanding the attention of those who hadn't yet turned. Realizing who was speaking, the bartender paused the music and waited for me to begin. "As you all know, my brother was murdered earlier this month."

A round of hissing broke through the crowd, like a disgruntled hive of bees.

"He had his throat slit and he was hung upside down to let the blood drain from his body."

The swarm grew silent. A few faces paled at my words. The headlining news of Connor's death had hit Ireland moments after it had broken in America, but the reporters didn't know the details.

"The person who did this isn't a serial killer. He works for the Italian Mafia, and he's been picking us off one by one."

People exchanged nervous glances, eyes wide.

"People call him the Babau — named after a legend used to frighten children." A few men nearest my makeshift podium spat on the floor, their disgust evident. "Now, I don't know about you, but I'm not scared. I am fucking *livid*!"

The crowd erupted, screams and ale flying through the air. At my feet, an angry sea of red faces, scratchy beards and rosy cheeks churned, feeding off my emotion, ready for my demands. It was O'Connell money that had built this village from the ground up, wrenching the citizens out of poverty, filling their businesses and lining their pockets. Although we had never outright asked for help, these people would always answer an O'Connell's call.

"Who's coming to the Empire City with me to tear this bogeyman limb from limb?" I roared, tossing the remnants of my drink down my throat.

The energy was palpable. People slapped each other's backs, howling their loyalty. A chant of "For Connor" and "Emerald Devil" echoed through the small-town pub. Men and women grabbed one another as the bartender pumped music through the speakers. They began to move to Flogging Molly's *The Devil's Dance Floor*.

How fitting.

I surveyed, intestines twisting with hatred and grief and whiskey, as my army assembled in front of my very eyes.

Mick helped me down from the table, patting me on the shoulder as he did. A soft hand slipped into mine, a pair of lips at my ear. I jerked from the foreign contact. The woman who'd winked at me was trying to pull me into a dance. I cast her a reproachful glare, widening the distance between us. I might have been drunk, but I hadn't forgotten who I was or who I belonged to.

Bereft or not, no woman could hold a candle to Emma Marshall.

* * * *

Emma

Charlotte Aoife O'Connell wasn't two hours old, and I was already in love. With her wisps of shocking red hair, pink cheeks and pursed lips, she was everything a baby was supposed to be. She would break hearts and mend even more throughout her life.

Her breathing was soft and consistent, a miracle in and of itself, as I stood over her bassinet. Shannon was getting cleaned and stitched up but demanded that I stay by Charlie's side until she got back. It wasn't a difficult request. I could stare at the little treasure for days, although she hadn't even opened her eyes yet. Her eyelids were a pale lavender, twitching with movement.

When Shannon returned, the nurse lifted the swaddled baby and set her in her mother's arms. Shannon glowed, eyeing her child clearly for the first time in the absence of the turmoil that was post-birth. Without any direction, Shannon tugged at her hospital gown and guided Charlotte's rooting mouth to her breast.

My heart burst with aching warmth as I snuck a picture with my phone. Shannon would want it eventually. I left the room soon after to give them a chance to bond in private. Once I'd secured the door, my fury returned at the sight of Faye Walsh.

"Where the hell have you been?" I whisper-yelled.

Faye sauntered into the maternity ward, designer handbag swinging from her arm. She was dressed with precision, not a single auburn hair out of place. The buoyancy that'd existed in my chest moments before was gone, replaced with an icy hate.

She appraised me, unimpressed. I felt like a child in front of her in my ripped jeans and sneakers, my hair messier than before. I was exhausted. Two hours of active labor. Two hours of baseless encouragement while Shannon screamed in agony.

"Babies take forever to come." Faye shrugged, nonplussed. She picked at her fresh manicure, coming to a stop in front of me. We were the only two people in the clean, clinical hall.

"Well, she's here," I bit back, arms crossed. It was an animalistic defense mechanism, the intuition to guard my underbelly. The woman made my blood run cold, and it was more than the fact that she hadn't been here for her niece. It was unwarranted jealousy.

Faye's brows skyrocketed. "*She*?"

"Charlie," I clarified. "Short for Charlotte. It's uncommon, but the doctors got it wrong. Gender aside, your niece needed you and you weren't here."

Faye rolled her eyes, straightening. "You're an uptight little bitch. I don't know what Jack sees in you."

"What the fuck do you know about Jack?"

She gave me a meaningful look, almost glowing with mirth. "Oh, I know a *lot* about Jack."

And there it was. The reason for my jealousy. I had suspected it the first time I'd met Faye but hadn't wanted to believe it. The way she spoke about my boyfriend, there was an intimacy behind her words. And it enraged me.

"You two slept together," I confirmed.

Faye just smiled.

"Aren't you a little old for him?"

She chuckled at my snub, but her eyes narrowed. "It was a long time ago."

"Oh, so statutory?"

Faye took a step in my direction. She was taller than me by a few inches, the height difference worsened by her killer heels. She made me feel small and vulnerable — something I disliked very much.

"Connor's body is already in the ground." Faye's grin turned malicious. "So, why is Jack still in Ireland? Why hasn't he returned if you're so special to him?"

Her words hit close to home. I fought to maintain my self-assurance, although I'd been wondering the same thing. "He's busy."

"Yeah." She scoffed. "Busy shoving his dick down someone's throat."

I flinched at her vulgarity.

"Jack is too much of a man for just one woman. Even I know that. And the O'Connells are as good as kings in their hometown. Women will be throwing themselves at his feet."

"It must be difficult, being hung up on someone over a decade younger than you."

She reeled back a fraction. "Better than kidding myself into thinking he's in love with me. Jack doesn't love anyone. He *hates*, and he's good at it."

I was done—with her, with this conversation, with everything. I needed to get the hell out of this hospital before I did something to Faye that would have me committed to the psychiatric ward.

"Go take care of your niece," I advised. "And if you feel the need to bail on her again, have her call me."

With that, I spun on a heel and left to find my father. I needed pizza.

And a stiff drink.

* * * *

Jack

Crouching, I swiped at the set of keys on the stone floor, my hand missing them by a good few inches. Blood pounded in my head, making my brain feel twice its normal size. My body pitched forward precariously. I straightened, striking my temple on the brass doorknob.

"Fucking hell!" I cursed, glaring at the keys on the ground. Why were there three sets? I was positive I had just one.

Taking a deep breath, I tried again. The floor tilted and I lost my footing. Mumbling another swear, I caught myself on the inside of the massive front door.

Lord, help me.

I was obliterated. I had a vague recollection of Mick dropping me off at the manor's doorstep—his shoulder supporting my half-dead weight — but I had no clue how long I'd been standing in the entrance hall, fumbling as I tried to lock the door.

Why lock the door? Our family's farm was in the middle of nowhere. The closest neighbor was two miles away, and our grounds were gated and guarded. I'd been in America too long. I was accustomed to double checking that my cars and apartments were secured. Not that a thief would walk away from me with anything, their life included.

Huffing, I left the door unlocked and my keys on the ground. When I turned toward the sitting area, I bumped into something. No, not something.

Some*one*.

"Mother of —!" I broke off midsentence, not wanting to get slapped.

My grandmother was practically a ghost, but she still packed a punch. The short decrepit woman was eyeing me up and down, clicking her tongue in disapproval.

"You scared the shite out of me, Nan! What're you doing awake?" I didn't know the exact time, but it was well past dark when I had left the pub. Much too late for a hundred-year-old to be stalking the halls of the manor.

"I'll sleep when I'm dead," she bit out, her voice just as strong and deep as her emerald eyes. She gave me a cursory glance, then shuffled into the sitting area. "Got too many things to do before then."

Stumbling, I followed her retreating form, guiding myself along the hallway with a hand. I had to pay close attention not to disturb any of the ancient family photos adorning the sandstone walls.

"Oh, yeah? You trainin' for the Tour de France?"

When I entered the elongated sitting area, Nan pushed me onto a red velour sofa. Just a small nudge from her and she had me toppling, useless.

"Don't get on me nerves, boy," she threatened, jabbing her bony finger into my pectoral. "I dealt with yer father's shite all me life, and ye aren't him."

"Look at me." I grinned, although there wasn't an ounce of humor in my tone. The embers of a once-roaring fire cast an orange glow onto Nan's translucent skin, but they did nothing to soothe the chill in my bones. "I've been pissed for three days straight. Look at my face and tell me I don't remind you of your pathetic son."

Nan bent over me, glaring into my eyes with her identical ones. She held my slackened jaw in her firm grasp, squeezing so hard that my lips pursed.

"I've been lookin', boy, and all I see is sorrow. The cracks in yer foundation are bleedin' ye dry. Ye'll need to start patching them up."

When I jerked my head, Nan let go. She mumbled something unintelligible, sitting on the edge of a solid coffee table. The way she perched there made her seem younger than she was. Nimble and vicarious weren't words I'd use to describe Nan. Hard-headed and strict, more like. How the hell my father had broken free of her mold was beyond me. I couldn't comprehend how someone raised by such a fiery woman could be such a waste of space.

Without a doubt, her bony ass was hurting on that table. I wanted to offer her my seat, but was unsure if I'd be able to stand. Now that I was down, my limbs were heavy, my mind a fog.

I wasn't lying. This had been my state of being for three days. When I awoke in the morning, the pain in my chest ached for immediate relief. By the end of the day, I aimed to be so far gone that sleep was the only way out, the only true repose.

"You're in love."

From under my heavy lashes, I studied Nan. Her sallow skin and bright eyes were latched onto mine. She rested her hands in her lap, her spine ramrod straight. I felt her opposite — three times her size yet smaller in every other way, crumpled into a heap before her.

"I don't deserve her," I slurred, inhaling as I gave breath to the statement that'd been haunting me for months. From the first time I had laid eyes on Emma, I'd known she was too good for me. Too good for anyone. Too good to be true.

"Tell me, boy," Nan commanded, her tone harsh. "Is she a stupid woman?"

I glared at her from my sunken position on the sofa, anger boiling at the insinuation. No one, not even my ancient grandmother, insulted Emma. "Fuck no."

Nan huffed with something akin to satisfaction. "Then why don't ye let *her* fret about what she does and doesn't deserve?"

"Because I don't want her to fret about anything!" I growled, a wave of energy cresting with my temper. I leaned forward, a moment of clarity seeping into my thick skull. "Fuck, Nan. I love her, and it's making me weak."

The slap came out of nowhere. The sound echoed off the stone walls of the sitting room, forcing my head to the side. Jesus, she was a powerful woman, and moved faster than I thought possible. My jaw was pinned between her fingers again. She towered over me, a rage

I knew too well adorning her features. The O'Connell blood ran as hot as it did toxic.

"I will not sit idly by and listen while ye talk about yerself in such a manner," she seethed, her thin face an inch from my own. Her nose almost brushed mine, her eyes lit with ire. "Love is not a plague on yer soul, Jack Arden O'Connell. Love—*real* love—isn't a weakness, boy. If ye truly care for her, don't discredit her by thinking she's anything other than yer greatest source of strength."

Her words stung more than my cheek. "I'm too drunk for this conversation, Nan."

"Tough shite," she spit, releasing my jaw and coming to a stand at my legs. I rubbed my palms along my face, chafing the overgrown stubble there. "The best conversations take place in the bowels of a bottle."

I groaned, leaning my head back and shutting my eyes. "I'm not going to remember this."

"Ye'll remember it when ye need to," she muttered from farther away. I sat up groggily, squinting at her tiny back as she slunk into a dark hallway. Her suite was on the ground floor.

"How did you know?" I called after her, my throat hoarse and broken. I was going to black out any second. "How did you know I'm in love?"

Her blurry form turned to face me. I couldn't make out her features. There were three of her peering at me from across the sitting room.

"I looked in yer eyes, Jack," she said, her voice echoing in my eardrums. "There's an ocean of sorrow, but there's also a glimmer of hope. I've never once seen them shine like that, not even when ye were a wee lad. Hold on to that hope, boy. Hold on to *her*."

Chapter Eleven

Emma

Dinner with my dad was just what I had needed after the day — no, the week — I'd had.

We went to an Italian restaurant in Lenox Hill. While I ate, Dad talked about the selling of our family home in Stonerose, the odds and ends of packing our entire lives.

Stonerose was all I had known growing up — a safe, friendly village on the eastern coast of Connecticut. A town where everyone knew each other's names. A place where a person could get sucked into a lengthy conversation while out buying milk from the family-owned market.

A smile pulled at the corners of my lips, memories flitting through my head like a roll of film. I saw Ella's flaxen hair and Nate's wide grin as we ran through the garden, armed with squirt guns... My mom coated in flour, asking me to tuck a strand of hair behind her ear while she baked Dad's fortieth birthday cake... Myself sitting cross-legged on my bedroom floor during a thunderstorm, pouring through a book while Nate spun on my desk chair singing along to Franz Ferdinand. With each recollection, my mind went somewhere darker.

In the same town where I had experienced endless amounts of joy, I'd also witnessed horrors beyond the realm of my adolescent comprehension. Four years ago, I'd awoken in the dark, staring into Nate's cold, dead face. Just this past November, I'd stood in shock while Mark had swallowed the barrel of a shotgun.

My dad regaled me with Ella's latest rebellious stunt involving blue hair. I took a sip of spiked cider, pondering my recovery. I'd suffered a lot, but I was stronger than people gave me credit for. Sure, I was small and fidgety, but I was tough. I'd seen more death than most. Maria, Nate, Mark, Connor. Morbidity surrounded, but I could and would continue to battle for happiness, for peace. There was no other alternative, not when I was set on Jack. To survive in his world, I had to wear my armor well.

"You okay, Em?" Dad asked, pulling me from my thoughts.

He'd just given me the dates for their relocation— the last week of August. My parents were moving into a regal brownstone in Carnegie Hill. I'd agreed to help my little sister get situated in our apartment. She was going to visit once beforehand to attend NYU's orientation.

I nodded, clearing my throat. "Just tired."

Dad wrinkled his chin with a grimace. He reached across the table, giving my hand a squeeze. "You should go home and get some sleep."

I shook my head, setting a pizza crust to the side. "I need to get back to the hospital."

"No, you don't," he argued. "Shannon has her aunt. You can see her and the baby tomorrow after you've rested. You look dead on your feet."

I didn't have the energy to fight him. As much as I hated Faye Walsh, she was with her niece now. Shannon had promised to call if she needed anything. And Arthur was standing guard outside Shannon's room, finding new purpose in protecting what his boss had left behind.

My dad drove us west to my apartment, making sure I got in safely. He kissed my forehead, ordering me to stay in bed until I'd spent a solid eight hours with my eyes closed.

Thirty minutes later, I stood in the shower, letting the water drill into my neck until my skin went numb. As the smell of antiseptic and latex gloves washed away, I allowed myself a small cry, a necessary expulsion of stress.

When I got out of the bathroom, I threw on a pair of sweats and an old T-shirt of Jack's that I kept hidden at the back of my sock drawer. It was from the first night I'd spent at his apartment, and it still smelled like him. Rain and fire. My personal storm.

I poured myself a glass of chilled wine and sent a quick text to Jack, congratulating him on becoming an uncle. I didn't expect a reply.

I attempted to make headway on my summer reading, but my mind had other plans. Those warm recollections from lunch caught up with me once more. I would miss our family home in Stonerose, but my memories weren't confined to the walls of a house —

they were embedded into the tissues of my heart. They'd be with me wherever I chose to go.

Giving up on the reading, I scrolled through luxury nursery vendors on my phone, ordering new supplies for Charlotte's room. I might've splurged on a Chanel tutu, but Shannon would love it. I fell asleep with a smile on my face and my phone in my hand.

* * * *

I immersed my energy in the mundane to keep my thoughts from straying to Jack. My stomach plummeted and my chest constricted every time he entered my mind, which was often. I felt like I was missing a vital protein in my blood, but I did my best to combat it.

He never called, and I followed his lead. Even though I ached to hear his voice, I'd remind myself that he needed space. He would take whatever amount of time he needed, then I'd have him back. Despite my effort to banish the insecurities, Shannon's warning kept ringing through my ears.

"He'll push you away."

Mick and I talked twice more. They were short conversations. Apart from repeating "he's been busy" and "I know he misses you," I didn't get any additional information.

Faye stayed by Shannon's side at the hospital. When she needed a break, she called and I filled in for her. We had an unspoken agreement not to mention our altercation in the hallway. Shannon was stressed enough. She didn't need us making it worse by bickering over her brother-in-law. Not that there was much to argue about. I'd known since the moment I'd met Jack that he'd been with other women before me. Many, many other women. That I hadn't run into one of his rendezvous before now was shocking.

Kieran arrived the day after Charlotte was born. Although I wanted to, I didn't ask him about Jack's well-being. He'd returned early to meet his niece, not to quell my anxieties.

In the middle of the week, I was summoned to the swanky Midtown offices of Trevor Gallagher, the O'Connells' finance officer. He was in his seventies but had a youthful vibe. He wore a large suit and rimmed glasses, his gray hair meticulously combed. He was professional but kind, like an overworked grandfather. I imagined overseeing the O'Connell accounts was a full-time job. He mentioned they were his sole clients and had been ever since Connor O'Connell had been gifted Uncle Henry's fortune upon his passing. Since then, the accumulated wealth was staggering.

He informed me that, with Shannon incapacitated for the foreseeable future, Roisin's needed a manager. Someone that knew how the men truly made their money. Someone who would be able to handle the capital flowing through the restaurant. I put two and two together. Although Roisin's was a legitimate business, it was also used for laundering money. The brothers had multiple establishments across the city that processed their illegal cash flow, but Roisin's was the only one without current management.

Jack had spoken with Mr. Gallagher regarding me, prompting him to enlist my help with the high-end establishment. The next day, Trevor and I convened in Shannon's modern office at Roisin's. The media had all but dissipated from the block, frustrated that they couldn't get a quote from anyone entering or exiting the building. The New Yorkers that lived at the Shannon were of a superior mindset and wouldn't give press the time of day. And the employees were paid well for their silence regarding the O'Connells.

Mr. Gallagher and I spent hours reviewing the books. He taught me how to use discretion when up-charging a ticket so that the feds wouldn't flag it, which was paramount now that the FBI was poking around.

"A couple on a date night?" the old man asked, tapping his pen against a ledger. "Charge them for their meal, then alter the bill. Add a lobster and dessert. If it's a busy night, maybe even tack on an appetizer or an extra steak. Then, we funnel the dirty money through. Simple as that."

Over the past few months, I'd wished to be more involved in Jack's work. This was an opportunity to prove myself. I ignored the illegality of it. It wasn't like I was dealing drugs — the O'Connells stayed out of the drug trade. This was behind-the-scenes stuff. I wanted to help where I could, so I shoved my morality down and powered through. With working late nights at Roisin's, I didn't bother going home. I kept a bag packed with essentials and slept at the Shannon's penthouse.

Later in the week, I called Eoghan and asked to have a chat. I wanted to make sure he was copacetic after our discussion. He sounded distracted, so I offered to go to him. He reminded me not to use the subway, but I assured him I'd use one of the O'Connells' drivers.

When he sent me his location pin, I was confused. Kieran owned a high-rise in Soho and lived on the top floor. I'd been there on multiple occasions but hadn't realized Eoghan lived in the building as well. Right when I was about to ask him for details, he sent another text.

Fifth floor.

* * * *

An hour later, I exited the back of the hired car and approached the building. A well-built man in street clothes was leaning against the iron door, smoking a cigarette. He appeared inconspicuous, but I'd been around Jack too long not to recognize an armed guard. The man dipped his cap at me and slid a key into the door, holding it open. I smiled a thank you and crossed the empty warehouse. It was never in use, but the adjoining room was often utilized for underground street fighting.

As I neared the service elevator, another guard looked me over with a nod, handing me a heavy metal keycard. I'd only ever been to Kieran's loft, which was on the top floor. The keycard I now held had a bold '5' etched onto it. Thanking the man, I entered the elevator and inserted the key into the slot.

I gnawed on my bottom lip, watching the panel light up with each passing floor. As usual, when I had a moment to myself, I thought of Jack. I opened our text chain, seeing a disconcerting message he'd sent a few days ago. It was a quote from *East of Eden*. He'd stolen and read many of my books, but this one was his favorite.

"Monsters are variations from the accepted normal to a greater or lesser degree. As a child may be born without an

arm, so one may be born without kindness or the potential of consciousness."

I'd yet to reply, not knowing what to say. It'd been radio silence for days, then one of Steinbeck's most morbid quotes. Jack thought he was a monster, but evil didn't recognize the darkness in itself. It simply festered in it.

When the doors slid open, I was blinded by the sudden intrusion of light. I tucked my phone into my back pocket, then held my hand in front of my face, squinting.

"Eoghan?" I hedged, stepping off the elevator.

"You must be Emma Marshall."

I blinked a few times, adjusting my eyes.

A tall, curvaceous form appeared before me. She looked to be in her late twenties, had platinum blonde hair and wore an impossibly white dress that ended just beneath her knees. Her skin was flawless, and her blue eyes danced with the impression of a smile. I'd never met her before. I was positive I'd remember someone so striking.

Much like the blonde bombshell, the waiting room-foyer hybrid was impeccable with white walls, a matching marble floor and a receptionist's desk. The rear of the room was a solid barrier of frosted glass, concealing whatever was beyond. The door behind the sleek desk was shut. Compared to the dusty warehouse below, this room looked like the entrance to a space-age heaven.

Had I stepped into an alternate reality?

"I'm Zara," the woman continued, unphased by my frozen state. "Eoghan is expecting you. Just beyond the door you will find his lab."

Lab? What exactly did Eoghan *do* when he wasn't driving me around? When he said he liked to tinker, I thought he meant on old cars or something. I couldn't imagine finding a '70 Chevelle behind the glass door.

And I didn't.

When I entered the room behind reception, I halted, taking in the massive space in front of me. Vaulted ceilings, large picture windows and white lab tables. Dozens and dozens of lab tables — all covered in what looked like tech equipment. Really, *really* high-end tech equipment. Computers, motherboards, RAM chips. Wires dangling, lights blinking, various metals and glass pieces awaiting assembly. The back wall was lined with large monitors, all blank at the moment. I didn't dare think of how much money I was gaping at.

"Oh my God," I whispered to myself. "He's like Bruce Wayne."

"I prefer to think of myself as more of an Alfred." Eoghan sidled up next to me. "But even that's a stretch."

He was in his usual grungy form, which I found laughable. I'd been expecting a white coat and goggles, but his worn jeans and T-shirt were a welcome sight. His hair, however, was uncapped, revealing a charming mess.

"What is all this?" I asked, walking farther into the room. He'd said he was a hacker, but this was in a different stratosphere.

Eoghan chucked. "Tinkering."

"This is more than tinkering. Does the mob fund it?"

"Partly."

Eoghan followed me into his pristine lab, watching as I neared table after table. I had no idea what any of this stuff did. I knew how to use a computer and I owned the latest model smartphone and all that, but this was out of my league.

"I started it," Eoghan continued. "I was awarded the MacArthur Fellowship when I graduated high school."

I knew what the MacArthur Fellowship was. Often referred to as the MacArthur Genius Grant, the organization gave a person a ton of money for being insanely smart. With no strings attached.

"And you chose to do this with it? No MIT for you?"

"I hate school." Eoghan wrinkled his nose in distaste. "Too structured."

I raised an eyebrow, holding some sort of square equipment in hand. "And the mob isn't?"

Eoghan took the object out of my hand, placing it where I'd found it. "It's more interesting."

"Is your receptionist an AI?" I asked, half joking. She was too perfect to be human.

"No, Zara is private security."

Had I heard him correctly? The blonde woman on the other side of the door was akin to a supermodel. She wasn't a beefy guard like the ones below.

"Zara is a sharpshooter," Eoghan explained, noting my incredulity. "And she never misses."

"I'll take your word for it." There were millions of dollars' worth of equipment in here. If Eoghan thought Zara was capable of protecting his assets, so be it.

A glitter nearby caught my attention. "What are these?"

There were about fifty small metal chips lining the lip of a table, each the size of my pinky nail. They were the most inconspicuous item in the room by far, even smaller than a SIM card.

"Subcutaneous trackers," Eoghan answered, circling the other side of the table. "Still in development."

Careful not to drop it, I picked one up, holding it between my thumb and forefinger. "Don't these already exist?"

"Not these bad boys." His grin was magnetic. He was enjoying this, I could tell. "They'll monitor location, heart rate, oxygen levels, blood pressure, toxicity. They go beneath the epidermis. Undetectable in a pat-down or body scan."

"Do they need to be under the skin if you're just trying to track location?"

He furrowed his brow. "Well, no, but they're not ready yet. They don't transmit underground. And the tracking doesn't work until it's broken for some reason."

I narrowed my eyes, brain whirring. "Explain."

"They only send a location ping when snapped." He retrieved a small tablet out of his back pocket and loaded a program. "Look."

I set the chip down and rounded the table, peering over his shoulder.

"These are the trackers." On screen, there was a list of about fifty trackers, all numbered. "No location yet. Now break one."

"Really?"

The eager gleam in his eye sent a wave of excitement through my veins. "Really."

I grabbed a chip, held it between two fingers then bent. Hard. It snapped clean in two, and I cupped the tiny pieces in the palm of my hand.

"Now, watch," Eoghan ordered, calling my attention back to his tablet.

On screen, one of the tracker's tags went red. Next to it, a set of coordinates popped up. Eoghan tapped on the coordinates and was directed to an aerial view of the city. A red dot appeared in Soho, right where we were standing.

"That's awesome," I breathed, impressed.

Eoghan shook his head. "They aren't done yet. I need them constantly sending a signal. And with the subway system in this city, they've got to work underground."

"They don't work underground?" I clarified.

"Not yet, but they will."

I shrugged. "Still amazing what you can do."

He smiled, blushing. "Come look at this…"

He walked off, invigorated that I was showing interest. I made to follow him but stopped in my tracks. While Eoghan's back was turned, I nabbed one of the trackers from the table and slipped it into my pocket. He said they didn't do what he'd designed them for, but I might be able to find a use for it just how it was. And in the mob world, it was always good to have a trick up my sleeve.

* * * *

That evening, as I exited through the reception area, Zara said a polite goodbye. I returned her farewell, then stepped into the elevator, opening my messages with Jack. I'd finally thought of the perfect response, one of Steinbeck's more optimistic ruminations.

"We have only one story. All novels, all poetry, are built on the never-ending contest in ourselves of good and evil. And it occurs to me that evil must constantly respawn, while good, while virtue, is immortal."

Three little dots appeared, letting me know he was typing.

If I were suffocating, I'd miss you more than the air in my lungs.

My inhale was sharp, the sound circling around the enclosed elevator. My retinas burned and my nose itched with unshed tears. I licked my lips, replying just as fast.

I miss you too, devil of mine.

Chapter Twelve

Emma

"I'm surprised you haven't asked about Jack."

Eoghan offered me one of the iced coffees in his hand. Thanking him, I sipped the vanilla-infused drink, resuming our walk. It was another lonely Saturday, but the sun was beaming and a lazy breeze made its way across the Hudson. Battery Park was full of life. In the distance, a ferry crossed toward Liberty Island, packed to the hull with tourists.

Eoghan stood on the boardwalk, one hand in the pocket of his jeans. I shrugged, twisting the end of my sundress between my fingers.

"Why would I?" I asked, feigning nonchalance.

"Because I know you miss the shit out of him. I've seen the way you two look at each other. You can barely keep your hands to yourselves for two seconds." He pretended to gag. "It's sickening."

Rolling my eyes, I made my best attempt at deflection. If thinking of Jack was painful, talking about him was agonizing. "You said you're from Louisiana. Why the change in scenery?"

Eoghan's humor disappeared in a flash, the tendons in his neck tensing. "I don't like talking about my past."

Nodding, I bit my lip. "From my experience, that's a common trait amongst humans."

A pair of siblings raced by — in the throes of a thrilling game of tag — and we were forced to dodge them. Their mother charged after, giving us a polite apology before threatening her children with no tablets for a week if they didn't rein it in.

"I'm sorry, Em," Eoghan said once we'd settled onto a nearby bench. I picked at the lid of my plastic cup, keeping my gaze downcast. "I really am, but we're all a little damaged. A kid with well-rounded parents and an infallible support system doesn't just up and decide to join an international criminal organization, you know? We've been fucked by circumstance and we're trying to fill a void. I love the mob. I finally feel like I belong. It's the closest I'll ever get to a family."

I tossed my empty cup into the recycling bin, pondering his words. Family. At its heart, that was what the mob was about. Loyalty and trust were what bound the men together, not blood and steel. I had my own family, but I wanted to be a part of Jack's, too. If that was greedy of me, so be it.

Crossing my legs, I leaned back on my hands to let the vitamin D soak into my bones. "Any updates on the dating front?"

Eoghan started to groan, but it was cut off by his ringtone. "Saved by the bell, eh?" He winked at me, pressing the cell to his ear. "I've got Wings, but she can't hear."

I straightened, my heart pounding. "Jack?" I mouthed to Eoghan, maniacally pointing at his phone.

"Got it," he spoke, then shook his head toward me. I sighed, deflated. "Uh...how about ten?"

A flush came over Eoghan's cheeks. I tilted my head, wondering who the hell he was talking to. It didn't take long before he ended the call, and I asked him just that.

"Kieran," he replied. He stood, widening the distance between us with purposeful strides. "They're back."

I catapulted out of my seat, catching up with him. I clapped my hand onto his shoulder and spun him toward me, drawing the attention of a few people. "*What*?"

"Relax, Wings. They just landed. Jack and Kieran are heading to a meeting with the heads of house. They'll be there in a couple hours."

My excitement morphed into anger. "Where?"

Eoghan sighed, glancing skyward at the canopy of trees. "Scarlett's Closet."

My mouth popped open. "The strip club?"

"It's a gentleman's club, yes."

"Jack just returned after two weeks in Ireland and he's going straight to a *strip club*?" I clarified, crossing my arms over my chest. Eoghan didn't confirm, but there was no need. "Take me there now."

"To the club?" He hollered after me because I was already jogging toward the parking garage. "Emma, I can't take you. *I'm* not even allowed at this meeting. It's heads of house only."

"I don't give a flying you-know-what!" I screamed over my shoulder, aware that there were children in our midst. I spun around, thinking of something else. "If you refuse to take me, I'll get a cab."

His features hardened, a threat passing his lips with ease. "Good luck trying to hail a cab while I fireman carry you to the car."

"We're surrounded by people," I pointed out, not at all phased by his challenge. "Try to pick me up, and I'll scream rape."

Eoghan's jaw dropped in horror. "That's a low blow."

"Pat yourself on the back, then," I retorted, annoyance spewing from my every word. "You've all taught me how to play dirty."

An hour later, Eoghan pulled into a vacant alley in Turtle Bay. Scarlett's Closet was an upscale gentlemen's club. It was dark and classy. Stripper poles, yes, but the stage was set well out of reach from grabbing hands. The women would dance to one song, then wealthy onlookers would bid for a private showing. The bidding started at a thousand for ten minutes and rose from there. Experienced and drop-dead-gorgeous dancers only, of course.

Eoghan pointed toward the employee entrance, uneasy with the situation. I ignored him, focusing on my plan. I wouldn't let Jack push me away. He'd never let me into the meeting willingly, but he would if there was no other option.

Determined, I stomped through the blood-red hallway and spoke to the manager. He was a McKenzie and didn't know my name, but he knew Benjamin Franklin. He inspected me up and down, brows raised. In my frilly sundress and sneakers, I wasn't exuding any sexual prowess. He muttered something along the lines of "if you can handle it" before counting the cash I'd handed him with greedy eyes.

Not long after, I stood in front of a mirror in the greenroom. A familiar stranger stared back at me, and I was proud of her appearance. I'd always known I was aesthetically pleasing, but my looks were antiquated — classic, I supposed. I was more Audrey than Marilyn, but not tonight. My reflection was a hybrid of them both. Emma, the old and the new. Demure, but alluring. Elegant, but sexy. Soft, but known to bite if provoked.

Confidence. That was what was radiating from my skin, giving me an unearthly glow. I smiled, one side of my mouth hitching higher than the other. Confidence looked pretty damn good on me.

"You came to kill tonight, baby girl," one of the dancers cooed, her long eyelashes waving as she dusted my body and curly hair with green glitter. Although our vacation in Santorini was long over, I still wore the evidence of it on my tan skin.

"That's exactly what I came to do," I answered with a wicked grin.

Jack wouldn't know what had hit him.

* * * *

Jack

"We've heard nothin' since Connor's death," McKenzie continued. "Not so much as a rumble from the Nicolettis."

My tumbler of whiskey began to sweat as I twirled it in my hand, pushing myself backward into the leather chair. I was trying to hide my impatience, but I could feel how close she was now. I rubbed at my chest to disperse the ache. Emma was somewhere in the city — minutes away — but I needed to be briefed before I lost myself in her. It was paramount that I knew my men, my family, were safe.

Over the next few months, an influx of green blood would be joining our ranks, coming to the city by the double. With the FBI investigating Connor's death, it all needed to be done aboveboard, so we were making a gameplan for obtaining work visas.

We would house the men in various hot points across Manhattan. Apartments and safe houses I once used for business and meaningless fucking would now be devoted to our war with the Nicolettis. A war that Luca Nicoletti had no idea was coming. I was grateful for the element of surprise. We needed everything on our side to get through the Mafia and take out the Babau.

"...may be an amateur, but what she lacks in experience she more than makes up for in motivation." A voice announced another dancer over the speaker.

We were seated at an oblong table on the private balcony in Scarlett's Closet. The dark floor of the club and the elevated stage were in clear view, but I ignored it. I needed to get this meeting over with so I could see my girl.

"Gentlemen, please join me in welcoming the Emerald Angel to our club," the voice said, catching my interest. I tilted my head at the coincidence of the name, but only just. Bryan Murray had started talking again and my attention was drawn back to the heads of house.

"How are you handling the shipment to Seoul?" I asked him. The Murrays had taken over operations at the waterfront for the meantime. They were dealing with the increase in work well, but our partners in South Korea were particular. They liked things done a certain way and paid extra for it.

Bryan's attention was lost along with a few of the others. He was staring at the stage as a unique, alluring song began to play—an ominous remix of one of La Roux's hits. Bryan's immaturity showed on his face. It was infuriating that he couldn't get through a simple briefing without glancing at the dancers.

"Holy shit, she's hot," he muttered, eyes glued to the stage.

I took a swig of my drink, looking to the heavens for help. "Next time McKenzie suggests we gather at his club, may we all remember that Murray can't keep his dick in his pants for an hour."

The men laughed, but Kieran stiffened out of the corner of my eye. *Really? Him too?*

"Is that..." Kieran trailed off, an incredulous smile adorning his gaping mouth. "Emma?"

At the mention of her name, I froze. My gaze followed his down to the rest of the club and, in particular, the stage. There was a small girl on it, wearing a short white dress that I recognized. It flowed around her as she twirled, hand on the pole. She bent at the waist in one languid move, then stood again, twirling her long dark hair around a finger. Her gaze melted when she looked out into the crowd of black suits—a room filled with dozens of men who were bidding on her for a private dance.

She reached behind her body, undoing the childlike bow at her lower back, then let the dress slide off. Underneath she wore practically nothing, just a silver mesh bra and a diamond thong. Her heels were at least six inches high, but she danced like she'd been doing it her whole life. She wrapped a long, toned leg around the pole and spun, her head tilted back, her hair a sexy mess.

"Jesus, what did her daddy do to her?" Sweeney chuckled.

Kieran watched in disbelief as I jumped from my seat, letting the door slam after I burst from the room. I flew down the stairs and onto the main floor, refusing to take my sight off Emma.

It'd been two weeks since I had laid eyes on the light of my life. I wanted to wrap her in my arms and never let go. Another part of me wanted to circle my fingers around her throat for her behavior. She was dancing onstage, naked and swaying her hips for a room full of horny executives. She was *mine*. I reached a vacant lounge chair near the stage and pushed the button on the arm, holding it down so that my bid could catch up to the others.

Emma faced the intricate backdrop, her backside to the crowd. She squatted down, her decadent ass on full display, and traced a line from the strap of her heel to her neck, teasing the crowd. She turned around, sucking her finger into her mouth, hollowing her cheeks around the digit.

God help me, if I wasn't rock-hard. I was imagining all of the ways I could punish her for this. I wanted to begin now, but the stage was elevated to prevent horny men from grabbing the merchandise. The club made its money from private dances. I had to pay to get the girl.

The patron next to me noticed my interest. He moved a hand to up his bid, but paused at the look on my face.

"If you press that button," I snarled, "I'll cut off your fingers, one by one, and feed them to you raw."

He pulled his fat hand back, moving it to adjust the hard-on in his pants as he watched Emma. I considered pulling the pistol from my waistband and shooting him in the kneecap. But the song was almost over, and I had the highest bid.

As her dance came to a merciful end, Emma's eyes finally found mine, lighting with fire as she took in the sight of me. It softened my heart a little, but not enough. She opened the locked gate at the edge of the stage and descended the steps with care, her delicate fingers held out toward me. I grabbed her wrist, hauled her avian-like body over my shoulder, and deposited her in one of the private rooms. I slammed the door behind me to block off the other men's stares. Their attention was diverted as another dancer got onstage.

I was fuming, but unraveled in front of Emma's deep, sultry stare. With one glance, she could scatter my brain. She was more beautiful than I remembered, although my fantasies never did her justice. The diamonds of her panties twinkled, refracting the subtle green lighting in the room. She stood demurely, one long leg crossed over the other.

As I neared her, her gaze raked over me, ravenous. When I towered over her, within arm's reach, she skated her hand down my chest, past my buckle, then wrapped her fingers around my pulsing cock.

That was all it took. I lost my internal battle. Lust first, fury second.

Spinning her toward the wall, I ripped that stupid thong off. The Swarovski diamonds skittered across the stone floor. I bent, kissing her glittery ass before sinking my teeth into it — just enough to let her know who she belonged to. She let out a high-pitched moan, a mixture of surprise and impatience. She braced herself against the wall, arching her backside into my face. Kicking her legs farther apart, I had my cock out in the next second.

I sank into her heat with ease, my eyes rolling into the back of my head. "Fucking hell, Emma."

Her core sucked me deeper, pulsing around my length. She was dripping, arousal coating her thighs. I pressed her head against the wall, burying myself to the hilt. She gasped at my greedy intrusion, her breathing uneven. I'd been envisioning this moment for weeks, praying for the break in my nightmares in which Emma played a starring role.

The rest of the world disappeared as I slammed into her, over and over and over, chasing my need like a starving wolf. All that mattered was this, the moment our two bodies became one. Like magnets, we'd always find each other.

Wrapping her wild hair around my fist, I pulled her back against my chest, supporting her weight. Pinpricks of light danced inside my brain at the adorable sounds she made. Her whimpers turned into low moans, followed by my own feral grunts.

"Don't you fucking come, Emma," I growled into her ear. "You take your punishment like a good little dove."

"Punishment?" she gasped, her head falling onto my shoulder. I was almost as shocked as her. How could she not understand why I was upset?

"You're *mine*," was all I could muster, my breath becoming hard to catch. I pulled her earlobe into my mouth and sucked hard. She squirmed in response, but I pushed my free hand flat against her pelvis, keeping her still against me, feeling my hard cock thrust inside her. "You don't parade yourself in front of other men."

She scoffed. "I do whatever I fucking want."

Her disobedience sent me over the edge. Emma was an expert at toeing the line that was my patience. She transformed my anger into the ultimate form of pleasure. I pressed her flush with the wall, pistoning into her. I was a madman, seeking release at any and all cost. Words were flying from my lips, but I couldn't recall what they were—or if I was even speaking English. I'd been dipping in and out of Irish for weeks.

My spine tingled with heat, my balls drew up, my fingers grasped at her silky skin. With scrambled thoughts and buckling knees, I poured myself into Emma. Her walls thickened around my cock as I continued to pump, my release exploding like a bullet from a gun.

When I was sure she'd emptied me, I pulled out before she could reach her own climax. She slumped against the wall, perspiration beading along her spine.

I wiped myself off with my handkerchief, speaking with nonchalance. "Mick will take you home."

Emma turned around, frustration clear in her eyes. She reached for my handkerchief, but I tucked it into my pocket. I wanted my cum to be a reminder of my ownership, so I wasn't going to clean her like I normally did. She wouldn't forget her lesson anytime soon.

"No," she argued, her jaw set in defiance. "I'm done being kept in the dark. You either take me with you to your meeting, or I'm getting back on that fucking stage. Your choice, Jack."

I ground my teeth to keep from roaring. What the hell had gotten into her? My body was alight with rage, but an idea occurred to me. If Emma wanted to be in that meeting, I'd fulfill her wish. I didn't feel like letting her go so soon anyway. But I would make damn sure she didn't hear a single word that was said.

"Fine," I bit back at her. Her eyes widened, as though she'd been expecting a fight. "Put this on."

I threw my suit jacket at her. She caught it, scrambling to slide her arms through.

Chapter Thirteen

Emma

Jack led me up to a private room above the balcony, his grip on my arm firm.

When we entered, every face turned to us. *The heads of house.* I recognized them all from the wake, but I'd never spoken to any mobsters outside the O'Connell family. Apart from the knowledge that one of them was a Murray, I didn't know their last names. They watched as Jack guided me to his empty seat at the head of the table and sat down, hauling me onto his lap in one fluid motion.

"Everyone, meet Emma." Jack gathered his tumbler of gold liquid. I recognized the smell. It was a vintage Macallan single malt—about three hundred dollars a glass. "Emma, meet everyone."

I forced a shy smile, my cheeks flushing. Four pairs of eyes stared back at me, incredulous. My hair was a mess and I was wearing nothing apart from stripper heels and Jack's suit jacket. I also happened to be the only female in the room. The misogyny of the Irish mob knew no bounds.

"Jesus," a man sitting on the right side of the table whispered, his gaze briefly meeting mine. He looked younger than me, perhaps still a teenager. "She's with you?"

"Keep it in your pants, Bryan," Kieran said, making me cringe. I'd forgotten he would be here. I had all but blocked out every man in the room while I danced. It was easier to pretend I was alone or dancing just for Jack. Now I realized that all of these men — including Jack's brother — had seen the whole thing. They'd seen more of me than I was comfortable with, but it'd been my choice.

Jack might be furious, but I didn't regret my decision to get on the stage. It had gotten me in this room. He was going to let me be a part of his world, if just for a moment.

"She belongs to me," Jack warned, directing his anger toward the young boy, which shut him up. Jack's possessiveness could be exhausting, but I was grateful for it in moments like this — when every eye at the table was on me.

I was Jack's, and he was mine.

"Can we trust her?" one of the older men asked, his accent as thick as his copper beard. He gave me a suspicious glare. I returned it, growing tired of them talking about me like I wasn't here. Still, I kept my mouth shut. Jack was ruffled enough already.

"*Anam cara*," Jack muttered, taking a sip of whiskey.

The answer seemed to satisfy the group, who stopped ogling me. To my left, Kieran met my gaze, a twinkle in his eye. I had a feeling '*mo anam cara*' didn't mean 'I love you' like Jack had said. I would have to research it when I got home. Whatever its translation, it refuted any suggestion that I wasn't trustworthy.

As the ruddy Irishman started talking again—something about Seoul—I relaxed against Jack. The comfort I found in being near him after such a long time apart was immeasurable. And he looked so yummy in his expensive three-piece suit, his hair disheveled after our short but effective tirade. My little stunt garnered the reaction I wanted from him.

As I settled in, Jack adjusted the leg I was straddling and an electric current shot from my core straight into my fingertips. Jack hadn't let me finish, so I was still hot and slick. I'd almost forgotten my discomfort, but his sudden movement awakened me, making the heartbeat between my legs throb once more.

Out of my peripheral vision, I thought the side of Jack's lip twitched in a shadowy smirk, but he took a sip of his drink before I could be sure. I squirmed, trying to get relief, but Jack held me still. His arm wrapped around my torso, pinning me down to his thigh.

Oh, fuck.

My so-called punishment wasn't over yet.

Jack flexed his leg. My clit pulsed like mad, seeking any way to get off, but Jack stilled himself. I dug my fingers into the solid flesh of his forearm, trying to find my bearings. That time I was positive I saw a smile curve along his mischievous mouth.

Oh, my God. He was going to torture me in front of all these people. His business associates. His *mob*. And he wasn't just doing it to punish me for stripping. He was making sure I couldn't focus on anything but him—that I couldn't hear a word being said over the blood rushing in my ears. No wonder he hadn't argued when I had demanded a seat at the table. My body might be here, but he had no intention of letting me use my brain for anything other than a silent plea.

Jack adjusted himself again—imperceptible to the rest of the group—and I was pushed to the brink of orgasm. Sinking my nails into Jack's iron-like grip, I fought with everything in me to keep the gasp from escaping my lips.

"Don't you dare," he purred, so low that his voice came from deep within his chest. He didn't want me to climax, that was obvious. He wanted me to sit here and take it. But even his tone, utterly dominant in its command, had me salivating—panting like a dog in heat.

He wasn't going to let me go. Not that I could *go* anywhere. Jack's semen was dripping down my leg, along with my own wetness. It was dark in the room, but I wasn't going to chance the heads of house seeing it if I tried to escape.

Jack shifted once more. I almost slapped him, hiding my groan with a cough. I turned my head to catch his eye, but he was staring at one of the men, doing a wonderful impression of paying attention to what they were saying. Or maybe he was interested in the discussion—I didn't know.

It wasn't until I glanced down that I realized he couldn't be listening—at least not fully. He was hard as a fucking rock, straining against the fabric of his luxurious suit pants. Smiling to myself, I knew what I would do.

Two could play at this game.

I pretended to wriggle away, forcing Jack to pull me back. I let him, my ass coming to rest next to his arousal.

His nostrils flared, letting me know he was becoming frustrated as well.

Sliding my hand under the table, I rested my palm on his zipper. Jack trailed his fingers across my thigh, cupping the heat between my legs. I licked my lips, tightening my hold on his rigid cock. He was so solid that I could feel the outline of his throbbing crown.

"All right, I think that's enough for today," Jack boomed, interrupting Kieran. He lifted his glass in a half-salute to the other men. "Now get the fuck out."

Oblivious to what was going on beneath the table, the mobsters were slow to rise, finishing off the last of their drinks and taking their time to shoot the breeze. Jack's fingers tapped a rhythm against my pelvic bone. Sweat broke out across my brow as we waited for them to leave.

Kieran was the last to go, telling Jack he planned to visit Shannon and Charlie at the hospital. Jack nodded once, remaining silent. His erection, still cupped in my palm, engorged as the seconds ticked by.

"By the way, bro," Kieran added, his hand on the doorknob. We glared at him, but Kieran was unphased. In fact, he looked as though he was barely containing his amusement. "You've got glitter *all over* you."

When Kieran shut the door, Jack pushed his chair away from the table and spun me around to straddle him. I didn't have the brainpower to be embarrassed by Kieran's insinuating comment, although Jack did have glitter on his chin.

"You're a fucking savage, lass," Jack growled, his mouth descending on my neck.

He was pure, unadulterated sin. The way he kissed and grabbed made me feel sexier than any stage or dance ever could. He'd missed me, that was clear. He peeled the jacket from my arms, unzipped his pants, and I lifted my hips to give him full access.

"Guide yourself, dovey," he cooed. His anger was absent, replaced by raw need. He traced his tongue over the pulse at my throat, sending goosebumps skittering across my skin. "I've ached for this. For you. I won't last long."

Doing just that, I impaled myself on his length. My body welcomed the pillar that nearly split me in half. I braced my hands on his shoulders, slow to lift. Jack's green eyes shimmered, his chest heaving as he tried to control himself. His fingers twitched, delving into the plump flesh on my ass. I rolled my hips, sinking down to sheathe him completely.

"Dammit, Emma," Jack cursed, transfixed by the spot where our bodies linked. He groaned at the sight, brushing his thumb over my swollen clit. I went off like a rocket, greedy as ever. My lips met his in a tangled rush, our tongues sliding in and out of each other's mouths. He tasted like whiskey and warm caramel, driving me wild.

"Shit, shit, shit!" I moaned as Jack's ministrations became more frantic. I cupped his jaw, running my fingers along the thick stubble there before fisting my hands in the curls at the nape of his neck. It felt amazing to have him in my arms again—like I was complete. I'd been living the last two weeks with half my soul missing.

But it was home now. Jack was home.

"You with me, dove?"

"Always," I panted, sinking my teeth into the sensitive skin at the base of his neck.

Jack grabbed my torso, slamming me down onto him. I screwed my eyes shut, a fierce growl erupting from my throat, the sound echoing across the club. I didn't give a shit who heard us. Jack grunted, pulling my hair back so he could see my face as he came. His hot cum spilled into me, his pupils blown, his jaw slack. God, I loved it when he looked at me like that—like I was the only thing he knew was real.

When we were sated, he pulled me to his built chest, his arms locked behind me in an earth-shattering embrace.

"That was a hell of a welcome home," he joked, patting my ass. He lifted me off him and set me on my feet. "Let's go home and get cleaned up, baby."

"I can't," I replied, legs wobbling. These heels were killing me. "I'm meeting my parents and Ella for dinner in Midtown."

Jack wiped my inner thighs with a fresh cocktail napkin, grinning up at me. I bit my lip—just to be sure I wasn't dreaming—at how handsome he looked. He was all refreshed and satisfied, almost buoyant. I'd been worried about what mood he'd be in upon his return, but this was better than expected.

"Then we'll go to the greenroom and get changed." He stood, taking my hand in his. "Mick will bring my bag in from the car. And let's tie your hair back. It looks like you just had the life fucked out of you."

I laughed at that. "I think I did."

Chapter Fourteen

Jack

The steakhouse in Midtown was black tie only, but I had slipped the manager a wad of cash and he had let us through. I'd thrown on a fresh pair of jeans and Emma was back in the flowing white sundress that crested her knees. She'd switched her heels for sneakers, thank fuck, and was looking more and more like my innocent little dove.

It was past nine, but Emma's family was still there. We joined them in a booth at the rear of the restaurant. They were dressed to the nines. Emma's sister, Ella, eyed us with curiosity as we sat down. She was just as perceptive as her older sister, although she hid her wit behind ignorance because she thought it made her more approachable. At least, that was what Emma had told me. I'd had a few conversations with Ella, inclining me to believe she knew more than she let on.

The Marshalls were already eating dessert, but Emma was famished. Once we were settled, she ordered a prawn and polenta dish. I followed suit, not wasting time with the menu.

"Congratulations on the sale of your house." I nodded toward Gregory and Katherine, Emma's parents. "Glad to see you're getting out of that town."

Stonerose, Connecticut. I'd been there twice, but the first time had been a train wreck. I'd been detained and interrogated by the local sheriff after Emma had been forced to watch yet another man kill himself. I knew Gregory Marshall was impatient to get his family away from there, once and for all.

"Oh, Jack," Katherine started, and I braced myself for her sympathy. "We're so sorry to hear about your brother. It's such a horrific tragedy. If you need anything at all, please let us know."

"Thank you, Mrs. Marshall."

I'd heard similar sentiments since my brother's passing, but Emma's mom clearly meant every word. Her eyes glistened as she looked me over, giving my forearm a maternal squeeze—almost like she was comforting her own wounded child. I relaxed into the booth, heart warmed.

Katherine's attention was then diverted. She licked her finger, rubbing at something on Emma's neck. "Is this glitter?"

Shit. I'd missed a spot. Emma blushed, batting her mother's hand away. Ella cleared her throat, coming to her sister's defense.

"Oh, that's from me. I sent Emma one of those joke cards. It was a trend on TikTok. When the receiver opens it, it explodes in a puff of glitter."

"Why would you send your sister a prank greeting card?" Katherine inquired, aghast.

Ella shrugged, dipping her spoon into the chocolate lava cake. "Because it's funny."

Katherine gave her youngest daughter a reproachful glare but dropped the subject.

"Thank you," Emma mouthed to Ella.

I was surprised. I didn't even know they made prank greeting cards. And Ella had come up with it on the spot without question.

"We were just about to take Ella to Times Square." Gregory patted his breast pocket, searching for his wallet. "You guys want to join?"

Emma grimaced at the idea. The waiter was just setting our food in front of us, clearing the rest of the party's dessert plates.

"You three go ahead," I replied, gesturing to Emma. "She hasn't had dinner yet. I'll settle up." Gregory protested me covering the bill, but I stopped him. "I feel horrible for making Emma late tonight. Why don't we meet for dinner when you three officially move to the city? You can grab that check if you'd like."

With plans for a dinner in September set, the Marshalls left the restaurant. I turned to Emma, who was wolfing down her meal. I'd underestimated how famished she was.

"You've lost weight," I commented, taking a bite of my own food. The stress of the past few weeks had taken its toll on her. I didn't like that the reason she was getting thinner had everything to do with me and my fucked-up world.

She gazed at me from across the table, a dark look in her eyes. "So have you."

I knew I'd slimmed down. I had been drinking my calories in Ireland. I was by no means slight, but I'd lost a small amount of muscle. It seemed my brother's death and our ensuing separation had been hard on us both. Just having her sitting across from me now eased my grief over losing Connor. Her presence was soothing to my frayed nerves.

I smirked, changing the subject. "Emerald Angel, huh?"

"I thought it'd be fitting," she mused, sipping at her water. She wasn't drinking tonight, so neither was I. It was the first time I'd felt sober in a week.

"I thought I'd died and gone to heaven when I saw you. Until I realized every other man in the room thought the same."

She scrunched her nose in distaste. "How much did you pay to have me?"

"Fifty thousand, but it was worth every penny."

She balked, which I had expected. Emma came from a comfortable family in financial terms, but she had no idea how much I made. Nor did I, to be honest. But Trevor Gallagher never told me to slow down on the spending, so I didn't think of money as an issue. Early on in life, I had made it a goal to be in the position I was now — to have more wealth than I knew what to do with. Money was something I needed for comfort and I wasn't ashamed to admit it.

She sat back in her seat, arms crossed in front of her. "That makes me feel like a whore."

My temper rose at her words. "Don't talk about yourself that way, Emma. If you'd come straight to me instead of that stage, I wouldn't have had to outbid anyone. Not that money is an object where you're concerned."

"I wanted to surprise you...and prove that I can handle myself."

"Point taken. I'll try not to doubt how much you can handle in the future." An image of her standing on that stage came to mind, hips swaying as she sucked on her index finger. "Where the hell did you learn to dance like that?"

She blushed. "I took lessons when I was younger."

I raised my brows.

"Ballet, not pole dancing. But if you have rhythm, I guess any form of dance feels natural."

"You'll never do that again," I warned, "unless it's for me."

She smiled, but something was holding her back. "Point taken."

I reclined in the booth to mirror her. "You still seem upset."

We'd finished our meals and the waiter was bringing the check. I handed him my card, not bothering to look at the bill. I was impatient to have her to myself in private. He grabbed it and thanked us before stalking off to make the charge.

Emma waited until he was out of earshot before speaking. "Yes, I'm still upset with you."

I fought to conceal my smile. I would never get over how cute she was when she got all riled up—like a tiger cub with its fur sticking on end.

"For punishing you?" I asked. I couldn't see why else she would be upset. I, for one, was content now that I had her with me. It'd been a long two weeks of Emma withdrawal.

"No," she said, enunciating the word. "If that's your form of punishment, I'll try to piss you off more."

"Then not calling you?" I floundered. "I knew if I heard your voice, I'd come straight home. And I had things to take care of."

Like recruiting an army.

"No, I'm pissed because the first thing you did when you landed was work more! Shannon and the baby are still in the hospital. They should've been your first stop."

The mention of my niece was akin to an ice cube sliding down the back of my throat. "I'm not going to that hospital."

She sighed, sweeping her dark ponytail over one shoulder. "Well, they're being discharged tomorrow morning, anyway. We can head to the Shannon together."

"I won't be visiting the penthouse either."

"And why is that?"

"I'm not going to look my niece in the eye until the man who took her father from her is dead." My voice was thick and laced with the hatred that burned in my eyes.

"Are you serious?" Emma asked, incredulous. "She's a *baby*, Jack. She doesn't care about your vendetta. She needs her uncles. And Shannon needs you, too."

I wasn't changing my mind. "All Charlie needs right now is a nipple and a dry diaper."

Emma threw her hands in the air. "You are so stubborn! Babies form bonds before they even leave the womb. You can't miss out on such an important thing."

"How do you know so much about newborn bonding?" I had a feeling this subject would arise often if I didn't kill the Babau soon. Which I planned to, once

I discovered the bastard's real name and whatever cave he was hiding in.

"I volunteered at a children's hospital in New Haven when I was in high school," Emma replied.

I rolled my eyes as the waiter returned with my credit card. "Of course you did."

"What's that supposed to mean?"

"Angel," I muttered, rising from the table.

Emma was a good person. She stayed out of trouble and volunteered. Not just to get into Columbia, either. She'd spent this past spring working at a soup kitchen in the Bronx for no reason other than she wanted to give back.

I placed my hand on the small of Emma's back, guiding her toward the front of the restaurant. We were almost to the door when someone called her name, and she halted.

"Emma Marshall?"

The voice belonged to a young man around Emma's age. He was good-looking in a preppy, generic sort of way—styled blond hair, deep blue blazer, clean hands. He walked toward us from the sunken dining area, a grin engulfing his face. I had to bite the inside of my cheek at the way his eyes were glued to Emma.

"Jamie?" Emma answered, surprised. "What are you doing here?"

Much to my chagrin, she let go of my hand and gave the little git an affable hug. From the way he closed his eyes and wrapped his arms low, he didn't want a simple friendship. Who the hell was this guy? Emma only had one boyfriend in her past and he was dead.

Emma broke the hug before I could give into the urge to rip the stranger's hands off.

"My parents came to town for my birthday," he explained, glancing somewhat nervously at me. He'd just noticed that I was standing right beside her. "I'm more of a pizza in the park kind of guy, but they insisted."

"Same," Emma agreed, turning to me. "This is my boyfriend, Jack O'Connell. Jack, this is Jamie Carlyle."

Reluctant, I held my hand out for Jamie to shake.

"Jesus," Jamie said, eyeing me with trepidation. "You're... I mean... Do you work out?"

"I fight," I said, hoping he got the memo.

"He owns a gym," Emma clarified, pulling my hand from Jamie's and inserting her own. There was a warning in her tone. "Jamie and I take a lot of the same classes at Columbia. He's a history major as well."

"Wonderful," I replied bitterly, but Jamie's attention had already returned to Emma.

"A few of us are going through the course catalog in a couple weeks if you want to join," Jamie said. "I'm trying to avoid Professor Callahan this semester if I can."

A blush crept up Emma's neck. I knew where her mind had strayed—we'd fucked on Professor Callahan's desk at the beginning of the year.

"Sure, I'll see if I can make it," Emma rasped.

Jamie's face lit up like a goddamn Christmas tree. I wanted to stomp on that hope with my heel, irked that Emma had a common interest with this bloke. She was serious about her education. It was something I was proud of her for, but I never quite understood the appeal. Clearly, Jamie did.

"I have your number. I'll send you the details."

"Thanks. Good to see you, Jamie."

Jamie opened his mouth to say something else, but Emma turned around, yanking my arm toward the door. I guided her onto the busy street. It was sweltering even with the absence of the sun. I wanted a cool night with Emma all to myself. I hadn't even been to my apartment yet. I could still feel the jet's circulated air on my skin. And I missed my damn cat.

"Why the hell does that beta have your number?" I asked, keeping my tone level. It wasn't Emma's fault she was attractive, and I didn't want to ruin the evening I had set aside. I didn't know how much time I'd be able to devote to us in the near future.

"It's for *school*, Jack. I had to borrow some notes last year because I missed a few classes."

Internally, I slapped myself. She'd missed those classes because she had been with me. Unbeknownst to me, I'd put her in connection with the kid — and now he was foaming at the mouth.

"He wants to jump your bones."

Emma sighed. "I'm not going to whatever study group he has anyway. I can read a course catalog all by myself, thank you very much."

Fine. I would drop the discussion, but I'd have Eoghan run a background check on the bastard just in case. If Emma was going to be in the same classes as him, I wanted to know who was fawning over my girl.

"By the way," Emma started as I texted the driver to let him know we were ready, "even if Jamie does have a crush on me, you have no right to be jealous."

I narrowed my eyes. "Why is that?"

"'Faye is unreliable at best'," she snarked, repeating my words from weeks ago. "You know her on an *intimate* level, don't you? Thanks for the heads-up. She couldn't wait to throw that in my face the moment you left."

My confusion blurred to anger. What the hell had Faye Walsh said to Emma? We'd fucked over ten years ago, for Christ's sake. It was drunk, ancient history. A mistake, though I hadn't given it much thought at the time. Or ever.

"I was a kid, Emma," I placated. It didn't seem to calm her. If anything, she looked more furious. "I was wasted every time."

Her jaw almost hit the sidewalk. *Shit*. I definitely hadn't said the right thing.

"*Every* time?" she shrieked.

A cab whizzed by. The driver honked his horn at a bicyclist hogging the lane. A few people turned to look, but most kept walking. It was Midtown in Manhattan, after all.

"A few times," I said, hoping to put her qualms to rest. "Like I said, I don't remember."

Emma scoffed. "My opinion of this woman keeps dropping and I thought it was already at its lowest. Statutory *and* you were under the influence?"

Her protectiveness was one of the things I loved most about her. My family was always in my corner but having Emma at the bat was an anomaly. Like God defending Lucifer.

"It was consensual," I explained, "but I regret it now that it's upset you."

Emma held the bridge of her nose between her fingers. She'd never done that before she met me. We were becoming more alike without even realizing it. The image of my dark mixing with her light both thrilled and sickened me.

"You're a piece of work, you know that?" Her eyes were still scrunched shut, but I knew by her tone of voice that her anger was waning. We were blocking foot traffic, but I didn't care. People could step out of the damn way.

I pulled her hand from her face, stepping closer to her. "I love you too, dove."

I leaned down for a kiss. She kept her lips snapped shut at first but melted after a bit of prodding. I parted her lips with my tongue and slid into her sweet mouth, her taste like apples and lavender. She put her hands on either side of my face, holding me to her. I let my fingers tangle in her curls, trailing them to the small of her back.

"One more thing," Emma mumbled against my lips.

She pulled away to look me in the eye. She was so goddamn beautiful — sexy and demure all at once. Her long lashes cast shadows over her cheekbones. I wanted her in my bed. Now.

"My parents and Ella are taking over my apartment for the night," she said. "I told them I would crash at your place, but I didn't know you'd be home, so I didn't think to ask."

"Dove, you never have to ask to come over." I peppered a kiss to her button nose. "The apartment is just as much yours as it is mine."

She grinned with full force and I could have sworn the lights of the city brightened. The girl could devour my soul with that smile. I would do anything in my power — move mountains, slaughter villages — to keep that unabashed, euphoric look on her face.

And all it took was letting her know my apartment was hers, which I'd been trying to do for months.

Jesus, lass.

Chapter Fifteen

Emma

"Oh my God. Are those what I think they are?"

Jack chuckled, amused by my reaction. He'd stopped to pet Fiagaí, who was purring so loud I could hear it from where I stood. The house panther had missed his daddy.

Cute as Fia was, he was far out-shadowed — at least in my eyes — by the mustard-yellow box on the kitchen island. On either side of it were two glass flutes and an iced bottle of Armand de Brignac.

"Cronuts from Dominique's?" I squealed, hopping onto the counter and pulling the box onto my lap. My nose almost orgasmed when I opened it. He'd ordered my favorite flavors — and I had at least eight.

Fia scampered down the southern hallway, content with his greeting. Jack rose from his knees, a wicked smile on his lips. "I know you live off sugar and carbs."

"Coffee and carbs," I corrected, unashamed as I spoke around a mouthful of the delectable treat. "But sugar is a close third."

Jack set his hands on my bare thighs, coming to rest between them. Even from my seat on the countertop, he was taller than me. He bent down, licking the cinnamon-apple crumble from my bottom lip.

"How fitting you chose the apple one first," he murmured.

My heart skipped a beat. "Why is that?"

"You taste like apples." His voice was deep and raspy, like gravel. He sounded starved. I would've offered him a cronut, but I knew he wasn't hungry for food. "And lavender," he added as an afterthought.

Ignoring his strange insight and seizing the moment, I pulled another piece of pastry into my mouth, closing my eyes and savoring every hidden flavor. Jack had assumed I was coming to his place tonight, otherwise he wouldn't have had Steven shop and set out my favorite dessert. Not to mention an insanely expensive bottle of champagne — but that could wait.

I almost choked as something hot and wet touched the inside of my ankle. Gasping, I dropped the half-eaten cronut into the box. Jack had disappeared under the skirt of my sundress, wrapping his fingers around my thighs, nudging my panties aside with his nose. He darted his tongue out, parting my slit.

He groaned, his warm breath making my toes curl. "Fuck, I've missed this."

I leaned back on my elbows and went with it. Sugar *and* he was going down on me? I felt like a well-attended princess.

Jack was skilled in many ways but this, by far, was my favorite. He could live between my legs and we'd both be happy. He spent his time licking the length of my folds, delving his fingers inside to find my most sensitive spot—a spot no one else, not even me, had been able to locate. I would've fallen off the counter if he wasn't holding me so tight.

He sucked and swirled and nipped at the tiny bundle of nerves, pushing me to the edge he'd taunted me with earlier. My lips parted, my head rolling along my shoulder blades. The marble of the kitchen island was cool against my flushed skin. I churned my hips, shameless as I rode his face. He grunted, spurring me on.

"Please, please," I whispered, the words barely leaving my mouth. But Jack always heard me. He palmed my thigh, signaling that it was okay to let go. On the next curl of his fingers, I did just that. Moaning his name, I reached forward to sift my hands through his chocolatey locks. As I came, he snarled into my flesh—the vibration heightening my raw senses. Jack lapped greedily as I clenched around his fingers, his facial hair rubbing at the insides of my thighs.

"Holy Mother," I breathed, attempting to copy his Irish accent. Jack peered up at me, his tongue caught between his teeth, my wetness coating his chin. "That was a hell of a welcome home."

He licked his lips, eyes half-lidded. "I seem to recall you owe me a dance."

My mouth popped open in mock outrage. "You got more than a dance, Jack!"

He walked backward toward the living room, taking a seat in the leather armchair. His movements were lazy, but I knew he was waiting, his patience wearing thin. Over the past ten months, I'd learned that Jack was a man of instant gratification. He made exceptions for me—barely.

"Still, I want one of my own." He wrinkled his chin in a fake pout. "Just for me, dove, please?"

"There isn't any music."

Jack hit a few buttons on his phone, then tossed it aside. Seconds later, a song by Rosenfeld filtered through the surrounding speakers, the deep bass rattling the walls.

Realizing he was far from kidding, I jumped off the counter and entered the living room, standing a few feet in front of him. I held a finger up—signaling that I needed a moment—and turned to face the glass wall of Jack's living room.

The lights of the city were familiar, helping me find that girl from Scarlett's Closet again. The sultry woman in the mirror who didn't give two fucks about performing for a room full of men. If I could do it then, I could do it now. Jack's eyes burned into the bare skin of my back, his gaze traveling the length of my body.

We were only allowed the present. I didn't want to think of the dead that lay in our wake or bogeymen that hid under false names. I didn't care to predict when Don Luca would ask for proof of Nate's suicide note, which would end the security I'd garnered for Jack and myself. For one night, I wanted to let the worries go, to give Jack the control he craved. To fully submit, to grant him his every wish.

Listening to the slow rhythm of the song, I lifted my hands over my head and let my hips sway back and forth, getting into the mood. Before I turned around, I undid the bow at my lower back. Instead of letting the dress fall to the floor as I had at the club, I pulled it over my head, dropping it from my outstretched fingers. It pooled into a heap on the large white rug.

I glanced at Jack from underneath my lashes. He appeared drunk on my presence alone, his thighs spread, the thick length of his erection straining against his jeans. The way he observed, relaxed but enraptured, lit me up from the inside out. A fire roared in my belly, spreading to my fingertips and toes.

"Jesus Christ, Emma," Jack cursed, wiping a finger back and forth across his bottom lip. His emerald eyes were bottomless pits. "Get on your knees."

I sank to the floor, untying my hair from its elastic.

Jack swallowed, a dark cloud descending over him. "Now crawl," he growled.

The satisfaction I felt from demeaning myself surprised me. I was naked, crawling, yet an overwhelming surge of power sluiced through my bloodstream. Jack was looking at me like I was the answer to every question he'd ever had, like I was the angel who would grant him entrance to heaven. He shifted his hips as I neared, like he hoped the fabric on his jeans would be enough to get him off. The rug chafed my palms, awakening my nerve endings. Jack bit his lip, digging his teeth into the plump flesh. When I reached him, I placed my hands on his thighs, awaiting further instruction.

"Sit on my lap, Emma," he ordered.

For the second time that night, I straddled him. He leaned back, studying the swivel of my hips as I ground on his erection, getting lost in the song, the moment, my desire.

"I wasn't very kind to you today, was I?" he ruminated, cupping my breasts, weighing them in each hand like a prospector.

I shook my head, then dove in to bite his neck, delving my fingers into his hair.

He skated his fingers to my backside, reaching around to sink into my pussy. The heel of his hand pressed against the bud of my anus, which he knew was off-limits for now, but Jack had a way of making me question myself. The pressure against that virginal area was foreign, but not unwelcome.

I dry-humped his dick, fucked myself on his fingers and massaged my puckered ass into his hand. Sweat broke out along my upper lip, my skin itchy with the need to release. My body was rubber, pulled to its greatest length. At any moment, I would snap.

"You hear how wet you are, baby?" Jack hummed, drawing attention to the squelching sound of my arousal. He curled his fingers as I bobbed up and down, lost in my own lust. "You're making a mess on my lap. I fucking love how sopping your pussy gets. So greedy for my cock."

"Jack," I whimpered, lungs burning.

"What do you need, dove?" He grunted, sucking my nipple into his mouth, surely leaving a bruise that I'd see tomorrow. Some people woke up to love notes on their pillows. I woke up to the physical evidence of Jack's dominance—and I wouldn't have it any other way. "You were such a good girl today, not complaining when I edged you in public. Tell me how you want to come."

"Around your cock," I pled, yanking at his hair, holding him to my breast. "I want you to feel it when I orgasm, then I want you to finish inside me."

Without hesitation, he lifted me off him as if I weighed nothing and situated me so that I was lying face up over the arm of the chair, my butt and legs

Jennifer Luna

dangling off the side. I looked down my torso at him, trying to get my bearings.

That was how it always was with Jack. He could do what he wanted — because everything he wanted felt so damn good — and it was up to me to take whatever he had to give. At times, like tonight, he gave more. Other times, not so much. I lived for nights like this. When the world stopped spinning, everyone and everything disappearing apart from us. We were drawn together like magnets, fiery passion raging wherever our bodies met.

"I missed you so much, Jack." Tears sprang to my eyes. I hadn't realized just how much his absence would pain me — the weight of it was lonely and cold. Now, I could breathe again. After two long, grueling weeks, oxygen blessed my lungs, stretching them to their fullest extent.

Jack pressed his lips to the dip between my collarbones, playing with the charm on my necklace. He twirled the miniature handcuffs around his tongue, sliding inside me with ease. We gasped in tandem, my channel stretching to accommodate him.

"Without you," he murmured against my skin, emerald eyes boring into mine, "I may as well be six feet underground."

Chapter Sixteen

Emma

The following morning, I awoke bright and early. A lazy grin plastered itself to my face as I showered, getting ready for the day. Jack was exercising and I decided not to bother him until I had brushed my teeth, at the very least.

Ella texted me as I exited the rainfall shower, inquiring about the night before.

U gonna explain the glitter?

My sister had covered for me, but her assistance had come with a price — the truth.

I danced at a strip club. Jack wasn't too happy about it.

Her reply was instantaneous.

Surprised he didn't spank U.

My cheeks heated. Jack would never lay a hand on me like that—his form of punishment was both forcing and denying orgasms—but Ella didn't need to know the specifics of my sex life. I cleared my throat, fingers flying over the keyboard.

Don't give him any ideas.

I laughed aloud when her text emerged.

Gross. He's hot but…gross.

Dressed in jeans and a thin blouse, I followed the sound of weights dropping. At the frosted glass entrance to Jack's home gym, I paused, careful not to alert him to my presence.

Apparently, I had been wrong about Jack losing weight. With a snug pair of training sweats wrapped low on his hips, he was still my strong, toned Jack. Beads of sweat ran down his powerful back and sculpted abs, his hair dripping with exertion. He had AirPods in, lost in thought despite sprinting at over ten miles an hour. I knew the routine well enough to recognize his cool down, so I decided to make him breakfast. I wasn't much of a cook, but an omelet didn't sound too complicated—crack a few eggs, throw them in a pan. Besides, I needed something more productive to do than stare at him.

I found a carton of eggs and some pans, which was a miracle because I'd never cooked for Jack before and the kitchen was huge—state of the art, with all the fancy gadgets and gizmos. Jack could be a professional chef if he wanted, but I was sure it wasn't as lucrative as running a criminal enterprise.

As I made breakfast, my thoughts strayed to Eoghan's lab and, in particular, the little tracking chip that was hidden in an old sock at my apartment. Hopefully, Eoghan wouldn't notice its disappearance. They were so small that one of them going missing wasn't inconceivable.

"What on *earth* are you doing?"

I spun around, spatula in hand, as Jack strode into the kitchen, eyes wide in alarm. His skin glistened from exercise, but he wiped it away with a hand towel before tossing it into the sink.

"Cooking breakfast," I replied. "I wanted to do something nice after you got me the cronuts."

Jack bit his lip in consternation. "Dove, you can't even boil water."

I unhinged my jaw, pretending to be insulted. Technically, he was wrong. I boiled water all the time to make ramen noodles.

Jack held his hands up in retreat, taking a seat on the bar stool nearest me. He interlaced his fingers on the island, looking down at the pan with a wince.

"Have a little faith," I reproached, tending to the hot pan. The edges of the omelet were dark brown. I didn't know if that was good or bad, but figured it was time to flip it. I held the pan above the blue flame and tossed the eggy mess into the air. Half of the burned omelet splatted onto the kitchen floor.

"Ah fuck, Emma, this is torture!" Jack whined, fisting the hair at his temples. "Please, for the love of God, let me make the damn food. You're going to poison us."

I pursed my lips. Poison was a high probability. I hadn't thought about that. It was dangerous to eat raw eggs, right? Or was that just the chicken itself?

"Fine." I sighed, rolling my eyes like I was doing him a favor. I supposed I was.

Jack jumped out of his seat and circled the counter. He put his hands on my hips and guided me out of the kitchen, a stern look on his face that said I was not to help him in any way.

"You'll have to teach me to cook someday," I said, taking the stool he'd vacated.

Jack chuckled, throwing the smoking pan into the sink and grabbing a fresh one. Fia was licking the runny egg from the floor, but Jack tapped him aside with his foot. It was for the best—I didn't want to be responsible for killing his cat.

"There are some things even I can't do," he replied, smiling sardonically as he prepared our meal. Before I could respond with a comeback, he changed the subject. "What are your plans for the day?"

I hadn't known whether Jack would want to stay in with me today. Optimistic, I'd left my schedule open, not that I had much to do besides paperwork at the restaurant. But, upon his question, I realized he would be busy. Our one night of peace was over.

"Shannon and Charlotte are getting released from the hospital soon," I reminded him, watching the muscles between his shoulder blades tense when I mentioned their names. "I should check in and make sure they're doing okay. Then I have some stuff to finish at Roisin's."

"How's that going, by the way?" He loaded a huge pile of eggs onto his own plate before dishing a smaller amount on mine. He knew there was no way I could match his appetite. For food, at least.

"You mean laundering your dirty money?" I teased as he set the mushroom omelet in front of me. It smelled better than anything I'd eaten since Santorini, which happened to be the last time I'd experienced my boyfriend's cooking.

Jack hummed, choosing to stand and eat at the island so he could face me. "Why do I feel like I'm a terrible influence on you?"

"Because you are," I joked. "No one else could get me to break the law but you."

A shadow eclipsed his features as I finished my sentence. I straightened on the barstool, the food heavy in my throat while Jack's jaw twitched in aggravation. But, as quickly as it had appeared, the strange darkness was gone, a soft smile taking its place. *What the hell was that about?*

"I've got quite the schedule today," he continued, donning the mask that hid his emotions. "I won't be home until one or so. Will you be in bed when I return?"

One in the *morning*? I was used to Jack keeping long and strange hours, but I hadn't thought he'd be jumping back on the horse so soon. He clearly wasn't wasting any time trying to find the Babau. The pain in my stomach worsened. It was selfish of me, but I hoped Jack wouldn't make any progress. If he did, Nicoletti was bound to push my hand.

"You okay, dove?" Jack asked, his hand warming my forearm. He'd taken note of my distress.

"Just be safe, all right?" I peered up at him in earnest. I didn't want him going out into the city with Don Luca's pet assassin lurking around. Even if the don had informed the Babau that Jack and I were off-limits, nothing was certain.

Jack leaned forward, planting a kiss on my cheek. "I always am."

"And yes," I added, trying to hide my concern. "I will be in bed when you get home."

Jack's smile almost snapped my heart in two. There was relief in that grin—like he wasn't positive I'd come back. As if there were any other place I'd rather be.

* * * *

After careful consideration, I decided to get my work at Roisin's done before visiting Shannon. It would be easier to complete before the Saturday lunch rush arrived. If the restaurant was slammed—as it always was, especially on the weekends—I would be guilted into waiting tables. By my own conscience, of course. My fellow employees knew I'd taken over Shannon's role as manager and didn't bother me when the door was closed.

The work was easy once I got the hang of it. Placing food orders with local vendors, handling our liquor account and making the schedule were the simple things. It was the laundering I paid close attention to. If it was slower than usual, I had to be careful how much I added to a ticket. I tracked the guest list for the previous days and pored through every tab to see where things could be altered. Despite it being a background job, I took pride in my new responsibility. Jack and Trevor Gallagher were trusting me not to draw suspicion, and I wouldn't fail.

Altering the books was also a great way to take my mind off things. I'd always received stellar grades in mathematics, but I was first and foremost a reader. Keeping track of tickets and their changes, then funneling the correct amount of money into the till took my concentration away from nefarious thoughts.

Around four, I rode the private elevator up to the penthouse. Kieran had stopped by Roisin's to say hello an hour prior. He'd just been to see Shannon and Charlotte, so I knew they were home from the hospital. The doors opened and I entered into the foyer.

Arthur stood guard just outside the elevator, nodding once. "Miss Marshall."

"Just Emma," I corrected, noting his demeanor had brightened since I'd last seen him at the hospital. With his black hair and gray eyes, I wouldn't have described Connor's first lieutenant as bubbly, but he looked slightly less constipated than usual.

Turning, I was disheartened to see Faye striding in my direction. Her heels—*does she ever wear anything else?*—clacked against the marble as she came to a stop in front of me.

"I hear Jack's back," Faye said by way of greeting, her tone malicious. She looked behind me to emphasize the fact that he wasn't by my side, altogether ignoring Arthur's presence. "Where is he?"

"I'm not his keeper."

She chuckled, stepping around me toward the elevator. "That's what I thought."

I spun, anger rising. I wasn't jealous anymore. Jack had made it clear that their hookups had meant nothing to him. They were a long time ago—when he had been a kid and she'd taken advantage of him. It didn't matter if he said it was consensual. He had been a drunk teenager and she'd been an adult. End of story.

"What the hell is your problem with me?" I fumed, causing Faye to stop with her back to me. "Connor is dead, your niece is grieving with a newborn yet you're still throwing your drunken lay with Jack in my face every chance you get."

Arthur lifted his heavy brow, eyes widening like he wanted to praise me, but he dropped his gaze once more.

Faye turned on her heel, wearing a surprised smile. "Jack mentioned something?"

"We've spoken about it, yes. It was a short conversation. Apparently, you didn't leave a lasting impression."

Her glossy mouth popped open and fire danced in her eyes. She looked as though she planned to say more, but she snapped her lips shut and left the foyer. *Emma one, Faye zero,* I thought as the elevator doors closed. Hopefully that would be the end of that.

"Excuse my outburst," I apologized to a stoic Arthur.

His expression remained neutral, but his response almost sounded like a joke. "Don't be. That was the most satisfying part of my week."

My grin fell when I entered the living room.

Shannon stood by the sofa, holding a sleeping Charlotte in her arms. Shannon still looked ill with grief, but she'd been getting better day by day due to the bundle of love strapped to her chest. Now, she wore an expression of shock and regret, having obviously overheard my discussion with Faye.

"I'm so sorry, Em," she whispered, soothing the sleeping Charlotte. Her little red curls shone bright, having doubled in thickness over the past week. "I had no idea about Faye and Jack."

"It's not a big deal." I shrugged, leading her to the couch so she could sit. "Jack is over it and so am I."

Shannon handed Charlotte to the live-in nanny — a quiet but tenacious Sweeney daughter — so she could sleep in the bassinet. When the baby was settled in the corner of the room, resting under the thrum of the busy city, Shannon turned to me and held my hand.

"Jack would've been just a teenager." She looked horrified and disgusted. "I don't know what the hell Faye was thinking. And she shouldn't be mentioning this now. She's clearly trying to hurt you."

I pulled Shannon in for a hug, biting back an ugly retort. Faye was Shannon's aunt. I didn't want something so petty driving a wedge between us. And Shannon was still recovering from labor. As I held her, her T-shirt — wet with leaky breast milk — soaked mine.

"Don't worry, Shan. You have enough on your plate. I can handle this."

She fell backward onto the couch cushions, exhausted. Dark circles had taken up residence under her eyes and the whites of them were red. She'd been crying.

"What does 'mo anam cara' mean?" I blurted, remembering I hadn't had a chance to Google it. I hoped Shannon would know. She didn't speak the language, but she was Irish. "Jack told me it means 'I love you,' but I'm not sure if I believe him."

"It means a little more than that." She sniffled, a morbid smile lifting her ashen cheeks. "Irish folklore states that the soul exists just outside of the body, enveloping it. Kind of like an aura. Souls encounter one another throughout a lifetime, but when two souls are matched, they commingle. Mixing. Inseparable and forever changed. Your soul has met its permanent match. It *literally* means a friend of the soul, but the English translation is, more or less, 'soulmate'."

I recalled something Jack had told me last November.

"I want to make you as dirty as me. Ruthless, with twisted morals. I want to take your dark and my light, and mix it so there's no beginning or end to us. We'd be forever entwined, shrouded in gray."

Jack had explained what he thought would happen when our souls mixed, but that had been months ago. We'd already changed one another irrevocably. My world was so gray, I couldn't see my hand in front of my face. There were so many twists and turns, I no longer knew which direction would lead to a happy ending.

I was stunned by Shannon's description but saddened by the innate sorrow in her eyes, the bottomless pit of loss. Connor must've called her '*anam cara*,' and that was why she knew the translation.

"I'm so sorry, Shan," I whispered, my voice cracking. "I shouldn't have asked."

"It's fine. I just miss him, you know? You never really understand how empty a room is until you'd give anything to have someone in it." She shook her head, stifling a sob with a false laugh. Still, twin rivers of agony carved a path down her cheeks. "Charlotte helps. I have a little piece of him with me, like you said."

I nodded, unsure what else I could say. No words could heal a widow — or anyone who lost someone they loved so deeply. A part of me had decayed after Nate had killed himself. I wondered which pieces of Shannon were withering, and what she would be able to salvage years from now.

A *soulmate*. I shuddered at the thought of losing Jack forever. I wouldn't survive something so excruciating, so final. My deal with Luca Nicoletti was the one thing keeping him safe.

Chapter Seventeen

Emma

The last Thursday in July was humid, but I was escaping the heat at the Emerald. After extensive groundwork with Mick, I jumped on the treadmill for a cool down, reflecting on the past month.

I'd moved in with Jack until the end of August. Although he left early and always got home late, we had the nights together—and that was something.

As the weeks had passed, Jack's demeanor had grown darker. It had nothing to do with me and everything to do with the fact that he couldn't find any information on the Babau. He had been a brooding person even before Connor's death, but he had usually relaxed when he was with me. His shoulders would shake with unbridled laughter, he'd sigh in content when I gave him a back rub—which ended in him pinning me to the bed. Those cherished moments were long gone and there was nothing I could do as he slipped further and further into a near constant state of internal turmoil. Shadows danced behind his eyes. When he didn't know I was watching, his expression would become frighteningly blank. In some ways, it reminded me of Nate after his mother's murder. That was more than enough cause for concern in my eyes.

Most of my time was spent at the penthouse, helping care for Charlotte. Her eyes, once the trademark newborn black, were now a brilliant blue — like a tropical ocean. They were Connor's eyes, which both pleased and saddened Shannon.

Shannon was struggling, but motherhood suited her. I had found — and Eoghan had vetted — a postpartum therapist to help her work through the mixed feelings of single parenthood. The pediatrician was also making house calls, which told me Jack and Kieran didn't want Shannon and the baby leaving the building under any circumstances. I considered myself lucky that Jack hadn't put me on house arrest as well.

Jack cared about Shannon's and Charlotte's well-being, but he refused to speak to me about them, let alone see them. I offered to go to the penthouse with him, but he merely responded with a warning glare. He even refused to look at the pictures of Charlotte I had on my camera roll, which was now full of them. I mentioned Jack's absence to Shannon once while we were folding laundry. She brushed me off, saying it was what she expected from him. As she said it, I was reminded of her prediction — *"He'll push you away."*

She was right on the money. Jack's goal to avenge his brother's murder was becoming a dark obsession. I didn't know what to do, apart from be there for him in any way he saw fit to have me.

I was at the end of my third mile on the treadmill when my music was interrupted by a phone call. Tapping the AirPod in my ear, I answered. "Hello?"

"Hey, how you doin', Em?" an unfamiliar voice rang through the minuscule speakers. I furrowed my brow, pressing the button on the console to slow down the belt.

"Who is this?" I huffed, trying to settle my breathing. I was a solid runner, but the day had taken a toll on me. Jack was insatiable this morning, waking me with his stiff cock and not so much as a word. Once he knew I was up, he'd flipped me over and fucked me hard until I was screaming his name. He had finished with a groan, kissed my forehead then left for work — and that was all before the sun had risen.

"It's Jamie," the person answered. "From school?"

"Of course!" I said with a little too much enthusiasm, setting my feet on either side of the belt. "I'm good. How are things?"

"Great!" He matched my tone. "I was calling because my friends are having a small pool party this evening at Syndicate Tower."

My forehead wrinkled in impressed shock. Syndicate Tower was a skyscraper in Midtown with unobstructed skyline views. It was an expensive piece of real estate, which I knew because the O'Connells had had a hand in placing it with its current owner.

As a result, I knew the words 'small' and 'Syndicate' didn't go hand-in-hand. There were multiple pools on the property, filled with enough water to combat a drought in some third-world countries.

"I know the study group wasn't up your alley," Jamie continued when I didn't respond, "but I hoped cooling off on a rooftop was better suited to your tastes."

I made a small noise at the back of my throat, fiddling with the miniature handcuffs resting between my sweaty collarbones. "I'm afraid rooftop shindigs are another no from me, Jamie."

I'd been avoiding anything school-related for the past month. It felt pointless to worry about academics when people were being slaughtered on the streets — when my boyfriend was becoming a different man before my very eyes.

"So, what *are* you into?" Jamie prodded.

Heat rose to my cheeks at the suggestion in his tone. I stepped off the treadmill, glancing around the gym. The Emerald was never too inhabited. Most of the patrons were involved with the mob in some way. Those that weren't — people training for the UFC — kept their mouths shut.

Jamie knew I had a boyfriend, a threatening one. He wouldn't be seeking anything more than friendship. My little scholarly sidekick had never once given me the impression that he found me attractive. Still, I decided to err on the safe side — for Jamie's sake.

"I'm into reading and spending time with Jack," I answered, emphasizing *Jack*.

"All right, all right," he joked. I pictured him holding his hands up in retreat. "No worries. Just thought you might want a break from all that shit going on with his brother. Connor, right?"

I swallowed, cursing myself. Why the *hell* had I mentioned Jack's last name at the steakhouse? I'd forgotten how far of a reach the media now had on our lives. According to the public, the O'Connells were luxury real-estate developers. Jack was a silent partner in all endeavors, clinging to his anonymity. It had been careless of me to let that slip.

Mick's blue eyes caught mine as he headed toward the octagon. He was accompanied by a burly fighter but stopped when he saw the look on my face.

"I'm sorry, Emma," Jamie said, sounding genuine. "I'm sure his family is going through a tough time. I'll put your name on the list in case you change your mind."

"Thanks," I muttered, ripping the AirPods from my ears and ending the call.

My heart raced, and not from exertion. Jamie had connected my boyfriend's last name to the most recent victim of the Babau. It was easy to imagine that my worlds were separate—Jack and his mob, then school and my family. But they were bleeding into one another, spilling across lines. I was splintering. There were two Emmas—the fierce woman who fought for the man she loved, and the coy girl who fought for no one. Not even herself.

"You okay, Emmy?" Mick cocked his head as he approached. He wore jeans and a black vest, as per usual. He always looked the same—shredded, tattooed, a few inches taller than me and hair a natural shade of deep red.

"Where's the boss?" I asked. Jack was the only person who could soothe me at a time like this, erase my panic. Sure, it'd blur my worlds more, but he was what I needed. Just one moment of serenity.

Still, it wasn't common for me to try reaching Jack during his work hours. Sometimes he'd shoot me a text to check in, but our conversations were mundane—asking what I'd had for lunch, whether I was naked in bed, if I wanted a coffee on the days he didn't get home until five in the morning. He wouldn't talk about his work, so I had no idea what he did when he wasn't home.

Mick shuffled his feet on the mat, uneasy. "He's in the office."

"*Here?*" I squeaked, glancing toward the hallway at the back of the building. "And he didn't say anything?"

How often had I been training at the Emerald while Jack was in his office? I didn't give myself time to dwell on that as I jogged toward the hall. I needed him. He could take a break to see me — to fuck me on his desk, to touch me while the sun was still well above the horizon.

"He's not to be bothered, Em." Mick grabbed my wrist before I could get closer. "He's in a meeting."

I quieted my voice. "With who?"

Mick's pale cheeks turned pink. He cast his gaze downward, looking anywhere but me. "I'm not sure."

I almost laughed. Mick not knowing who Jack was meeting with was asinine. He was his first lieutenant, his second in command, his closest friend. Mick knew where Jack was at all times of the day. They'd grown up together in the Bostonian projects. If anything, he knew Jack better than anyone apart from his brothers.

Brother, I corrected myself.

"Let go of my arm, Mickey," I ordered.

Mick grimaced, releasing me from his hold. I spun, opening the door to Jack's office.

"I need you to —"

Jack stopped midsentence, turning his head toward the door as it swung open, clanging against the wall. He stood behind his desk, fingers splayed on the wood as he leaned toward a familiar woman. She shifted, her eyes wide like a rabbit caught in headlights.

Oh, shit.

It was the Italian informant. The same one Jack had cornered at Roisin's. The woman I'd accused him of fucking before we'd found Connor. Jack glared at Mick over my shoulder, his nostrils flaring.

"I told you I didn't want to be disturbed," Jack growled.

The gorgeous woman turned, her gaze sliding over my sweaty, disheveled appearance. She didn't appear smug, as I would've expected based on our first encounter. This time, I could smell the fear pouring off her skin. She didn't want to be here.

"So, I'm a disturbance now?" I volleyed, betrayal thick in my throat.

Jack sighed, running his hand through his messy hair. "Mick?"

Mick took my arm, tugging me into the hall. Once he shut the door to Jack's office, I yanked my elbow from his grip.

"There's no need to be jealous, Em," Mick pandered as I stalked down the ill-lit hallway.

I turned around, walking backward. "I'm not jealous because she's a woman, Mickey! I'm jealous because she's useful to him."

Mick's ocean eyes widened, aghast. "You're useful, Emma. Not in the same way, but you *are* useful."

"Oh, fuck off, Mick!" I hollered, entering the main floor. A few men glanced in our direction, trying to hide their amusement as I stormed through the building. "I'm not just a wet hole!"

I called that last bit over my shoulder, shoving into the women's locker room and ripping at my sports bra.

Hell, I sounded belligerent and desperate—and I hated it. I wanted to mean something to someone who only valued money and information as a form of currency. Sure, I had a quasi-relationship with the don of the New York Mafia, but that wouldn't get me anywhere with the leader of the Irish mob.

Because I knew nothing about Don Luca, apart from his love of billiards and his sadistic streak. He'd murdered his own daughter, but I didn't have any proof. I wasn't even sure where the man lived. I had no way to pin him down. And it was wreaking havoc on my nerves.

I had no business being in this world. I was a shy schoolgirl who was better at shoving her nose in a book than up someone's ass. I dealt in CliffsNotes and excavated lives, not underground armies and sliced throats. I'd never felt more out of place than I did now.

My phone dinged with a text from Jamie. It was a QR code, followed by a short message telling me to wear a swimsuit. I bit the inside of my cheek, the forced air in the locker room shifting my ponytail. If Jack didn't want me to be a part of his world, why was I attempting to force my way in?

I quirked my lips upward, thinking of how Jack responded to Jamie that night in the steakhouse. *He wants to jump your bones.* Whether Jamie was attracted to me didn't matter, but Jack's reaction to him did.

Damn it, I knew I was being a brat, but I couldn't help myself. After weeks spent waiting for the other shoe to drop, I wanted to let loose, to stage my own quiet rebellion. I would go to this stupid pool party and I would meet with Jamie, if only for a minute.

Besides, Jack would be too distracted to notice my absence.

Chapter Eighteen

Emma

"Holy shit, I can't believe you came!"

It was hard to hear much over the music, but I could make out Jamie's voice, seeing as he was yelling right in my ear.

The roof of Syndicate Tower was, indeed, a sight to behold. The pool itself was small and intimate but filled to the brim with bodies trying to beat the heat. Cream-colored loungers and cabanas dotted the edge of the terrace. Atop a glass stage, a reputable DJ was blasting a popular hip-hop song and there were two fully stocked bars, one of which was submerged in the water. People queued in front of the DJ and the bartenders, requesting drinks and tracks.

"Yeah, I'm, um…" I trailed off, thankful that I didn't have to finish the sentence when another girl spoke up. Jamie was still waiting for me to continue talking, but I kept my gaze focused on the woman.

She was Latina and curvy as sin, her breasts on the verge of spilling from her turquoise top. I didn't understand why Jamie wasn't staring at her, like the three other men in our posse. I didn't recognize her, but I assumed she was the same major as me by what spilled out of her mouth.

"How can we *not* talk about agricultural erosion when Callahan mentions Karahantepe?"

The small group surrounding the glass table erupted in laughter, but I was elsewhere. Graphic memories hijacked my brain at the mention of dear old Professor Callahan—namely, being pinned to his desk with Jack thrusting between my legs.

Jamie placed his hand at the small of my back. "You okay?"

I flinched at the foreign contact. His hands were too soft. They hadn't known an honest day's work in his life. I rubbed my thumbs across my own silky palms. *Just like mine.*

"Yeah, good," I replied, giving him a friendly smile. *Friendly* being the operative word here. I hated to admit that Jack had been right about him. He wanted to be more than just classmates. I began to wonder if one of the reasons Jamie had let me borrow his notes last year was so I'd feel obligated to return a favor.

Jamie's desires were written, clear as day, on his boyish face—the way his eyes had feasted on me when I first approached the group. I was scantily clad in a pale pink bikini, a chemise wrap and white espadrilles. In the mirror in my apartment, I had looked fantastic. Standing among seventy of my peers and partygoers, I was self-conscious. How was it I could strip for a room full of men, but a pool party made me feel exposed? Maybe I *didn't* belong here, after all.

"Did you guys hear about Emily Schaffer?" A guy in board shorts and a Ralph Lauren polo looked around the group, grinning with excitement. "She got a transfer to Dartmouth after her dig in Venezuela, but everyone knows it's because she's fucking Professor Blanch."

Ah, hell. *I* blanched while taking a reluctant sip of my Long Island Iced Tea. No, that wasn't enough. I tilted the glass and poured the rest down my throat, setting it on the table. No one noticed, apart from Jamie, who signaled to one of the waitresses that I needed another.

He was trying to get me drunk, but I couldn't care less. I wanted to be drunk for this conversation. Gossip and upper-class Ivy League bullshit. Would this be my life if I'd never met Jack? No, I'd still be with Nate. And he wouldn't have been caught dead at a party like this. A shiver ran down my spine.

Poor choice of words, Em.

Jamie slipped another chilled highball into my hand. I nursed it, pondering my predicament. Coming here had been a terrible decision. But if I felt out of place everywhere I went, where did I belong?

"Emma?"

"I'm sorry, what?" I asked, my cheeks warm. I'd zoned out, watching the condensation on my empty glass drip onto the table. It pooled there, creating a ring before I lifted it to my lips and chomped on a piece of ice.

"You all right?" Jamie asked, concerned. He was handsome, I supposed. In a well-groomed, proprietary way—with white teeth and light eyes. His coiffed hairdo was made to look like he didn't give a shit, but he did. He most definitely did.

Five pairs of eyes were on me. I widened my grin to compensate for the awkwardness. "Sorry, I just got off a long shift," I lied.

"You work at that swanky place on the Upper East Side, right?" the beautiful Latina woman asked.

"Yeah, Roisin's," I confirmed.

Another guy grimaced. "I hear they charge, like, three hundred dollars a steak there."

One person gave a halfhearted laugh at the joke, as almost everyone else at this event could afford a meal in that price range.

"Something like that," I murmured, my smile plastered on my lips like putty. I didn't eat steak, but food at the restaurant was free for employees and family. The head chef made me custom vegetarian dishes on the fly, teasing me about my diet as he did.

"The O'Connell guy that was on the news owns it, right?" a girl asked. "Did you know him?"

A heavy stone dropped into my stomach. The warmth drained from my cheeks, replaced by a coldness so bone-deep I shivered. I did not want to have this discussion with what amounted to basic strangers, peers or not.

"Wait, that hot guy that was murdered in Brooklyn?"

I couldn't decipher who had spoken. My throat dried and my vision tunneled as panic gripped me. I tried to remember my therapist's advice. *Identify three things you can hear in your reality.* But my ears only latched onto their conversation, forcing me to visualize the trauma I'd buried over the past months—years, even. Loose pills, a billiard ball, the gaping wound on Connor's neck.

"Not just *any* hot guy. The O'Connells own, like, a third of Manhattan."

"I heard it was a serial killer."

"I don't know… The news says the FBI doesn't have any leads."

"Yeah, they *say* they don't. I think it's some feminist with an agenda, you know? Out to kill rich white guys."

"Emma?"

"A feminist with an *agenda*? Do you hear yourself? God, I hope you're next, Chad."

"Emma?"

"It was just a theory. No need to get emotional."

"Emma, are you all right?"

"Stop!" I screamed.

Silence descended on the group. Everyone stared as I abandoned my belongings, tripping over my own feet in haste to get away. I was dizzy, and not just from the alcohol. An anxiety attack was rapidly approaching like fire licking the edges of a forest. I hadn't had one in so long, but the terror was familiar—as if it'd never gone away, but lay dormant.

I widened the space between myself and Jamie's friends. Lost among sweat-dampened skin and overpriced swimwear, I began to feel better with the knowledge that I was anonymous again. That was what had drawn me to Manhattan in the first place—the anonymity. At home, everyone knew their neighbor's dirty secrets. Here, I didn't even know the name of the man in the unit across from mine. In New York, no one cared about anyone other than themselves.

Everyone was selfish and it was an easy rule to live by. I didn't need any more connections than I already had. I had my family, I had Jack, I had Eoghan and Shannon. I didn't need anything else.

I didn't know where my skirt went, but I was suddenly wading through the pool in just my bikini. The water felt like warm butter against my skin, bringing welcome relief from the evening heat.

I'm buzzed. Ten months with the Irish and I still can't handle my liquor.

What the hell had I been thinking, coming here? The panic was a result of trying to live two lives, be two people. Trying to immerse myself in the mob scene while grasping at this outdated model of myself—a version that studied every hour of the day and only cared about getting good grades and passing finals with stellar marks.

I wasn't her anymore.

I'd changed and there was no point denying it. I was a money launderer. I'd held my high school sweetheart's cold, dead face in my hands. I had been present while a man shot himself, blowing his brain matter onto my skin. I'd witnessed a man hanging upside down from a rafter, a sea of blood beneath him. I'd struck a deal with the don of the New York Mafia. I'd performed in a high-end strip club. I had done things with Jack that would make my grandmother, God rest her soul, blush in her grave.

At this very moment, I realized just how much I no longer cared about my mainstream education. It paled in comparison to Jack and the world I was now so deeply ingrained in. Ancient history and the discovery of it were insignificant in the light of everything going on in my present. A war was looming and no one on this rooftop was aware of it apart from me. It wasn't a war that would make history books, no. But lives were being lost. People were being hurt. Forever changed by it.

At least four men were dead.

And it was infuriating to stand among people who didn't give a shit about any of it. Who would never know how it felt to be separated from someone they loved. Because that was it. Jack hadn't been drafted overseas—he wasn't missing from my life physically—but he was just as distanced from me as if he had been. He was a commander in chief of an underground army, fighting a battle where law and order had no say. Where morality was a spectrum—and it changed depending on whose eyes we were looking through. It was impossible to know how depraved our enemies were. Especially when they moved like smoke—like the Babau, who struck, then disappeared into the shadows.

As if on cue, a hand moved through the water and snaked around my waist, squeezing my side. I jolted at the playful tickle, spinning to find Jamie had joined me in the darkening pool.

We were surrounded by flesh, but I was only aware of his—and not in a good way. As I moved backward, the bottoms of my shoulder blades hit the lip of the pool. I just wanted to go home. No, I wanted to go to Jack's apartment and wait for him until *he* came home. Even if he'd been in an atrocious mood as of late, I'd take any version of him I could get my hands on. That was always my motto—any Jack was better than no Jack. Somewhere along the line, I'd forgotten that.

"I'm sorry about them," Jamie said, treading closer. His caution was endearing, but I refused to let my guard down. "They love to gossip."

"Yeah." I crossed my arms in front of my chest in defense. "I got that."

Jamie bit his lip, glancing down at the swell of my breasts. *Ah, shit.* Jamie might've been a good person, but he was still a man. That Y chromosome was currently wreaking havoc on his system. I fought the urge to roll my eyes, dropping my hands to my sides instead.

"Why did you come tonight?" Jamie asked, bringing himself a little closer to avoid a group of girls splashing behind him. "I mean, don't get me wrong, I'm glad you did. This just doesn't seem like your type of place."

I chewed on the inside of my cheek. "I guess I don't know where my place is anymore."

People bobbed in and out of the pool, creating waves as the DJ spewed Kendrick Lamar. Those nearest us pressed closer, the alcohol swimming through their veins as the water churned around their bodies.

Clearing my throat, I turned back to Jamie, who was smiling with a furrowed brow. "I'll be honest with you, Jamie. As petty as it sounds, I came here because I knew it would piss off my boyfriend."

Jamie tilted his head, breaking out in a short laugh. "I appreciate the honesty. And I'd love to help you with that."

"Um, wait," I stammered, holding up my hand as Jamie drew closer. His body was inches from mine now, his hands caging me to the edge of the pool, his head angled down as he waited for me to continue. "That wasn't an invitation. I shouldn't have come."

He smirked, his light blue eyes dancing with mischief. "If coming to a party makes your guy angry, what would kissing me do?"

My mouth dropped open at his audacity, then I snapped it shut, clenching my jaw with a warning. "That would be your death sentence."

Jamie clearly didn't understand the truth to my words. He thought I was egging him on. Did my hand pushing against his chest mean nothing? But he was drunk. We both were. He wouldn't be making this type of outlandish move under any other circumstance.

As his face neared mine, I reeled back. My rigorous defensive training crossed my mind, but a swift knee to the groin wouldn't work underwater. My hesitation cost me useful seconds, during which Jamie managed to press his average erection against my hip. *What the actual fuck*? Did he plan on having sex in a public pool?

Oh, no. I had to get out of here before I got Jamie killed.

* * * *

Jack

The muffled shot flew through the underground room, echoing off the bare cement walls. I dipped the barrel down, inspecting my target with narrowed eyes. Shot to the heart. Angling the barrel, I fired two more rounds, which overlapped themselves on the forehead of the paper dummy.

I set the gun on the metal shelf and snatched the Macallan, not bothering to pour myself a glass—I was sipping straight from the damn bottle. Pressing the button that triggered the belt, the paper dummy flew toward me. I tore the sheet off, crumpled it, then tossed it over my shoulder.

"What are you doing down here, Jack?"

I groaned, rubbing the heels of my palms on my jawline. Mick tossed the crumpled paper dummy into the air, waiting for my reply.

"Target practice," I bit back, knowing that wasn't the answer he was looking for.

There was a shooting range under the Emerald. The door to the basement was in Mick's office and no one got in without him handing them a key — except me.

"No," Mick said, throwing the paper ball at me, where I clutched it against my chest. "You're avoiding her."

"Where is she?"

Mick shrugged. "She left a few hours ago. Stormed through the gym like a firecracker."

Heading toward the metal bench at the back of the basement, I threw the paper into a nearby trash bin. Mick followed, bottle of Macallan in one hand, my pistol with an empty clip in the other.

"I'm fucking this up, aren't I?" I could talk to Mick like a brother. We'd grown up on the streets of Boston together. He'd arrived in America a year before us. His family reeked of poverty, just like mine. We'd been forced into the same groupings in school because of our accents.

We hadn't gotten along at first. In fact, we had despised one another — hated that everyone assumed we'd be friends because we were from the same country. We had gotten into a brawl on the playground. Beaten and bloodied in the principal's office, we'd burst into laughter as we awaited the announcement of our suspension. As it turned out, he liked fighting just as much as me.

"Yeah, you're probably fucking it up, but what do I know?" Mick huffed, sitting on the cement floor. He took a sip of the Macallan, then passed it to me. "My longest relationship was three months."

"Hey, that sophomore had you for a bit, Mick."

My best friend laughed, leaning back on his hands, his legs stretched in front of him. "Yeah, trouble was she had about four other guys, too."

I took a sip of the whiskey, recalling Mick's short high school tryst. She'd been his date to the prom and wound up going home with another senior. When I'd gone over the next afternoon with a string of jokes prepared, he had clocked me in the jaw before I got through the first one.

"You've been different, you know," Mick said, pulling me from my reverie. My childhood didn't have a lot of good memories. In fact, the few that I had were with my brothers and Mick. Maybe one or two with Shannon. She had never let me take myself too seriously. "You've been a lot easier to work for since Emma came around. Until—"

"Until we found Connor hanging from that rope," I finished, casting him a glare.

"Yeah." Mick scuffed the toe of one boot with the other. "Until that."

I took another drink and leaned against the cement wall, hitting my head against it. "You know what kills me?"

It was a poor choice of words, but I had to get this out to someone. Kieran wouldn't understand. Hell, Mick might not either, but he wouldn't judge. This had been haunting me for weeks, the image always at the back of my mind.

"What's that?" Mick prodded, sliding the bottle from my loose grip.

"Every time I see Connor hanging from those rafters, my mind strays to Emma," I admitted, allowing shame to cloud my chest.

"How so?"

"It's this rage, right? I've been angry for as long as I can remember. Frank always said the O'Connell blood ran hot. But mine is constantly at the risk of boiling over. It's like my foundations are cracked."

"Your foundations are cracked. Time to patch them up."

The words were accompanied by a blurry image of a dying fire and the smell of fermented rose perfume. What the hell? I rocked my head back and forth, shaking it clear as Mick waited for me to continue.

"I see my older brother dead and I feel red." I powered through, my voice raw with emotion. "Then I see Emma hanging from those rafters and all I feel is darkness. A black hole where I cease to exist. If she ever went missing, fuck... I'd burn cities to the ground to get her back. She didn't choose this life, Mick."

"No," he agreed, eyeing me with caution. He rested his elbows on bent knees, the half-empty bottle dangling from his fingertips. "But she chose you. And everything that comes with you."

I rolled my eyes, my temples pounding with a migraine. "She doesn't know everything that comes with me."

"Don't you think you should tell her? Lay your cards on the table? She deserves as much, Jackie."

No, Emma deserved more than the remnants of my tattered soul, but I couldn't let her go. I was more selfish now than when we had met. At the thought of her slipping through my fingers, my heart began to race, unease latching onto my bones. I needed to see her. Like, right fucking now.

"Did Emma say she was going home?" I asked, rising from the bench. I grabbed my empty pistol from the floor beside Mick, tucking it into the back of my jeans. Offering my first lieutenant a hand, I helped him to his feet as he answered.

"Nah, she was going to a pool party in Midtown."

The fuck? Emma wasn't a party girl.

"Where in Midtown?" I shoved through the door, pounding up the basement stairs.

Mick was hot on my tail. "Syndicate Tower. I figured you knew about it. She said it's just a bunch of kids from Columbia."

I stopped walking and turned toward Mick, putting everything together. Emma was pissed at me. I hadn't been the nicest guy to be around. That was why she was going to a party with...what the hell was his name? Jamie, right.

His background check had unearthed nothing of value. No arrest record, nothing to cover up. He was a good, boring kid. And he was currently being used by my girlfriend as payback for neglect.

I clapped Mick on the shoulder, jogging out of his office. "Have Eoghan meet me there in fifteen."

"Don't fuck it up, boss!" Mick hollered.

Chapter Nineteen

Emma

No, no, no, no, no.

Jamie's face neared mine, his eyes half-lidded from either the alcohol or his horniness. He ran his hands along my upper arms. I cringed at his touch. This was, by far, one of the stupidest ideas I'd ever had. And I'd had a lot of them over the past year.

I flexed my fingers, preparing a palm heel strike. This wouldn't be pretty, but maybe Jamie would learn a thing or two about unwanted advances. All I'd done was accept an invitation to a party, but Jamie thought I was giving him one of my own.

Before I could jam my hand into his nose, a shoe was suddenly covering his entire face. I gasped in shock, faint recognition rolling over me—I knew that black Converse with the frayed laces. I knew that enticing smell. A storm had come for me.

I was hauled out of the pool by strong hands and thrown over his shoulder without so much as a word. A string of curses and splashing ensued, and I assumed Jamie was resurfacing after taking a kick to the forehead. He'd have the diamonds from the bottom of Jack's shoe imprinted on his face for days.

"You can put me down, Jack," I muttered.

He gave no indication that he'd let go. My arms dangled below me, the fabric of his T-shirt scratching my cheek. Something hard hit the crown of my head. It took a moment to discern it was his pistol. I moved my hands to the hem of his tee, keeping it from riding up. This was embarrassing enough without everyone seeing that my boyfriend had a Glock tucked into his jeans.

Despite dozens of heads turning in our direction, no one made a move to assist me. I imagined the murderous look on Jack's face was enough to keep the hazy partygoers at bay. I buried my nose into Jack's back, slamming my eyes shut while humiliation coursed through me.

Childish.

Disoriented, I didn't realize I was standing until Jack pinched my chin between his fingers, tilting my face. I snapped my eyes open, taking in my surroundings.

We were in an elevator, but it didn't have the same design as the one I'd ridden up in. This lift was simpler, with steel and mirrored walls. The black granite floor was like ice under my bare feet. My skin pebbled with goosebumps from the air conditioner. Jack had my cell and skirt tucked into the back pockets of his jeans, my heels dangling from his tattooed middle finger.

He looked irate, but heart-throbbing as usual. Jaw clenched, dark hair a mess of curls, eyes glowing a forest-green. Those orbs roamed over every inch of me, searching for possible injuries, cataloging my appearance. I knew what he was thinking. This outfit wasn't any better than the one I'd stripped in. But, still, it was just a bikini—a pink, girlie swimsuit.

He towered over me, his body emanating the heat mine so desperately needed. His scent was intoxicating, calming my nerves despite the situation. Before I could make a move, he stepped backward, slamming his fist into the elevator panel. The lift came to an abrupt halt. I leaned against the handrail for balance, teeth chattering in anticipation. I could *feel* his wrath in the air.

"On your knees," Jack ordered, his voice gravely.

He was pissed, but I reminded myself that this was the whole reason I'd gone to the party. To let him feel how angry he sometimes made me.

Childish.

As I knelt, Jack's gaze never left mine. He was shooting daggers at me, but I didn't bow my head. I wasn't a puppy being scolded. I was a grown woman facing the consequences of my actions.

Jack wasted no time showing me what he wanted. He unfastened the button and fly of his jeans in a flash, his thick erection inches from my face. I couldn't help myself from licking my lips. This cock and I knew each other well. We'd become fast friends and, more seldom, mortal enemies.

When I made no move to touch him, Jack let out a low growl. I looked up at him from under my lashes, giving him a glare of my own. I wanted him in my mouth, but I knew he wasn't going to make this pleasurable for me. I needed him as impatient as possible so he wouldn't last long.

Jennifer Luna

"Do I need to spell it out for you, Ivy League?" Jack's chest rose, his pupils dilating. His lust was taking over, which was good—better lust than rage. "You knew exactly what you were doing. Just how far were you going to take it?"

I glanced at my hands, which were resting on my thighs. My cheeks heated, shame hot in my blood. "I didn't plan on him following me into the pool. I was about to leave when he cornered me."

"I told you that kid wanted to fuck you. And yet you led him on. Coming to a party in the skimpiest bikini known to mankind, then drinking more than you ought to. You know better, Emma."

"You've been drinking, too," I challenged. I could smell that expensive whiskey on him. He wasn't drunk—I'd never seen Jack that far gone. He could drink his weight in liquor and still be able to recite the alphabet backward.

Jack narrowed his eyes, squeezing the tip of his awaiting cock. "Suck."

I smirked, giving my head a slow shake. I had every intention of making this easy for myself. Just the sight of me on my knees was getting him off. A bead of precum slid over his knuckles.

Expecting another order, I was surprised when he slapped my cheek with his dick. My jaw dropped in outrage and Jack took full advantage of that. He was in my mouth before I had time to yell at him.

The disrespectful little shit.

I placed my hands on his powerful thighs, attempting to push him off, but it was no use. He had me pinned against the mirror of the elevator, my head pressed against the wall. He slipped a hand behind my hair, protecting my skull from the hard surface as he thrust into me.

I choked, spit flying from my mouth, coating my lips and chin. My eyes watered, but I didn't take them from his. His temper was controlling him, but those emerald pools were getting hazy, becoming lost in the way my tongue flattened against his shaft. I gripped his base with both hands so he wouldn't be able to go as deep. I was still tipsy and I didn't want to chance my stomach emptying if he gagged me again.

"Mine, mine, mine," Jack chanted, throwing his head back, the tendons in his neck straining. There was no point in answering him, even if I could. He knew my answer — *always, always, always.*

He needed this reassurance more than I did. I knew who I belonged to. Mind, body, soul — they were all Jack's. And if he had to reclaim his territory to feel better about himself, so be it.

Technically, we were fighting. This was how we argued — him desperate for my obedience, and me making him work for it. I was upset, but so damn turned on. My clit throbbed. In response to him taking his pleasure from me, arousal further drenched my wet swimsuit. His rough jawline was in perfect view, his six-pack tensed through his shirt, every muscle racing toward his goal. And I wanted to give it to him.

When the head of his cock engorged, I knew he was close. I hollowed my cheeks, letting him feel the soft walls of my mouth as he slid in and out. When I nicked him with my teeth, he whispered a string of curses. I readied myself for the taste of his cum at the back of my throat. He always came in my mouth.

Which was why I was bewildered when he yanked himself away. I opened my eyes just in time to see a stream of white cream jet from his tip, hitting me directly in the face. Ropes of cum burst from him, coating my lips, neck and breasts. He fisted his length, continuing to mark me with his essence as he stroked himself.

"You asshole!" I rose from the floor, shoving his shoulders with as much power as I could muster. He moved, but not because of me. He pressed the button on the panel, springing the elevator back to life before tucking his dick into his jeans. He slid a hand through his hair and scooped my shoes off the floor before straightening his clothing in the mirror.

Flabbergasted, I took in my own appearance. Bikini shuffled around, hair wet and messy and a rosy face covered in cum.

Jack leaned against the elevator wall, smug. He pressed his tongue to the inside of his cheek, surveying me. When his eyes met mine, I saw a hint of a satisfied smile. I let out a snarl when he took a step toward me, tapping my collarbone with his finger. He adjusted the charm on my necklace, placing the handcuffs at the base of my throat.

"Mine," he whispered just as the elevator doors slid open.

Then I was off my feet again, thrown over Jack's sturdy shoulder. I let out an angry howl as Jack paraded through the lobby. I wanted to use the back of his shirt to wipe off, but I'd reveal Jack's pistol in the process. We were already drawing enough attention — no need to scare everyone on top of it.

The Midtown sidewalk was bustling, but Jack parted the traveling crowd with ease. Once people got a look at what he was carrying — an angry, almost naked woman — they stepped out of the way.

I pounded my fists into his solid ass. "I cannot believe you just did that!"

In a series of quick movements, Jack had deposited me into a familiar vehicle, tossing my belongings by my feet. My head was spinning, but I didn't have to look over at the driver to know it was Eoghan. Jack slammed the door with finality.

Oh, hell no.

I pressed a button, rolling the window down. "Are you *insane*? You think you can just jizz all over my face, then throw me in a car without so much as a word?"

Jack ignored me, tilting his head to address Eoghan. "Take her to my apartment and make sure she stays there. I'm meeting Cathal, then I'll be back to relieve you of Wing Duty."

"Go to hell, Jack!" I fumed.

He walked backward toward his Icon Sheene, which was parked in front of Eoghan's Tesla. Jack held his hands out at his sides, shouting, "Where do you think I came from?"

I crossed my arms, seething. Eoghan rolled my window up, studying me as he did. His attention was pissing me off. I wasn't upset with him, but he was the closest outlet and had just so happened to catch me at a bad time.

"What?" I snapped.

He rolled his lips, hiding a smile. "There's something about Emma."

I narrowed my eyes. "I'm sorry?"

Eoghan raked a hand through his dirty blond locks, knocking his ball cap off in the process. "There's something about Emma...?"

I pondered that for a minute, then cursed and flipped the visor down. I bent my head, searching for… Yup. I had cum in my hair.

Disrespectful little shit.

With shaky hands, I swiped at the substance, depositing it on the center console, much to Eoghan's discontent. He yelled and I rolled my eyes, refusing to comment. There was an entire fleet of vehicles he could choose from while this one got detailed.

"Why'd you even go to that party?" he asked once he'd calmed down. We were crossing Broadway and traffic was heavy.

"To piss him off." I watched a group of tourists who were taking photos of the towering block. I felt like an idiot. I'd acted out because I could feel Jack slipping away, but all I had managed to do thus far was shoot myself in the foot.

Eoghan made a small noise at the back of his throat, throwing his blinker on. "So, you went to the party to piss him off…and now you're upset because he's pissed off?"

"Don't try to reason with me."

"Jack isn't Nate," Eoghan mused, hand draped over the steering wheel. I glanced at him, waiting for more insight. "You're terrified of losing Jack to grief, like you lost Nate, and you're desperate to avoid that pain again."

"Do you take psychology courses in your free time?"

Eoghan powered through, ignoring my sarcasm. "When Nate became depressed, you said you didn't know what to do, apart from let it take its course. You regret inaction. Now, you're acting irrational, trying anything and everything to get an emotional response from Jack. You feel as though you failed Nate, so you're seeking redemption by not letting the same thing happen to Jack."

I squeezed my eyes shut, astounded. Of course I was comparing the two situations, as the similarities were frightening.

"You're forgetting that Jack and Nate are two different people," he continued, turning at the intersection toward Lincoln Square. "Jack isn't depressed—he's fucking livid. He's not going to commit suicide."

"I know Jack would never kill himself. I'm worried he'll do something stupid and get himself killed."

A telling silence filled the air. Eoghan didn't have any words of reassurance for me, which only gave my anxieties a solid foundation to grow upon.

"Any updates on the Babau's identity?" I asked.

"No." Eoghan groaned, tightening his fist on the wheel. "We've partnered with the Russians to block the Mafia's skin trade, but Nicoletti doesn't know who's compromising his merchandise."

My upper lip curled in horror. "By merchandise, you mean…"

"People, yes," Eoghan confirmed with a grimace. "We've raided three shipments destined for foreign shores, and safely returned the victims to their homes. Since our mob controls a majority of the arm and tech market, the Italians make the bulk of their income in drugs and sex."

Apparently, mobsters and militaries used similar tactics in war. *Cut off trade routes, form alliances, infiltrate enemy territory.* I rubbed my palms on my thighs, processing the information.

"Is that why Jack was meeting with Sofia?" I asked.

"Yes and no. I tracked the victims to the cargo ships and Jack organized the strike teams, making sure the Mafia didn't recognize any of our men. Sofia has been helping us understand the Nicoletti mindset. She's also keeping an ear open for information on the so-called bogeyman."

An image of Sofia's pale face and trembling hands came to mind. "She's terrified of Jack."

"The Emerald Devil has a reputation that inspires nightmares." Eoghan paused, seeming to consider how much he could tell me. When he spoke, his tone had softened. "He's our leader, Wings. I know he can be an asshole, but he never wanted this responsibility. Maybe you could take it easy on him?"

It was no wonder Jack was stressed. He wanted to strike directly at the Babau to avoid more bloodshed, but he couldn't find the monster. If he would tell me about his work, I could prepare myself for his mood swings. Instead, I was walking on eggshells half the time. My anger was dissipating, leaving exhaustion in its wake. I leaned back into the seat, placing my bare feet on the leather dashboard.

"Don't put your feet on my dash," Eoghan barked.

I peered over at him, dropping my legs to the floor. "Your boss's ejaculate is on the center console, and you're worried about my feet?"

His lips twitched. "Don't try to reason with me."

Chapter Twenty

Jack

Tiny needles pulsed into my chest, but I didn't register the pain. My skin had long since gone numb and this wasn't my first tattoo—or even my tenth. My right arm was covered in them, each one connected with smoky lines. The Roman numerals on my middle finger had been my first, soon followed by the family skull.

"We've got Tony Greco in the dungeon below Murray Hill," Cathal said, rapping his knuckles on the counter.

I turned my head, giving him my full attention.

I'd left Cathal behind while I was in Ireland, and for good reason. My third lieutenant was a black Scotsman with an English accent who could walk through Italian neighborhoods in every borough without drawing suspicion. He knew how to blend in as a tourist—sports cap, camera bag slung over his shoulder, confused look in his eye.

Each of my lieutenants had their own unique qualities, which was why I had chosen them with great care. Loyalty was a given — I wouldn't stand for anyone disobeying a direct command. Trustworthiness was next. Also, obvious. We were brothers, in a sense. Bonded by spilled blood.

After Mick and Eoghan, Cathal was the newest addition to my personal ranks. He was my age and had worked his way up from Willie to lieutenant in the matter of a year — his background in Scotland Yard's espionage unit had helped. He was excellent at feigning an American accent, and he was the one I turned to when I needed intel straight from the streets. From people who didn't know — and would never know — who was overhearing them.

As the tattoo artist placed the plastic wrap over my pectoral, I nodded once. Cathal rose from his seat, calling for my driver. He knew exactly where I needed to be. Because Cathal had just told me — without much explanation on the how — that there was a prominent member of the New York Mafia being interrogated at a safe house nearby. Tony wasn't talking, but he hadn't met me yet.

* * * *

"All right, Tony." I paced the small, unventilated room. The sweat dripping from my pores wasn't good for new ink, but this was important. "I'm going to ask you one more time."

Tony Greco was tied to a metal chair in the middle of the otherwise empty dungeon. Until recently, the floor had been covered in dust. Now the dust hung in the air, tickling my nose. It mixed in with the blood, sweat and drool on Tony's face. His skin resembled an abstract painting — the kind that made a person ill when they looked at it.

Tony had been here since early morning. My men hadn't held back in their interrogations. Still, they hadn't covered any solid ground.

"What is the Babau's real name?" I asked, feigning nonchalance.

"I-I don't know!" he shrieked. "None of us do! The don keeps his identity a secret, I-I swear!"

Biting the inside of my cheek, I threw him a disappointed glare. He opened his mouth to protest, but I met his words with my fist. The hit was hard, but not detrimental. I didn't want him passing out on me just yet. If he did, I would be here for hours. And Emma was undoubtedly still upset. Eoghan assured me she hadn't left the apartment, but I had to get to my girl. We'd both acted rash tonight, but I might've pushed her a bit too far. I'd been an asshole, but I'd do it again in a heartbeat if she ever put herself in danger like that again.

The fracture in my right hand was almost healed, but I didn't want to aggravate it. So, I used my left as I dealt another blow to Tony's stomach, knocking the air from his lungs. The blood he'd been holding behind his lips flew at my face. I grimaced, wiping it away with the back of my forearm.

"That was rude," I deadpanned. Now I would have to thoroughly bathe before seeing Emma. It was past midnight and she'd be sleeping. I'd wash, then wake her to apologize.

"Do you know who I am, Tony?" I asked, massaging my knuckles. I would wear bruises on them for a few days.

He made a disrespectful noise at the back of his throat. I glanced at him, brows raised. He knew I wanted more of an answer than that.

"The fucking devil," he spoke through clenched teeth.

He balled his tied hands into fists behind his back. He was trying to hide his fury, but his eyes were fearful. I might have been an arrogant bastard, but I could read a man well. The subtle cues his body lent told me just how far I had to push — how much longer it would take to break him. This man, however, couldn't be broken. He didn't know anything about the Babau. He was being honest, which I found impressive. Honesty was hard to come by in an enemy. He could've falsified information, which would have set me back a solid week.

"Close enough, Tony." Although he'd meant the name as an insult, it made me chuckle. Tony's eyes widened at the malicious sound, terror flitting across his features. "Close enough."

The middle-aged mobster shifted in his seat, assuming what would come next. He could see the resolve in my eyes, but I was conflicted. Should I return this man to Nicoletti with a warning? I wanted to send a message to the bastard, but I still had the element of surprise on my side. If the don knew I was blocking his trade routes and interrogating his men, he would respond with his own attack, which could pull the Babau from his hiding place. It would give me the chance to take him out — or, at the very least, gather a name — before more people got hurt.

But my anonymity was on the line as well. Tony knew me by reputation alone. Once people got a good look at my face, I didn't let them go. I relied on the fact that my enemies couldn't describe or document my appearance.

Decision made, I turned to face Tony. He flinched, a whimper escaping his lips. I pulled the pistol with the attached silencer from my waistband, aiming it between his brows.

"I do apologize for this." My words were clear and without affectation. "I wish you had information, so your death wasn't for nothing. I'll be more careful next time."

"Please!" he screamed, his voice hitting a pitch only a man begging for his life could. His eyes were round orbs, the whites glowing as he leaned forward in his restraints...and right into the barrel of the gun.

Without so much as a blink, I pulled the trigger and left the room.

* * * *

Emma

The arrival of the elevator pulled me from my slumber. I'd fallen asleep on the couch watching infomercials, but the television screen had gone black. I slapped the coffee table, searching for my phone. When I found it, I saw it was after two in the morning. Jack was late.

The apartment's sound system roared to life. Metallica shook the tiny hairs in my eardrums. I straightened, peering over the back of the sofa. Jack was fumbling with the interactive screen in the foyer. I rubbed the sleep from my eyes, struggling to see in the dark.

"Shit!" Jack cursed, slamming his palm against the touch screen. I put two and two together — Jack had been listening to music and his phone had automatically synced to the speakers. "Fucking hell..."

"Jack?" I stood, brushing my hand along the wall, probing for the light switch. The music cut off. "You okay?"

"I'm sorry for waking you up," he muttered, still hidden in shadow. "Please don't turn on the lights."

"Okay," I answered, brow furrowing. "*For Whom the Bell Tolls*, huh? Does that mean you're still angry with me?"

Jack sighed, ruffling the hair at the nape of his neck. "I'm not angry, baby, and I apologize for what I did."

"Can we talk?" I asked, hope bubbling in my chest. I didn't expect him to be so receptive. "Preferably not in the dark?"

Jack gave me a wide berth, heading toward the hall. "I have to shower first."

"Okay..." I trailed off, unnerved. Under normal circumstances, makeup sex was in order after an apology. Jack liked to jump on that at the first opportunity. Standing in the living area wearing nothing more than a white tank top and panties, I was a siren. So, why was showering so important?

I followed the sound of running water, pausing when I reached the master bathroom. Jack's clothes were on the ground, but the white of his T-shirt was tinged with red. I bent, heart pounding as I examined the article of clothing for holes. Nothing.

Dropping the blood-splattered shirt, I entered the shower. Jack was facing the opposite direction, scrubbing his hands over his face. I raked my eyes over him, searching for signs of injury. The thick muscles along his shoulder blades tensed under my perusal.

Jack looked toward the ceiling, letting the suds rinse from his dark hair. "Are *you* still mad at me? You have every right to be. I was acting the maggot."

I couldn't help but smile at his choice of words. It was the moments when he let his guard down and an Irish phrase slipped that made my heart warm, even if I rarely knew what he was saying. I understood this one, though. He was admitting that he'd been out of line.

"No, I'm not still mad at you." I trailed my finger down his spine. "But next time, do you think you could keep your cum out of my hair?"

Jack hung his head, his shoulders shaking with a laugh. "Sure, dove. Next time, I'll aim for your tits."

My mind traveled to the dirty clothes on the bathroom floor. "Whose blood?"

He huffed. "It doesn't matter."

As he turned to face me, I was prepared to argue. *It doesn't matter*? He expected to come home covered in blood and not face scrutiny?

But a very large something that was pasted to his upper chest cut me off. I froze, analyzing the clear plastic protecting the fresh ink underneath. I held a hand over my mouth, tears springing to my eyes.

"It looks better without the wrapping," Jack muttered, grinning at my reaction. "But I can't get it wet."

Shushing him, I refocused on his newest tattoo. It was a bird—about the size of my palm and intricately detailed. Plumage in different shades of gray and black, its head upturned toward his shoulder as though it was about to fly from his skin. Feathers floated off its outstretched wings, trailing down his ribcage with delicate grace.

Jack got a tattoo of a dove right over his heart.

"You like?" he asked, biting his lip.

"*Mo anam cara,*" I whispered through the tightness in my throat. I glanced between Jack's face and the tattoo. It was so realistic I thought it might burst through the plastic and take flight.

Jack reached forward and tugged at the hem of my soaked tank top, pulling it over my head. When I looked up at him, he had his arms on either side of my shoulders, pinning me against the shower wall. A tear broke free and slid down my cheek. Jack watched it, not bothering to wipe it away. It was then that I realized how dark the circles under his eyes were getting.

I reached up, rubbing the pad of my thumb over one shadow. Jack closed his eyes, nuzzling into my palm.

"I can't keep doing this, baby," he whispered, his voice cracking. My heart wept for him — for the agony that lay below the surface of his skin. "I'm so fucking tired. I'm trying to be two different people."

"Please, Jack," I begged, leaning forward to kiss his plush lips. He returned it, but only just. "You don't have to pretend with me."

Jack groaned, tucking his nose into my neck. I wrapped my arms around his narrow waist, pulling him into me. He was so warm, so comforting. But I didn't know if I was enough of a solace for him anymore. It was terrifying to think I was out of my depth. Connor's death was destroying him. What could I do now that vengeance was Jack's greatest desire?

"I'm not pretending. I'm holding back." He caught my gaze with his bloodshot eyes. "I love who I am when I'm with you, and I hate who I am when I'm not."

His words were a vice, constricting my throat to the point of pain. "I love who you are at all times, Jack."

He grimaced, like my statement was an insult. "You don't know the other man I can be. I'm not all bubbly and full of laughter. Not when I'm out in my world."

"As I recall, I met the Hyde to your Jekyll last Christmas," I reminded him. Jack gave me a dark look before continuing his oral exploration of my throat. "Let me in, babe. I'm not afraid of you."

"*I'm* afraid of me!" Jack roared, lifting me up by the backs of my thighs. He had me pressed to the chilly marble wall within the second, my legs wrapped around his torso. His erection was evident, the head of it nudging my heat. My sex clenched on the steamy air, begging for him to take what was his.

"When are you going to learn that you don't have to pin me to hard surfaces to keep me?" The question burst from my lips right before Jack sealed his mouth over mine, devouring my gasp. He delved his tongue in, angry and hungry — maybe even a little desperate.

"Never," he replied huskily, trapping my bottom lip between his teeth and pulling it toward him. His hooded eyes locked on mine, a smirk adorning his sinful mouth. "Besides, you love being tossed around."

"Yeah?" I challenged, raising a brow. "And how do you know that?"

Accepting the challenge, Jack swiped a finger along my pulsing clit, bringing the glistening digit up between us before putting it in his mouth. My body ignited in flames.

"That's how I know," Jack answered, his voice low with a threat. And Jack didn't make empty threats.

Without warning, he sheathed himself inside me. I cried out at the fullness, digging my nails into the muscle at the base of his neck. He made me feel whole whenever we were together. Every day, I waited for this—for anything he could give me.

I wiggled, begging him to move. Sometimes, he liked to stay still like this. While I adjusted to his size, he regained composure so he knew he wouldn't hurt me. He loved testing the boundaries of his own self-control, waiting until he absolutely couldn't stop himself from going further. It was maddening and oh-so-very hot.

"Shh," Jack cooed, retaking my mouth with a slow, sweet kiss. "I want to fuck you so hard, baby. Until you can't walk even five feet away from me. And then I want to do it again and again until we're too old and stubborn to entertain the idea of leaving one another."

I screamed when, on cue, Jack lunged into me, rocking his hips so that his groin massaged my clit. I was a live wire, wriggling and clawing, barely capable of keeping the plastic on his tattoo away from my nails. I was certain Jack had just said he wanted to grow old with me—but in his own way.

"Again, again, again..." I begged.

Jack did as he was told, gripping my hips and pulling me down onto his thick cock. I loosened my legs and arched my back, allowing him better access to do what he did best.

"That's right, dove," Jack encouraged, rocking deeper and deeper with each thrust. "Let me in."

I groaned, equal parts turned on and frustrated with this man. "Let *me* in!"

"No!" Jack barked, hitting the end of me.

"Jack." I moaned, my lungs ragged. Sweat and water drops coated my body, running in rivulets down my slippery skin. "I'm not going anywhere. I won't survive it. Please stop pushing me away just to pull me back again. I'll never recover from losing you. You've completely obliterated any preconceptions that I had of love. I can't live without this. Without you."

Something shimmered in his eyes when I finished my confession, but what I thought was a tear was gone in the next moment. His forehead collided with mine, throwing me back into the wall. Oh, he was moving so fast, guiding us both to that highest of highs — hearts pounding against one another, tongues dueling, legs trembling. Jack ate my moans, pushing me farther up the wall with every flex of his hips. I was going to be sore as hell tomorrow, but this was worth it — *he* was worth it.

"Are you here, baby?" Jack asked, his voice strained with impending release.

"Always," I whimpered, going slick around him as my own orgasm crested.

He buried his face in my neck, his jaw tight. "Oh, fuck, fuck, *fuck*!"

The sound of pleasure ripping through him was my undoing. I fisted my hands in his hair, yanking at the roots as a scream erupted from my belly. Warm heat shot from my sex to my fingertips and toes, goosebumps following in its wake.

Jack's legs gave out and we slid to the marble floor, latched together. We kept our arms wrapped around one another as our breathing settled. *Oh. My. God.* At this rate, we were going to destroy each other.

"I killed a man tonight."

My grip on him tightened and, in response, his still-hard cock twitched inside me. I thought about my response, grateful that he couldn't see my face while I bit my lip, my eyes narrowing.

"Do you want to talk about it?" I prodded, knowing what his answer would be.

"No." He was shutting me out again. No explanations. His muscles stiffened, his arms becoming iron bars around my petite frame. "Are you going to leave me?"

I leaned back as much as his grip allowed. *Oh, Jack...* His head was hanging, his eyes screwed shut. He looked to be in even more pain than before.

How could he think—after everything we'd been through, after everything I just said—that I would ever leave him? I knew Jack was a killer. He had admitted it to me on one occasion. I liked to imagine it was in his past, but that was wishful thinking. Over the course of our relationship, I'd caught evidence of his work—bruised knuckles, bloody towels, cuts along his forehead from where he'd met the blunt end of an object. With Connor dead, it was only going to get uglier.

"Open your eyes, Jack," I demanded, interlocking my hands behind his neck.

"I can't. You're too beautiful. It's like trying to stare at the sun."

Tears muddied my vision. "You're mine, Jack. As much as I'm yours. You could've killed a thousand men tonight and it wouldn't change anything."

He finally looked up at me, eyes wide in disbelief. His gaze roamed my features, as if begging me to take it back—and wishing I never would.

"You're fucking perfect," he croaked, signs of hope stirring in the grassy depths of his irises. "You wreck me, Emma. I love you so much it hurts."

I sniffled, struggling to speak around the lump in my throat. "I feel it too."

Jack pulled me to him and I sobbed into the crook of his neck. He ran his soothing hands along my back, sending tingles up and down my spine.

Everything I had said was true. I just had to keep reassuring myself that Jack would stay on the right side of the barrel of the gun. If he didn't... I couldn't fathom the outcome. There would *be* no outcome.

I didn't care about the damn blood or who it belonged to. If he didn't want to tell me, that was fine. All that mattered was that it wasn't Jack's.

Chapter Twenty-One

Emma

Jack was home late again. It was August, and I still hadn't grown accustomed to his unorthodox schedule.

As he gathered my sleepy form off the couch and carried me to bed, I nuzzled my lips into his neck. In a daze, I watched his impressive silhouette move into the closet. When he exited, he slipped into a pair of briefs and spooned me beneath the cool sheets.

"You should be asleep," he murmured, his teeth grazing the tender flesh behind my ear. I shuddered, pushing my backside into his groin. He responded by wrapping his arms around my middle, holding me to him. "How was your day, dove?"

He knew something was wrong. I'd fallen asleep on the sofa watching British reality TV, trying to take my mind off the anxiety. Every time I thought about returning to school, dread gripped me. I had concluded that I no longer wanted to go back. School used to be my sanctuary, my stress outlet. That was no longer the case. Plenty of people deferred. If I wanted to go back, it would be there. I had more important places to be than the hallowed halls of Columbia.

"Horrible," I answered, "but revealing. You?"

"It's better now." He splayed his hand, moving it up the length of my torso toward my breasts. The pulse between my thighs quickened and I closed my eyes, shutting out the lights of the city.

"You want to talk about it?" I asked, my breathing hitched.

"No. You want to talk about yours?"

Surprising him, I hooked my leg behind one of his and had him on his back in less than two seconds. Thank goodness Mick had covered groundwork with me. I straddled him, his erection bare and in my hand. I moved upward, pumping him. His head fell back onto the pillows with a harsh groan, his hips flexing.

"I take that as a no." He moaned, reaching for me. He took my shoulders and pulled me down onto him.

Our lips met with such ferocity that our teeth clanked together. Jack lifted me into position, his fingers digging into the flesh at my hips. The one thing that could make me feel better about my day was losing myself in Jack. *He* was my sanctuary now.

* * * *

Jack was gone when I woke up. He was only getting a few hours of sleep each night. He couldn't maintain this routine for long—shower, fuck, sleep, exercise, work, repeat. He admitted to being exhausted just once, but still refused to take a day off until he caught the Babau.

I poured myself a cup of coffee and grabbed a yogurt from the fridge before the television caught my attention. Walking to the living room, I sat down cross-legged on the couch, eyes glued to the screen.

"'...city's violence is reaching new levels as another body is discovered in the Hudson. Channel Nine was first on the scene and reporters have confirmed that this body also had wounds to the neck and appeared to be drained of blood. We will send you over to Villanueva, who has just been briefed by the FBI... Villanueva?'"

I dropped my yogurt-coated spoon on the floor. The feed switched to a reporter standing on the steps to the NYPD Midtown Precinct. With frantic reporters milling about behind him, it looked as though a press conference had just ended.

"'Thank you, Denise. Yes, the FBI just held a briefing for members of the press in which they stated they are *not* relating this death to the murder of Connor O'Connell as of yet, despite the similarities between the two heinous crimes. When asked about the possibility of a serial killer in the city, Supervisory Special Agent Matthew Wallace said they are merely considering it as a lead among many, nothing more. The name of the victim is being withheld upon notification of the family—'"

My phone rang. I tore my eyes away from the screen, jumping to answer. It was from a blocked ID, but sometimes Jack called from strange numbers.

"Hello, little one."

A chill skated down my spine at Luca Nicoletti's voice. My throat dried instantly, and I gulped to moisten it. Fia, unaware of anything but his own little world, prowled by my feet, licking yogurt from the spoon.

"H-how did you get this number?" I stammered.

"Is that the most important question you have for me?"

I tried again. "Did you tell the Babau to kill that man?"

"As a matter of fact, yes," Don Luca replied, aloof. "In response to what Jack O'Connell did to one of my men. Did your boyfriend tell you about that?"

I chose not to respond. Perhaps it was better for Don Luca to be under the impression I was kept in the dark—which, I suppose, I was. But I knew a bit more than I let on.

"Just as I thought," he surmised. "Mr. O'Connell still doesn't trust the girl who lays down her life for him, I see."

"Is this why you called?" I asked, pressing his point. I had a sick feeling he was going to ask me to visit with him again—to provide proof of Nate's letter. "You wanted to explain why you had your assassin mutilate someone?"

"It's funny you use that word, Emma. *Mutilate*. Because my friend Tony Greco, the one your Irishman killed, could be described the same way. Face and ribs broken, bullet hole between his eyes, washed up like a piece of trash on the beach at Dead Horse Bay."

I shuddered, but kept quiet.

"No, Emma, that is not why I called. I don't owe you an explanation."

"Then why are we speaking?" I asked, holding my breath. If he asked for evidence, I didn't have anything. And I couldn't forge Nate's suicide note. Not only was it immoral to feign Nate's last words, I knew in my heart that Don Luca would be able to tell.

"I rang to let you know that, if I am forced to choose between sparing your lover's life or the Babau's, I will not hesitate to slice Jack O'Connell's throat myself. Do you understand what I am telling you?"

Panic. My heart, once frozen, raced to catch up on the beats it had missed. I couldn't find my voice to reply. I had to stop Jack from getting to the Babau — and I had to do it on my own. I couldn't tell Eoghan about this conversation without him filling Jack in on everything. This was an open threat against his boss.

"Emma, I am waiting for you to tell me you understand," Don Luca prodded, impatient.

"I understand," I answered.

"Good. As always, it has been a pleasure speaking with you, Emma."

* * * *

Jack

It was after two in the morning when I got home. Emma was still awake. She sat at one of the bar stools in the kitchen, typing furiously into her cell phone, tongue caught between her teeth.

"If you're texting me because I haven't called today, let me apologize before your thumbs fall off," I said with little humor, pulling the revolver from its holster at my side. I dropped it in the drawer next to the five-range.

Emma jumped up at the sound of my voice, relief washing over her. She'd obviously seen the news and come to the correct conclusion. It'd been a long day.

"I was talking to Ella." She looked wary — like she couldn't decipher what mood I was in. I felt terrible about putting her on edge, but my control was slipping. We both knew it. Hell, everyone did. "She's coming to the city this weekend, so I need to go home for a few days."

Nodding, I poured myself a drink and took a sip. I was already tipsy. Sweeney had cleared out his pub in

Murray Hill and I'd been there since midday—strategizing, planning, making calls, dealing with yet another grieving family.

Emma's gaze burned a hole in my profile as I stared at the city view, drink in hand. Manhattan hadn't changed, but it looked less vibrant to me. Central Park lay beneath the dizzying lights like an abyss.

"Who was he?" Emma asked, her tone blanketed in empathy. I ached to wrap my arms around her, to lay my head on her chest. She was ready to comfort me, but I couldn't bring myself to accept it.

"A Sweeney," I answered. "New recruit. He was only nineteen."

I tore my gaze from the view and looked at Emma. She was so warm and inviting that it made my heart hurt. She wore black silk pajamas, her hair falling in natural waves.

She was still slight, but her muscles were showing definition. Mick had informed me Emma was throwing herself full throttle into fitness. I was proud of her. She was far too selfless to begin with. Even if it was as simple as exercising and eating better, she deserved it. She deserved more than that—more than anything I could give her.

She was out of her seat, rounding the counter that separated us. She took the drink from my hands and set it down. "It wasn't your fault."

"I killed one of Nicoletti's men to save face. I knew the consequences, and I killed him anyway. I thought I could handle his retaliation."

She placed her hands on either side of my jaw, massaging the tension there. I'd been grinding my molars all day, fighting the growing rage. And fear.

"I have hundreds of lives in my hand, dovey," I continued. She lay her head against my chest while I talked. "Someone dies, and it's on me. Hundreds of lives, Emma, and the only one I give a shit about is yours."

She looked up at me, frowning. "I'm safe, Jack. Please don't worry about me so much."

I scoffed. "That's like telling me not to breathe. Every second we're together, you're risking your life. And the worst part is that you think I'm worth it. You think being with me is worth putting yourself on the line. I'm a horrible, fucked-up human being. You should've never given me the time of day."

Tears sprang to her eyes, her hold on me tightening. We were so attached to each other it was sickening. I knew the consequences of our relationship the minute it started, but I brushed them off. Now I was dealing with them and I wasn't ready for it—just like I wasn't ready for a war with the Mafia.

"You had a hard day," she offered, her voice low, trying to bury her sadness. I was doing a terrible job at keeping her happy. She hadn't had a genuine smile on her face in weeks—and neither had I. "I can't even imagine the stress you're under. But that man was killed by the Babau, not you."

I didn't even bother asking how she knew about the Babau. I had probably let it slip when she was within earshot or she'd overhead someone speaking at the Emerald.

"And if you keep up with this self-deprecating bullshit," she continued, "I will personally slap you."

Her expression was stern, shining with a sorrowful determination. I knew, without a doubt, she would follow through on her threat. But it wouldn't hurt. Even when she tried her hardest, I was numb. Hell, I deserved a slap to the face. Not just for the Sweeney kid's death, but for letting her fall in love with me. For choosing to pursue her when I knew it wouldn't end well.

"Stop it," she ordered, poking me in the chest with her finger. She'd known what I was thinking — or close to it.

"I love you, dove," I murmured, leading her to the bedroom. I was exhausted and unnoticeably drunk. I just wanted to hold Emma as I drifted into an alcohol-laden slumber. Maybe watch her sleep for a few minutes, looking innocent and angelic.

"That's better." She applauded, climbing into bed. She peeled the white comforter back, hitting my pillow with a shy grin.

Chapter Twenty-Two

Emma

Seeking to expel my bad mood, I decided to run one of my longer routes through Central Park. It was still early — the sun had just crested the skyline of the Upper East Side — but the humidity was killer. Even sticking to the shade, I labored along the off-beaten path, trekking through Belvedere Castle. Once nine o'clock hit and the park became too congested for my liking, I called it quits.

After my run, I grabbed an iced coffee from a street vendor and walked the rest of the way to my apartment — no point in calling Eoghan for what amounted to a few blocks. I hadn't been home in a while and the little two-bedroom needed scrubbing. Ella would be visiting this weekend and I didn't want it to look like I never used the place. I didn't want to make it obvious that I was only moving back for her, which I was.

Showered and clothed, I arrived at the penthouse to find Shannon in one of her better moods. She had good and bad days, which her therapist had told her was normal. We munched on Guillermo's berry and quinoa salad at the kitchen island as the nanny put Charlotte down for a nap.

Shannon was out of her usual sweats and, most shocking, her lips were a cherry red. I was glad to see her signature makeup, if just for a day. She examined me from across the counter, smirking.

"For once, you look worse than I do," she joked, popping a baby carrot into her mouth.

I mustered a chuckle. "I feel like it."

"Jack?" she guessed.

My response was a heavy sigh. I fiddled with my fork, poking at a blueberry. The salad was delicious, but too much effort to eat.

"What did I tell you?" she asked. It was an 'I told you so,' but without the mirth. "Jack is a hard person to know."

She repeated her words from last November. I had thought I'd understood what she had been talking about, but I'd clearly had no idea. Now, the sentiment took on a whole new meaning.

"I see darkness in his eyes." I balanced my chin on the heel of my hand. "It's more prevalent than ever before. Why does he keep trying to hide it from me?"

"Because if Jack gives into his demons, he's scared he'll lose you. He's scared you'll run and never look back."

"But I've seen him at his worst!" I yelled, exasperated. "At Christmas he almost killed Frank. What could be more horrifying than that?"

Shannon grimaced, giving my shoulder a gentle squeeze. "I know you won't run, Emmy. But you haven't seen him at his worst. Not yet. Soon, I think. He's crumbling. From what Kieran's said, he's not far off."

"Is there, like, some timetable I don't know about? A Facebook event to alert me? Has he done this before?"

Shannon shook her head, giving me a meaningful look. "Never at this magnitude. Never when he's got so much at stake."

"What do I do when he reaches rock bottom?" I pleaded.

"I don't know, babe. Jack's been a different person since he met you. You know him better than any of us at this point. My best advice is to follow your intuition."

Head in my hands, I groaned. "That's not helpful at all."

Shannon rummaged around in the fridge, pulling out a bag of green grapes and setting them in the sink to wash. "Then you're going to hate what I'm about to tell you."

Oh, God. I didn't know if I could handle any more bad news. What could it be? Another murder? Ours or theirs?

"Charlie and I are moving to Ireland," she said, turning to watch my reaction. "I've been talking with Roisin. We're going to live with her on the O'Connell farm. I'm sick of being cooped up in this penthouse. Charlie hasn't been outside since the ride home from the hospital. She can't grow like this. I want her to breathe fresh air. To be able to play outside without a security detail. To make friends without needing a background check on their parents first."

Shannon's face brightened at the picture she painted. A smile spread across my face as well. This was the best news I'd heard all summer.

"That was not the reaction I was expecting," Shannon said, laughing at my expression. "Are you that sick of me? I mean, I know you've changed more dirty diapers than most—"

"I'm going to miss you guys so much." I rose from my stool, circling the counter to pull her into a hug. "But that sounds amazing, Shan. When do you leave?"

"Thursday morning."

I understood the rush, but still—a week? "So soon?"

"I was waiting on Jack to meet his niece, but I can't hold off any longer. I found Guillermo an executive chef position at a restaurant in Chelsea. He starts in a little over a week. And I've paid the nanny out through the year. She's been so helpful."

I tugged her into my arms once more. "I understand."

God, I was going to miss her. She was the first real friend I'd made since moving to the city. She was my closest friend since Nate.

"Wait. What about your Aunt Faye?" I'd been so wrapped up in Jack's darkening mood that I'd forgotten about Faye Walsh. Our little scuffle seemed like years ago.

Shannon waved her hand like she was shooing a fly. "We got in a huge fight after I confronted her about sleeping with Jack when he was underage. She got on some cokehead's jet and is off in Aruba or Bora Bora or who-the-fuck-knows."

"You should've told me she left! I would've been here to help more."

"Em, you're here damn near every day. I need to learn to take care of Charlie on my own. I'll have Roisin's help in Ireland, but she has an entire farm to run. Besides, you have enough on your plate with Jack and the restaurant."

Oh shit. The restaurant.

"What?" Shannon asked, noticing my alarm.

I swept my phone from the counter, shouting over my shoulder on my way toward the elevator. "I forgot to put the liquor order in."

"Go, girl, go!" Shannon called. "God knows Wall Street will come crashing down if those stockbrokers are actually sober!"

* * * *

Roisin's was buzzing. I would have my work cut out for me fixing the books over the next few days. People flooded in dressed to utter perfection — silk neckties fastened snug, Harry Winston diamonds twinkling with pride. The high class of Manhattan had emerged for the weekend.

Around eight, Anna entered the office, flustered. I'd mistakenly understaffed for the evening, and it was time to pay for that error. *Good thing I keep a pair of heels under the desk.*

I set to work, tending to the tables that were unmanned. After a few minutes of hustle, time began to blend. My brain was preoccupied, memorizing orders and alterations as I made my way to the kitchen to write them on a ticket for the expediter. I hammered the bartender for extra olives or if — God forbid — a drink was supposed to be on the rocks. Reprising my waitress role was as simple as slipping into an old pair of jeans.

A hostess named Claire approached me as I waited at the bar. "Uh...Emma?"

I moved an assortment of drinks onto a sleek glass tray. "What's up?"

"There's a guy in the lobby asking for you." Judging by her consternation, it wasn't someone she recognized — meaning it wasn't Jack. Everyone in the building knew who the O'Connells were. "He says his name's Jamie."

I groaned, brushing the hair away from my face. *I don't have time for this shit.*

"Want me to tell security to kick him out?" Claire asked, intrigued. It'd been a while since we had been forced to remove someone from the building. They were rare occurrences—a guest getting too drunk or making a sexist remark to a waitress. The O'Connells were anal about security and didn't stand for anyone getting hurt or disrespected while under their wing.

"No," I sighed, handing her the tray.

Her eyes widened as the weight of it landed on her arm. Being underage, she wasn't supposed to run alcohol, but that was the least illegal act occurring under the Shannon's roof.

"Just take this to the six-top," I told her. "I'll handle it."

She nodded, accepting her new task, and we departed in different directions—her to the table of three couples on a date night and me to the lobby, our heels clicking on the stone floor.

When Jamie came into view—hands in the pockets of his jeans, hair wiry—I steeled myself and channeled my inner Shannon. I was the manager. I couldn't have people dropping in to chat during the dinner rush.

"If you want a table, we're booked for the night," I said, mustering a polite smile. "And there's a strict dress code."

Jamie's gaze alighted on me. His mouth broke out in a grin, and his cheeks flushed with what I assumed was shame.

"My parents have me paying my own tuition this year. I don't think I could afford a glass of water in there," he joked, nodding toward the opening of the restaurant. Out of the corner of my eye, I saw Claire slip behind the hostess stand. She busied herself with cleaning her workspace, but I knew she was eavesdropping.

"How can I help you, then?" I asked, all too aware that I had tables waiting. I didn't care about the tips — they would be split among the staff. My managerial pay bump was incredible, not that I needed it. Jack's black Amex was still burning a hole in my wallet, untouched. I was conservative with money for someone who had never needed to be. There were just too many people suffering in the world for me to be spending thousands of dollars on things I didn't need.

Jamie glanced around the Shannon's exquisite lobby, which had been designed by Shannon herself. It seemed as if he didn't want to meet my eye, which was understandable. Our last interaction had been awkward — what with the drinking, his hard-on and Jack's foot in Jamie's face.

"I came to apologize," he explained, his gaze downcast. "I was drunk, but that's no excuse for pushing myself on you. I'm glad your boyfriend was there to stop me from making an even bigger ass of myself."

Before I had a chance to respond, someone burst through the revolving doors and latched onto my upper arm. His grip was familiar, but gentle this time.

"You're coming with me," Eoghan commanded, tugging me across the lobby. He was agitated, which must mean this was something important. The restaurant staff would have to survive without me for the night.

"Thanks, Jamie," I called, pausing at the revolving glass doors. Jamie was frozen in shock, staring at Eoghan like he was Hades emerging from the underground to abduct Persephone. "Consider yourself absolved!"

Eoghan yanked open the backdoor to the SUV and guided me through, climbing in after. Mick nodded once from the passenger seat, signaling for the driver to pull into traffic. The driver cut a taxi off, forcing the cabbie to switch lanes with a long, drawn-out blare of his horn.

"Where are we going?" I asked, like being dragged out of a building with no more than a six-word explanation was common. It was for me, but it was usually Jack barking the order.

Mick glanced back, raking his gaze over me. I was still in my little black dress and heels, the standard uniform at Roisin's.

"Moscow," Mick muttered, his expression grave.

My pulse raced. Had I heard him correctly? He'd said Moscow, right? As in Russia? I couldn't go to Russia. What the hell was in Russia?

Eoghan grabbed my hand, reassuring me. "The Moscow Vodka Room. It's in Midtown."

"Oh, thank fuck!" I breathed in relief. The men snickered, shaking their heads. "Any reason in particular?"

"Why do you think?" Mick grunted.

"Jack," I answered, lacing my fingers together and squeezing hard.

Judging by the apprehensive energy in the car, tonight was going to be long. If Mick and Eoghan were enlisting my help with their boss, it wasn't going to be pretty, either.

Chapter Twenty-Three

Emma

The SUV pulled to the curb of a dark side street off Broadway. Despite the summer heat, a chill doused my bones when we entered the Moscow Vodka Room.

The restaurant was...red — red walls, booths, chairs, lighting. One side of the space housed a lengthy bar with over two dozen giant jugs of flavored vodka, everything from lemon to horseradish. A traditional Romani band was performing, strumming their instruments and singing jovially. Every seat was taken, but that didn't stop people from standing arm against arm, drinking and shouting to one another. Over half the room was speaking Russian, the other half Ukrainian.

It was after ten and everyone in the room seemed well watered. They didn't notice as we shoved through the restaurant. Eoghan held my hand, parting the crowd with aggression. When we reached the back door, a giant bouncer stepped in front of it.

"Emerald Devil," Mick shouted at him.

The bouncer sneered, opening the wooden door to let us pass.

The Emerald Devil was Jack's alter ego, so to speak. He used the nickname when he was participating in underground street fights. If that was why we were here, why were Eoghan and Mick so distraught? Jack was an excellent competitor.

We descended a spiral staircase, coming upon an elaborate barrel room. It was dusty and ill-lit with medieval wall sconces. Eoghan prodded me in the back with his finger. I sighed in frustration and continued after Mick, teetering in my heels. If Eoghan wanted me to go any faster, I would be tumbling the rest of the way.

When we leveled out, I realized I was right. About the fight, at least. The dingy storehouse was as congested as the restaurant had been, but the zeal down here was violent. Most of the men were yelling in Russian.

"Finally!" Kieran emerged from the crowd, animated. His eyes landed on mine and relief flooded through him. "You ready, Ivy League?"

"For what?"

Someone had better tell me what the hell was going on—and soon. Where was Jack? I couldn't see the octagon through the throng, but I assumed it was somewhere in the middle of the room.

Instead of answering, Kieran guided me through the horde toward the center of the basement. As we neared, I could hear blows being thrown and masculine grunts in response. Jack was handing someone's ass to them.

When we reached the front, the blood drained from my brain.

Jack was fighting, but it wasn't the bout I was expecting to see. His face was coated in thick blood. His wrapped knuckles were shimmering with the substance, so much so that it dripped down his forearms and off his elbows. His ribs and toned abdominals were beginning to show welts. His worn jeans were stained in a deep red and his bare feet were flat on the ground, a clear sign of fatigue.

Jack's opponent, on the other hand, showed no signs of slowing down. He had a few facial abrasions and bruises on his ribs but looked healthy by comparison. He danced circles around Jack, who struggled to keep his enemy in his line of sight.

I'd only been watching for a few seconds before the Russian landed another blow to Jack's face. Jack staggered backward, arms dropping to his sides in an attempt to steady himself. As he stumbled, the Russian advanced. Jack recovered and shoved the man off him, releasing himself from a hold on the fence surrounding the octagon.

I'd seen Jack take a hit before, but he was almost pulverized. The previous times I'd watched him, the fights had been manned by a third party—someone who called time to give the participants a break—but there was no referee in sight. And if there wasn't an official, that meant the men brawled until a knockout, or worse.

"You're gonna have to go in there and get him," Kieran said, his voice betraying genuine concern and raw fear. Not just from tonight—it was a culmination of everything. As Jack's control slipped, Kieran's worry grew. It was like looking in a mirror. Kieran recognized the same fright in my eyes as well.

A flash of movement caught my attention. The Russian let his fist fly, hitting Jack in the same spot as before. Jack hunched like a wild animal, a wide grin overtaking his bloodstained mouth. *Jesus Christ.* He was letting the man beat the shit out of him. And he was *enjoying* it.

I kicked my heels off, my bare feet sifting through spilled beer and discarded blunts. "Give me a lift."

Kieran bent down, interlocking his fingers. I stepped onto his hands and he stood, boosting me toward the top of the fence. I grabbed the rail and hoisted myself over, landing on the rubber surface inside the ring.

The fighters were unaware of my presence, but the crowd erupted in a mixture of boos and encouragements. Half of them wanted me out of the octagon, while the rest urged me to join the men in battle.

I circled the outer edge of the ring, well behind the Russian. There was no hope of taking him down, but that wasn't why the three O'Connell men brought me here. They knew there was no one apart from myself that could get Jack's attention long enough to talk him out of whatever the hell he was doing. I'd done it once before at Christmas when Jack had tried to kill his father, my voice cutting through his rage.

It was horrifying to see him so bloody and beaten, but I wouldn't let myself look away. If my gaze called even half as much attention as his did to me, he would know I was here.

And he did.

Jack's unfocused eyes shifted toward me, looking over the Russian's shoulder. The smile curving his lips disappeared, his expression turning to stone. I couldn't tell what he was thinking. Angry to see me? Happy? Panicked?

The Russian—noticing Jack was unaware—aimed a high kick. The top of his foot met the side of Jack's head, knocking him straight to the ground like he was nothing more than a bag of sand.

The crowd erupted in cheers. The Russian lifted his arms above his head, chest heaving with the effort of his victory. He turned, triumph fading to confusion when he saw me in the ring.

Ignoring him, I ran toward Jack, a scream clawing at my throat. It looked as though that kick had enough force to break his neck. I knelt, laying my head on Jack's chest. I couldn't hear his heartbeat over the turmoil, but his bruised ribs rose.

He's breathing.

Mick appeared on Jack's other side, removing my hands so he could examine his best friend, probe him for injury. Mick had been a medic in the army. He was the person Jack turned to when wounded. It wouldn't be easy to explain his various injuries to the average doctor. Most would file a police report if Jack entered a hospital looking like he did now.

"Let's get him out of here," Mick yelled.

Eoghan and Kieran made their way into the ring as the rabble congratulated their winner, not paying us any mind. Money was transferred back and forth. More than a few men were bitter, having bet on Jack to win.

It took all three of them to carry Jack's limp body up the stairs. My stomach lurched as his head lolled toward the ground. After resecuring the straps of my heels, I ran behind our group and held Jack's thick curls in my hands, supporting his head.

In the barrel room, Jack stirred. Mick had us pause, setting him on his feet. The men held him there for a moment as his eyes fluttered half-open, his head shaking as if he could rattle his concussion away.

"M'fine," Jack said groggily, pushing himself away from his brother and lieutenants. He was...*laughing* as he crossed the room, using the barrels for support. The insane sound made my chest constrict. He walked with a slight limp, holding the side of his ribs where the bruising was centered.

"What the fuck is your problem?" Kieran roared, anger winning out over concern once he saw his brother was alive and on two feet.

We followed Jack to the dirty alley behind the restaurant. He staggered, muttering incoherently to himself, as though he'd forgotten he wasn't alone.

"Hospital?" I suggested to Mick, who was nearest and knew the extent of his injuries best.

"He's not concussed, just fucking hammered."

"As in drunk?" I asked, flabbergasted.

Mick nodded. "He drank about four thousand dollars' worth of Macallan and refused to let us stop him from getting in the ring. That's when I knew it was time to get you."

Mick rushed forward to catch Jack before he ran headfirst into a dumpster. Kieran and Eoghan, ahead of the pack, turned around, spewing curses. Everyone wore an expression of controlled pity, apart from myself. My eyes widened, my mouth dropping open.

Jack had gotten wasted before a fight — then had let someone kick the shit out of him. He was a more experienced fighter than the Russian. Even buzzed, he probably had the upper hand. So *why*?

We were on a main street now, people rushing by. A few pedestrians glanced in our direction, alarmed, as Kieran and Eoghan loaded Jack's beaten body into the backseat. But they kept walking, whispering either to one another or into their cell phones at what they'd just witnessed.

"Jack's been taking that Sweeney kid's death hard," Mick explained, gesturing for me to get in the passenger seat. "I'm sure you've noticed."

I nodded, entering the vehicle. Eoghan and Kieran saluted us as the driver pulled away from the curb. When I turned to the backseat, Jack was leaning against the window with his eyes closed, head rocking back and forth.

"He decided to give himself a punishment for it tonight," Mick continued, deadpan.

So, Jack had let the Russian knock him around because he felt he deserved it. Hence the laughing every time he took a hit. He *liked* it. If I wasn't so worried, I'd be furious with him. Maybe that would come later, once Jack sobered.

"Didja see Em?" Jack mumbled, struggling to focus on Mick, who was sitting right next to him.

"Yeah," Mick grunted.

Jack clearly had no idea I was in the car with them. I wouldn't be surprised if Jack even knew he was in a *car*. Or on earth, for that matter. He had a silly grin on his blood-streaked face.

"She's so goddamn pretty," he slurred, closing his eyes. Was he dreaming? Or hallucinating? "We're gonna make beautiful babies someday…"

"Ye sure are, Jackie Boy," Mick agreed, wearing a grim expression I was sure matched my own.

"I love her so much." Jack moaned. It was a matter of time before he passed out again. "She puts up with all m'shit."

"That she does, Jackie Boy. That she does."

When hot liquid fell from my chin and onto my shoulder, I realized I was crying. "He's losing it, isn't he?"

Jack gave into his exhaustion, or intoxication. His head lolled once before nestling against the backseat. This was a turning point. I could feel it in the air. Jack had lost control tonight, and I didn't know if he was going to get it back. The city blurred past us, the noise drowned out by the malignant energy in the car.

The driver didn't exist in that moment and, with Jack dead to the world, I felt closer to Mick than I ever had before. We'd spent countless hours at the gym together, but tonight had bonded us. Mick, someone who'd known his boss since childhood, had turned to me for help. Even though I hated seeing Jack in pain, my presence was useful. I'd found a place I belonged — by Jack's side, through thick and thin. I was his sedative, capable of snapping him out of the dark.

Mick glanced at Jack, grimacing. "Frank really fucked his son up."

He was referencing Jack's past — something no one had ever done during the course of our relationship. Maybe I'd have the chance at last to ask the questions that were burning a hole in my head.

"He abused them, didn't he? All of the boys."

"Yeah, but Jack got it the worst. Always showed up to class with a black eye or a sprained wrist. And those were just the visible wounds."

My fury catapulted at his words, but I reined it in. This was a rare moment. I didn't know when or if I'd get another opportunity like it. "Jack got it the worst," I repeated. "Because he looks the most like Frank. And Frank hates himself."

"Aye," Mick confirmed.

"So, Jack wanted punishment for that kid's death, right? He wanted a beating for it?"

"Aye."

The pieces were falling into place. Jack had been abused as a child. He'd escaped, but trauma lines were hard to break. As a result, whenever Jack felt he'd done something irreparably wrong, he sought physical punishment to pay for it. He thought that was the way to redeem himself.

"Does no one see how completely fucked that is?" My voice wobbled around the lump in my throat. I felt Jack's pain like it was my own. If I could carry the burden for him, I would do so in a heartbeat.

"We all do, lass." Mick scrubbed a hand over his tired face, the bristles of his red beard scratching. "But it's not our place to make him acknowledge his demons."

Was it mine?

"Why are you telling me this? No one in the mob has been forthcoming with me, least of all Jack."

"Because I don't want to lose my best friend." He shrugged, but a world of torment brewed in his eyes. "And I like you. You're good for him. You've given him something to fight for."

I sniffled, breathing life to my insecurities, my fear. "I don't know if I'm enough anymore, Mick."

"Ah hell, lass," Mick swore, handing me a handkerchief from the pocket of his vest. "I saw it in Jack's eyes the moment we put his brother's body in the ground. He wanted to give up then, but he stuck around for you."

I was sobbing now, my head in my hands.

"Shit, I didn't mean to upset you. Jack will have my head on a spike…"

I straightened, dabbing my cheeks with the warm cloth. "He won't find out you spoke to me. I swear."

Mick exited the car to open my door. I was so absorbed in our conversation that I hadn't realized the vehicle was parked in Jack's private underground garage.

Mick held out his hand and helped me from the SUV. The gesture felt like it came from a brotherly figure. I'd always appreciated Mick, but now I understood why he was Jack's first lieutenant. There was a calming effect about him that I'd never noted before.

"Look at me, lass," Mick commanded. I wiped my remaining tears before meeting his gaze. "Jack's going to be angry we brought you tonight. The Russians know about your relationship with Jack now. We have a deal with them while the Babau runs rampant, but they're still our enemies. So, you stay strong and don't take his shit."

I attempted to smile, but my lips twitched with the effort.

"Just remember," Mick continued, his heavy brow lined with concern, "you don't owe him anything. We all care about you, Emma. If this is hurting you too much, we'll understand if you choose to part ways. We'll take care of Jack...and you'll always be protected."

I stood taller, my chin lifting a notch. "I'm not going anywhere, Mick. My place is by his side."

Chapter Twenty-Four

Jack

The room was spinning.

Somehow, I'd gotten home and into my bed. My body ached like I'd been hit by a truck. I wished it had been a truck that hit me. It would've been a quicker punishment, but not as fun.

I rose, groaning as my feet touched the floor. My bedroom was dark. I was shirtless and my jeans were covered in bloodstains. I probed myself, pressing gingerly to discover where I was injured. Or, better yet, where I wasn't.

The taste of blood and whiskey washed from my mouth as I brushed my teeth, wincing at the bathroom's harsh lighting. I didn't know if it was my injuries or the hangover, but my head was killing me. My brain had grown too large, throbbing against the inside of my skull. My reflection was grotesque. Blood, swelling, cuts and bruises. I looked almost as horrific on the outside as I was on the inside.

Arrogant fucking bastard.

I had thought I could handle the consequences of killing Tony Greco. Sure, I'd murdered before. Seventeen people, to be exact. But a kill had never caused this much retaliation. A fucking kid. I was responsible for the death of a kid.

You can't keep this up, Jackie Boy.

Meetings, surveillance, raids. Drinking from sunrise until well after sunset, working out before four a.m. The only time I let myself have a break was in sleep, with Emma beside me.

All of that had to change.

No more Emma. I didn't deserve the solace she offered. No more meetings. No more anyone. This was my vendetta and no more of my men were going to die for it. I was supposed to be protecting them, but I'd failed thus far.

I had to go underground. I had to go rogue — just like the Babau — if there was any hope of finding him. Cathal had discovered a spot where the Mafia played cards in the evenings. We were sitting on it, tracking who was coming and going. I would start there. Sofia told me of another, but it was riskier, so I'd kept it to myself.

First, I had to deal with Emma. I had to get her to go back to her apartment. She would be starting school soon. I couldn't risk her getting caught up in everything. I'd rather she be safe and away than in danger by my side.

After my shower, I dressed in a T-shirt and jeans, careful to avoid exacerbating my injuries. I looked better now than I had before. Head wounds always bled a lot, but with the blood gone I looked close to human. More human than I felt, anyway.

I entered the kitchen, pouring myself a large drink to curb my migraine. As I held the cool glass to my forehead, I realized with malice that the bottle I'd poured from had a red bow tied around its neck. It'd been a Christmas gift from my father. He had given it to me hours before I'd tried to kill him.

Merry fucking Christmas, Dad.

I toasted the bottle, tilting my glass back and emptying it. The alcohol burned its way down my throat and up into my head, easing some of the pain. I poured another.

"It's six a.m., Jack."

Fuck.

Emma was standing right behind me. Her words carried no judgment, just concern. I thought I'd imagined her last night. The way she'd bent over me in the octagon, her chocolate eyes troubled. The lights on the ceiling had blurred, forming a halo around her head. *My angel.*

But if I hadn't imagined her, then that meant she truly had been at MVR last night. She had been in the dungeon. She'd seen the fight. And every single person in that room had watched her enter the octagon. They'd seen her dote on me. The Russians would know we were together. It gave me more resolve to do what was necessary. *For Emma.*

"Shouldn't you be studying your course catalog?" I asked, taking a sip. I refused to face her. I needed a few moments to gather my mask. If I met her gaze now, I would melt. There would be no doing what needed to be done. We would never make it out of the apartment.

Her warm breath glided over my neck. "I'm not going back to school."

I circled the island, putting the counter between us. For once, I didn't want Emma near me. I would shatter into a million pieces at her touch.

"What do you mean?" I asked.

She wasn't going back to Columbia? Emma was a scholar. She always had her head stuck between the pages of a book. It was one of the things I loved about her. Her beautiful brain whirred behind those wide eyes, soaking everything in. She was too smart for her own good.

"I mean I'm not going back," she restated, setting her hands on the counter in resignation. She had on one of my white T-shirts and nothing else. The hem of it came to a stop mid-thigh. Her long hair hung down over her shoulders, a mess of dark curls. I fought the urge to lick my lips. I needed to stay focused.

I kept my gaze fixed on my drink. "It's your last year."

"It'll be there when I'm ready to return." Her voice was stiffening, but not with anger. She was frustrated that I wouldn't look at her.

"What brought this on?"

The whole basis of my plan relied on Emma going home. Going back to the normal life of a college student. The life she had before she met me.

She shrugged, her delicate shoulders inching up. "It's not who I am anymore. There are more important things."

"Like what?" I retorted, losing my internal battle and looking her in the eye.

"Like *you*, Jack," she argued, her voice thick with unshed tears.

Cursing under my breath, I drained my drink. Hell, I knew I would have to make her cry. I just didn't think it would be this soon. She was ripping me apart and I hadn't even broken us yet.

"I'm not important, dove," I growled, slamming the glass tumbler down.

She rounded the counter, nearing me, but I held my hand up. She halted, the wounded expression on her face a punch to my already-bruised gut. If I didn't do this now, I never would.

"I fucked someone in Ireland."

My words hit her as if moving at a glacial speed. She cycled through a myriad of emotions. Shock, disbelief then — rather surprisingly — rage. Her face reddened, tears spilling over her lids. I felt each one like they were dripping onto my own heart, sizzling the organ there, burning me alive from the inside out.

I hadn't fucked anyone else. I was positive I'd never get it up for a woman after Emma, but she didn't know that. I could see doubt creeping in, niggling at the back of her brain. She'd been quick to jump to conclusions about Sofia, so I knew her insecurities well, although I'd tried to banish them. I felt horrible for using them against her now.

Hating me was the best way for her to move on. She couldn't spend the rest of her life wondering what if. Emma was a proud person. Despite her confidence issues, she wouldn't stand for being cheated on. It was the one thing that would make her leave. Hell, even knowing I had murdered someone hadn't scared her off. Infidelity was her hard limit.

I'd been praying for months that Emma wouldn't abandon this relationship. That she wouldn't realize I was a terrible person. That I could hide part of myself from her. Now, I couldn't wait for her to turn heel and run as fast as she could in the opposite direction.

"You're lying," Emma whispered, her voice cracking like a whip.

"I'm not. It was the day after I put Connor's body in the ground. I was drunk and lonely. She was more than willing to solve one of my issues."

God damn. It was like kicking a fucking puppy. A helpless, defenseless puppy. Her face crumpled, but she maintained composure. She closed her eyes and pursed her lips, steadying her breath while I waited for her to respond. When she opened her eyes, I was in no way ready for the fury lying there.

"You're telling me," she snapped, baring her teeth, "that while I was cutting your niece's umbilical cord, while I was laundering your dirty money" — she began to flit around the living room, chaotic and wild — "you were *fucking* someone else?"

As she paced, the sun rose above the skyscrapers of the Upper East Side. It was bright and hot, outlining her willowy silhouette underneath my shirt. She was ethereal, her hands balled into fists at her sides. Her long legs forged a path, searing betrayal into the white rug. I snapped my eyes shut, making sure this was the last memory I had of her. It was tragic, but beautiful in its own way. Tiny, furious Emma and the view of the awakening city behind her.

"Yes," I confirmed, the lie burning a hole in my tongue. "It was a lapse in judgment."

"Oh, for God's sake, Jack!" She whirled, throwing her hands in the air. "Why not tell me when you got back? Why pretend to be in this relationship when you clearly checked out months ago?"

I couldn't hear my own voice over the pounding of my pulse. "I didn't want to hurt you."

"You son of a bitch!" She stalked in my direction, pointing her finger at my chest. "I trusted you. I closed myself off from everything and everyone after Nate's suicide. Three *years* I grieved, then you came along and pried my chest open with a fucking crowbar. And for what? So you could turn around and stomp on it?"

"I'm sorry, baby, I—"

"No!" she shrieked, angrier than I'd ever seen. She no longer looked like the adorable tiger cub with its fur puffed up. I wouldn't be surprised if steam started rising from her skin. "You don't have the right to call me that anymore. I was yours, Jack. I stood by your side through *everything*. All your controlling bullshit and half-answers and secretive past."

I bit the inside of my cheek, drawing blood while she continued her attack.

"God, and you were so upset about Jamie making a move on me when you've been seven inches inside another woman!"

Emma crossed the living room. I hadn't seen the pair of dark jeans hanging from the couch, but she slid into them quickly. She shoved her cell into her back pocket, coming to a halt in front of my steel form.

"If I mean so little to you, why did you even get that tattoo?"

I was blocking her path to the elevator. Despite my resolve and what I'd just told her, I didn't want to let her go. I wanted to take it all back. Tell her I was lying. That I was an asshole for even trying to push her away.

But I didn't.

"Because I love you," I said, but she was having none of it.

"Fuck you, Jack!" Her anger rolled off her in waves, and it smelled like apples and lavender. "You don't cheat on someone you love."

Taking my silence as an answer, she scoffed and pushed me aside, her hand landing on the dove tattoo. My skin blazed with heat where she touched. I reached out involuntarily, catching her as she brushed past.

She stopped, looking down at my hand on her wrist, her teeth peeled back in disgust.

"Don't ever touch me again," she growled, ripping herself from my grip.

I let go, my lips pinned shut. I was going to lose it any second. I could already feel the separation snapping my heart in two. I was a cancer in Emma's life. I'd latched on and sucked everything good from her — her energy, her innocence, her softness. I was changing her and I didn't know if it was a good thing. I had to end this before she had nothing left. I'd cut myself off from her, even if it killed me.

"I love you," I whispered as she got into the lift.

She faced me, pushing the button for the doors to close. Her bottom lip trembled as she took a deep, shaky breath. "I hate you, Jack."

Once I was sure she'd descended a few floors, I fell to my knees, pressing my bruised knuckles into the marble ground. My soul was being torn in two, half of it plummeting to street level with Emma. She'd always carry the best pieces of me, the parts I hadn't known existed until I met her.

Emma had kept me sane over the past couple of months. I wanted to be a better man for her. I'd been holding onto her by my fingernails, but I had to let her go. It was time to shut it off, to give in to the monster I truly was.

I pounded my fist into the floor, releasing an exhausted groan. "Goddamn it!"

I would give myself an hour to grieve.

Then I would find the bogeyman and finish what I had started.

Chapter Twenty-Five

Emma

My legs buckled. I landed in a heap on the elevator's cool floor, huddled in the corner. I bit down on my kneecap, letting out a violent scream.

I should've trusted my instincts. I had known Jack was out of my league. And the moment he didn't have me to comfort him, he'd sought someone else. A beautiful, curvy Irish woman with auburn hair and bright eyes, no doubt. I could picture them perfectly—matched better than Jack and I ever could be—fucking in the bathroom of a seedy pub.

"Stop," I begged my own mind, willing the images to vanish.

The doors would be opening soon. I wanted to stay in that little box forever, refusing to accept my reality. Nonetheless, I forced myself to stand. There was no point in hiding from the world—it'd already fucked me.

It was just a few blocks to my apartment, but my legs protested. With every step I took away from Jack, I trod on my own heart. Faye Walsh had been right. Men like Jack didn't know how to love. I had fooled myself into thinking he did. I was blinded by his looks and words, by how he made me feel — confident, sexy, worshiped.

It had all been a lie.

I'd been so lost in my own thoughts that I didn't remember walking home. Trancelike, I stood in front of my bed. The yellow quilt my grandma made two years before she passed, the framed photo of Jack and I leaning against his bike, my schoolbooks — it was too familiar. Like nothing had changed.

Everything has changed.

My sobs came out broken and hollow like I was being strangled. I reached for my neck with trembling hands. When my fingers met the golden handcuffs resting between my collarbones, I ripped off the choker and threw it into the corner by my closet. The rational part of my brain attempted to calm itself, but the panic was crippling.

You stupid girl.

You were never going to be enough for him.

He's a player. He played you.

"Stop!"

I was kneeling on all fours on the bed, head bowed and dripping sweat. My heart raced, but it was slowing now. I focused on my breathing, channeling the yoga I hadn't practiced in months. Inhale for eight seconds, hold, exhale for eight seconds, hold.

After a few minutes, I kicked off my shoes and jeans, crawling toward the pillows. I was exhausted. I hadn't slept all night, opting to sit cross-legged beside Jack, worried he wouldn't wake up due to his injuries.

Flashbacks of Nate's body had plagued my mind as I monitored Jack's pulse.

I just had to take this one step, one breath, at a time. The deepest connection I'd ever had with a human being had just been severed, but the world wasn't ending. I'd feel better once I got some rest. *Sleep now, life later.*

* * * *

So. Many. People.

After staying cooped up in bed for two days, I was sluggish. There was too much noise, everyone speaking at once. The atmosphere was energetic, and I was a fish out of water.

For Ella, I reminded myself.

My little sister had arrived at my apartment bright and early this morning. I set an alarm so that I had time to shower, hide the dark circles and chug a gallon of coffee. I ignored the notifications on my phone—eight missed calls from Eoghan, three from Mick and one from Shannon—and managed to get through breakfast without succumbing to hysteria.

On the taxi ride to NYU's campus, a wave of guilt hit me. I sent Shannon a text to make sure she and the baby were okay. She replied immediately, asking if I'd heard from Jack. My grip on the phone tightened and I blackened the screen, swallowing my discomfort.

Ella and I crossed the campus toward orientation. She spoke a mile a minute, her blonde hair tied up in space buns. Coupled with her denim dress, mustard-yellow Chloé backpack and a fresh pair of sneakers, she was every bit the quirky college freshman. My smile was genuine, if only for my sister's benefit.

I refused to make my sorrow obvious. Ella had seen me at my worst after Nate died. My family had breathed a sigh of relief last November when they discovered I'd recovered from depression. I'd given them three years of hell. I didn't want to worry them again.

Not that I was sinking back into a depressive state. This was heartbreak. A heartbreak I'd never experienced before, but at least Jack was alive. He'd chosen another woman over me, while Nate had chosen death. Still, the pain was similar — anger, betrayal, devastation, loss. I'd never given much thought to 'the one' until I had met Jack but if it did exist, he was it. I couldn't see myself moving on in any way.

One step at a time, Em.

"Em!" Ella shrieked, running through a crowd of teenagers. She was decked out in NYU swag — hat, flag, tote bag — and carried a powdered donut like a ring. "For the sugar fiend."

"Thanks." I chuckled, taking the donut from her finger. The powder fell onto my jeans, leaving a trace that I stared at a little too long.

"You okay?" Ella gave me a curious look, her brown eyes shimmering in the sunlight. The courtyard was beautiful, even with all the commotion. It was a tiny oasis in the concrete jungle.

I smiled, but it didn't lift my cheeks. "Totally."

"Fine, don't tell me. Can we get dinner? I'm craving pizza."

"That works," I replied, relieved that she wasn't going to push the subject. "I don't have anything at home, anyway. Are you sure you don't want to hang out and make friends?"

Ella waved her hand, dismissing the youthful crowd. "I'll wait until the semester starts. I'd rather hang with my big sis."

My shattered heart warmed at the sound of that. I slipped her tote bag from her shoulder and slid it over my own, interlinking our arms. She giggled as we exited the courtyard.

"The Marshall sisters take New York!" Ella chimed, drawing attention from a group of guys nearby. They grinned, eyeing my little sister lecherously. I glared at them, pulling her tighter against my side. "Hey, isn't that Jack's friend? What's his name?"

"Eoghan," I whispered, freezing on the spot.

Ella looked at me with a furrowed brow, but my gaze was locked on Jack's second lieutenant. Eoghan was leaning against a tree on the sidewalk a few yards away, blending in well with the college students. He was staring straight at me, his normally kind eyes icy.

"Is he okay?" Ella asked, sensing tension.

"Give me a second," I answered, passing my sister the powdered donut. I patted her hand to let her know I had this handled, then stomped toward Eoghan, anger boiling beneath my skin. Tailing me was one thing, but he didn't have to make it obvious in front of my little sister.

When I reached him, I cocked a hip and crossed my arms over my chest. "I'm assuming Mick sent you."

It was the only reasonable explanation. They'd been trying to reach me for two days, but I didn't have it in me to face Jack's men. It was too fresh, and I was furious with them. Mick *knew* his boss had been unfaithful. He had been with Jack in Ireland, after all. He'd also said he would understand if I wanted to call it quits with Jack. It made sense now.

"Yeah, he did," Eoghan said, narrowing his eyes. "So, you know about Jack, then?"

The betrayals just kept coming. Eoghan knew *too*?

"Yes," was all I could muster.

Eoghan shuffled his feet, peering at me from under the lid of his cap. "You haven't heard from him?"

"No." I had a feeling Jack wouldn't be calling. I'd made it pretty clear that things were over between us. Still, his lack of persistence was another blow.

"You seem upset."

That almost had me laughing. "Do I?"

"I thought you'd be worried," Eoghan said, crossing his arms so that our stances were mirrored. "Not angry."

I furrowed my brow. "Why would I be worried?"

His confusion matched my own. "Why do I feel like we're talking about two different things?"

I'd already given this conversation too much energy. Ella was waiting for me. We were going to have a normal night with some not-so-healthy food. She wanted to spend time with me, and my assigned 'guardian' was preventing that.

I took a step backward, emphasizing my point. "I'm with my sister."

"Okay." He drew out the word, hurt flashing across his boyish features, triggering my own guilt. Eoghan was just being loyal to his boss, which I couldn't fault him for. "We'll stop bothering you, if that's what you want."

"Y-Yeah," I stammered, clearing my throat. "That's what I want. Jack made his decision, now I'm making mine."

Eoghan nodded, eyeing me with concern. "That's fair. Take care, Wings."

"You too," I muttered, heading toward my sister.

Ella gave me a wide-eyed look, glancing over my shoulder. The street was far too noisy for her to have overheard, but by her anxious expression, Eoghan and I were giving off some serious vibes.

"What was that about?" she whispered, powdered sugar lining her lips.

Relinking my arm with hers, I gave a noncommittal shrug. "Just stuff with Jack."

"Is that why you look like you've been crying for a week straight?"

Dammit.

"Yeah. We broke up."

"What?" Ella gasped, almost walking headfirst into a street pole. I tugged her aside just in time. "You two were, like, goals. End-game status. Oh, shit! I'm so sorry, Em. What did he do? Do I need to kick his ass?"

Tears were running down my cheeks, so the laughter that bubbled up took me by surprise. Ella attacking Jack was a comical image. The blonde firecracker might even give him a run for his money.

"No, El." I sighed, the echo of a laugh hurting my lungs. "I'd rather not discuss it. It's sister weekend and I'm in need of a distraction."

Ella clapped her hands, accepting the challenge. "Pizza and candy and wine and movies and pedicures and—"

"You had me at wine," I said, attempting to hail a cab. "As long as you don't tell Mom and Dad."

"Please." Ella scoffed. "By the way, why are we taking taxis? The subway is faster."

She was right, of course. It was so ingrained in me— the promise I had made to Jack about not using underground transportation. But he'd obliterated the biggest promise of all by sleeping with another woman. Besides, my safety was no longer a priority to him.

"You're onto something, little sis." I stepped back onto the sidewalk. "Let's take the fucking subway."

Ella giggled at my change in attitude. We walked, hand-in-hand, to University Station.

* * * *

Something woke me, but I couldn't pinpoint what. I kept my eyes closed, hoping my body would settle back into sleep. My head was throbbing. Getting drunk with my eighteen-year-old sister had been a bad idea. Getting *drunk* had been a bad idea. I seemed to be full of them as of late.

We'd started the night off with *Spaceballs*, eating pizza, sipping wine. By the time we'd finished *Dumb and Dumber* and started *Bridesmaids*, we were hammered. I couldn't figure out which button to push to "make the movie *go*!" So, we ate gummy bears and danced, screaming our heads off like maniacs. I owed my neighbors an apology.

Something cool tickled my neck. I swallowed, but the necklace didn't shift.

Wait.

I threw the necklace off two days ago.

"Aw, *topolina* is finally awake."

I attempted to sit up, but a sharp pain bit at my throat. I opened my eyes, taking in my surroundings.

Luca Nicoletti's niece hovered over me, holding a blade to my skin. She looked pale and skeletal, her red lips thin. It was the beginning of August, but she wore all black, including a lightweight trench coat.

Was I having a nightmare? How had Amara gotten into my apartment? I always locked the door. I was drunk, but not that drunk.

"There's a blonde girl asleep on your couch." Amara inclined her head toward my closed bedroom door. "Is she your sister?"

"Don't hurt her," I whispered, but it wasn't a plea — it was a demand. I could guess why Amara was here, but this had nothing to do with Ella. If Amara tried to harm my little sister, I'd launch myself onto the bitch, knife be damned.

"You know," Amara conversed, "for the Upper West Side, your building's security is pretty lax. It wasn't difficult to pick the lock."

"Congratulations," I bit back. My heart raced, but I kept my tone low. "Now, what the hell do you want?"

"My uncle has decided he wants to see his grandson's letter for himself. You have three days to get him the evidence." Amara twirled her braid with her free hand, that stupid butterfly barrette resting on her bony shoulder. "A little generous, in my opinion. I would've given you all of three seconds. But like I said, soft spot and all..."

Tears sprang to my eyes, but I blinked them back. I knew this day would come and I'd done nothing to prepare myself.

"You are to meet us after sundown on Tuesday at this address." She slipped a piece of paper into my hand, her blade nicking my throat. "And come alone."

I said nothing, letting the anger in my heart fester.

"Personally, I can't wait for you to show up empty-handed." Her laugh was laced with scorn at the mere idea. "I hope Don Luca makes your death a slow one. It'll be a pleasure to watch."

The walls were closing in on me, the generic beige paint clouding my vision. "Is that all?" I asked.

"I noticed you have a picture with your Irishman on the table here." She nodded toward my bedside table, but I couldn't look without deepening the cut at my neck. "But it's facedown. Love life not going well?"

"You can't kill me, Amara," I reminded her. She narrowed her black eyes on me. "I'm untouchable. Don Luca will be furious if you break the promise he made. So, get your knife off my throat and get the hell out of my apartment."

Amara's glare was pure hatred. If I hadn't made a deal with her uncle, she would—without a doubt—have stabbed me. Then again, if I hadn't made a deal with her uncle, I wouldn't be in this colossal mess.

She pulled the switchblade from my skin, flicking it around her fingers before tucking it into the pocket of her trench coat. "Three days."

I followed her out of my bedroom, my gaze bouncing between Amara's shoulders and Ella's sleeping form. Movie credits were rolling on the television, otherwise Ella might've woken up.

Amara didn't spare me another glance as she sauntered into the hall, closing the front door to my apartment behind her. I put one foot in front of the other, holding my breath while I paced back to my room. When I shut the door, I slid down the back of it, trembling from head to toe.

After the week I'd had, I didn't think I'd have any tears left to cry. Alas, something hot and wet dribbled down my cheek. I smothered the sobs, covering my mouth with my hand. Oxygen was being sucked from the room, leaving me a withering corpse. I was heading straight for a panic attack.

Not wanting to wake my sister, I crawled toward my closet, my heart a blur inside my chest. I sat in the corner, shutting the door behind me. I grabbed a sweater from the floor, stuffing the cashmere between my teeth before letting out a long, hopeless scream.

Chapter Twenty-Six

Emma

Ella babbled around a mouthful of French toast, but I'd checked out of our conversation thirty minutes ago. The ominous sound of a clock ticking down rattled my already-sore brain, reminding me I had three days.

Once Don Luca realized I'd lied to him about Nate's suicide note, he'd kill me without hesitation. I needed to get a hold of Jack. Broken up or not, it was the right thing to do. The don would be coming for him as well, if only just to hurt me. I wanted Jack to live a safe, happy life. I no longer felt bitter about the cheating, not when I'd done so much worse.

Lives would be ruined. My sister—who was now prattling about her course catalog—couldn't move in with me. She wouldn't be able to attend her dream school. My family would have to stay away from Manhattan—maybe even the country—for a while. I wasn't sure how far Don Luca's wrath would extend, but I wouldn't put their lives at risk with my idiocy.

Where would they find my body? Would Don Luca kill me or would he have his Babau do it? I would discover the bogeyman's true identity, but it'd be too late to do anything about it. Either way, I was destroying lives. My death would hurt my family to no end. Would they have to identify me? Would I be identifiable?

Three days, then nothing.

"I need you to defer Tisch for a year," I blurted, interrupting Ella's stream. The noise of the boisterous diner threatened to burst my eardrums — the clanking of dishes, the scraping of cutlery, the chatting at nearby tables. No one had a clue they were sitting among a girl marked for death.

"I'm sorry?" Ella asked, eyes widening. I stared at her fork, watching a piece of egg dangle from a tine before falling with a *plop* onto her syrupy plate.

"I need you to defer Tisch for a year. This is important, Ella."

She searched my face, parting her lips in disbelief. "You're scaring me, Em."

"I've made a huge mistake." I took a deep breath, rubbing my temples. "Like, really huge."

Ella set her fork down with purpose. "I'm waiting."

"Defer Tisch, go abroad, try to convince Mom to go with you." If my mom traveled with Ella, then I'd just have to worry about my dad's safety. He'd be harder to lie to. "I'll pay for everything. Hotels, planes, trains, food — you name it."

Ella drew her brows together as I spoke. "Are you... What's going on?"

"I can't go into detail," I answered, praying she would give me some grace—not that I deserved it. "But I've pissed off some dangerous people. I don't know what lengths they'll go to for revenge. If they can't find me, I'm scared they'll hurt you. Or Mom and Dad."

Ella bit her lip, rolling the paper from her straw between her fingers. I knew she was analyzing my words and inflections, trying to piece the puzzle together. She wouldn't be able to. It was too convoluted.

She cleared her throat. "Has Jack threatened you?"

I should've assumed her mind would jump to Jack. "God, no. This is on me. I made this particular bed without anyone's help."

And now I have to lie in it, forever.

Ella glared at me from under her lashes, but it wasn't with anger. "Then what are you going to do about it? Because from what I'm hearing, it sounds like you've given up."

"I haven't given up, El. I'm just playing a game with someone who is always five moves ahead of me."

To my surprise, Ella scoffed. Her shoulders tensed and she narrowed her eyes at me. This was not the response I had been expecting. I thought she'd be prying for more information or—at the very least—fuming at me for ruining her life.

"Emma, you're the strongest person I know." Ella leaned forward, pinning me with her ferocity. "You recovered from Nate's suicide. You survived after Mr. Ranucci blew his *head* off in front of you. I don't care who this person is or how dangerous they are. They obviously don't know what you're capable of if they're threatening our family. When someone comes after us, we don't give up and hide. Five moves ahead, my ass.

Get your shit together and play ten moves ahead of *them*."

She slapped her hand on the table, and a fork fell to the checkered tile. I stared at it, Ella's pep talk echoing around my empty skull.

"I'll take a year off," she continued, her voice softer and reassuring. "I've always wanted to see the West End, anyway. Mom and Dad will throw a fit, but I'm eighteen. They can't stop me. If it'll make you feel better, I'll stay out of the city."

"It will," I croaked in relief, reaching across the table and grabbing her warm hand.

"My bus will be at the terminal in an hour," Ella said, eyeing me wearily. "I'll go home and break the news to Mom and Dad. I'll say I've had a change of heart and want to take a gap year. Plenty of people do it before college. But I'm calling you in a few days. If you don't have a solid plan and a better attitude, I'll come back and light a fire under your ass. Got it?"

"I got it."

After the bill was paid, I watched my sister disappear into Port Authority. Ella wasn't the same little girl I'd grown up with. Somewhere along the way, she'd matured, blooming into a tenacious young adult. As outgoing as she was, she'd been paying attention to the world around her—studying people, their habits, their dilemmas. She was a true artist, a student of the human condition. She was also right. It wasn't like me to concede. Not after everything I'd been through. My situation might seem futile, but I'd been hopeless before.

Don Luca wasn't just threatening me—he was threatening everyone I loved. What kind of person would I be if I didn't retaliate? I wasn't a fighter, but people could change. If I approached this like a huge test to study for, maybe I'd get a better result. I had to think of every possible outcome — every question — and have a countermove — an answer — for each. First, I needed an ally, a study buddy. Preferably one that had no clue what I was up to.

"Hey, Em," Eoghan answered after the first ring, expectant.

I tossed my empty to-go cup into the recycling bin, not bothering for the light to change before I crossed the street. I didn't have much time. I'd wasted the morning in panic and self-pity. If I was going to do this right, I needed to prepare for every eventuality.

"Eoghan," I replied, clear and concise. I had a goal — beat Don Luca, ace this test. "My sister has a summer assignment for Tisch. She's studying film and they want some sort of provocative, artsy bullshit to start the year off with a bang." The lie rolled off my tongue like syrup. "She has an idea, but it's not technically *legal*. I told her I'd help, but I thought of you first."

Eoghan hesitated, but I'd piqued his interest. "What does she have in mind?"

"It's a documentary on the food industry. She can't use her own camera because it's traceable. I'm assuming you've got a nice one in that nerd lab of yours?"

"I do," he said, drawing out the 'o'.

"Relax, Eoghan. It's just an activism thing. If I give you an address, could you install a hidden camera within the next day or so? It's in Jersey, but I'll pay you for your ti—"

"Shut up, Emma. I'll do it. Text me the address."

I bit my lip at my luck. "Thanks."

"Yup," he answered with a *click*.

Holy shit.

This could work. I might be able to take down the New York Mafia.

I, Emma Marshall, was going to end Luca Nicoletti's reign of terror.

* * * *

Two hours later, I stood in the elevator of Jack's building.

It was time for me to tell him about my deal with Don Luca. I'd hidden it from him for months because I feared it would push him over the edge, but it was too late for that. He needed to know what was coming — maybe hire extra security for himself, although his pride would make that difficult. Some women would write a guy like Jack off after he had cheated on them, but I wouldn't be able to sleep knowing I'd put him in danger and didn't at least make him aware of it.

When the doors slid open, I knew Jack wasn't there. His presence always made me hyperaware, a type of magnetic pull that prickled my skin. Alas, the apartment was empty. I would have to leave a note. It'd be easier that way.

"You've been avoiding us, lass."

I jumped, hand to my heart. The lights of the city cast an eerie glow over the living room. Mick sat on the leather armchair, ankle resting on his knee as if he'd been there awhile.

"How'd you get in here?" I asked.

"Steven let me in," Mick answered, standing as I entered the room. Steven was Jack's housekeeper. "I didn't give him much of a choice, given the circumstances."

Jennifer Luna

I headed toward the hallway, planning to comb Jack's desk drawers for a pen and paper. "When will he be back?"

Mick followed. "I have a feeling Jack won't be returning for a while."

I stopped mid-stride, turning to face him. The hallway was darker than the rest of the apartment, casting a menacing shadow across Mick's grim expression.

"What do you mean?"

Mick shuffled his feet, staring down at them. "Jack's gone rogue."

"What the fuck does that mean?"

"He's been dark since Thursday. That's why we've been trying to contact you. To ask what the hell happened that morning."

"Dark?" I repeated.

Blood thrummed in my ears. My legs shook. Connor had gone dark and, two days later, we'd found him nearly decapitated. The warmth fled my body at an alarming rate. I placed a hand against the wall, steadying myself.

"Calm down, Emma." Mick approached with his hands raised like he was cornering a rabid animal. "Jack's alive."

"How do you know?" I choked, almost bent in half. If he wasn't in communication, how could anyone know he wasn't being held captive or hurt? Or dying alone in the streets. Shit, I was going to faint.

"Because he cleaned one of the Mafia's safehouses," Mick explained. "I know his style. He doesn't leave any evidence behind, but it was him."

Cleaned a safe house? Did that mean what I thought it did? Was this what Eoghan had been referencing when he caught up with me outside of NYU?

"I thought you'd be worried, not angry."

We *had* been talking about two different things.

I sprinted down the hallway into Jack's bedroom. I slammed into the armoire, punching the code to the safe as fast as my numb fingers could move. I opened the door, relief washing over me.

One of the cases—one million in cash—was gone along with a few different weapons. A sniper rifle and a pistol with accessories. There were other things missing from crates, but I couldn't remember what had been there before.

He was alive. For now.

Exiting the closet, I found Mick waiting for me in the bedroom. "Why aren't you looking for him?"

"We are," he insisted. "We've been searching for days, ever since Cathal got word about the seven Nicolettis found dead. We've hit all our own safehouses and every apartment, but there's no point. He won't be at any of them. He doesn't want to be found."

"S-seven?" I stammered, trying not to display my horror. Jack had murdered seven people. On his own. He could've been killed.

"Jack can handle himself," Mick clarified, but I recognized the doubt in his voice. "But we need to find him soon before the don puts two and two together."

"How does Don Luca not know who killed his men?" I asked, incredulous.

"Jack thrives in the shadows."

I returned to the closet, digging through drawers in search of sturdier clothes. Dark jeans, combat boots, lightweight leather jacket. I changed quickly, not bothered that Mick could walk in and find me indecent. Regardless, he gave me privacy.

"Are you going to tell me what happened between you two?" Mick asked as I walked into the bedroom, tying my hair into a high ponytail. "You were the last one to speak with him."

"Don't play coy, Mickey," I reprimanded, still feeling sour toward Jack's first lieutenant. "You know why I ended things."

"Ended things," he repeated. Despite saying he'd understand if I called it quits, Mick's tone was one of disbelief and anger. "Just like that?"

"No, not 'just like that'! I ended it because he confessed to cheating on me while you two were in Ireland."

Mick furrowed his brow. "Are you *insane*? Jack hasn't so much as glanced at another woman since you walked into his gym."

I rolled my eyes, leaving the room. He followed me, his footsteps much heavier than my own. I jogged ahead, reaching the kitchen well before him.

"He did a lot more than glance, Mick!" I yelled into the hallway, yanking open the drawer next to the stove. "And you're a bastard for not telling me."

"There's nothing to tell, lass!" Mick argued, coming into view seconds after I'd stuffed Jack's revolver into my jeans. I stomped toward the elevator, but the persistent bastard still followed. "Where are you going now?"

"I may hate his guts for what he did to me, but I'm not going to let Jack get himself killed searching for the Babau. Either we find Jack, or we find that fucking assassin and deal with him ourselves."

"Do you even know how to use that thing?" he huffed, pointing to my torso.

My anger dissipated when I realized Mick knew exactly what was tucked into the waistband of my jeans. I pulled the gun from behind my back, studying it like one would study an ancient artifact—with the utmost care and sensitivity. It was heavier than it looked. I'd never held a gun before. My dad kept a shotgun in a lockbox underneath my parents' bed, but I'd never seen it.

"I'll YouTube a tutorial," I muttered, trying not to let my nerves show.

He sighed in resignation, holding his hand out for the gun. "I'll break it down for you."

Setting the metal contraption in Mick's calloused palm, I watched with narrowed eyes. If he took it from me, there was an entire panic room full of weapons I could peruse.

"It's loaded," he began, his tone instructional. "You can tell by the weight. Now, never put your finger on the trigger unless you know you're going to shoot."

I nodded so he knew I was listening.

"Watch. You click the hammer back once"—he clicked it as he spoke—"and you can open the cylinder."

He opened the little rotating thing, sliding a bullet about half the size of my pinky from the chamber and into my hand. I rolled it in my palm, then slid it back in, waiting for him to continue.

"Then snap it like this." He snapped the cylinder closed and I watched, intent on committing his movements to memory. "You click *twice* and it's ready to fire. Always put the hammer back in place or you'll kill yourself, Emma, you got that?"

"I got it," I confirmed, meeting his sparkling blue eyes.

As he secured the weapon, Mick's expression turned curious. "Jack really never taught you how to shoot a gun?"

I shook my head, taking the revolver from his outstretched hand. I slid it underneath the back of my jacket. "I don't think he ever wanted me to be in a situation where I needed to use one."

"That's wishful thinking."

"My thoughts exactly," I agreed.

Mick's smile was sorrowful. Despite the dire situation, the corners of my lips twitched in response. I was formulating my plan. There was a fifty-fifty chance I would die, but that was better than my odds from this morning.

Chapter Twenty-Seven

Jack

Heat rose from the asphalt in blurry waves. Sweat had plastered my black thermal to my chest. Discomfort aside, I kept still, eyes trained on the back door of the card club. It was midnight, and I'd been watching it for hours. My presence in Little Italy was risky, but I was discreet. Few knew what the devil looked like, so I could walk the streets of New York without anyone noticing.

Five men had entered the unkempt building two hours ago. One of them would be stepping into the alley to take a piss any second. I stretched my gloved fist, then cracked my neck. My vision had long since adjusted to the darkness and the glare of city lights off passing cabs.

The door swung open. I narrowed my eyes as one of the Italians stumbled into the alleyway. *Good, he's drunk.* The man faced the building on the opposite side, hidden from the street by a dumpster. He pulled his dick out and started to piss.

I gripped my set of brass knuckles, waiting for the oily bastard to tuck it into his jeans. Enemy or not, I wasn't going to attack a man with his pants down.

He turned, stopping when he spotted me standing behind him. He opened his mouth to call for his crew, but I was fast. I shoved the brass knuckles into his face, hearing teeth pull away at their roots. My fist came back in a flash and I hit him once more in the nose with an uppercut. There was an audible crack as the cartilage shot into his brain, dropping him to the ground. *Four left.*

I located a key inside his pocket, then fitted it into the lock. I entered the building, shutting the door behind me without a sound. Smoke and light filtered through a hallway to my left. I could hear voices, but I had to clear the rest of the floor before I went after them.

No one noticed as I slinked past the card room. I kept to the shadows, gliding down the hall. The storefront was a deli, but it was well after closing time. None of the clerks or butchers were there, for which I was grateful. I didn't kill innocents. If any were here, I would have to return later and try again.

"The fuck is Joe?" someone asked.

Pivoting, I freed the silenced pistol from the waistband of my jeans. A man exited the card room, not bothering to glance in my direction. He made a beeline for the back door, most likely to check on the man in the alley. He would find him bloody and beaten as soon as he opened it.

I waited until he did so, watching as his shoulder tensed in shock. Then I pulled the trigger, the bullet hitting dead center in the back of his head. *Three.* The door shut with a slam, hiding his body from the rest, but it didn't matter. It was time to make my presence known.

I entered the card room, immediately firing another round at the man nearest me. He'd been laughing at something one of the others had said. The bullet entered at his temple and he went limp, cards fluttering to the ground. *Two.*

"Royal flush." I tsked, nudging the playing cards with the toe of my boot. "Pity."

I turned to the last two men, the barrel of the silencer pointing at each in turn. They didn't say anything, their faces ashen. Even though they were armed, their empty hands rose to the sides of their heads. They didn't have time to pull out their weapons, and they knew it.

"The Babau," I commanded, voice low. They withered under my glare. Or was it the name I spoke that they were afraid of?

The man on the right twitched, one of his hands dropping a couple inches.

I tilted my head, eyes narrowed on him. "Careful."

"I'd rather the don kill me than the untouchable." He snarled, reaching under the table for his gun.

The moniker was interesting, but not enough to make me hesitate. I pulled the trigger, silencing him, then aimed the gun at the man on the left. A rancid smell permeated the air. He'd wet himself. *One.*

"The Babau," I repeated, detached.

"P-please," the man begged, tears mixing with the perspiration on his cheeks. "I have a wife and daughter!"

I didn't so much as flinch. "So did my brother."
Zero.

* * * *

Emma

"I'm just sayin', the next time ye decide to go an' murder a dozen men, I want some kind o' heads-up!"

Peter McKenzie paced around the warehouse in Soho, fuming. The rest of the men that had gathered at Scarlett's Closet were there, as well as a few additions. Eoghan, Mick and Cathal stood by my side, their arms crossed. It wasn't customary for non-heads of house to be at these meetings, I assumed, but rules were being broken by everyone.

"So would we," Kieran snarked, casting a glare at the older Irishman. "Unfortunately, my brother doesn't answer to anyone but himself."

"And Emma…" Eoghan joked, trying to lighten the mood. Mick gave Eoghan a fierce look, shaking his head to quiet him.

"Nicoletti is grasping at straws," Bryan Murray, the youngest of the group, added. "He can't figure out if it was the Russians or us."

"Good," Kieran replied. "Let's hope he takes his wrath out on the Russians."

Jack's little brother looked more stressed than I'd seen since Connor's death. With Jack having gone dark, the mob was now his responsibility. He was just as ill-prepared as Jack had been, but Kieran was a different breed from his brother. He was irresponsible, yes, but he had a positive attitude. He was social and people liked him. Maybe he was better suited to the role. It wouldn't be the first time the thought had crossed my mind.

I gripped the flash drive in the pocket of my jacket, twirling it around, studying its exact dimensions. I'd programmed a file from my laptop onto it after asking Eoghan to set up the camera. It wasn't much, but it comforted me—reminded me to maintain focus.

"Hope isn't going to keep us out o' the ground," McKenzie growled. "We need more men."

"We've recruited eight from the homeland," Cathal informed, "and two more will be arriving next week."

"What homeland?" McKenzie scoffed, turning on Cathal. "Ye're a fucking Scot. And from London to boot!"

"We are *not* arguing over bloodlines right now!" Kieran yelled, infuriated. Eoghan shuffled his feet beside me. I glanced at him, curious. "We need to find Jack before anyone else does."

"Has the FBI said anything?" Michael Sweeney—the quieter one—asked.

Mick shook his head. "They're tasked with catching their serial killer. Jack's MO won't match. NYPD will be handling this. Organized crime unit, no doubt."

"And?" McKenzie asked, impatient. "Will they find anything?"

"Jack is very thorough," Mick replied, clearly perturbed that his boss's work was being called into question.

Mick and I had been scouring the streets all night. Everywhere but Italian neighborhoods, which we were careful to avoid. I wanted to go in, but Mick wouldn't let me. Now I wished he would've. We'd found out we had been just a few blocks from Jack's latest attack. If I could've been there...

I didn't care if it was before or after he had killed the five mafiosos. He wouldn't want to see me, but I just needed to be sure he was uninjured. I'd let him go after that.

Everyone was scrambling, trying to formulate a defensive strategy. It was a matter of time before Nicoletti responded to twelve of his men being taken out. Mick was positive he wouldn't know it was Jack, but I didn't have as much faith. I didn't see how it was possible to kill twelve people on your own and not leave a trace. Jack had been missing four days now. He wasn't thinking straight. He was bound to mess up, especially if he kept going at it.

"Then why the fuck are we lookin' fer the rogue bastard?" McKenzie asked, speaking to the rest of the group. "Let him do his worst. If he catches the Babau, great. If he gets himself killed, good riddance."

There was an uproar from the O'Connells, but my voice rang loudest.

"Shut your fucking mouth."

Peter McKenzie had been grilling everyone in turn for the past hour. It was seven in the morning and I hadn't slept again. I was growing impatient, pouring myself into the search for Jack. Whenever I wasn't thinking of Jack's well-being or location, my mind was devoted to surviving Luca Nicoletti. I was forever stuck inside my head, meticulously planning for my meeting with him.

One and a half days, Emma. Tick-tock.

McKenzie moved nearer, his glare vitriolic. Beside me, Eoghan and Mick tensed. I lifted my hand, signaling for them to back off. They were my words, and I alone would pay the price for them. I was slowly but surely learning to own up to my actions, to face the consequences with my head held high. Ella had helped me realize I was more than capable of surviving whatever these men threw my way. Irish or Italian, it didn't matter. They all wore the same cloak of arrogance. False bravado would always be their downfall.

"You think..." McKenzie started, stopping with his nose a foot from mine. Everyone's eyes were on us, but I didn't falter. "Just because Jack's been dipping his dick in your little *cunt*...you can speak to me like that?"

Punching a man was nothing like hitting the bag at the gym. Lightning exploded across my knuckles and into my arm, but I didn't let the pain show. I hit McKenzie right in the mouth and his head snapped back. A few others had been about to do the same, but I beat them to it. This was my fight. Not to mention, good practice for what was to come. If I couldn't take on the likes of Peter fucking McKenzie, I had no hope of surviving Don Luca.

McKenzie probed his bottom lip. When he pulled his fingers away, I was proud to see blood staining them.

"*Go n-ithe an cat thú*," I hissed in Irish. "*Is go n-ithe an diabhal an cat.*"

It was a phrase Jack had taught me during our vacation in Santorini. *May the cat eat you, and may the devil eat the cat.* Reserved for enemies, it meant the utmost disrespect.

For a moment, I thought McKenzie would strike me. Instead, his mouth broke into a wide grin. He tilted his head back, laughing riotously, both hands on his gut. A few others began to chuckle, but Jack's three lieutenants stayed silent and still, at the ready.

"Ye really are the Emerald Angel, aren't ye?" Peter McKenzie wheezed, his eyes shining with amusement. "Ye remind me o' me wife!"

I forced a polite smile. McKenzie returned to his spot in the circle. Kieran winked in my direction. Mick cleared his throat from behind me, patting my shoulder once.

"Well." Kieran clapped, drawing the attention back to himself. "Anyone else have any misgivings about finding Jack?"

Everyone shook their heads, eyes on Kieran.

"All right." Kieran rubbed his palms together. "Let's get to work, fuckwads."

Chapter Twenty-Eight

Emma

Eoghan and Cathal led the Murrays on the first combined shift to find and subdue Jack. When he was found, I would be the first call. Although I was adamant that we were broken up, Mick believed I was the only one who stood a chance at talking Jack down from his homicidal ledge.

Kieran, Mick and I spent most of the day at the pier. A shipment of arms due for Shanghai needed to be prepared. The Triads were an account the O'Connells couldn't lose. Mick let me tag along, saying he wanted to keep an eye on me anyway.

I walked around with a tablet, making sure the numbers on the military-grade crates matched the ones on the screen. It was Willie work, but I was grateful at having something to do. No one would let me join the other crew until it was absolutely necessary.

When the sun began to set, Mick forced me into the back of an SUV, ordering me to go straight to Jack's, eat something and rest. He warned that the front desk would call him if I chose to leave. I couldn't help but visualize the clock ticking down. I knew I would be more beneficial if I got some sleep, but even blinking seemed wasteful at a time like this.

The elevator doors slid open, and I stumbled into Jack's apartment. I rummaged through the pantry for a Pop-Tart—Jack kept junk food on hand for me—and shoved it in my mouth. Fia roamed around my legs, seeking affection, but I was scared if I bent down to give him a scratch, I would pass out on the floor.

The shadowy cat followed me around his home. I checked the panic room to see if Jack had returned for supplies, but everything was as it'd been the night before. I took the revolver from my waistband and placed it on the bedside table next to a bronze-framed picture of Jack and I from St. Patrick's Day. He'd refused to wear anything but black, assenting to green eyeliner when I wouldn't stop pinching him.

When I climbed into bed, Fia joined me, hunting for a comfortable spot. I grabbed one of Jack's pillows and buried my face in it, smelling sweet smoke and earthy rain. It brought back memories that made my heart ache. He'd cheated on me, but I still missed him with every fiber of my being.

Please, God, I prayed, wondering if there really was a man floating in the clouds, listening to my laments. *People call him the devil, but he's not all bad. Please keep him safe.*

I succumbed to the bone-deep pain, tears wetting the pillow. Fia lay in the hollow behind my knees, his warm body vibrating with a purr. As a means of comfort, I reached into my pocket and gripped the flash drive. I fell asleep with my hand wrapped around it. When I awoke hours later, it felt as though I'd hardly blinked.

"I found him."

My speakerphone startled a sleepy Fia, who scampered into the closet. I glanced at the ornate clock on the wall. It was two in the morning.

I jumped out of bed. "Where?"

"An old police contact called me a couple minutes ago," Mick explained. I listened to the sounds of traffic on his end of the line as I ran to the bathroom, splashing water on my face. "He was just arrested in Boston."

I paused, turning off the water. "For what?"

"He got into a fight at a pub in Roxbury. We need to leave now."

"I'm heading to the elevator." I grabbed the revolver from the nightstand, sprinting down the hall. I jammed my finger on the call button over and over, willing the elevator to arrive. "Where should I meet you?"

"I'm in the garage."

* * * *

Mick sped to Boston, the city fading to New Jersey suburbs, which turned into miles and miles of thick forest. We stayed quiet for most of the drive. I closed my eyes but was unable to sleep. My nerves were frayed. I didn't know what condition Jack would be in. It would take a psychopath to kill twelve people in a matter of days and remain unaffected. Jack wasn't a psychopath.

"Why do you think he went to Boston?" I asked Mick. Of all places, I wouldn't expect Jack to show up there, given his horrific childhood.

"Probably to lie low." Mick glanced in my direction, his hand resting on the base of the steering wheel. "Who knows? Maybe he was feeling sentimental."

"Sentimental?"

Mick shrugged. "Henry O'Connell is the only family member not buried in Ireland. He chose to be laid to rest by his wife in Bunker Hill."

"The Uncle Henry who gave the boys their fortune?"

It was because of Uncle Henry's accumulated wealth that Jack and his brothers had been able to get out from under their father's shadow, to form their own branch of the Mob in Manhattan. They'd used the money to purchase the Shannon and Emerald Gym. From there, they had joined high society — invested wisely, bought and sold real estate, made international contacts in the black market. As they had risen to power, more and more members had joined their ranks.

"Aye, that's the one," Mick confirmed, slowing to the speed limit when a red light on the police scanner flashed. Seconds later, we passed a cruiser hiding between a pair of thick pine trees, its hood glinting in the moonlight. Once the scanner turned green, Mick revved the engine of the SUV again.

"I didn't know Henry and Jack were close. He never talked about him."

"Jack doesn't talk much as it is." Mick grunted, smirking. "Anyway, Henry wasn't very close with the boys, but he taught Jack a few things back in the day."

"Like?" I pressed.

"You'll have to ask Jack yourself," Mick replied, effectively sealing his lips.

"Jack doesn't want anything to do with me. He made that clear."

"Yeah, I've been thinking on that." He put his signal on to pass slower traffic. "Did it ever cross your mind that Jack *wanted* you to believe he cheated? He'll have told himself that he has to lose you to protect you."

"*He'll push you away.*"

"It may've crossed my mind," I replied, staring out of the window so that I didn't have to meet Mick's eye. "Either way, his goal was to hurt me. And he succeeded."

"You're a tough one, lass. You may have more pride than Jack, even."

I fought to keep the heat from pooling in my cheeks as Mick continued.

"I've seen the way he looks at you. Like you shit gold. He's convinced you're an angel."

"I'm not an angel," I argued. "No one's perfect. I'm capable of doing bad things."

"Aye, but you try not to." Mick tapped his temple. "That's the difference. You try to be a good person. And I think that's what makes you one."

"Jack tries to be good. Usually."

"He didn't used to try. Not until he met you. Didn't give a shit who he hurt as long as he got his way. You've changed him. He thinks about consequences before he makes a decision. Thinks about *you* before he takes a breath. You're his lighthouse in a storm, lass."

Mick's analogy struck close to home. I'd always thought of Jack as my storm — unpredictable, chaotic, passionate — but I'd never envisioned myself as his lighthouse.

"He's changed me, too," I murmured. "Only I'm not sure if it's for the better."

"You're stronger."

I looked at Mick, raising my brows. He could still snap me in two with his fingers.

"When I started teaching you self-defense, you were scared of everything. Flinched at the sound of a dumbbell being dropped. There's something different about you now, lass. It's hard to see. You get a certain look in your eye every once in a while. Like when you told McKenzie to go fuck himself. It's not all from Jackie Boy, though, so don't give him credit. I think it just took you a while to realize what was in you all along."

I hadn't known Mick was the type to pay so much attention. Especially to someone like me, who wasn't a member of the mob. He was insightful as hell. And confident with what he saw.

"It takes an ungodly amount of pressure to make something as tough as a diamond," Mick related with a soft smile. "You've adapted. And that's the best quality one can have in our world. The ability to survive. I know how difficult it is, but you've been remarkable."

I sniffled. "Stop. You're going to make me cry."

"I think you deserve a good cry, Wings."

"Believe me, I've cried enough."

Mick's phone screen lit up, the ringtone interrupting our conversation. He gathered his device from the cup holder, his expression stoic. "Hi, Donovan."

I didn't know who Donovan was, but Mick wouldn't answer unless it was important. Kieran, Eoghan and Cathal were still in the city. Kieran couldn't leave at a time like this — it would look to the rest of the mob like he was fleeing Nicoletti's wrath. But I hoped Don Luca wouldn't be retaliating until after our meeting, at the very least.

"You let him go?" Mick yelled, pressing the pedal all the way down. The engine revved, vibrating my eardrums. "Jesus Christ… Fine. Thanks for telling me."

Mick dropped his phone into the cup holder with aggression.

"Why the hell was Jack released?" I demanded.

Mick ran a hand through his hair. "Technically, he was never being held under an official charge."

We were going well over a hundred miles an hour, but the roads were almost empty. It was after four in the morning. We'd passed a few suburbs and the trees were thinning. We couldn't be far now.

"The Roxbury precinct is known for its corruption," Mick explained. "I wasn't the only one on Donovan's call list. Jack was bailed out an hour ago."

Acid rose in my stomach, burning my throat. "By who?"

Mick exited the highway, thinning his lips. "Frank O'Connell."

"Fucking Frank," I cursed, wincing at the sound of his name.

Connor's wake had been the first time I'd seen Frank since Christmas Eve. The memory of that winter night still gave me chills. The look on Jack's face as he'd choked his father had been enough to weaken my knees—black eyes, pale skin, jaw clenched with decades of unreleased fury. It had been a miracle he hadn't killed him.

"Fucking Frank," Mick agreed.

* * * *

Jack

"Never though' I'd see the day," my father's voice rang through the hallowed halls of Boston's finest, "when my son called *me* for a bailout."

Frank O'Connell staggered into view. He was all blurred edges, hungover as hell. He'd lost a bit of his gut, but the puffiness around his face was permanent from the alcohol. He reeked of it as he neared, forcing me to swallow the bile in my throat.

The fluorescent lights of the precinct were blinding. I leaned my head against the bars, gritting my teeth. My ribs were healing, but my migraine had amplified over the past few days. Gunshots echoed inside my skull, driving me insane. Twelve people were dead by my hand, yet I was no closer to finding my brother's killer. *Carnage*. That was all I had unearthed.

"I didn't fucking call you," I growled.

Keys clanked against metal. I opened my eyes as Officer Donovan unlocked the door to the cell, which I had to myself. Knowing who I was, they'd separated me from the other inmates in the drunk tank.

"Is that any way to treat the man who just saved yer skin?" Frank asked in a singsong voice, winking at Donovan.

I pushed past them, rounding the corner to the other cell. The victim of last night's brawl was looking worse for wear. He held an ice pack to his swollen eye, glaring at me with malice. I flipped him off as I passed his cage, trailing my finger on the bars. I couldn't remember what he'd done to anger me. Given the week I'd had, it wouldn't take much.

Frank signed the paperwork, but it was for show. It would go straight into the shredder when we left. He hadn't paid to get me out—he was paying for their silence.

Miraculously, it was the first time I'd seen the inside of a cell—and for something as petty as a pub brawl. If they had any idea how many people I'd killed since Thursday, they'd be shipping me back to New York to serve life and then some.

"Tom's in the car." Frank grunted, working to catch up as I slammed through the precinct's glass doors.

I eyed the Jeep, wondering if I should even get in. Abhorrence was an understatement when it came to my father, but it'd be smart to cool off for a few days. God only knew how many people were searching for me. My own men, definitely. Nicoletti would be hunting for someone to answer for the massacres. Organized Crime was another, but they'd be easier to dodge. Police were predictable and had to follow protocol.

The one person *not* looking for me was her, which was bittersweet. I wanted her to hate me, but it still stung. I had to block my mind from going down that route. I needed to finish what I started, then I would allow myself time to lick my wounds, although there wasn't enough time left on earth for me to recover from losing Emma. Men like me didn't get second chances. When we committed, we gave it our all. Emma Marshall might not know it, but she'd always have my heart. I'd never love again.

"I hate you, Jack."

I hopped into the back of the Jeep, shivering at the harrowing memory. Tom glanced at me over his shoulder, nodding once. I must have looked wrecked, though I'd won last night's brawl.

Frank clambered into the passenger seat, passing back a fifth of whiskey. "Hair o' the dog?"

I eyed the bottle, imagining hitting my father over the head with it. Instead, I took it from him.

Frank chuckled, the sound like a semitruck failing to start. "Though' you might need it. Ye gonna thank yer father, boyo?"

I poured the liquor down my throat, wincing from the cheap brand's burn. I was normally pickier with my choice of drink, but not today. I would take anything to ease the pain in my head. As well as the ache in my heart.

"Fuck off, Frank." My voice cracked with the heat from the alcohol. I took a few deep breaths, then tilted the half-empty bottle back again. I didn't recognize the street Tom was driving down, although we were likely headed to Frank's trailer park.

Frank's expression betrayed the slightest sign of concern. "I know it's the pot callin' the kettle black, but you migh' wanna slow down, boyo."

I ignored him as the alcohol sluiced into my belly, dulling my senses. If I were going to lay low in Boston, I didn't want to be conscious for it.

Chapter Twenty-Nine

Emma

"Is this where you guys grew up?"

Mick pulled into a dilapidated trailer park in the neighborhood of Roxbury. Dumpsters were overfilled with garbage, attracting droves of flies. There were potholes every ten feet, forcing me to take hold of the leather seat. Broken-down cars littered the skinny driveways. Shattered windows, liquor bottles, cigarette butts, torn screens—I'd never been anywhere like this.

It wasn't even dawn, but people sat outside on lawn chairs. They drank from paper bags, joints pinched between their fingers. A few residents stopped talking, staring as we passed them. Mick parked in front of a periwinkle-colored trailer with a Jeep beside it.

"No," Mick answered, unbuckling his seatbelt. "We grew up somewhere much worse than this."

I exited the vehicle, my boots crunching on the gravel driveway.

It wasn't a secret that I'd lived a sheltered life. I'd known the O'Connell boys had been raised in squalor, but seeing it firsthand was eye-opening. Jack had grown up in a place *worse* than this? I wanted to grab him and get the hell out of here as soon as possible.

Mick didn't bother knocking on the dirty front door, which was unlocked. I followed him as he walked straight into the trailer, his movements stiff like he was expecting retaliation. Jack's revolver pressed against the damp skin of my back, hidden beneath my leather bomber jacket.

"Where is he?" Mick demanded, coming to a halt in the living area.

I stood behind him, studying the room. There wasn't much to see — stained purple carpet, peeling wallpaper, thick smoke in the air. Frank O'Connell sat in a worn armchair, a mug of black coffee steaming in his hand. I knew him well enough to assume there was more than coffee in the cup. An older man I didn't recognize eyed me with curiosity, ignoring Mick.

"Oh, let the boy sleep." Frank cracked his neck, setting his mug on the wooden coffee table as he rose from his chair. "He's had a rough day."

"Like you would know anything about the type of day he's having." Mick's tone was colder than I'd ever heard it before, but I was no longer giving them my full attention. Frank had mentioned Jack was asleep. If he wasn't in the living room, he must be down the hall somewhere.

"We just lost Connor," Frank argued as I inched across the living room, keeping my back to the wall. "Give the man a break."

I didn't hear Mick's response. My eyes had traveled to a half-open door in the hallway, light pouring through the crack to illuminate a small bedroom. There was an unmade twin bed, but not much else in it.

Apart from Jack.

Oh, Jack...

He was much too big for the bed. One arm and leg dangled off the side, lifeless. He was clutching an empty liquor bottle to his chest. His face was unshaven, his dark beard thicker than normal. His face was turned toward the door, his jaw slackened.

Swallowing the lump in my throat, I knelt by the bedside, pressing my fingertips to the soft skin of his neck. His pulse fluttered beneath my touch, but he didn't stir. I lifted his tattooed arm, sliding the bottle out from underneath it. Shadows had made a home around his closed eyes. His hair was an absolute mess, umber curls going this way and that. Even on his worst day, there was a savage beauty about him.

"You need to get him home, lass."

I spun, almost losing balance. The older man I hadn't recognized was leaning in the doorway. He wore a pitiful expression.

"That's why I'm here," I answered, my voice stiff with heartbreak.

Worried I'd been too loud, I glanced at Jack, but he was dead to the world. For once, I was grateful for it. I wasn't sure if he would want to return to the city. Seeing how far down he'd fallen into his darkness, I would drag him back if I had to.

"Are you Emma?" the man asked.

"Yes."

I rose from my crouch, careful to keep my body between his and Jack's. It was a subconscious move, but a protective one. It didn't matter whether Jack had cheated on me. Together or not, I would protect him with my dying breath. Especially when he was in such a vulnerable state—oblivious to the world and unable to defend himself.

"I'm Tom. Frank's first lieutenant."

"Wonderful," I snarked, peering over his shoulder. Mick was still arguing with Frank, but they spoke in hushed voices.

"I've known Jack since he were a wee lad," Tom continued. "He's always been troubled, but nothing like this... Do you have a plan?"

If Tom answered to Frank, he wasn't trustworthy, but there was something about the way he looked at Jack. His face was wracked with guilt, and it seemed as though Tom wanted to pay back a debt.

"I always have a plan," I answered.

Mick entered the room. When his gaze landed on Jack, he cursed and glanced at the ceiling, asking God for help.

"You get his legs," Mick said to Tom.

Tom stared at me a moment longer, then helped Mick with Jack. I left the bedroom, not wanting to watch his lifeless body get hauled around again. I pushed through the screen door, taking the plastic stairs two at a time, when I ran into Frank.

"Jesus," I muttered. His cigarette had nearly poked my eye out. Frank grabbed my wrist, his grip tight. My temper flared, taking control of my mouth. "If you don't let go, I'll shove that cigarette up your ass."

Frank's forest-green eyes were so similar to his son's—except they were bloodshot and the skin around them had begun to droop.

"Ye take my boyo back to that city, he's yer responsibility, woman," he growled, his dark teeth clashing. "If he gets his throat slit, I'm blamin' ye."

I glared at him, a thousand retorts flying through my mind. Before I could settle on one, Frank spoke again, his rancid breath churning my stomach.

"I've already lost one son. If I lose Jackie, I'll kill ye with me own two hands."

I twisted my arm, grabbing onto his wrist. The new angle gave me leverage, allowing me to spin Frank, pinning him against his own trailer. With his arm bent crookedly behind his back, I could dislocate his shoulder without breaking a sweat.

Someone started clapping to my left.

"Nicely *done*, Wings!" Mick congratulated, the sound of his footsteps pounding down the stairs. They must've already loaded Jack into the SUV. Maybe there was a back door to the trailer I hadn't seen. "You're an excellent student."

Frank spit, his brow furrowed in pain as I leaned my weight into him. "Ye taught her this, ye bastard?"

Mick grinned, proud of me. "Damn right I did."

I released Frank, letting him fall into the dusty flowerbed. He let out a grunt, his breathing labored. He scrabbled in the dirt, trying to stomp out the glowing cherry from his cigarette. It burned a hole in his soiled jeans.

"I suppose that's close enough to your ass," I deadpanned, leaving Frank behind to join Mick in the driveway. "All set?"

Mick handed me the keys. "You drive."

I raised my brows. Mick was a much faster driver than me and he knew the way home. My internal clock was ticking. I had thirteen hours to get back to Manhattan and prepare myself for the meeting with Don Luca.

Mick ignored my hesitation, holding open the door to the SUV. I climbed behind the steering wheel, taking a moment to adjust the seat and mirrors to my height. The rearview mirror settled on Jack. Mick and Tom had buckled him in, but he was still in a deep, drunken sleep. His head lolled against the headrest, and I wanted to reach out for him. Why the hell did I have to drive?

Mick hopped into the backseat beside Jack. "Hand me the black case inside the glove compartment."

I opened the console, grabbed the leather case then handed it to Mick.

"It's a sedative," Mick explained, unzipping the container to reveal an ominous syringe and a small vial with medical jargon on its side. "Just in case he wakes up. Trust me, we don't want to deal with him in a confined space."

"Is it okay to give it to him when he's had so much to drink?"

"He's sleeping like a rock, so I shouldn't have to use it. But if I do, he'll be fine. It'll knock him out for a few more hours. Enough time for us to get him back into his apartment. And then you'll call me when he wakes up."

I nodded, knowing very well that wasn't part of my plan. Sure, I'd get Jack back to his apartment. But Mick couldn't know what happened after.

As I closed the glove compartment, my gaze snagged on a manila folder resting in the passenger footwell. It must've fallen when I had retrieved Mick's case. Bending my body at an awkward angle, I grabbed a black-and-white photograph peeking out of the envelope.

"It's the only lead we have on the Babau," Mick said, noticing my attention had drifted. "Cathal took it a couple nights ago."

There were three people in the picture, dressed head to toe in black, their faces covered. The slim man in the middle faced away from the lens, pointing at something in the distance. I narrowed my eyes, studying his back. There was a strange object resting between his shoulder blades, catching a beam of light at just the right angle.

It was impossible to discern unless I knew what I was looking at, but I'd seen that insect-like shape before. Chills skated down my spine.

"Can we get on the road, Em?" Mick asked, eyeing Jack.

I dropped the photograph, throwing the vehicle into drive. The picture was useless to them, but not to me. I knew exactly who the Babau was.

Chapter Thirty

Emma

Mick placed the unused sedative on Jack's bedside table, showing me where to inject it if necessary. I shuddered at the thought, but listened carefully.

"Call me when he wakes," Mick ordered. "We don't want him running off again. I'll be at Roisin's getting briefed with Kieran. So not far, okay?"

I swiped a loose tendril of hair behind my ear, nodding. Once the elevator doors had closed behind Mick, I set to work. I filled a few gallon jugs with water, one with orange juice and another with ginger-ale. I grabbed a bag of rolls from the pantry, an entire box of protein bars and sliced fruit. Feeling contrite, I threw some beef jerky in the bag and carried everything into Jack's closet. It took a few trips.

As I moved around the apartment, I kept an eye on Jack, hoping I wouldn't need to give him the sedative. I didn't like needles. While I was piling supplies into the panic room, Eoghan called to let me know he'd set up the camera.

"What the hell is your little sister up to? The address you gave me was to a slaughterhouse. Is she working undercover for PETA?"

"I told you, it's a short documentary on the food industry. I didn't ask too many questions, Eoghan." I felt bad for lying, but this had to be done. Hopefully some good would come of it, even if I was killed.

"How's Jack?" Eoghan asked, sounding exhausted.

"Still asleep."

Eoghan grunted. I thought I recognized a voice speaking in the background, but Eoghan ended the call before I could come to any conclusions.

Pocketing my phone, I entered Jack's bedroom. He was sleeping atop the comforter. It took a few pulls, but I was able to move him. His body hit the floor with a sickening thud. Jack moaned, turning his head left and right. When his eyelids fluttered, I swiped the leather case from the bedside table, fumbling with the zipper. By the time I knelt by his side, syringe at the ready, he was nearly awake.

Jack's expression was wrought with pain, but when he saw me, his frown disappeared. He looked at the syringe in my hand, his eyes widening.

"Emma?" he slurred, fumbling over my simple name.

"I'm so sorry, baby," I whimpered, pulling up the sleeve of his T-shirt and sticking the needle into his tattooed shoulder.

He flinched, but I felt it more than he did. Having to do this to him was a necessary evil. Jack's eyelids drooped, his muscles relaxing as I pressed my lips to his forehead. My eyes burned with tears I refused to let fall. There wasn't enough time.

I returned the syringe to its case, then tightened my ponytail. "You can do this, Em."

Jack was close to one hundred pounds heavier than me, so moving him strained muscles in my body I hadn't even known existed. It took over thirty minutes, and I was drenched in sweat by the time I'd laid him on his side in the panic room, a blanket wrapped around his large frame.

I grabbed a pen and paper from his office, having thought about what I would write on the drive back from Boston. Still, seeing the stack of novels on his bookshelf made my chest constrict. They were books that Jack had stolen from my apartment over the months. Steinbeck, Angelou, Vonnegut, even Stephen King — we'd read them together, lying side by side, our heads touching.

Pushing the memory down, I taped a note to the inside of the panic room door, making sure Jack had all he needed until I returned. If I didn't survive, he could push the panic button. The entire mob would descend, just to realize his ex-girlfriend had locked him in his own panic room. Jack would feel like an idiot.

Because that was exactly what I was doing. I changed the code to the safe so Jack wouldn't be able to escape until he guessed it right.

"Sweet dreams, Jack," I whispered, shutting the heavy door.

When I turned to face the interior of the closet, Fia startled me. The dark cat sat upright on the island, his green eyes brimming with what I assumed was judgment.

"Don't give me that look," I said, scratching him under the chin. He dodged my hand after a few taps, sinking onto his belly. "I'm trying to help him."

* * * *

Jack

My dreams were relentless. I fought with all my might to pull myself out of them, but had no such luck.

They started off with Emma, as most did. She was warm and soft, asleep in bed after I got home from another late night. Stripping down to my black briefs, I crawled under the blankets to join her, pressing my hard body against her supple one. She sighed with contentment—the best sound a man could come home to—but when she faced me, it wasn't Emma. Faye Walsh smiled at me, her white teeth glowing in the city's lights.

"Fuck!" I scrambled backward, falling off the bed.

Instead of hitting the plush rug, I landed on a cold linoleum floor. I recognized the cheap, beige-and-white diamond pattern. I was in the tiny kitchen of my family's old Boston subsidized apartment. My father towered over me, younger than I remembered. He held a black pistol in hand, his gaze withdrawn.

"Shoot him, Jackie Boy," he ordered.

I rose to my feet, taking the Ruger from him. The metal weapon was unfamiliar in my grasp. My arms were skinnier, the limbs of a child.

My gaze roamed the face of Tony Greco, the mobster. In my dream, he was foreign to me. I didn't know why my father wanted him dead. "What did he do?"

"It doesn't matter. If I tell you to kill someone, you do it without hesitation."

"I'm not a child anymore," I argued, the gun growing heavier in my grip, dragging me down. I strained to keep myself upright. "I decide who dies, not you."

"He tried to kill Emma."

As the man opened his mouth to protest, I aimed the gun and shot him. He'd tried to take Emma from me. That was a death sentence in my book.

The room disappeared in a plume of smoke, skulls forming from the ashes. Dark shamrocks floated in front of my vision. Coughing, I swiped at the particles in the air until they dissipated.

"Don't ever let anyone tell you who to kill, son," Uncle Henry's voice whispered in my ear. "And don't ever tell anyone else to kill for you. If you think someone's life is worth taking, you take it yourself."

Now I stood in a large warehouse, night visible beyond the skylights. The rubber of the octagon beneath my bare feet was familiar. On instinct, I raised my fists to guard my face, my toes dancing on the mat.

"Give it up for the Emerald Devil!" the announcer yelled.

When I glanced at the crowd, fear struck my core. They were all dead—skeletons with flesh hanging off their faces, their clothes tattered. I nearly fell to my knees. All twenty-nine of them were men I had killed. The oldest and most ragged was in front, stoic and silent, watching me. His was the first life I had taken. Eighteen years ago. It was something I'd never told my brothers. It was a secret between my father and me. That bullet might as well have gone through my heart. That was when I'd forgotten I had one.

"And, without further ado," the announcer continued. "The Emerald Angel!"

The dead parted, revealing Emma. A skeletal hand assisted her into the octagon. She smiled, thanking the monstrosity. As she neared, my knees buckled, my heart bursting from my chest.

"Jack," she breathed in that soothing voice she reserved just for me.

She wore a short white dress, and her skin was sprinkled with green glitter. Her curly hair tumbled to her hips. On her back, sprouting where her shoulder blades should be, was a massive pair of white wings. They spanned the width of the octagon as she knelt, her face inches from mine. The horde of bones vanished. It was just my dove and me.

"Emma?" I asked, a knot welling in my throat.

My own personal angel. *She came back to me.* Her delicate face floated above mine as if she'd fallen from heaven itself. She cocooned me in her wings, her feathers tickling my spine.

"I'm so sorry, baby," she whimpered.

Tears welled in her deep, brown eyes, but she wasn't looking at me. I tried to raise an arm to stop her, but my muscles weren't functioning properly. Before I could object, she slid the needle into my deltoid. I winced at the sting, only to see my pain reflected in Emma's eyes. The last thing I remembered was the press of her lips to my forehead.

When I awoke, the fluorescent lights were blinding. I groaned, pressing the heels of my hands into my eye sockets. The dreams had been so real, like an alternate reality. My hell.

My arm was sore, but it was nothing compared to the pounding in my head. I crawled across the floor, wondering where the hell I was. Last I had checked, I was in Boston. But this place didn't look anything like Frank's dingy trailer. It was too clean and clinical. I rested my hand on a plastic jug and I pulled it to me. I sipped at the water, taking in my surroundings.

Fuck.

I was in the panic room, which meant Emma had told someone the code. Probably Mick. I wouldn't have put it past him to stick me in here and wait for me to sober up.

After a few minutes, my legs felt steady enough to hold my weight. I stumbled to the safe's door, then punched in the code. A red light flashed, followed by a deep beeping sound. *Dammit.* I must've forgotten a number. Sighing in frustration, I entered it again.

Beeping and a red flash.

I slammed my fist into the door, although it wouldn't make a difference. If Mick was on the other side, he wouldn't hear a thing. The room was soundproof. Nothing could get in or out. Apparently, 'nothing' now included me.

Something white flitted before my eyes and fell to the floor. I bent down, losing my balance when I saw the neat scrawl on the piece of paper. It even smelled like her. Apples and lavender.

Jack,

If you haven't already figured it out, you're home. Mick and I picked you up from Boston earlier this morning and, quite frankly, I think you've earned a timeout. I changed the code to get out of the room, but I'm sure you realized that. Don't worry. I've left you food, water and a shiny gold watch from your collection so you can keep time. I'll be back

*tomorrow night around nine to let you out if you haven't
done so yourself.*

A little hint? The code is in the room with you.

Emma

The Rolex was next to a sawed-off shotgun on a
nearby shelf. I picked it up, cursing as I read the time —
ten p.m. Emma wouldn't be back for another twenty-
three hours.

"Fuck!" I roared, the hoarse sound echoing off the
walls and shattering my bruised skull. I reread Emma's
note, turning it over to search for clues. There was
nothing written on the back, but she'd said the code
was in the room.

Where could she have left it?

I glanced around. Shelves, locked cabinet, food and
drink on the floor. *Jesus…*

I had to get out of this room. I wasn't going to be
locked in here, useless in my own pity, for the next day.
I would tear the place apart inch by inch. I would be
free before Emma arrived, whether she liked it or not.

Chapter Thirty-One

Emma

The address on the card Amara had given me was in the industrial section of Jersey. The buildings were rundown and lifeless, nestled in between the outskirts of the two states. The murky waters of the Hudson River sloshed nearby, separating me from the city I called home.

The cabbie dumped me a block down, asking for clarification when he did so. Since it was well after the end of the workday, the neighborhood was abandoned. The driver eyed me with reasonable concern as I nodded, exiting the taxi.

The sun had just dipped below the horizon, casting a macabre, purple hue to the night sky. It was starless, as all nights were. In Connecticut, the sky was full of distant galaxies, but I had grown accustomed to the suffocating feeling that came with Manhattan life. Even relished it on evenings like tonight when it felt as though I could be swept into space at a moment's notice.

The cabbie shook his head in exasperation, then drove off down the street. He obviously didn't want to be here any longer than he had to.

As I made my way down the block, counting the buildings, I wondered if Jack was awake yet. Wasn't that funny? Out of all the things I could be thinking of – family, Don Luca, war, the never-ending list of existential crises happening around the world – my mind was clouded with Jack. Replaying every perfect detail of the short amount of time we'd had together. I'd never love another man like I loved Jack O'Connell. If I survived the evening, I would have to spend the rest of my life coming to terms with that fact.

At the fourth warehouse, I came to a stop. It was large and rusted, with double doors lined in sheet metal. It was the exact address Amara had provided, but the building looked vacant. No one stood guard outside, as I'd expected, and none of the lights were on that I could see.

Just when I thought I might have counted the buildings wrong, the heavy doors were pulled apart from the inside. *Stick to your plan, Em.* I steeled myself, trudging into the dark warehouse. Two men flanked either side of the door, a wolfish look in their eyes.

"Come to die, *topolina*?" the skinnier one asked, his voice jarring my memory. I'd seen him before at the Booker Hotel. He had been the first to call me *topolina* – *little mouse*. The skinny man smirked, nodding at his partner to follow him out of the building.

As they exited, I moved in the opposite direction, determined. I wasn't dying unless I took the bogeyman with me. The doors snapped closed behind them. I waited for my eyes to adapt to the darkness, listening for signs of life.

There was a faint scuffing sound, like slippers snagging on ragged cement. Metal clinked in the ominous abyss, followed by a desperate whimper. But it wasn't from me.

Suddenly, my pupils were doused with light.

The Italian informant—the call girl I'd accused Jack of hiring all those weeks ago—was standing in the center of the vast room, her mouth gagged with a dirty cloth. Her hands were tied behind her back and a rope was wrapped around her feet. I glanced up, following the rope to where it was tethered high above our heads in the rafters. Dozens of rusty meat hooks hung from the ceiling, drenched in years of uncleaned blood. If I hadn't been a vegetarian already, the sight would be enough to turn me into one. A slaughterhouse. Eoghan's comment about Ella joining PETA made perfect sense.

At the presence of light, Sofia caught my eye and screamed in terror, mascara-stained tears carving a path down her dirty cheeks. Her knees bent, as if the strength it took to scream made her weak. I stepped forward on instinct, fumbling with the rope around her wrists.

"Don't touch her."

I froze as Amara's voice cut through the silence like a knife. Or, better yet, like the switchblade she'd held to my throat three days ago. Her slim form came into view. Her pale skin gave her a ghost-like quality. A loose braid cascaded over her shoulder, the diamond barrette winking at me from the tip of it. She wore all black, her cloak dirty from where it flitted along the floor. With her height and clothing, she could easily be mistaken for a man.

"Do you know her?" Amara asked, nodding toward the bound and gagged girl.

I took a step away from the informant, avoiding her gaze. Sofia's eyes pleaded with me, begging me to continue my previous action, to let her go. Even if I did, she wouldn't get far.

To Amara, I shook my head.

"Her name is Sofia Fiore," Amara explained, her hands clasped behind her back. "She is a friend of a Mr. Bryan Murray. Does that name ring a bell?"

Amara stopped pacing and turned toward me, waiting.

"I don't know who either of those people are," I answered, void of emotion.

"Sofia is a whore. She deals exclusively with the Mafia's...*distinct* tastes. But she also feeds information to your mob, yes? She just confessed to revealing the location of one of our safe houses to none other than Jack O'Connell."

I glared at Sofia, my temper flaring. *Traitor.* Don Luca now knew who had murdered his men. After he realized I held nothing over his head, he'd go after Jack.

"I don't belong to any mob," I stated, hating to admit it. I was no more a part of the Irish mob than Don Luca was.

Amara tilted her face toward the rafters, laughing. Her mouth was a black hole, her teeth sharp and deadly. She removed her hand from her pocket, switchblade at the ready. Moving faster than I thought possible, she pressed the blade to Sofia's neck.

The look in Sofia's eyes was enough to make my battered heart shatter further. I'd never seen that expression on someone's face before—the way the brow furrowed, the cheeks rose, the pupils dilated, the forehead beaded with sweat. It was the look of someone who knew they were going to die. Even if I was angry at Sofia for her lack of spine, I didn't think she deserved death for it.

"Stop!" I screeched, betraying my calm demeanor. "If you kill her, I'll never give Luca the letter."

Amara reached out with her opposite hand. "Hand it over."

"Don Luca," I clarified, recoiling at the sight of her long, dirty fingernails. "I'll only give it to him."

"No one sees the don without clearance. You know that." Amara brandished the switchblade at me, her eyes black and greedy. "Time for a strip search, *topolina*."

Fuck that.

Amara would find my weapon eventually, so I pulled Jack's revolver from the waistband of my jeans. I aimed it between her thick eyebrows, clicking the hammer back twice. Amara didn't waver under the barrel. Instead of fear, a small smile formed on her thin, dry lips.

"You don't have it in you," she goaded. Sofia fidgeted, but my stare was fixed on the monster in front of me. "When did you figure it out?"

"This morning," I answered, my finger hesitant over the trigger. A thousand thoughts flew through my head—*I can't do this, I'm not a murderer*—but Jack would get himself killed trying to find the Babau. And I had the bastard at gunpoint.

"It appears you're as smart as my uncle gives you credit for," Amara whispered, her gaze flitting to something over my shoulder.

I stiffened, aware of a demonic presence behind me.

Not a moment later, the cold steel of a gun furrowed its way through my thick ponytail. Every nerve in my body stood at attention as Don Luca's pistol nestled against the seat of my brain. I glanced upward, knowing now was the time, if any.

"Don't look to the heavens for an answer," Amara teased, that sickening smile marring her chalky face.

I reached into my jacket pocket with my free arm.

"Careful, little one," Don Luca cooed from behind me.

I grasped the flash drive and handed it back to him. His cold fingers grazed mine as he gripped the small piece of data. I glanced once more at the rafters, hoping Eoghan had done his part. Otherwise, I would have sacrificed myself for nothing.

Luca Nicoletti's breath skated across my neck. "A flash drive?"

He exerted more pressure on the gun, forcing my head to tilt forward. My eyes watered, but I didn't flinch. Amara's malicious glare was fixed on me, evaluating.

"There's a copy of Nate's suicide note on there." My palms began to sweat, the revolver's handle threatening to slip from my grasp. "I'm not going to give you the real thing. It was addressed to me and I'm keeping it."

"Fine."

Luca's voice was terse but compliant, revealing a weakness. Amara had said he had a soft spot for me, but his Achilles' heel was the grandson he'd never know. Nate's suicide was something no one, not even Don Luca, could have anticipated. He would grasp at any remnant of Nate, even something as vague as a flash drive. Anything that would give him an insider's view into his grandson's world which Maria Ranucci had cut him off from.

"Put the gun down, little one," Don Luca ordered. "You've given me what I want."

"Babau," I whispered, catching Amara's attention. She'd been looking at her uncle like she was expecting something from him — probably hoping he would shoot me now that he had his evidence. "Why Connor?"

"The eldest O'Connell was an enemy," she answered. "The Emerald Devil is more elusive and, therefore, a greater challenge. I wanted your Irishman, but my uncle informed me he was off-limits."

"Amara," Don Luca warned, his weapon still pressed to my skull.

"Someone should've told you, *topolina*." Amara tsked, unaffected by the barrel pointed between her eyes. "Children shouldn't play with guns."

"Who said I'm playing?" I asked, gritting my teeth as I pulled the trigger.

Before I knew it, I was on the ground. My ears were ringing, the pulse fluttering in my neck. A searing pain rocked my head. Moaning, I ran my fingers through my hair. Had I been shot? No. I would be dead. I didn't feel dead. In fact, I felt very much alive.

A silent scream burned my throat. A pale woman lay on the ground before me. Her eyes were open and vacant, her black hair shocking against the white of her face. And in the middle of her forehead was a bullet hole.

I murdered someone. I killed Amara. The Babau is dead.

"Is that the first time you've shot a gun?"

Don Luca circled me, his weapon pointed down and at nothing in particular. I didn't have the voice to answer him, so I nodded, pulling my hand away from my head to examine it. My fingers were trembling and covered in my own blood.

"No one ever told you about the recoil?" Don Luca asked with little affectation, as if this was all a joke to him, just another day in the life. He wore leather driving gloves, which peeked out beneath the stiff arms of his tailored suit jacket. He bent down, rummaging through Amara's pockets. When he stood again, the switchblade was in his other hand.

"I have a lot of nieces," he continued, opening the blade. "One less is no skin off my back."

The following events happened so fast, I couldn't be sure if they were real. I thought time would slow, like in television, but death was immediate. I was beginning to realize that.

Don Luca stepped behind a trembling Sofia, whom I'd forgotten was there. She squealed, squeezing her eyes shut as he slid the blade across her throat. Blood spewed from the gash. She fell immediately, her body dragging along the floor before the pulley system was triggered, lifting her into the air by her feet. She hung upside down, suspended from the rafters, blood gushing from the wound at her neck.

Don Luca avoided the crimson spray with grace. I crawled backward, bile rising in my throat. My vision blurred, whether from the loss of blood or the shock to my system I didn't know. Once I'd inched away from the bath of blood, I stopped trying to escape and gasped for air.

Don Luca squatted in front of me, elbows braced on his knees. He held the flash drive between his fingers, forcing me to look at it as well.

"If this doesn't have what I asked for," he began, his tone casual, "I will destroy you and anyone who tries to protect you. You won't know when or how, but your death will be slow and imminent."

"Don't worry." I swallowed a mouthful of vomit, meeting his dark glare with my own. "It has exactly what you asked for."

He nodded, his face grim and stony, before rising once more. He exited the slaughterhouse with elegance, as if he hadn't just been part of a massacre. I heard the metal doors slide open, accompanied by the rumble of an engine.

As the tires rolled away — not at all how I imagined one would leave the scene of a crime — I tried to bring myself to my feet. I needed to get the camera, but in all my careful planning, I'd forgotten to ask Eoghan where he'd hidden it. The warehouse was huge. It'd take me hours to search, all the while leaving traces of myself at a double homicide.

The camera had filmed everything, but not what I'd hoped for. I hadn't gotten a confession from the don. He was getting antsy and I knew my time was running out. I'd had to euthanize his little pet before anyone else, including Jack, fell victim.

"Jesus fucking Christ."

Jumping to my feet, I spun to find Eoghan standing by the doors to the slaughterhouse, his chest heaving. He had his phone in hand, his hazel eyes wide and shimmering.

"Are you okay?" he asked, horrified. "Oh fuck, Em, that was torture to watch."

My mind wasn't working correctly. I blinked at him, bewildered. A layer of blood coated my lashes, making it difficult to see out of my right eye. "You...watched?"

Eoghan neared, holding my shoulders in his hands. His frightened gaze ran over my body, taking inventory, then drifted to the wound on my forehead. "Are you good for a sec?"

I nodded. Eoghan disappeared into the darker part of the room, rummaging around. When he returned, he had a small camera in hand.

"I had a feed straight to my phone," he explained, shaking the camera for good measure. "I knew you were lying through your teeth about Ella's school project. I didn't think *this* was what you were up to. When I saw them drag that Sofia girl in, I came from SoHo as fast as I could. Christ, Emma. What the hell were you thinking?"

"I wanted to get a confession," I whispered, prodding the wound on my head. "I wanted him to admit to ordering the hit on his daughter so I would have something against him for real this time."

"Stop touching it." Eoghan pulled my hand away from my face. He wrapped an arm around my torso and helped me walk out of the slaughterhouse. "We need to get you to Mick."

"What about the...bodies?" I didn't want to say their names aloud.

"Let the police take care of it. That's what they're paid for."

"But Jack's gun," I protested. "If they find it —"

"They won't. I grabbed it. Either way, it's untraceable." He sighed, lifting me over an uneven section of the sidewalk. "Why were you shooting with one hand?"

I tried to shrug, but it was impossible with Eoghan carrying me at such an awkward angle. "That's how the cowboys do it in movies."

"Are you a cowboy, Emma?" Eoghan asked, his concern quickly turning to anger.

"I don't know what I am…"

My vision doubled. The ache in my head was reaching an apex. My center of gravity was off, the pavement tilting. I needed to sit, or I'd collapse.

"That makes two of us," Eoghan countered. He paused to examine me, furrowing his brow. "Emma?"

Pushing him away just in time, I spilled the contents of my stomach onto the pavement between us. Eoghan cursed, pulling my ponytail out of the line of fire.

"How are we going to explain my injury?" I asked a moment later, wiping my mouth with my sleeve.

"Are you joking? You still think you can keep this from Jack?"

I shook my head, but that was a bad idea. I closed my eyes to stave off the nausea. "I can't explain…"

"Oh, stop thinking so hard. You're making *me* sick. I'll come up with something good."

"Thank you."

He muttered something incoherent under his breath, guiding me toward the vehicle. He buckled me in, then circled the hood. I took a few shaky breaths. I still felt dizzy, but my stomach was settling.

Eoghan threw the car into gear. Within seconds, we were hurtling through the darkened streets of New Jersey. I couldn't stop shaking. I twisted my fingers in my lap, my knees bobbing. After a few minutes of silence, he spoke.

"Do you have a death wish?"

"I was hoping *not* to die, actually."

"It's not your place to be taking out our enemies, Wings!" Eoghan yelled, slamming the breaks when a light turned red.

"Well, no one else had a chance! That bitch killed Connor and irrevocably scarred Shannon. And she was threatening my relationship."

He gunned it through the empty intersection. "How is that?"

"Jack has been agonizing over the choice between keeping me in his life and seeking vengeance for his brother. He chose vengeance, so I've taken it off the table."

Eoghan looked at me like I was spewing insanities.

"What?" I asked, annoyed.

He shook his head, refocusing on the road. "You really fucking love that asshole, huh?"

Laughter bubbled up from my lungs, but it wasn't funny. It was my coping mechanism working harder than it ever had before. Months of stress and worry and anxiety burst through my mouth in long peals. Tears fell from my eyes, commingling with the blood. I gasped for air, hitting my knees with the heel of my hands.

"You're a lovesick lunatic."

His comment did nothing but tickle me further. I didn't know if I was sobbing or laughing, or perhaps dying. "I sh-sh-should g-get that ta-tattooed somewhere."

"Please don't make any more stupid decisions tonight," Eoghan begged, resting a hand on my shoulder. "I need a break, or you'll do me in."

Chapter Thirty-Two

Emma

Mick tugged on the thread. My entire scalp moved in response. I kept my eyes shut, careful not to squint too hard as he worked. He'd numbed me, but I felt the heat from the wound and the pressure from his hands.

"Just a couple stitches," Mick murmured, concentrating. "I'll take them out in five days. Shouldn't leave a scar."

My reply was stiff. "I don't care about the scar."

"Next time you want to go to the shooting range, ask me." Mick grunted, pursing his lips. "If you have a computer problem or you need to be babysat, that's what Eoghan's for. Got it?"

I had the decency to look embarrassed. Everyone had so readily believed the lie Eoghan had spun. That I had asked him to take me to the shooting range under the Emerald. And, when he wasn't looking, I'd shot the gun and it had recoiled, injuring me.

"Jack's gonna have a field day." Mick placed a second butterfly bandage on my head wound. "I thought I told you to call me when he woke up. We don't want him running off again."

"He's not going anywhere," I muttered, taking the little white pill Mick held in his hand. He poured me a glass of water from the tap, his brows raised, waiting for an explanation. "I locked him in the panic room."

Mick almost dropped the glass. I grabbed it, swallowing the pill without asking what it was. I trusted Mick—not like I trusted Eoghan, but still. He wasn't going to give me anything I couldn't handle.

"You locked Jack in the panic room," he repeated, casting a strange look at me. It was the same expression Eoghan had worn when I'd first told him about my deal with Don Luca. Disbelief and awe.

"I left him the code." I slid from the counter, my bare feet hitting the heated stone floor. "But it might take him a while to find it."

"You feeling better, Em?" Shannon asked, sweeping into her master bathroom. She wore satin pajamas and a matching robe. Her hair was piled up high in a bun. It was ten o'clock and, by the sound of it, Charlotte had just gone down.

"Emma locked Jack in the panic room."

Shannon let out a bark of a laugh, then covered her mouth with three fingers. "I'm sorry, but that just made my day. Oh, I'd pay anything to see the look on his face when he wakes up."

"I left him food and water," I clarified, glaring at Mick for ratting on me. "I plan on releasing him tomorrow, but I figured he needed a timeout."

Shannon bent over, her arm wrapped across her middle, and laughed so hard I thought she might cry. Upon seeing her reaction, Mick chuckled.

Eoghan sauntered through the archway, confused. He looked between Shannon and Mick, then at me with question. "Why are they giggling?"

"I locked Jack in the panic room earlier today."

Eoghan's face split into a wide grin. "You didn't!"

I shrugged, feeling giddy myself. I was exhausted in every way—physically, mentally, emotionally—but seeing Shannon and Mick in fits made the corners of my mouth twitch.

"Oh, Em, I fucking love you." Shannon resurfaced, wiping tears from her red cheeks. "Now, everyone with a dick between their legs get out. I need to clean her up."

Mick clapped Eoghan on his shoulder and they promptly left the room. Eoghan glanced back to make sure I was okay and I nodded once. I was as okay as I ever would be given the strange, violent night I was having.

"Sit," Shannon ordered, the humor gone from her voice. She pointed to the closed toilet seat, then grabbed a washcloth from a cabinet and wetted it. It was warm and soothing when she applied it to my forehead, careful as she wiped away the excess blood. "What happened with Jack?"

"I told you. I locked him in the panic room."

"Not that. I mean before. I heard he was in a fight at MVR and that he got pretty messed up. The next morning, he's AWOL and no one can reach either of you. What the actual fuck?"

The fight at the Moscow Vodka Room had occurred five days prior, but it felt like Jack had been missing five *months*. The agony and sleepless nights had made the time stretch on endlessly.

"We got into an argument," I admitted. This was something I could talk with Shannon about. After all, she'd seen it coming. "And kind of...broke up."

She dabbed at my wound. "Why?"

I curled my nails into my palm. "He told me he cheated on me in Ireland."

Shannon scoffed and I looked up to catch her rolling her eyes. "And you believed him? I told you he would do this, Em."

"I didn't know he was going to say he cheated on me!" I defended. It wasn't like Shannon to be angry with me.

She set the washcloth on the counter with a huff. "He only told you he cheated to get you to leave. He would know there wasn't any other way."

"Yeah, Mick said the same thing." I winced, heat pooling in my cheeks. "I went feral on Jack. I told him to never touch me again."

"Oh, Em." Shannon sighed, a frown puckering her lips. "Jack knows how to hurt people, to identify and utilize their weaknesses. He's an asshole and you shouldn't take him back."

"He's not asking me to."

"He will once he realizes what a huge mistake he's made. The man cannot *function* without you. He was just getting by before. Going through the motions. He has a purpose with you in his life. I mean, look what happened the second you left him! He went Rambo and practically drank himself to death in the process. Five days without you, girl! And he spiraled quicker than even I thought possible. You did good locking him up.

He needs some time to think about what he's done. Especially to you."

Shannon eyed me with curiosity, her brow furrowed. I stood and put my hands on my hips, looking away. *Shit.* It was too late. She'd seen something in my expression.

"There's more…" She trailed off, taking a few steps until she faced me again. Shannon was shorter than me, but I felt small in comparison. She was such a strong person. I hoped I had just a sliver of her strength to get through this. "What aren't you telling me?"

I looked down at my hands, gripping my hips until I knew I'd leave bruises. My teeth were clenched so hard that my jaw fired with pain. The throbbing on my forehead returned despite the pain medication.

"I—" My voice was cracked, hoarse. "I killed…the Babau."

Shannon's slipper stopped tapping the floor. I couldn't bring myself to meet her gaze. I wasn't sure why I told her. Perhaps I needed someone else to know what I'd done. Someone on a more even playing field with me. Eoghan was used to violence. Criminal activity was just an average day for him. Not me. Not us.

"It's strange," I continued, picking at the leather sleeve of my jacket. "I don't feel guilty. I just… I was given an opportunity tonight and I took it. Jack was destroying himself and you would have to go to bed every night knowing justice still needed to be served and—"

Shannon wrapped her arms around my waist, pulling me tight. She stood on tiptoe, her mouth at my ear. The force of her embrace almost knocked me over. She was shaking. Crying. Relieved, I let my own tears fall.

"Thank you," she sobbed. I hadn't expected her gratitude, not so soon. I'd thought she was going to question me, demand details, say that we had to tell Jack. "Who was he?"

"*He* was actually *she*. Her name was Amara." Saying it aloud was soothing, like aloe on a sunburn. "She was Luca Nicoletti's niece."

"And who else knows this?"

"Just me, you and Eoghan."

"We need to get you cleaned up and dressed for bed before the meds kick in." She let go, spinning around to turn the shower on. "You can borrow something of mine. Lord knows I have enough crap to pack as it is."

"Are you still leaving Thursday?" I asked, reeling at the transition back to casual conversation. Shannon was amazing at compartmentalizing. The first advice she had ever given me came floating to mind — "*Living in their world, you have to know when it's okay to talk... and when to just smile.*"

"Day after tomorrow, yeah." She pointed at my bloody clothes. I stripped without question. At this point, Shannon and I were beyond boundaries. I had watched a human come out of her, for God's sake. "You'll see us off at the airport?"

"I wouldn't miss it," I replied with a plethora of emotions. I was losing my best friend, my confidant. I'd have to survive whatever came next without her, but it was for the best. Things were only going to get worse once Luca saw what I'd left him on the flash drive.

"Jack's going to come around," she promised as I slid behind the glass of the shower. Her next words were convoluted from where I stood under the waterfall. "I wouldn't be surprised if he's on his hands and knees begging your forgiveness by tomorrow. Are you going to give it to him?"

"I don't have much of a choice on the matter."

I was hopelessly, unconditionally in love with the man. Fucked as it was, Jack had sacrificed his own happiness to protect me—the same way I'd gambled with my life to end his suffering. His absence was an ache deep within my bones. I was desperate to wrap him up in my arms, to kiss him all over, to let him know everything would be okay. At least between us.

"You should still make him work for it," Shannon replied, her advice making me smirk.

"Oh, I plan to."

* * * *

Jack

I cursed for the millionth time, glancing at my watch. Three a.m.

The room was an absolute mess. I'd torn the shelves down, cracked open the locked filing cabinet with the butt of a rifle, opened each and every case full of cash. I'd even tried the serial numbers on the gold bars, hoping against hope that one of them was the code.

Nothing.

My bladder was painfully full after I had drunk over a gallon of water. I could piss in one of the empty bottles, but if Emma found me with jugs full of pee, I would never let myself live it down. Talk about weak.

Six hours. That was how long I'd been trapped in a room of my own creation, in a mess of my own volition. I did deserve this. I deserved far worse. I realized that now.

This obsession with the Babau was killing me, destroying everything that I loved. And I loved but two things—my family, blood or otherwise, and my girl.

* * * *

Emma

Emma Marshall was first on my list. She had been from the moment I had walked into her apartment for the first time. When I'd bared my life to her, telling her I was a criminal. Instead of kicking me out like most sane people would, she had launched herself onto me and never once let go. Not until I had forced her hand.

Choosing vengeance over love. *What a fucking idiot.* If Connor were alive, he'd slap me upside the head. How could I salvage my relationship with Emma? I hadn't actually cheated, but what I *had* done was just as bad. I'd used her own weakness against her, fabricating a lie I knew would devastate. Confidence I'd spent months building had shattered before my eyes. She would never trust me again, nor should she. I had a lot of work to do.

Earning Emma's forgiveness was a challenge I could get behind. It would be easier to kill a thousand Babaus, but I didn't love Emma because she was easy. She constantly begged for more than I could give. She wanted to see inside my head, to know my darkest thoughts, my sordid past. I had to be willing to open up to her—to expose the secrets I'd kept hidden from everyone else—and pray she didn't run. I wasn't sure if I could do it, but I owed it to both of us to try.

I clenched my right hand into a fist, eyeing the markings there. My oldest tattoo mocked me, forever reminding me of my first kill. Eighteen years ago. The memory of it was haunting, but it hadn't stopped me from killing again and again.

Until Emma. My life had started once I met her. Before, I had just been a machine. Carnage and mayhem were the only activities that had brought a smile to my face. Even sex had felt forced at times. All in the past, pre-Emma. I was a better person now. Better today than I was yesterday. I simply had to be.

Oh, fuck.

She had said the code was somewhere in the room. What if it was written on *me*?

I punched the date of my first kill into the keypad — the same date that was tattooed on my middle finger in thick Roman numerals. A green light flashed in the corner and the latch clicked, unfastening. I sighed at her ingenuity and my own stupidity, pulling the heavy door open at last.

Fia was sitting on the island in the closet, squinting his eyes in judgment.

"Don't give me that look," I muttered, running my hand through his fur as I headed toward the bathroom to relieve myself.

But I didn't stop there. I looked like an absolute wreck. I needed sleep and some detailing before I had a chance at approaching Emma with a mere apology. I washed my face and shaved just enough to leave a thin layer of stubble, knowing that was how she liked it. I spent thirty minutes in the shower, cleaning and grooming. I was worn out, but I wouldn't be able to sleep until I felt better about myself. Physically, at the very least.

After setting an alarm, I crashed into bed. In a few hours, I'd start the day right. There was one stop I had to make before finding Emma, wherever she was.

First, I had to meet my niece. It'd been long enough already.

Chapter Thirty-Three

Jack

It was close to noon when I exited the Tesla. I crossed the lobby toward the elevator, nodding at the armed guards. Shannon would be angry with me. Her feelings were founded, but she'd get over it. She always did. I wouldn't be as lucky with my next challenge. After reconciling with Shannon and meeting my niece, I'd call Eoghan and figure out where Emma was, although I didn't know what I would say just yet. My shit was all over the place.

The bright foyer with its fresh flowers and crystal table triggered a warmth in my chest. The unchanged penthouse reminded me how much I missed my family—Connor, in particular. It was moronic to cut myself off from his wife and child as a form of punishment, and I was ashamed for doing so. Self-sabotage was a habit of mine, a trauma cycle I needed to break if I wanted to survive my own mind.

When I approached the large white sectional, I froze. The wind was knocked out of me, a hard lump forming in my throat. *Holy shit.*

Emma was cuddling with an infant on the couch, fast asleep. Charlotte was still wrinkly and new, dressed in an army-green jumper with a matching headband. Her cheeks were rosy. Her nose was a button adorning her round, cherub face.

Emma, on the other hand, looked even more angelic. I hadn't seen her in a sober state of mind in weeks. She wore Shannon's clothes. The acid-washed jeans were baggy and torn. The pastel pink, lacy corset top was so sweet it had me salivating. A creamy blue beanie sat atop her head, her dark hair loose and curling over bare, ivory shoulders. Despite being in repose, she looked troubled.

I ached to cross the room, to stroke her cheek.

The sight of the two of them, Charlotte resting on Emma's chest, was magical — as was every chance I got to see Emma, especially when she caught me by surprise. I should've considered Emma would be spending the afternoon with Shannon.

I stepped forward, eyeing the blanket on the back of the sofa. I wanted to cover the two of them, the first small act in my search for forgiveness. But Shannon's angry face and wild red hair floated into my vision, cutting me off from Emma.

"Nursery," she hissed, pointing behind me. "Now."

I turned, heading toward the baby's room. Shannon followed, entering the pink haven soon after me. The nursery had changed drastically from the last time I had been here. They had been expecting a boy. Emma and Shannon had decorated the walls with trucks and dinosaurs. Now, I walked into a little girl's dream —

cotton candy and unicorns, ballet slippers and tulle accents.

"Emma did it," Shannon said as I gazed around at the new room, cataloging everything. "If you think you can just waltz in here after two months and go back to life as normal, you've got your head up your ass."

Shannon wasn't the type to hold a grudge. She needed to purge her system in one go. And I knew it. "Get it out, Shan."

"Oh, Jack," she labored, rolling her eyes. "I wish I could slap you, but I'd probably break a nail on your stubborn jaw. We have been cooped in this tower of spit-up and dirty diapers and tears for *months* while you've been out there with some sick vendetta. Even Kieran had his shit together enough to be at the hospital the day after Charlie was born! What the hell is wrong with you?"

I bit my cheek as I listened. Shannon was breathless and her face was red, but she wasn't close to being done.

"Oh, and don't even get me started on Emma! Telling her you cheated? You're so obsessed with protecting her, yet you hurt her worse than anyone else ever could," she hissed, casting me a dark, loaded glare. Her eyes were a lighter green than mine, but shadows danced in them. "Emma would kill for you. Don't fuck it up."

"I already have."

"Yeah, you have." She sighed, running a hand through her hair. "I assume you've been kept abreast on my decision to take Charlie to Ireland? We're leaving tomorrow."

This was a good move, even though I'd miss her terribly. It had been my choice to forgo a relationship with Charlotte, and I was suffering the consequences.

"Yes, Mick told me last week."

Shannon took me by surprise with a tight hug. She smelled like baby powder and milk, making me smile. The last time I'd seen her, she had been comatose with grief. She had recovered miraculously, and it had everything to do with that baby in the other room. Motherhood had saved her.

"I've missed you, Jackie," she whispered. "Don't ever do that to us again or I'll fly back here and lock your ass in the panic room myself."

I widened my eyes. Emma must've told Shannon what she'd done. I didn't even have it in me to be embarrassed. Fuck it. Everyone knew I had earned my timeout.

Without a word, I handed the light blue box to my sister. If all else failed, something shiny would win her over. She took it, prying it open immediately. Like me, she hadn't grown up with money. We were greedy when it came to material things.

"Oh, Jack..." Tears pooled in the corners of her eyes. She fiddled with the silver chain, trailing her fingers to the small charm. "Thank you."

"A 'C' for Charlotte," I explained.

"And Connor," she added, setting it carefully back in the box and holding it to her heart. The lump in my throat threatened to return. She neared me and kissed my cheek, wiping a loose tear from her own.

"Change the Diaper Genie," she ordered, pulling away. "And I'll forgive all of your transgressions."

I furrowed my brow in confusion. "Okay..."

Shannon's ensuing grin was wicked. Shit, I knew that look. I wasn't going to like this form of punishment, but I would hold my tongue and do whatever she wanted of me. Nothing could repay the time I had missed — the time I was going to miss.

"Kieran will show you," she said.

My little brother walked into the room accompanied by Eoghan.

"Who the fuck is the Diaper Genie and why do I think I'm going to hate him?" I asked once Shannon left.

Kieran didn't speak, but inclined his head toward the corner of the room. A tall white contraption sat in the corner, a button on its side. I pointed to it, eyebrows raised in a question. Kieran nodded, his expression inscrutable. He was pissed at me as well, but he would get over it. We were brothers. I didn't have to try with him. No gifts or apologies would suffice — time and justice were the formula there.

The smell that wafted out of the thing was blasphemous. Gagging, I grabbed a stuffed bunny from one of the shelves and held it over my nose and mouth. Returning my attention to the hellhole, I set to work pulling the bag out. I cut it with a pocketknife and tied it off, holding the full bag of dirty nappies aloft.

"Oh, for the love of Mary, throw that thing out!" Mick hollered as he passed the nursery.

Both Kieran and Eoghan had their noses covered. When I approached them with the bomb, they turned on their heels and scampered from the room. I followed, heading toward the kitchen pantry with the vacuum-sealed bin. The nanny — one of Michael Sweeney's daughters — took the bag from me with a silent smile. Clearly, she thought my punishment was comical.

"How was your timeout?" Mick asked, the three men joining me in the kitchen when the smell had left the room.

"Jesus, does everyone know?" I asked. Shannon was one thing, but my men would never let me live it down.

"Emma's been on a roll this week," Kieran said. "A couple days ago, she clocked Peter McKenzie in the mouth after he disrespected you."

I set the plush bunny on the counter, giving my brother a double take. "Say that again?"

"And yesterday morning she put your father in a chicken-wing hold," Mick added, grinning at the memory. "Dropped his ass to the ground without so much as blinking."

"She..." I faltered, turning to Eoghan. "Anything you'd like to add about what Emma's been up to?"

Eoghan shrugged, grabbing an apple from a crystal bowl on the counter. "I think they covered it."

Mick snorted. "Eoghan took Emma to the shooting range to practice with your revolver. It recoiled and hit her in the forehead. I stitched her up, though."

I held the bridge of my nose between two fingers, almost breaking it with the force. Emma had punched Peter McKenzie, she'd gotten into a scuff with Frank then injured herself at the Emerald shooting range. How was it possible for my men to be so incompetent with Emma's safety? She was a tiny thing, for God's sake!

"Did you say stitches?" I asked Mick, but my fiery gaze was fixed on Eoghan. "Why the fuck weren't you watching her more closely?"

He looked contrite at having failed Wing Duty. "I'm sorry, boss. I didn't expect her to shoot with one hand. When I asked her why she chose that stance, she said — get this — 'that's how cowboys do it'."

Mick and Kieran snickered, but I didn't find humor in the situation. Emma could've been hurt far worse.

What the hell had Eoghan been thinking, taking her to our shooting range and not even giving her a demonstration before handing her a gun? Christ Almighty.

"Guys, get in here!"

Shannon's voice had the hair on the nape of my neck standing on end. We all dropped our discussion — Eoghan flinging his apple core into the sink — and ran to the living room.

My gaze immediately found Emma, but she was fixated on the television. It had been turned on and the volume was at a maximum level. I pondered the side of her face as she stared in terror at the screen. It took me a moment to hear what the reporter was saying.

"'…the serial killer's identity has been revealed as Amara Marino, an illegal Italian immigrant who arrived in the city last year. The FBI has confirmed that Marino is the perpetrator behind the six murders across Manhattan and beyond, including the death of real-estate mogul Connor O'Connell. Marino was found dead in a slaughterhouse in Jersey just hours ago, along with her most recent victim Sofia Fiore, a nineteen-year-old Italian-American woman from Queens. It seems New York can breathe a sigh of relief now that the monster has been caught. There is no doubt Amara Marino's name will go down in infamy for her terrible crimes, but it's important to remember the names of her victims as well. We will now take a moment of silence to honor those…'"

As Connor's face flashed across the screen, I turned toward the wall. I gripped my hip in one hand, running the other through my thick hair. Relief nearly brought me to my knees. Because if my time in the panic room had taught me anything, it was that beneath all of my anger was a world of hurt. For losing Connor, yes, but also for myself. For being no better than Nicoletti's assassin.

I screwed my eyes shut, focusing on that magnetic pull—the one that drew me to Emma, as if our heartstrings tied us together. It was with her in mind that I was able to face my family again.

I strode forward, stepping around the sectional, and turned the television off. Connor's handsome features, along with the faces of five others, disappeared as the screen went black. The room was so silent, I could practically hear everyone's hearts beating in tandem.

When I pivoted toward them, I glanced in Emma's direction. She was staring at me with wide, terror-filled eyes. Had I put that look on her face? Was she scared of what I would do? That I'd go off the deep end again?

Eoghan placed his hand on her bare shoulder, giving it a gentle squeeze. Swallowing back the jealousy at that tender act, I approached Shannon, who was holding the now-awake Charlotte. Those bright blue eyes—an exact replica of Connor's—stared back at me, as if she too were waiting for my reaction.

"So, this is the poop nugget?" I asked, my voice snapping the tension in the room.

There was a visible sigh as everyone broke into shaky smiles. Everyone apart from Emma, who shrank farther into the couch. I wanted to grab her, haul her over my shoulder and take her home to start my amends. We had a long road ahead of us, but I still didn't know what to say. I didn't want to destroy us further or, worse, scare her more than I already had.

Shannon stood, her arms outstretched to pass Charlotte off. Upon seeing me holding the tiny human,

Emma left the room. I watched from my peripheral vision as Eoghan followed her down the hall.

I didn't think Eoghan had it in him to swoop in after me. He wasn't that type of person, but I shouldn't put it past anyone. Emma was a fucking prize. Rules were broken when it came to her. Mine had been. Eoghan might be breaking them as well.

I'd have to keep an eye on them—monitor and assess. On a good day, I could woo any woman away from the young, boyish heartthrob. But I was already in Emma's bad graces.

Eoghan was invaluable to the mob, but if my hunch was correct, I wouldn't be able to stop myself from tearing him to shreds.

Chapter Thirty-Four

Jack

Members from the McKenzie, Sweeney, Murray and O'Connell families filed into the penthouse in droves. Upbeat techno music blared, a product of Kieran's playlist. People had brought liquor and food, but Guillermo and a hired bartender were still working their asses off.

The August sun blazed through the eastern windows. Even with the air conditioner humming, everyone was dressed in light clothing. The liveliness of this gathering in contrast to Connor's wake was striking. It was hard not to be affected by everyone's bright mood, but I hid my skepticism behind an indifferent mask. I sipped at my glass of water, watching as everything unfolded.

When Peter McKenzie walked in, the party was in full swing. He clapped Emma on the back, pulling her in for a hug, which I was surprised she reciprocated.

She'd ditched the beanie and her hair was tied into an artful updo, leaving tendrils to grace her thin shoulders. The stitches along the line of her scalp were immaculate but they made my stomach churn.

I kept my distance, watching and listening. For now, it was enough to be in her presence. I was enthralled but horrified by how she had integrated herself into the mob without my knowledge — and in less than a week. Everyone said hello, everyone knew her name, everyone adored her.

"This is the girl I was tellin' ye about, love," Peter said, speaking to his wife. She was small, warm and crass in a way only an Irish woman could be.

"Oh, so ye gave me husband a smacking, didja?" she asked, laughing as she swept Emma into yet another embrace. She had to be the fiftieth person to hug her, yet I couldn't bring myself to go near out of fear of rejection. "Ye must have some green blood in ye, no?"

Emma's smile was coy as she shook her head. "I'm not sure. I'm an American mutt through and through."

The sound of her voice made my throat catch. She'd spoken so little, despite everyone wanting to engage her in conversation. The soft words that left her mouth were a gift in and of themselves. I watched her lips as they twitched, structuring themselves around her sentences. Her brown eyes gleamed every once in a while with something like happiness, but it was short lived. The haunted look would return and she'd glance around, searching for Eoghan.

He would meet her gaze. Occasionally, he'd smile back with reassurance, then his eyes would find mine. He knew I was watching them like a hawk. The glare I cast should've stilled him, but he simply sipped at his pint and continued chatting with Kieran.

* * * *

A couple hours later, Kieran was standing on the bar in the kitchen, using his foot to push aside dishes filled with a vast array of traditional Irish food. Emma stood near Shannon and, of course, Eoghan. Shannon had spent a majority of the afternoon on the phone with the FBI, who were a little behind the media on 'alerting the family first.' I situated myself so that I could keep an eye on the three of them while still watching my brother.

Someone turned the music down and all eyes drifted to Kieran.

"Ding dong, the bitch is fucking dead!" he yelled, pumping his hips on the last word. He held up his pint, smiling. The crowd roared, mimicking his salute. "This one's to all the men we've lost because of that cunt."

The people in the room drank collectively. Emma sipped at the mimosa in her hand, but she wore no smile. Neither did Shannon, whose cheeks were wet with tears.

"This one's to the Emerald Angel and Mick for bringing my brother back to us."

I looked to the floor as everyone toasted. Someone clapped me on my back, but I ignored the sentiment.

"This one's to the bastard that had the balls to take the monster out."

My gaze returned to Emma, whose face drained of color. I took a hesitant step in her direction, but Shannon leaned her head on Emma's shoulder, and she regained her composure.

"And, last but not least, we drink to the war to come. Nicoletti is undoubtedly going to blame this on us. May our pints always be full and our guns always loaded!"

The crowd erupted and I lost sight of the trio. Eoghan had wrapped an arm over Emma's shoulders right before my line of sight was cut off. Jealousy burned through my body like a wildfire, but I fought to control it. I wouldn't be doing myself any favors if I acted irrationally.

"Now, drink like it's your last day of peace!" my brother roared. "Because it fucking very well is."

Kieran drained what little was left of his pint, then hopped from the island with easy grace. Eoghan approached him, his height allowing him to split the crowd. The mob dispersed as a song by Phantogram came on.

I set my water on the counter and circled the penthouse, looking for her. It was now or never. I had to factor Eoghan out of this situation. If I let jealousy get the best of me, she could very well run. Still, it was killing me not to know how those two had grown so close over the past few days.

"Come here often?"

I froze in place. She was standing directly behind me. That she'd been able to find me first was surprising. When I turned, she took my breath away yet again. In her oversized jeans and lingerie top, she was a dream. Luscious hair framed her delicate face. At her back, the picture window made her skin glow with an unearthly light. I coughed to clear the thickness in my throat.

"Not recently," I said, catching on. "You?"

She smiled, happy that I was playing along. "Too much. I work at the restaurant downstairs, but the owner can be a dick."

"I'm sure he doesn't value your level of commitment as much as he should."

She shrugged, sipping on her orange glass. "I like to give him the benefit of the doubt."

"Dove." My chest expanded despite the air that left it. I was unstable on my own two feet. She was sweeping me off them. Wasn't that my plan for her?

When her smile faltered, the fantasy disappeared. Our tiny bubble, our short exchange, faded and the presence of everyone else in the room came crashing down.

"I'll see you around," she said, brushing past me.

"Emma." I caught her wrist before she could get too far. The smell of her was intoxicating—green apples and lavender, always. "Where are you going?"

"Home," she answered, eyes open and honest.

"Let me walk you," I commanded, but it sounded more like a plea. I couldn't—wouldn't—let her go so soon. Not after she had approached, breaking the tension.

Her voice was sweet and unexpectant. It killed me, the aloofness, like she didn't care whether I accompanied her into the elevator. "Sure."

She set her flute on the table in the foyer and didn't so much as turn to see if I followed. The ride in the elevator—down sixty floors—was electric, but her expression didn't betray anything. I studied her profile, recommitting everything to memory. The way her chin jutted up just so, like she knew I was watching. Her long eyelashes fluttered as she watched the lights on the control panel descend. She had crossed her hands in front of herself in a protective stance, the only thing giving me insight into her state of mind. The way her breasts were pushed up in that strapless top was distracting.

It was five o'clock and the heat was excessive, but I'd slipped out of my blazer before the party had started. We walked toward Central Park. Emma didn't seem to mind the slow pace I'd set. The park was filled with people trying to find a way to beat the end-of-summer heat. Tourists enjoyed the beautiful day, snapping photos in front of vendors and statues. A few softball teams battled on the fields.

"You want ice cream?" I guessed, seeing Emma's attention drift toward a small bodega.

Her eyes were hidden behind dark sunglasses with rose-gold rims, so it was difficult to discern her emotions. "Okay."

As we stood in line, I caught Emma smiling to herself. It brought a warmth to my heart, and I couldn't help but reach out and touch her. The pad of my thumb tingled as I brushed a strand of hair behind her ear, trailing around the stitches on her head. My stomach clenched at the dark bruise beginning to form.

"If you want to go shooting again, let me take you."

Color rose in her cheeks at my touch and she looked down, embarrassed. "Mick already offered, but I think I'm done with firearms for the foreseeable future."

My lips thinned into a smile. "Good."

I didn't know why she had felt the sudden need to arm herself, but I was glad she'd changed her mind. Apparently getting pistol-whipped in the face was a deterrent. Eoghan was a fucking idiot.

"What's going on between you and Eoghan?" I asked, reminded of my second lieutenant.

She gave me a curious look, but it was our turn to order. She told the man behind the booth that she wanted a bomb pop. I followed suit, handing the vendor a twenty. Before he could reach for change, I tugged Emma aside.

"Eoghan is a good friend," she said, walking ahead of me.

I jogged to catch up, popsicle in hand. "He wants to be more than friends."

Emma licked her bomb pop and my mind was suddenly filled with images of her mouth on me — sucking, licking, fondling. I had a semi in the middle of the park.

She scrunched her nose, oblivious. "I'm not his type."

"You're everyone's type," I argued, unable to hide my jealousy any longer. She was dynamite on legs. Sweet smile, inviting eyes, killer body. And the way she was licking her popsicle, her lacy pink getup strapped against her chest, made me want to howl in frustration.

Emma angled her head toward me. Her cheeks hollowed as she slid the ice from her mouth with an audible pop. She looked to the side, licking her pink lips.

"Are you doing that on purpose?" I demanded, my voice husky.

She smirked, licking at a stream of syrup sliding down the stick. "Doing what?"

I couldn't stifle my groan. I also couldn't control what came out of my mouth next. "If you keep doing that, you're going to have to get on your knees and suck me off in the middle of the goddamn park."

"Don't threaten me with a good time."

"*Jesus*, Emma!" I yelled, exasperated. I couldn't pin down her mood. It was torture not to see her expression behind those sunglasses. *Was* she doing it on purpose?

Hiding her eyes in an effort to teach me a lesson? The way I so often hid behind my own mask…

"I forgive you," she said, changing the subject. "For lying to me about cheating. I forgive you."

I swallowed in disbelief, emotionally whiplashed. "Just like that?"

"Just like that," she answered, that fucking popsicle sliding back into her mouth. "But we have a lot to discuss."

"Come to my apartment?" I asked, impatient. She'd forgiven me, but I knew it couldn't be that simple. She wanted to talk more on the matter. A public place wasn't the best option, especially with her looking the way she did. We were quite a sight—drawing glances from passersby as we sucked on our popsicles, staring at each other ferociously.

"That was the plan," she breezed, dropping her unfinished treat into a nearby trashcan.

I followed, literally and figuratively five steps behind. "I thought you said you were going home."

"I am going home," she insisted. "To *our* apartment."

Realization hit. I interlocked our fingers, relishing the way her small hand felt in mine. I tugged her into my chest and my lips met hers, almost bruising them with the force. She slipped her cool tongue into my mouth, the artificial fruit from her popsicle dazzling my senses.

She sighed and I dipped her, smiling at my luck. We had a lot of shit to sort through, but she wasn't running. She was in this just as much as I was. We would figure the rest out later. I had to have her mouth. I missed it. I'd missed everything.

A few people hollered, issuing catcalls. I lifted my arm to flip them off, not breaking our embrace, but Emma beat me to it. Glancing sideways at her outstretched hand, I laughed when I caught sight of her middle finger. Then I let the rest of the world fall away, pulling my girl against me as we devoured one another in the heart of the city.

Chapter Thirty-Five

Emma

When we entered Jack's apartment, the sun was beginning to set. His glass walls, which faced the eastern twilight, compassed the giant living space in shadow. The warm lights and brass accents welcomed me, and I sighed in relief. It felt like home, but I had been too scared to admit it before—too focused on keeping my feet on the ground in my own apartment.

Not anymore. I took my phone out of my back pocket and set it face down on the kitchen island. If I got a call from a blocked number, I didn't want Jack to see it.

He stood in the middle of the living room, gazing at the view of the park. I'd grown accustomed to his suits from the past few months, but he was as immaculate as ever in jeans and a T-shirt. This look was more...him.

His hands were in his pockets, his abdomen flexing in anticipation. He appeared stoic, but he was far from it. His jaw was tense and his throat worked on a swallow. He'd been pensive all day. I knew he was watching me, though—could feel his stare following me everywhere I went.

"You're killing me, dove," Jack muttered. He hadn't glanced in my direction since we entered the apartment, but he turned the full force of his dominance on me now. "The air dropped about ten degrees the second we got in the elevator."

"I told you we had some things to discuss," I said, finding my voice. It was hard to do when he looked at me like that, when my body responded so quickly to the need in his eyes. Even now, my skin prickled with awareness, my nipples hardened with want.

"Let's discuss, then."

I neared him, keeping the sofa in between us. It was something we often did, maneuvering so the furniture stood as a barrier—to stop us from ripping each other to shreds in a frenzy. It was more of a mental barrier than a physical one. Jack could leap over anything and be on me in less than a second. He'd done it many times before, but we remained standing now, sizing each other up.

"I apologize—" I began, but he cut me off with a strict tone.

"You have nothing to apologize for."

I cleared my throat, casting him a withering look. "I apologize for lying to you as well. I was being dishonest when I told you I hated you. I don't. I could never hate you."

He took a deep breath, a crack in his façade. "I love you, too."

I rubbed a hand over my chest, dispersing the ache. His gaze followed my fingers, pupils dilating.

"Now I want you to answer me honestly," I demanded, trudging ahead before his singular mind got us off track. "Why did you lie to me about cheating?"

"Because I wanted you to break up with me," he answered. "Because it wasn't—it *isn't*—safe for you to be with me."

"Try again, Jack."

He tilted his head, examining me. "I'm being honest."

"Be honest with yourself. Why did you lie to me about cheating?"

The look he gave me was icy, but I stood my ground. His jaw twitched, his irises hardening like chips of jade.

"You're going to unravel me, Emma," he threatened.

"Good," I snapped. "Now tell me why."

"Because I wanted you to run."

"Why?"

"Because you leaving me is inevitable." His chest rose and fell, a clear sign of the anxiety I was causing him. This was his trigger, and I knew it. He always thought I was going to run, to abandon him. "And I wanted to make you do it on my own terms. I thought it would hurt less."

"Did it?"

"Fuck no!"

He mirrored me, putting his tattooed hand to his heart, gasping for air. This time, it was my turn to climb over the furniture. The moment I embraced him, he crumpled, and we fell to the floor in a heap. I held his face in my hands, forcing him to meet my eyes.

"Breathe, Jack," I soothed. "Just breathe, baby."

There was sheer panic in his eyes. I held him there, locked, until it began to recede. His breathing was still hitched, but not frantic.

"Fuck, Emma," he cursed, leaning his forehead against mine. "I thought I could do it. I thought I could handle watching you leave, but it shattered me. I can't breathe without you. I can't function. I'm a shell and there's nothing good inside me if I don't have you."

I pulled his head to my chest, his body melding into mine. With my back braced against the side of the sofa, I rocked him while he broke. I'd never seen him cry. Even when Connor had died, he'd shaken, but there had been no tears. He was releasing them now, grief wrapped in fear, tied with a bow of Frank's abuse.

"When have I ever given you the impression that I would run?" I whispered, threading my fingers through his silky hair. It was longer than usual. He hadn't had a cut in a while, but I liked it. *More to hold on to.*

"You ran when I told you I cheated."

"Because you *wanted* me to," I argued. "Because you identified and singled out my one insecurity and used it against me. I think you're too good for me and you think I'm too good for you. We're both convinced that one of us will leave the other. It's a vicious cycle and we have to stop it now."

"I don't deserve you, Emma," he insisted, pulling away. His tears had dried, and his face was back to its normal self-controlled mask.

"That!" I yelled, pointing my finger at his expression. "That is what I'm talking about. You shut me out every time I try to pry my way in. What do I have to do to convince you that I can handle your past? That I can handle your worst? You've killed thirteen people in the past *month* and I'm still here, aren't I? I've moved in with you. Chain me to your bed if that's what it takes. I don't care!"

Despite the volume of my voice, the corners of his lips twitched at the idea. "Don't threaten me with a good time."

"I'm serious, Jack!" I continued. "That's going to be a stipulation for me. You have to let me in. I need all of you. Not just the parts you choose to show me."

The smile disappeared from his face as quickly as it had come. "I'm fucked up, Emma."

"I know." I pushed back a curl that had fallen over his bright eye. "But no one gets through life without a few scratches. You've seen mine. We've discussed my childhood. I hardly know anything about yours."

"I have more than a few scratches."

I took a deep breath, searching for the words that would open him. If he didn't, this wouldn't work. We would be living a half-life. A half-love. He wouldn't trust me not to leave until he had told me everything he was scared to, and I had stuck with him regardless.

"I'm pleading with you, Jack." I rose to my knees so he would understand with my actions, not just my words. At this angle, I was a few inches taller than him. "I am asking you for everything. I know it's a lot and you have every right to say no. But that'll be it for us."

"Don't say that." He knelt as well, caging me in his arms. "Don't give up on me."

"I don't want to go, but you need to understand what I'm asking for. If you have a bad day, you can't just come home, fuck me senseless then pass out without so much as a conversation. If you're having a bad day, I want to have a bad day with you. If you're coming undone, I want to piece you back together. I want to solve problems with you. And if you feel like getting drunk and saying 'fuck the world,' I'll be right by your side. If you feel like going out and getting into a fistfight, I'll wipe the blood from your brow myself. I want to love you in the dark as much as I do in the light."

He stopped my mouth with his. The kiss was ravenous and demanding in nature, his tongue delving into my mouth like he was making love to it. He ran his hands through my hair, gripping the intricate braid at the base of my neck to unleash the tresses, letting my hair cascade around my shoulders.

"Yes," he breathed, his greedy mouth sucking and licking across the tops of my breasts. They were spilling out of the corset top. Air was hard to come by, but I didn't need it. I was drunk on the smell of him—rain and fire. My body lit up as he unlaced the back of my top, freeing me from its trap.

"What?" I asked, shaken. I'd forgotten how to use my brain.

His shirt was off now and I marveled at him, as I always did. Rock-hard body, lean and muscular. The V at his pelvis enticed me to look at the solid form straining against the denim of his jeans. The muscles of his forearm twitched as he unfastened the button on my pants.

"Yes to everything, dove," he said, his voice like gravel. There was hardly any green in his eyes. Just a black hole of hunger…for me.

He grabbed my legs, hauling them over his shoulders so that I was almost upside down. He wrapped his arms around the base of my thighs, planting a chaste kiss on my pelvic bone.

"Support yourself, Em," he ordered, his breath skating across my sex. Goosebumps broke out along my belly. I did as I was told, setting my elbows on the plush rug so my neck wasn't at a strange angle. "Good girl."

He slid his tongue into my folds, sending a delicious fizz of energy through my bloodstream. He groaned, the ferocity of it rattling my bones. He worked in quick, luxurious circles around and around my clitoris, blinding me with pleasure. My own moans sounded far off — like my mind was floating above my body. Fingers numb, nails digging into the carpet, I held on for dear life. I bent my knees, grinding my hips into Jack's face.

"You taste so fucking good," he growled, his nose nudging the tight pack of nerves while his tongue fucked my channel. The man didn't even need to breathe. "You taste like mine."

My soul was ablaze. Every sensation was magnified, made more important by the promise he'd made. *Yes to everything.* I choked on air as my climax roared through me. He held my trembling legs, his tongue guiding me through the mind-bending orgasm. He licked and sucked at my wetness, moaning like he'd been starving himself for it.

He set me down. Through a haze, I watched as he unzipped his fly and ripped his bottoms off. His erection hung hard and thick between his thighs. Even the veins had me panting for more. Jesus, how could his penis be sexy? I'd never thought of that particular appendage as visually appealing, but holy shit. Jack was lethal.

He picked me up and carried me to the couch, setting me on top of his lap. I straddled him and lifted my hips so he could position himself. He loved when I rode him right after I came. The flushed cheeks, the wild hair — it was all from him.

"Slow, dove," he hissed, but I didn't listen. He wanted me to go slow for my own pleasure, but I craved his release more than my own. I dropped myself down, sheathing him so that our two bodies became one. "Ah, fuck, Emma!"

"Don't look away from me," I commanded. I'd always been amazed that Jack could control his tone when we made love. Now I understood. There were some things more important than a race to the finish.

I slid up his length, then came shattering down again, knocking the air out of my own lungs.

"Goddamn, girl," he grunted, transfixed by the spot where our bodies met.

Grabbing his scruffy face in my hands, I met his mouth with a devastating kiss. Our tongues dueled, twirling and twining. Jack went very still, and an ominous chill came over me. His thoughts were going a mile a minute, his eyes cataloging my features — like he was deciding whether he could give me what I asked for.

"Everything, Jack," I whispered, kissing the tip of his nose. "I want to be a part of your world."

Before I knew it, I was flat on my back. Jack knelt on the ground in front of me, never once taking himself out. He shook his head, chucking darkly, then reached for my hand and kissed my knuckles.

"You *are* my world, dove."

With that, he started pounding into me. He moved so quick I was surprised we weren't just a blur, a speck in time that seemed to stretch on forever. The shock to my system dissipated, melting as he pushed me over again. His fingers gripped my backside, tugging me into his punishing thrusts. I bit his lip, eager to drive him wild.

"Always you, Em," Jack whispered, sweat beading along his brow. He looked manic and absolutely beautiful. "You're it for me, baby. You're everything."

I stared, slack-jawed, as he found solace within me. His gaze stayed locked on mine, and I could see the doubt disappear — replaced by euphoria and pure, unconditional love. The lines of his face hardened and my name ripped from his throat. I wanted to recommit every step of his orgasm to memory, but I couldn't hold mine off any longer — not when I had the devil coming apart inside me. He held me as my body trembled with the release of energy. Like a rubber band that'd been pulled too tight, I snapped in two. But this time, I had Jack to stitch me back together — and he had me.

"Was that everything?" he panted, collapsing on my chest.

"And more."

We lay like that for a while, entangled in every possible way. His familiar weight was a comfort. He was right — I loved when he pinned me down, hard surface or not. My muscles twitched with exertion and the pain in my head was returning. I would need to take something before my headache got too terrible. But it was nice just *being* for a while — shutting the impending shit storm out and focusing on us.

"What made you choose the Roman numerals on your hand?" I asked, disturbing the silence. We'd spent far too much of our relationship choosing to make love instead of talking. It was important we had time for both now.

Jack was silent for a minute. I thought he'd fallen asleep, despite his semi-hard cock inside me. "It's the day I killed for the first time."

I didn't need to glance down to know the numbers inked into his skin, but it still caught my breath. "That was—"

"Eighteen years ago. I was ten. My brothers were in detention. Miraculously, I wasn't. When I got home, my father handed me a gun. He ordered me to shoot the man tied up in the kitchen. I asked him why and he backhanded me. Told me never to question an order. So, I did it. Shot him right between the eyes with no excuse other than Frank told me to do it."

"Then what happened?" I whispered.

"He took the gun and hit me over the head with it. Said I must never close my eyes when I kill, to always look at them until they take their last breath." Jack hesitated, then took a deep inhale and continued. "With every hit, every drug deal, every intimidation tactic, I hoped I was making my father's life easier. That, maybe, if I killed the men who were causing him trouble, he wouldn't be so angry. He wouldn't need to drink. He wouldn't hit us. But it never stopped. It only got worse until, one day, I realized I was stronger than him, and Frank knew it, too. He couldn't control me anymore."

Jack's voice was monotone, but I knew the retelling had an effect on him. His jaw was tense against my breasts, his head still burrowed between them. I reached for his face and pulled him up to me, forcing his erection to slide out. I kissed him, masking my agony at the picture he painted—a young, naïve boy who just wanted to make his psychotic father happy.

"Thank you for telling me."

"Fuck." He groaned, grinding himself into me. "I can go again."

"You're a fiend," I joked. His grin took my breath away. That Jack could still smile after surviving hell, after convincing himself *he* was the devil, was a miracle. He was my miracle. "I'll meet you in the bedroom. I have to take some Advil."

His gaze flitted to the stitches on my forehead. "Did I hurt you?"

"No," I insisted, rising from the sofa alongside him. "I just have a bit of a headache. I'll be fine."

"We can stop."

"I don't want to," I argued, making my way into the kitchen. "Besides, you owe me five days of orgasms. And we're seeing Shannon and Charlotte off at the hangar tomorrow morning, so go to our bedroom and get clocked in."

Jack burst into laughter. "I'll show you clocking *in*, lass."

He grabbed my hand and kissed my knuckles. I pushed him toward the master suite before he could distract me. As the sound of his feet meeting the marble faded away, I grabbed the Advil from the cupboard and poured myself a large glass of water.

While I padded down the hallway to join Jack, I gave myself a little pep talk. It was important for us to enjoy tonight. Like Kieran said, it was likely our last day of peace. I hadn't heard from Don Luca, but that didn't mean much. The man was diabolical—he'd make his play soon.

And me? Well, I would stay ten moves ahead of him. Killing the Babau was just the first step in my plan. Everything was happening as I'd predicted. I'd be ready for tomorrow, and the day after that. I had nothing to worry about.

Not with everything and more at my fingertips.

Epilogue

Luca Nicoletti was an impatient man. He didn't like to put things off, but the web of lies he'd spun for law enforcement and reporters alike had to be pristine. It helped that he controlled a large portion of the local media. Still, one wrong word — one insubstantial fact — and the story would come tumbling down.

Amara Marino was my niece, yes, but we were not close. You see, my sister was having financial troubles and I offered my assistance by taking her daughter in. Upon Amara's arrival in America, I checked her work visa and everything appeared to be in order. She was odd and distant, but I chalked it up to a difficult childhood. I hoped she would open herself to a new culture, new friends, new environment. I was just as concerned about this serial killer as the rest of the city. Until this morning's story, I had no idea what she was doing. This has come as a massive shock to me and my family.

That evening, Luca was at last able to sit down in his study, away from the prying eyes of his men. Away from the turmoil of police and FBI that had swarmed his building in Little Italy, pestering him for information. Don Luca had spent decades building relationships with influential parties, law enforcement being one of them. As a result, they took him at his word.

The flash drive had sat in his suit pocket all day, burning a hole through it. He was antsy to see his grandson's suicide note for himself. It was the one thing he had to remember him by, apart from Emma Marshall. That young woman had grown a lot since Christmas. Her eyes were sharper, her threats more lethal now that she'd proved she could follow through.

When the shot had rung out from her gun, the pride that had surged through Luca had surprised him. He'd come to think of little Emma as more of a protégée than an enemy. She was flourishing, adapting quicker than most people did in their entire lives. He only wished she was on his side, under his careful, guiding hand. She was a prodigy in the Mafia world — a twisted scene filled with underhanded deals, quick wit and blood. So much blood. He'd known her potential when he'd first laid eyes on her.

Jealousy — not for her body, but her brain — spiked his veins when he was reminded who she shared a bed with. Those pesky Irishmen couldn't keep their dicks to themselves. He'd wanted to kill Jack O'Connell the moment Emma had asked for his amnesty.

Feeling anxious — something Luca never did — he slid the drive into the slot on his personal laptop. He clicked on a folder titled *NATE.img*.

Jennifer Luna

An image appeared on his screen, but not the one he'd been expecting. Instead of Nate's suicide note, he was greeted with two middle fingers. It was Nate and Emma, but years ago. They were teenagers, sitting on the edge of a pool, the clear water lapping at their legs. Their bodies were tan, the whites of their teeth gleaming. Nate had his arm draped over Emma's shoulders. Emma had a bottle of lemonade in hand. They both grinned at the camera, hands out to flip its user off.

There was a caption.

In bocca al lupo.

Luca bit the inside of his cheek, eyes brimming with hate. His lips worked their way into a malicious smile. It was an expression that had his men running in opposite directions if he ever graced them with it. He leaned back in his leather chair, dialing the number on his cell. It was answered in a single ring.

"The Emerald Devil," Luca ordered, his voice in no way betraying the fury simmering beneath the surface.

"Of course, Don Luca." The man on the opposite line hesitated. "Respectfully, no one has been able to identify him. I'll need a rough sketch at the very least, sir."

Luca removed a frame from his desk drawer, brushing his thumb over the glass. Amara had been a loose cannon in many ways, but her greatest gift to him was a result of Emma's negligence.

The picture he held in his hand was priceless. Jack and Emma were dressed in leathers, leaning against a unique motorcycle. Emma gazed at Jack, glowing with admiration. Jack smiled crookedly at the camera, his relaxed body language portraying a false sense of security. A rare shot of the devil himself.

Jack O'Connell was no longer untouchable—no longer a shadow.

Luca slid a razor blade down the middle of the glossy paper, separating the happy couple. He tossed Emma's side back into the drawer, holding the solo image of Jack between two fingers.

"You will have a photo within the hour."

"Absolutely, Don Luca," the man gushed, apologizing for his doubt. "How much?"

"Five hundred thousand," the don answered, unfazed.

"Done."

Luca ended the call, setting his cell phone on the desk with a macabre grin.

Oh, little one, he thought. *And just when I was beginning to like you.*

He was going to obliterate Emma Marshall. He would take everything from her until she came to his doorstep, begging for death.

That was a promise.

Want to see more like this?
Here's a taster for you to enjoy!

Irish Mafia Kings: Deadly Sins
January Bain

Excerpt

Quinn

My brother and partner-in-crime knocked then strode into my office at my bark to enter. "The Cullen brothers are wanting a word." A slight twitch under Devlin's right eye told me the story. "You want me to keep them waiting?"

The Cullens were in deep shit for thinking they could get away with stealing from my family. I should keep them cooling their heels all night. But hell, it might be more fun to torture them. I could use a good workout.

"Give me five and send them up."

Devlin nodded and looked like he was about to say more before changing his mind and exiting. I shifted — the Irish king, ready for action.

Stepping up to the one-way glass overlooking the main venue of the Emerald Club, I scanned the crowd, alert for possible signs of trouble. Our family hadn't risen to the upper echelons of Montreal's crime families by turning a blind eye. No, we'd done it by an eye for an eye, the golden rule.

"Power isn't handed to you. It's seized, by whatever means necessary."

Amen, Dad. Rest in peace.

I was a true son of my father. To everyone else, I was a monster, mob boss, a killer, king of the underworld, a man who took what he wanted. *One exception to the rule — I don't hurt innocents.* But for clarity's sake, innocence was a rare commodity in my world.

I glanced over at the huge oil painting of my father painted at the height of his power, his posture stern on the straight-backed chair, his eyes dark and shadowed, a man never to be crossed. My mother stood behind him and his four sons lined up by his side.

"Family. Honor. Security. Protecting everything we had struggled for over the years — that always comes first, son."

I honored his words with a nod. We might have arrived on the shores of North America starving and in rags, but since then we'd fought tooth and nail to rise and take our proper place in society, aligning ourselves with people and places that mattered.

"Never forget where you came from, Quinn...or what you will die for."

I will find his killer, Da, I promised both my father and my baby brother, Mikey.

The door opened and the Cullen brothers, Red and Sammy, both considerably paler than usual, stood there waiting to be invited into my office. Neither was able to look me in the eyes.

"In. Sit."

Silently they both entered and took a seat. The scraping of the chair legs on the easy-to-clean floor grated on my last nerve. *Fucking. Cheating. Assholes.*

"What do you have to say for yourselves?" I kept my tone cool and my voice low, not giving any of my seething anger away. I'd been told that was far more intimidating.

Red, the older brother, licked dry lips. "I got myself in trouble with Lenny. My gambling got out of hand, I admit it. It's not my brother's fault."

Lenny ran an illegal gambling enterprise not in our territory.

"You should have come to me. Made things right." I got to my feet and circled behind the pair, standing over them. Sweat dripped down both their necks and dampened their shirt collars. Huge wet patches bloomed under their arms. Both men stank of fear.

Red twisted his neck to look up at me, the white of his eyes visible. "I have something to trade. Some intel. About Conn Byrne."

I grabbed Red by the scruff of his neck, twisting the skin tightly in my fist. "What about him?"

"Please, let Sammy go and I'll tell you."

"Tell me now." His brother was just as much to blame for not stepping up and doing the right thing.

"Conn Byrne ordered the hit on your brother Michael."

The words were lobbed into the room like an incoming missile. The air itself vibrated around me, sending all my senses as taut as a high wire. I glanced over at the painting of the family again, seeing only my baby brother. Mikey. The only one of us able to make my dad smile with his sunny, mischievous ways, seeming unaffected by the dark trials of being raised in the pressure cooker that was the criminal underworld.

"And you know this how?" Maybe this pair of assholes did have something to trade. Thoughts of revenge burned ice-cold in my blood.

"Overheard it. Me and Sammy were hanging around Hazel's waiting for Shania to be finished with a client last night." *Euphemism for a whore Red liked to fuck.* "When in comes Lann Gallagher. You know, he's connected to the Byrnes—"

"And Conn's right-hand man," Sammy broke in.

"He didn't see us but he was talking to Nico Accardi and they were laughing about pulling one over on us. They were both drunk out of their skulls, otherwise they wouldn't have spilled it. But I heard Nico say that one less Lyons was fine with him. That Conn had the right fucking idea. And now that their families were going to be connected through marriage, things were only going to improve for them with such tight connections. More territory to milk."

My gut burned with anger. *Revenge.* It screamed my name, filled my body with the strength of twenty men.

I punched Red a solid blow on the jaw and he took the pain, knowing he had that and more coming. I reached in my jacket pocket and pulled out a switchblade, freeing the blade with a press of my thumb. The point gleamed in the overhead light, a proper weapon for gutting fish. *Or humans.*

My cell phone rang, interrupting my workout. The name on the screen had me snapping out a "Lyons," in answer.

"Sorry to bother you, boss, but we have a situation at the front door."

I growled. "Isn't Ian there? Ask him."

A slight hesitation made my gut roil. "It's about Ian. He's not himself tonight."

Code words. "I'll be right there."

I shut down the call. "Don't move," I warned the pair and stalked from the room, taking the stairs two at a time in my agitation. Favors expected by family members always burned. *Ian gets out of rehab, again, and everyone cheers. Then I'm begged to give him a job and this is how he returns it?* And right now, with the Italians trying to gain hold on our turf, we needed to stay sharp, provide a strong united front to protect our clan. *Those damn Accardis and their homing in on what's ours.*

Arriving late to the party with open beaks didn't entitle them to the same share as those that came first. *Us.* Hell, we were in America three decades before them and paid in blood, sweat and fucking tears for the price of admission to the American Dream by digging ditches in fetid conditions in New Orleans, making things easy for the Italians.

History, it's a bitch. But no point in changing it to suit the political times—what happened, happened. To suggest anything else was pure shite. And now learning that Nico Accardi knew about my baby brother was the last straw. A new plan was called for, one that took out Conn Byrne and crippled Nico.

I swept by the patrons at the bar on my way to the heavily guarded front entrance. The constant threat of possible retaliation by our sworn enemies remained high since we'd been actively pushing them all back toward the west end of Montreal where they damn well belonged. Everyone needed to be on full alert, not jerking off.

I stormed out through the front doors, the cold winter blast of air no brake on my anger, focused only on hauling Ian up by the short hairs. There was no line at the entrance this early in the evening...no witnesses.

"Where is he?" I asked John, a good man who knew the score.

John gave me a respectful nod, pointing at the alleyway across from the club known for drug dealing. "He's been in there for the past thirty minutes or so. I saw some piece of shit go in and come out again. I'd check, but I can't leave my post. I know he's your cousin, so I thought I should call you."

I placed a heavy hand on his shoulder as reassurance. "You did right. I'll handle it from here."

Undoing the buttons on my suit jacket, I pulled my gun from the holster, clicked off the safety then hurried across the narrow one-way street. Slowing down to allow my eyes to adjust to the dimness, I walked into the darkness, scanning the area for my bastard cousin. In the quiet, the scurrying of small creatures, probably a rat or two due to the restaurant that always overfilled their garbage containers farther down the alley. The stench of rotting food filled me with disgust. What kind of animal shot up in a place like this?

"Ian's not quite right. Keep your distance."

Words from my dad about his brother's boy came back. Some incident with a teenage girl years ago that cost the family dearly. But Ian had been young as well, probably just sowing his wild oats. I'd always kept an eye out for Ian, never sure who he was going to be on any given day. He was the guy most likely to be voted his own worst enemy.

Shit. There he was. Passed out. *Overdose?* I leaned down to check his pulse, noting it was steady.

"I should just leave you here for the rats to gnaw on," I said, putting my gun back in its holster. I pulled the twenty-nine-year-old to a sitting position before hauling him to his feet. "But your mother deserves better."

"Whatyadoing?" Ian slurred, obviously in a drug-induced haze as he leaned heavily on me.

"Hauling your ass out of here."

No answer to that. I steered the idiot across the street and pulled out my key fob from my jacket pocket, depositing him in the back seat of my Mercedes that was always kept at the curb.

"And don't you dare throw up," I warned, tossing a wool blanket over him.

"You know we…we met before. In…my past life. When I was king of all of Ireland. You know I didn't mean to do those bad things, right?" he babbled.

I snorted. "But you just can't stay off the coke." My anger burned cold again, and I wanted nothing more than to knock some bloody sense into him. But I'd tried that numerous times, to no avail. And tonight, I had other things on my mind that mattered far more than this junkie piece of shit.

Michael and revenge.

He didn't argue but slumped back in defeat, closing his eyes.

Slamming the car door, I handed the keys off to John. "Check on him from time to time."

"Will do. Thanks, boss."

"I'll send Fletcher right away. It'll be getting busy soon."

Stepping back into the club, I scanned the bar, focusing on a dark-haired man in a cheap suit with a weaselly look about him as he leaned in too close to a woman, hogging her personal space. Her expression was frozen, her eyes begging for help.

Without hesitation I strode toward the pair, my urge to jerk the man to his feet and haul his ass to the curb so strong that I clenched my fists in anticipation of doing just that. I was suited to what I did, more than I would have liked at times. I did what has to be done and damn the consequences. But this was an easy one.

I drew closer. He was begging her for a second chance, saying that he had changed, that they were good together. "Please, Kennedi, I need you. So help me, I can't live without you. You're my — everything."

Pathetic really, begging a woman. I want a woman, I take her.

He reached out to grab her arm and she shrank back, drawing in on herself. My vision narrowed, the edges of the club vanishing in a red haze.

"What's going on here?" I demanded, stopping right in front of the pair.

"Nothing. Who the fuck are you?" the perv asked, turning his focus onto me. *Good.* I was the only individual he should be seeing right now. *Judge and jury.*

"Is this man bothering you, miss?" I asked, turning deliberately to speak to the woman as if she were the only person in the room that mattered.

"It's all right," she said in a flat tone of voice that most definitely said she was not fine. "My lawyer was just leaving."

"Kinney, please, don't be like that. I just want to buy you a drink."

Lawyer. Figures. Probably defends murderers. The woman wanted me to know that. My estimation of her rose several more notches. She'd warned me off, so that I would know what was at stake. To save me. I hid a smile at the very idea.

"Time to hit the road, Jack. The lady's been pretty clear about the fact she wants to drink alone. Shall I call someone for you? A friend to take you home? Or a cab?" *Always give them a choice.* Most times it worked, gave them something else to occupy their little minds.

The man's mug twisted into a snarl. "I'm not going anywhere. You do realize who I am?" He gave me a look of disgust. "And I know your type. You got gangster written all over you, *paddy.*"

"My name is Quinn, not Patrick," I said smoothly, though my blood heated a few degrees. "And it's time for you to leave, buddy."

"We're just fine, *buddy*," asshat said, his mouth downturned. "I'll take care of the lady's needs."

I picked the man up by the scruff of his neck and marched him to the side door, his feet dragging on the ground. At the entrance, I slammed my foot into his ass for good measure and sent him barreling into the alley. When I got back to the table, the hassled woman had vanished. Good for her.

As soon as I sat down, the bartender sent my favorite whiskey sour over.

"Anything else, boss?" Kelly asked, leaning forward so that her breasts came into my direct line of sight. *Yes, I think so.* I needed to fuck something but a blow job would do.

"Come upstairs in five. Bring the bottle. Just got to take out the trash first."

Kelly nodded, looking eager.

Ten minutes later she was sucking me off. I held her head tight between my hands while she used her tongue and lips to good advantage. My cock hardened further with each hot, inviting stroke. She was a damn good cocksucker, her eyes never leaving mine. She opened her throat to me, greedily lapping up my cum a few minutes later when I shot my load, then licking her lips to catch every last drop.

"You want another drink?" she asked, getting off her knees.

"Pour one, then leave." She pouted at the dismissal but knew better than to complain. Seconds later she had gone and I had time to think, now that my body was eased, if only for a short while.

Thoughts about how to enact my revenge rose to the surface as I sipped the strong malt whiskey. *The marriage.* I had forgotten Red mentioning it in my need to squeeze him about Michael. Something from the newspaper came to mind. Yes. The engagement of Nico Accardi and Aria Byrne. My gut burned at the idea of my enemies' joining hands, but a wedding offered opportunities to strike like nothing else.

I raised my glass to my father's image, promising him I'd do what he would expect his eldest son to do.

"Destroy without mercy those who dare to come after us," I vowed.

About the Author

Jennifer Luna is an author by night and renowned chicken nugget chef by day—just ask her son. She lives in Virginia with her husband, son, and two cats. When she's not reading or writing, she can be found cleaning the litter box or doing just about anything for a Klondike bar.

Her debut dark romance, *Dove*, is the first novel in The Emerald Mafia Series, which exposes the gritty underworld of the Irish mafia and the sacrifices one woman will make to keep her loved ones out of harm's way.

Jennifer loves to hear from readers. You can find her contact information, website details and author profile page at https://www.totallybound.com

Home of Erotic Romance

Sign up for our newsletter and find out about all our romance book releases, eBook sales and promotions, sneak peeks and FREE romance books!